The Coastgua
& other

John F Bennett

The Coastguard Cottages
and other stories

J

The JoFra Press
www.jofrapress.co.uk

First published January 2022
©John F Bennett 2022

Printed and bound in Great Britain by PurePrint Group
Crowson House, Bolton Close, Uckfield,
East Sussex, TN22 1PH
Tel +44 (0) 1825 768811
Fax +44 (0) 1825 768062

ISBN 978-1-3999-1491-8

Also in JoFra Press by John F Bennett:
The Girl on the Seventh Floor
The Lights in The Wood

All rights reserved: No part of this publication may be reproduced, stored in a retrieval system, or transmitted in any form or by any means, electronic, mechanical, photocopying, recording or otherwise without the prior permission of the author/publisher.

This book is supplied subject to the condition that it shall not be, by way of trade or otherwise, be lent, sold, hired out or otherwise circulated without the author/publisher's prior consent in any form of binding or cover other than that in which it is published and without a similar condition including this condition being imposed on the subsequent purchaser.

JoFra Press
www.jofrapress.co.uk

publisher@jofrapress.co.uk
(Publisher and writers may be contacted at the above email address)

Dedicated to my brother Ian

Contents

1	The Coastguard Cottages	7
2	Ruby... and Me	20
3	The Girl in the Field	28
4	Castle of Discomfort	38
5	Reincarnation	43
6	But You Never Can Tell	48
7	The Final Victory	56
8	One Day While Out Walking	61
9	The Wiles of Women	77
10	The Lord of Caeragan Castle	81
11	Life With My Father	91
12	A Tale By Ann Radcliffe?	98
13	The Cricket Match	114
14	The Battle of Lewes	122
15	The Beautiful Songbird	132
16	Tammy	142
17	My Brother Bob	153
18	Stella Verity's Pendant	163
19	In Bessie and Arthur's Garden	171
20	The Ruined Cottage	182

The Coastguard Cottages

The way turned here and there; it was during its meandering that I discovered the gardens. The paths might have been made by years of feet, but discovering worn and broken paving stones suggested the relics of garden pathways.

What was most interesting about these paths were the flowers one encountered while walking. Surely no wood would contain garden flowers, but these did. While most of the green areas of the town had been subject to the demand for housing, this area had been allowed to go completely wild. Nature had flourished – and destroyed. It was one of the few areas which had been covered by a row of houses but which, on their demolition, had been permitted to return to nature.

The cottages had abutted the railway line to London; seaward had been the gardens which had presumably – at one time – been the delight of those who occupied them. Or was this romanticising the residents of the cottages?

Increasingly I made my morning walks in that direction, discovering more plants that were out of place on the public space of the hill on the cliff overlooking the sea. I walked among antirrhinums, montbretia, marigolds and chrysanthemums; even nerine. Roses were rapidly becoming wild. Soon all but the roses would become engulfed.

The pathways were even more enticing. Where did they lead?

Often a tree of mature appearance blocked the way to what once could have been the doors of the cottages. Had they been planted by the cottages' occupants? Or had they appeared since their evacuation, or their demolition? Had they grown from saplings which had made their appearance before the mature trees had been felled? Speculation was idle but my fascination with the gardens was undiminished. As I, with difficulty, made my way through the undergrowth of what had become woodland, I sought more signs of the gardens which had previously occupied the land. I watched the flickering sunlight which penetrated the trees and dispensed light like gold dust. And it heightened my sense of emotion. An emotion which prompted speculation to run wild. Who, I began to wonder, were the people who had lived in these cottages which had existed from a period before Victoria had ascended the throne.

It was weeks after I began my walks there that I began to be aware of movements in the wood. At first, of course, I attributed them to the wind, prevalent enough on this breezy spot overlooking the English Channel. Indeed, for some time, I challenged my growing belief that, although I had entered the gardens from a bright and sunny hill, I was encountering people who still made their ghostly presence evident in the gardens in which they had once walked.

Waving fronds and snapping twigs were one thing, voices were another. And it was not long before those voices in the small wood began to speak to me. Or not to me. To fellow inhabitants of that small world. Again I attributed this to my heightened awareness as I tried to imagine the people of a bygone age.

I admit to feeling alarm when a bird flew from its nest into my path or a tree branch made me stumble on my progress through another part of the gardens. But I was becoming more adept at distinguishing those sounds which should exist in such a wood – and those which should not.

The voices were not of the present day. And they spoke, too, in accents of the past – country accents which were once familiar in the county but which had long become subsumed into the speech of those – particularly from London – who had made the town their home. I began to think of these people – or ghosts – who had inhabited the cottages in earlier years, perhaps soon after they had been built to protect the coast and the shipping which had passed along the Channel at this point. And to combat the constant threat of the smugglers who, now much romanticised, had once attempted to defend their trade with the utmost ferocity.

But, initially, I heard no angry voices, only quiet ones which might have been aware of my presence, such was their edge of caution. Most frequently I discerned two particular voices and they became familiar to me. One was redolent of the accents of old Sussex. The other, sweet and mellifluent, I had tentatively ascribed to someone not raised within its boundaries. And, perhaps, to a stratum of society far removed from the male voice with which it cautiously conversed.

I became used to the voices: they became a part of my world as I walked into the gardens. I could see nothing of them, but I had heard the swish of long dresses and the roughness of male speech had brought about an image of coarse attire.

The walk became daily – and even more often on occasion – and I began to think of the cottages as if they still existed, and those who inhabited them as real people. I believed that I had begun to recognise them, although they could not hear me or know of my presence. Gradually, I began to hear not only conversation but to decipher the occasional word. And, eventually, phrases and sentences.

I felt an interloper, ashamed that I was listening to private conversations – sometimes words of love, sometimes of anger, but always of intimacy. Clearly the cottages housed a diverse group, even if they had in common the motive of assisting and acting as coastguards.

Listening I could hear devotion and yet discord. Increasingly I was able to form an impression of one man and one woman. I read as much as I could about the cottages' occupiers and even found lists of their names although I could not determine 'my' couple's period of occupancy and could therefore not identify them at this stage. The cottagers housed the coastguards – and their families. One, a grander dwelling, housed a lieutenant, his family of five and two servants. I believed that their lives were not easy ones; dangers were all around – rescuing those on foundered ships, tackling smugglers who, generally, had the support of the town where even the local worthies benefited from goods difficult to obtain, and available more cheaply than if they had carried duty.

The vague shapes I began to observe in the woods took to a new level my contemplation of a world gone by. My daily walks in them were beginning to show me more: a glimpse of female dress, a suspicion of a young man's figure. And, as the days – and nights – went by (for I was walking in the gardens during evening and even night time so great had become my obsession) the evidence of the past became more vivid. Until, on a bright July morning, more was revealed to me. I could discern now complete figures rather than shapes. I wondered what time of year it was in their world. I began to consider whether the progress of their lives took place in the order in which the 'scenes' – for as such I viewed them – were revealed to me. I concluded that I was witnessing their lives as they had played out, although it seemed to require an atmosphere, a heightening of their – and perhaps my – emotions to make them visible to me. And, given that I heard and saw them on my every walk, I concluded that I was only aware of that elevated plane, of the important scenes in their lives.

I was unable to witness the tending of their gardens and their other normal activities, a regret to me since I should have loved to have viewed such things. But backgrounds *were* becoming clearer. My 'wood' showed me a row a gardens beyond which, as I now began to see, was a terrace of seven cottages. I counted them. Seven cottages. Seven families or, at least, single inhabitants. But only two whose occupants' lives were becoming known to me.

Instead of momentary appearances, I began to see them as I should have seen them had I passed on the public path that had existed in Victorian times. For I could now see more clearly the person whom I had begun to identify as the heroine of the play I was witnessing – her swept back hair, with ringlets at each side. It told me nothing about the period of the world in which I was an uninvited guest; I was no expert on female fashion of any period.

I most often saw her alone; her facial expressions becoming clear and causing me concern. I found it difficult to see that worried face without strong emotion. While her cares were now subsumed in the dust of the past, they felt contemporary to me. Her beautiful face was marred – no, it could not be marred, but clouded – with sadness. With a grief that was difficult to contemplate unemotionally. For, absurd as it may now seem, I was beginning to love her.

And, with the empathy I was beginning to feel with her came a feeling that I was somehow part of her world, that I lived – for a time at least – in a period around one and a half centuries ago. Ironically I began to see no one during my morning walks – other than the fleeting pictures of which I had been aware when first I stumbled into their world. But, in the evenings and into the night time, the impression of these people was such that I felt I could reach out and touch them although, fearing to dissipate them, I made attempt to do so.

And the more I saw, the greater concern it gave me. I was able to hear their conversation and see their expressions. I could even see the man leave his garden one stormy night and proceed down to the beach, slithering down the cliffs as he had clearly done many times before.

I was able to follow him, always looking back to see if she was abroad. But she was not. I could go as far as the cliff edge and watch the man, head bent against the wind and rain, stumble across the pebbles to a boat from which a number of men came running, carrying boxes, sacks and crates. All, including the man who had drawn me to the shore, were weighed down with heavy loads. All took their spoils to a cave under the cliffs, while apprehensively watching the cliffs, which might have given cover to witnesses of their crime, but from which no movement could be discerned.

'Bevan' – I had heard his name spoken by the lady of the coastguard cottages – began to organise the group. Some of them were detailed to keep watch at the top of the cliff – to which they climbed with apparently little effort. Others, at obviously pre-prepared signals from them, began to move the boxes from the cave, while others rowed the boat from its moorings, presumably to a place of greater safety.

I should have been immensely ignorant of the history of the south coast had I not realised that I had just witnessed the landing of smuggled goods from across the Channel.

In the darkness the figures before me began to melt into a mist. I was surprised to find myself, not at the cliff edge, but at the point at which the cottage garden gates issued onto the grass covered cliff top. I felt my clothes, found them to be dry. Whatever conditions Bevan had encountered had not affected me. At least not physically, because what had made a great impression upon me was that a man whose purpose should have been to prevent such landings had assisted one and, from the regulated way in which he had marshalled 'his' men, organised and managed it.

But the evening's drama was not concluded. I slipped again into the past, and looked up at the cottage windows and, at one, stood a lady. I had imagined all Victorian clothing to be dark; she wore white. Her dress hugged her figure, something else I had not expected and, from my vantage point and, as she turned, I dimly discerned a bustle. Not the monstrous constructions that one sees in novel illustrations but little more than a prominent bow. Detail I could not see although I was able to see her better as she emerged from the cottage.

To my consternation, I saw that she was walking towards me, her long skirt trailing on the damp ground. I was worried that she might have played a part in the activities of her lover, of Bevan. But this fear soon evaporated. For I had seen the look on her face as she had passed me and it was one of fear, of utter astonishment. The more I stared, the more distinct her figure became – and the greater my love.

Suddenly I felt my head pounding; I looked down at the ground and then up. She, and the formal gardens had gone.

I shook my head, surprised to find that I had remained by the cottage gardens and had not proceeded to the cliff edge. Although I knew it to be much earlier in 'my' evening, the darkness indicated that the images I had seen had taken place at a much later hour.

For several days I saw on my walks the figure of the woman but, about a week later, I saw her with Bevan. It was an emotional meeting, and the distinctness of their speech was clearer than on any previous occasion.

'You went out,' she said. 'You took part…'

'Constance,' he said – and it was the first time I had heard her name - 'you do not understand. I am on the coast guard. I was engaged in joining the group in order to expose them.'

'You did not appear to be reluctant.'

'Of course not,' Bevan said. 'I should not then have been successful in giving the impression I need to give the men.'

'But I had heard nothing. None of those in the cottages had told me.'

'But of course they did not tell you; would it have been wise to reveal to the families here that an attempt to join a smuggling gang in order to destroy it was under way?'

Constance stared. I could tell that she was unconvinced and that her feelings towards Bevan were changing, whether because he had not considered her worthy of his confidence, or because he sought to mislead her I could not tell.

For the first time, I wondered why the other cottagers did not attempt to waylay the smugglers. I paid no more heed than Constance to Bevan's argument that they were in a pact to catch the criminals, rather that they were in league with them. And, later, on the only occasion that I saw anyone other than the two lovers, I saw a meeting outside her cottage between Constance and her 'lieutenant' father. I gained the strong impression that, while not a participant, he, too, knew of and condoned (or perhaps just sympathised with) the trade.

It was only days later, when I heard an argument with Bevan, that I became further convinced that her suspicions had become convictions. Their argument was long, and I moved forward as he lifted his hand to strike her.

My attempt to protect her was, as I should have guessed, a futile one. Never a man I had liked (absurdly I had experienced considerable jealousy) I now had even greater reason to hate Bevan – and I was unable to protect her from the blow that landed. She slumped to the floor and, perhaps motivated by remorse, he knelt beside her and lifted her head, stroking it.

'Always my anger,' he said. 'I cannot control my anger.'

He gradually lifted her and it was clear that she was not badly hurt.

'Always so angry,' he said – and the scene cleared, and I returned to my own times.

But, for some time, I could not leave her.

The absurdity of worrying about a woman who had lived over a hundred years ago, and whose fate had been sealed long ago was ever with me. But I had to know what that fate was. Whether the ferocity of her lover had resulted in her greater injury, and whether her life had become blighted when, as I suspected she would, she married a man so quick to strike.

My visits to the cottage gardens revealed little for some time. Whether through her forgiveness or her love – and her acceptance of his behaviour because of that love – I could not tell. But she clearly carried on as before – even if her face had become lined with worry.

It was about two weeks later in my life – I could not tell how long in theirs – that the next dramatic event occurred. As I approached the cottages, dusk was descending. As soon as my world changed to theirs, I could feel the cold that I had not experienced before.

The light wind had become a gale, the pleasant evening stormy. The wind and rain which lashed against Bevan's face could be seen but not felt. Constance was clearly in her cottage and my love engendered relief that she was protected from the elements.

I now became aware of the screams which appeared to be coming from the beach below the cliff. For the first time, I felt some sympathy for Bevan for I imagined he was about make an attempt to save those shipwrecked mariners from whom these wild cries came.

I saw him, indeed, make his way towards the cliff edge and make his adept descent onto the beach. But, here, were other men, the men I had seen on the night of the landing of the contraband. And, as before, they were retrieving goods from a boat, this time a foundered ship, a ship whose mast was still prominently above the waves but whose hulk was fast disappearing beneath them. Men were thrown by the unforgiving waves and only a few were lucky enough to reach shore.

These the smugglers ignored, intent on their task of recovering the ship's cargo. I watched powerless, and then I became aware, at the same time, of a man who had started to climb the cliff to escape the waves which would have torn him from it and returned him to the angry sea.

And I observed Constance, her ghost-like white figure watching the man. She was beseeching her lover to help him – and the other sailors whose lives were so clearly threatened.

It was difficult to make herself heard above the gale.

In horror I watched her scrambling down the cliff. This time he heard her cries and waved her angrily back. But she came on, slipping and stumbling to a ledge where she collected her breath. At last he acted, making light work – despite the conditions – of the treacherous ascent. When he reached her, the angry voice that I had remembered him using before could again be heard.

I could not hear their words but his anger, and increasingly hers, were evident. Her hand pointed towards the man who was now pleading for assistance. Finally Bevan's anger dissipated and he took her in his arms and, by an act I could not have believed possible, carried her up the cliff which she had descended with such difficulty.

And then he returned to where the sailor was still begging for assistance – and carried him with as little difficulty to a point at which he could scramble to the top of the cliff.

Constance watched them, her anxiety still evident. Her lover then returned for another man who was clinging to a ledge above the sea which was slamming against his back. This rescue was similarly accomplished, and Bevan returned to his colleagues who had, by now, filled the cave I had previously seen with the cargo they had managed to recover. Attempts to reach the ship were now abandoned, the danger of doing so as conditions worsened being obviously considered too much of a risk.

They would rely on the waves now to present them with their bounty. The mariners whose heads bobbed in the water they ignored – and it was unlikely anyway that they could have been saved. But one sailor, who had managed to secure a grip on the cliff, remained. He had been driven more by the waves than his own efforts onto the rock face where, again, Bevan effected his rescue. But Bevan's descent to the beach to assist the camouflage of the ship's cargo was hindered by a sudden change in the wind's direction. This drove the waves along the cliff and increased their intensity.

The smugglers continued to work while their colleague, for the first time, appeared to be in great danger.

Constance watched with horror as the wind and rain loosened his grip and consigned him to the waves. His colleagues looked on with similar horror as he joined the mariners whose heads continued to bob on the water before being sucked down.

My head pounded; the waves ceased to drive towards the shore. The wind returned to its previous benignity, and the rain ceased. The cliff top was empty but for a few late dog walkers, but I stood in horror. The cottage gardens returned to their overgrown state and I attempted to walk on, but found I could not. Eventually my head eased and I drove myself forward, away from the cottage gardens, away from the cliff, and toward my home where I attempted unsuccessfully to sleep. When I did, my dreams were invaded by the events of the night just gone. Or the events of over a hundred years ago.

It was many weeks before I could sleep without the horrors of that night returning and, during the time when they did, I changed the direction of my walks.

I never forgot that night; nor was I able to erase the horrific sounds of the screams of dying men from my memory. I remembered vividly the moment when Bevan's hands grasped for the safety of the cliff, and, unsuccessful, slipped into the sea. About Constance during this and subsequent moments I had no recollection. I had seen nothing of her after her lover's plunge into the stormy waters.

It was some years before I could even contemplate returning to the site of the coastguard cottages. But my retirement brought time to consider those days. To wonder just how my penetration through the ages had worked. Was there a correlation between the passage of time then and during my own life? Just as I had followed developments then, would there be a progression in the lives of the residents of the coastguard cottages?

My thoughts turned again – as they often did – to that fateful night. I prepared for my visit to the place I had included in my walks so many years before by visiting the local reference library in search of information about the events which must have made a significant stir in the town. Because I had never known the exact years in which these had taken place, I was unsure in which newspaper I should find a story. The loss of a man at sea would surely have been reported and, even if the smugglers had revealed nothing to protect their part in the event and failed to report a drowning, Bevan would not have been unknown and his death gone unreported. Constance herself must have made efforts to ensure that his body had been recovered. Most significant of all was the loss of what I remembered to be a large ship from which few of those who sailed in her could have survived.

For a time I found nothing. The local library had no records of the national press, although the local press seemed to pre-date the current title, and I turned to this. To my great satisfaction, I derived from this source that the ship had indeed gone down, although not at the exact point at which I should have guessed. Its name was Star of the Sea, an iron clad merchant ship. What it was doing and what it carried I could not discover, but I did learn that those who sailed in her, and were drowned, were buried in a simple grave in the parish churchyard, a grave marked by a small memorial which, despite all my years in the town, I had never before noticed. It was sad that such a minor headstone provided such an obscure final resting place for their bones.

I continued to search and located more reports of the shipwreck in the national press of the time. One even recorded the names of the dead. And the *Victoria County History* and other local histories referred to the tragedy.

I was ready to return.

My walk to the scene was plagued with apprehension and even doubts. I approached the gardens of the demolished coastguard cottages with disappointment. I could see that time had further erased what I had retained in my memory. As I plunged into the wood which had remorselessly replaced the winding paths and garden flowers, I found my progress hampered by the density of the woodland – such that I could not remember the ways I had walked before.

I do not know the significance of the point at which I had reached but I began to shudder. My body shook and my head pounded. It was as if I had been overpowered by an external force which brought darkness and horror. My fear increased as I tried to force my way forward. I stumbled. I could feel myself falling.

But the vision which enveloped me was – and is – clear in my memory. And the sight of Constance standing before me was accompanied by a wailing which caused pain in my limbs and in my head. I was helpless to resist her. Constance stooped, sat beside me and reached her hands towards me. In her eyes was a look of pain and concern. In her demeanour was a tenderness I had never before encountered. While the wailing continued, it appeared not to emanate from her. It was all around. I thought she attempted to touch me. But then I realised that her tenderness was not for me. Her eyes were trained not on my face but on a point beyond me.

It was my neighbour who found me and brought my unconscious self from the wood: I awoke in a hospital bed, and it took some weeks before I was well enough to return home. And, when I did so, I began to prepare for my return to the coastguard cottage gardens. I realised it would be unwise in my weak state, possibly detrimental to my health.

But I could not resist the pull that Constance exerted upon me.
So, I did return. With fear and apprehension, I returned.
Now I walk that way often.
But I have never seen her again.

Ruby... and Me

My name is Leslie Gannon. But this is a story about Ruby. Well, Ruby and me.

I should try to describe Ruby but it would be very difficult. How do you describe perfection?

Her face is lovely; her hair just sort of sweeps down in a glossy wave. Her body is heavenly. Her legs…

Well, I said how do you describe perfection and here I am trying to do it.

What I will do is ask you to think of your wife, your girlfriend, your favourite film star – whoever rings your bell or floats your boat. Whoever, if you haven't already got her, you would *love* to have as your soul mate. Whatever you come up with, you stick to it and imagine Ruby as being like her. Although, Ruby is… well, I won't go on.

Now, I live in Hendon; that's a place near London. Most people would say it's *in* London. And Ruby lives there too. That's where I met Ruby. She was walking round the shops – and I was walking round the shops.

And it was like two ships on a collision course. She stepped aside, and I stepped aside. And we collided. You know how it is. She laughed and I laughed and said something funny like 'shall we dance'? Not original but it made us laugh even more.

I said that we were obviously meant for each other and she said yes – and she laughed again. Anyway she was still smiling – and you can bet your life I was still smiling.

I asked her if she had time for a coffee – knowing she would have. And she said she supposed so. All hard to get – you know. She'd been knocked out by me. Not literally – we hadn't bumped that hard.

Anyway I looked up and saw one of those swanky coffee houses that people go to when they want to impress. I indicated by a nod of my head that we could go there – and she understood. So you can see that, right from the start, we were in tune with each other. We were like an orchestra playing beautiful music.

Anyhow, we went in and I ordered coffee. I asked what else she'd like but she said coffee was fine. I was pretty certain she only came in because she wanted my company. So I said – 'I'm having a pastry', so that she would have more if she wanted. And so that she could tell I wasn't a cheapskate. She just shrugged as if it didn't matter – confirming what I thought – that she was only interested in being with me. So, I ordered two pastries. Although I noticed she didn't eat hers. Obviously couldn't concentrate on eating while out with me. But she did sip her coffee.

And we talked. Boy, we really did talk. I talked about my life and my interests – about my motocross. And she listened and showed interest. I know she was interested because she didn't look bored. So I described all the ins and outs, the technicalities of the bikes and, of course, how many times I'd won. And how I'd done it.

She didn't talk much about herself. But that wasn't important because we were talking and that was all that really mattered. And she'd look up at me with those eyes. Did I mention her eyes? Well, if I didn't they were like limpid pools of light. I've read that somewhere or heard someone say it, and I memorised it. Now I think of it, the phrase suited Ruby's eyes down to a tee. And I expect you're thinking of your girl's eyes. Well, Ruby's were even more special.

Anyway, our chat went on for some time. She was obviously really interested in motocross because she never interrupted. So, since she didn't ask for any more information, my description of the bikes I'd ridden and my most outstanding rides, must have satisfied her, fascinated her. She just listened with those gorgeous eyes and sometimes smiled.

Since she was getting hooked, I suggested she'd like to come and see me riding. And, although I thought she was tempted, she shook her head. And I knew why. She'd become so fond of me that she couldn't entertain the thought of my being injured. You see I'd told her that it was a dangerous sport – very dangerous – and I could see why she'd think that way. So I didn't push it. I've never had an accident and, because I'm such a skilful rider, I never will – but she didn't know that. So, yes, I left it and we finished our coffee.

But, of course, that wasn't the end of it. It would be the end of the story otherwise and I can tell you're getting interested. In Ruby. And, well, I'm not a boastful guy but, in me too.

I saw her the next day and I thought – come on, be sensible, invite her to something where she wouldn't worry about my welfare. Cinema, show, concert: I gave her a choice. And she said – 'Well, I'm not sure'.

That wouldn't do. She would have to be sure, so I got more specific. A band I liked, Foot Loose and Fancy Free, were on at The Dominion. Would she like to see them? 'Well…' Yes, I knew, she wasn't sure; probably hadn't heard much of their music. I'd have to make up her mind for her.

'That's a date then,' I said. 'We'll go for that' – as if she'd said yes.

And we went. She wasn't into holding hands. Well, that was OK: some girls aren't. And she ducked away when I went to give her a kiss goodnight. And that was alright too. The best relationships start slowly – and those are the ones that develop into strong partnerships. It was a good sign really.

So I felt good: this beautiful girl was all mine, and I asked her where she lived so I could take her home. But, no: her mum wouldn't like it. Her mum had never seen me; if she had, she'd have been putty in my hands.

So, I didn't push anything so that our romance would blossom. And I saw her the next day. I knew where to look; I was getting quite used to where she walked. But this time I went up to her and she turned down a side street. I was going to say 'dived' but that would have been silly – almost as if she was trying to get away from me. Which would have been absurd.

I didn't see her for a few days on the streets I was used to seeing her. And why *should* she always do the same things in the same places? So I waited until I saw her again – and kept out of sight.

I followed her home; now I don't want you to get any wrong ideas. I wasn't stalking her or anything like that. I didn't mean her any harm – God knows I didn't mean her any harm. I loved her. Deeply.

So, anyway, I now knew where she lived. Or I thought so. Could have been her uncle's house or… But there are ways in which you go into your own house aren't there? Anyway I'd soon confirm it. And, the following morning I kept hidden again and, sure enough, she came out of the house.

Now, where could we go this time?

I sauntered over to her and smiled.

She smiled too but… you know a glimmer of a smile.

'Come on,' I said, 'don't I deserve a big, beautiful smile? I want to take you out again.'

She didn't answer me; just stood there.

'I was wondering where we could go – a show? Or do you like cultural stuff, like museums, art galleries?'

You see, I was being really helpful. No motocross or speedway. That's the way I am; I know how to treat a girl.

She still didn't speak but I knew she wanted to go somewhere, so I carried on.

'And when do you want to go? Any time – leave out the next bike meeting that's all.'

I couldn't say fairer than that, could I? But I needed to press home.

'Saturday? Saturday would be a good day. How about this Saturday?'

At last she spoke.

'Sorry, I er... I can't make Saturday.'

'OK, that's fine; some things are more important than going out with me.' I pretended to think about that – 'Well, perhaps they aren't but...'

'It's difficult at the moment. My mum's er... ill.'

'Oh, I'm so sorry,' I said. I didn't want to push it. 'Let's leave it for now. Until your mum gets better.'

I have to say I had seen a woman about the age her mother would be leaving her house not long before her. But it probably wasn't her mother. An aunt or someone.

So I left it this time but I kept an eye on her – or both eyes actually. And I followed her when she went out. Not that she ever saw me of course.

I have to say she never went anywhere interesting – the cinema, night clubs, pubs or anywhere like that – so I expect she was waiting to go out with *me*. If it were an aunt I saw her with, she seemed to go out with her a lot. And why not? It was to the shops mostly – but they went out most days together - she'd always gone out alone before.

Anyway, one day when I saw her out alone, I asked her again. Same excuse – and I bet you're thinking as I did.

She's playing hard to get.

I've been recording my life with Ruby. You can tell how I felt about her, but I'm now moving forward in my story. I've just met a guy who says he is Ruby's girlfriend. Well, she'd never told me about a Peter Shaw – that was his name. She would have told me if she had a boyfriend wouldn't she? So I ignored all that. But he was very polite and he said that he knew I wanted to ask her out and that was understandable given what a nice girl she was. But she was 'taken' (what an expression, 'taken') and he'd be really grateful if I let her alone. 'Let her alone', I ask you.

It was after meeting him that I got the impression that *I* was being followed. I'd look round and I would see someone was trailing me.

I even got as bit scared. Well, you do when someone won't leave you alone. This went on for a while. Of course I knew who it was. That guy who had 'taken' Ruby. And I didn't know what he would do. I could easily match him if he wanted to take me on – but not if he had the advantage of me. It was strange in a way. There was me following Ruby and him following me following Ruby. I even thought about giving up following Ruby. Not that I was *that* worried. But, if it were true that she was his girl, he could turn nasty. And Ruby hadn't agreed to go out with me again. Was it all worth the bother? I looked again at Ruby across the street. Oh yes, it worth it alright.

What *really* upset me was that I began to hear noises in my house. The door being opened… I always went down but there was no one around. I thought I was just being stupid but, one day, he was there in my living room. Sitting in my armchair large as life, reading a book I'd left on my table.

I was pretty shocked. I went for him but he got up and grabbed me by the throat. He pushed me down into a chair and stood over me. I could have thrashed him but my throat was hurting and he had the advantage of me. Standing over me like that.

I just stared at him. That was my nasty stare. It works on most people but it didn't seem to work on him. So I looked like I didn't care. Like I was used to men invading my house, sitting on my armchair, reading my books.

'You have gone too far,' he said.

'*I* have gone too far!'

'Yes, do you realise what you have been doing to Ruby?'

'Yes, I've been showing my love for her. And she's fine with that.'

'She's not fine with that.'

'Oh, and why should she come and have coffee with me? Why did she come to the show with me? Did I do anything that she could object to? And, when her mum is well again, she's going to go out with me again.'

'Her mother? Ill?'

'Yes, she's been ill.'

'Mrs Tallow is fine. She hasn't been ill.'

'Well, Ruby told me…'

The man shook his head, smiling. Nasty piece of work.

'Well, it's going to stop. I can follow you. I can enter your house whenever I want, and I will. Until you stop pestering Ruby. Until you stop stalking her.'

'Stalking!' I said to him. 'I haven't stalked her.'

'You have followed her and she is very worried about that; every time she goes out…'

'Not every time. And, anyway, she's flattered. Women are always flattered by attention, especially when they're admired like I admire them.'

'Well, if you won't listen, I'll continue to stalk *you*. And,' (he stopped my protest by putting his hand over my mouth), 'you can call it what you like, it will be nasty. I will appear wherever you are. I will not hesitate to show you how much I dislike you – and how far I can go with *my* stalking. You will see what Ruby has suffered all this time.'

'Suffered?'

'Yes, suffered. You *will* understand because I will make you suffer. I'm stronger than you and more determined than you. I'll…'

'I never did anything like that to Ruby; I'll call the police.'

'I don't think you will. I don't think you'll want to go to the police. Would you like to go and chat with the police now?'

Stupid. Ignore that. For a minute I thought about what he had said. I couldn't believe that Ruby thought that way about me. I was also beginning to wonder whether I really wanted him coming into my house – even if I knew that, when I knew where he lived, I could do the same thing to him.

But was it all worth it? I looked at his face. He meant it. And, no, it wasn't worth it.

I told him, in words that showed I wasn't backing down, and that I hadn't been worrying Ruby, that I'd leave Ruby alone in future. But only because I'd met a girl who seemed really interested in me. Rosa, what a lovely name. And she was begging for it – and

I could take her to motocross and she'd *appreciate* it. And I went home to think about Rosa.

Meanwhile Leslie's nemesis, Sergeant Peter Shaw, was discussing the matter with WPC Rosa:

'Can you believe he actually gave the story he'd written to Ruby?' he said to her. 'He was proud of his feelings for her and he just couldn't see why anyone – least of all Ruby – would be unhappy about what he was doing. But, that was only just after he had met a certain Rosa!'

Rosa smiled: 'Well, yes, I'll carry on, because I realise you wouldn't allow your precious Ruby to be the bait!'

'Of course not; this bloke is serious stuff – and I believe he'll turn nasty some day.'

'Thanks,' Rosa said. 'Thanks a lot.'

The Girl in the Field

The dust spiralled up as he walked; it had been a long period without rain. The sun shone onto the parched paths as he made his way to the field in which he expected to find the man he sought. But all he could see was a girl working in the heat of the day.

Near to the gate through which he passed was the girl in a red dress. Her bare arms glistened with the results of her toil. Her dress showed damp patches where the sweat had darkened it. All her attention was concentrated on the job she had in hand. She did not notice him until he approached her. He began to speak and, as she turned towards him, he recognised her. It was a familiar face and, because of its beauty, not forgotten.

Callum Henderson was the man he sought but this, his sister, had been his adolescent love.

He stared at the sun browned legs beneath the red dress, at the rise and fall of her breasts as she breathed deeply, briefly resting from the effort of her work. She returned his gaze. Then she continued her work.

'May I speak?'

She looked at him again – a piercing look which did not encourage him.

She looked significantly at the notice near the gate which informed walkers that they had entered private land. But she did not speak.

He was about to try again to speak to her. But she now had her head down, intent on her work.

Eventually he said: 'I wanted to speak to you, Amelia, I wanted to talk about…'

How could he broach the matter of the previous night? They had been very close. Her brother – to whom he wished to speak – had, on a foreign hill, saved his life. She had spent many of her teenage years with him, but he did not need to ask what had changed her. He knew that the shooting had changed her. He knew she had – as he had – witnessed the shooting. She held no animosity for him. He believed she still loved him.

He had seen the gun in her brother's hand and suspected that it had been he who had fired the shot which had brought down the foreman at the electronics components factory. He needed to persuade her that he would report nothing of what he had seen; he needed to show her brother that a man who had saved him, who had been as a brother to him, had nothing to fear from his friend.

He was reluctant, now, to speak further to the girl. He watched her for a few moments; then he began to move away. But he would return – when the man he sought was in the field.

He slightly raised his hand to her and approached the public footpath from which he had entered the field. As he returned the way he had come, he stopped on the path to look again at where the girl was still working busily. For a moment she looked up. He was again stricken by her beauty. How she had grown since they had meant everything to one another. But he realised that there was a wariness in her look. It was a look of fear. Once she returned to her labour he risked another look at her. She did not look up again. The sun passed behind a cloud in a previously cloudless sky. He felt as if the cloud presaged menace and walked on. As he did so, the sun re-appeared.

He sat at his desk during the evening feeling little motivation for the work at hand. He had to work; he could not let his concerns interrupt that. And now he had another distraction. He must see

Callum Henderson and he would do so, but his desire to see again the girl in the field was even greater.

And information about the events of the previous night was beginning to emerge from various sources. The local news caused him to leave his desk. During the robbery at Slanter's Electronics a man had died of gunshot wounds during the raid, and the police were investigating. There was no more information - which led him to believe that only he, and Amelia, were aware of the identity of the gunman. He had seen the gun in his hand, had seen him run and had seen the direction he had taken. It would have taken little effort to follow him to the farm, but he had not done so.

His decision not to report the incident (occasioned by the closeness of his relationship with Callum Henderson and his indebtedness to him) was not a difficult one to make. His attempt to contact him was to inform him of that decision. There must have been an explanation for Callum's actions which Walter Pearson did not understand, given what he knew of his friend. And he wished to hear it.

Walter Pearson viewed the coming darkness with concern. The fact that he held Callum's future in his hands was not the reason for his fear. He did not believe he was in danger - only that he might be held accountable for not reporting a crime - perhaps suspected of having played a part in the robbery given his association with one participant. Was he safe as he slept in his house? Were there others who had been involved in the crime who would wish to silence him?

Sleep, when it came, was invaded by dreams in which faces appeared amidst a welter of smoke and noise. Chief among those faces was that of Callum Henderson, a face showing horror and disbelief at what he had done.

Callum's eyes turned towards the sleeper, showing an awareness that his warning shot had, because of his lack of skill at using the gun, killed. They told too of the realisation that his act had been witnessed by someone who could identify him.

Re-living that moment, Walter wondered whether he had been unwise to seek his former friend; unwise to associate himself with a participant in the raid. Henderson, Walter believed, had found himself in a situation beyond his control. No man who had lived as Callum had lived, who had done for his comrade what he had done, could be a cold-blooded killer. There must be an explanation and, since he knew nothing of that explanation, he awoke amidst a welter of swirling thoughts.

And, although Walter closed his eyes again, he could not return to sleep. But he was unsure that he wanted to sleep and return to those images of turmoil.

The soft footsteps on the stairs could have been the result of his fevered imagination, but, sitting upright in bed, he realised they were not.

They were approaching his room.

He sat in the darkness, staring at the door. He waited.

He watched the door handle slowly turn.

His only hope was to act quickly and this he did, flinging himself against the door.

Whether because of the surprise this action occasioned or because the intruder had expected a sleeping victim, he could not tell, but the intruder fled. Rapidly leaving his room, Walter saw a man. He pursued the dark figure out of the house. As he left it, however, Walter realised the senselessness, of chasing the intruder across the field leading from his house.

Instead he returned upstairs to watch the retreating figure from his upstairs window. It was not long before he was out of sight.

Perhaps the aim of his visitor had been to create terror in Walter's heart. The intruder was not Callum. Walter knew this because of the home security system which had recently been installed. He knew now the face of the intruder and could see on the screen the intruder's hand, which held a weapon. He knew that he could return at any time, leaving Walter in a constant state of apprehension, not lessened by his recollection of the violence of the raid which he believed had occasioned it.

The news which Walter heard the following morning surprised him greatly. A man had been arrested in connection with the robbery at Slanter's Electronics. He believed that the face he had seen on his security system had been that man, although no representation of him was available to prove it.

He did what so many of us do when faced with a quandary. Nothing.

Whatever the reason for the intrusion, Walter now had confirmation that his visitor was not Callum. He realised that the situation had now altered so that he could renew his attempts to find Henderson, to explain that his secret was safe. He could also give reassurance to the girl he had loved for so many years.

And it was she to whom he directed his steps when he left the footpath in search of her brother. Having seen her on the night of the murder, he could, he thought, ease her mind. And he intended to do so. As he walked, he had visions of the adored face looking, like Walter, at the scene that night – of Callum, of the gun. The horror on her face as she turned to see that Walter, too, had witnessed the shooting showed him that she had a reason for her reticence. She, he knew, could not believe that her lover, and her brother's friend could report the incident. But, yes… he could understand her feelings.

As he approached, she eased herself to a standing position.

Walter smiled but his smile was not returned.

She backed away, fear in her eyes.

She raised her bare arms as if fearing him, but, as he made no attempt to get nearer, she seemed reassured.

'I just wanted to see Callum,' Walter said.

She looked surprised.

'Callum?'

'Yes, you know how close we were at school, and since school. I want to help him.'

The girl simply stared at him.

'I wanted to reassure him – but can you do it for me?'

'Why,' she said at last, 'should you need to reassure him?'

Walter smiled:

'I am no threat to him.'

The girl, realising the pretence of misunderstanding was no longer necessary, nervously toyed with the hem of her dress.

'You were there,' she said.

'I was there,' Walter confirmed.

'You can tell him yourself.'

She led him to the farmhouse, passing a large barn.

As she passed the barn, a look of terror showed on her face.

Walter looked in the direction in which her eyes had turned.

He felt bile rise to his mouth.

As he turned away and felt sickness overcoming him he could still see that dark shape hanging from the beam. There was no need to identify the hanged man.

He knew and she knew.

The dead man's sister did not cry. She raised her hands to her face and stood as if unable to move.

Walter, having slightly recovered, approached her. This time she made no attempt to back away. There was no need for speech; Walter took out his phone. Taking her hands away from her face, the girl gazed without expression as he rang emergency services.

He put the phone away.

She now appeared more animated.

'He could not live. He did not wish to live.'

She did not need to explain her words.

He was uncertain how to comfort her but perhaps no comfort was possible.

'We should stay here for when…'

She nodded.

The sun continued to shine, to create beauty and brightness in a world suddenly infused with grim reality.

The days passed slowly; the inquest found nothing about Callum which connected him to the robbery at Slanter's Electronics. Neither Walter, nor Amelia Henderson, found any need to mention Callum's guilt – although both feared what the future might hold. He did not hear from the girl and wondered if she would be able to renew her feelings towards him.

He constantly thought of her and her sad blue eyes and, after some months during which she occupied his every waking thought – and haunted his dreams – he walked purposefully to the farm and saw her in the distance. Her form reminded him of pleasant woods and sweeping fields. As he approached it was to an odour of her body which seemed to exude sun and open country. Her tanned skin and the golden hairs on her arms and legs reflected the sun.

The slight breeze rippled her dress.

When she saw him she walked towards the house; it was as if she were directing him, also, to move in this direction. She skirted the barn without looking towards it. He felt himself compelled to look inside to confirm that its occupant had been removed. It was absurd to think that the body might have remained and, instead, he looked towards her and followed those sun-browned legs into the house.

She did not offer tea, or even direct him to a seat.

She did sit, and he looked down at her.

He watched as the tears fell which had not been shed on the day at the barn. And he imagined that she would have often experienced these surges of emotion in the days since.

She seemed unsteady and he thought, again, to comfort her. But her tear-streaked face stared expressionlessly ahead of her.

'I tried to stop him. He had been forced along. He was given a gun and told how to use it; I knew he was going there and I went too. And I should have been able to stop him. But…'

He wondered whether to put out his hand to comfort her. But, despite their previous intimacy, he could not believe she would welcome it..

He came closer and she did not move away. But neither did she respond – either to his look of love, or his expression of compassion.

Walter drew comfort, himself, from her desire to speak to him. However he felt he could not intrude.

'Did he know I was there? Did he worry that I would…?'

She shook her head, her upper body moving rhythmically with it. She looked at him and stared into his eyes as if emphasising that he had had no part in the tragedy that had ensued.

'Of course he could not live with it. He was drawn in by that… that creature. That man who changed him.'

She looked now towards the barn. It was as if she could still see that form, hanging from its main beam. Her look showed that she could never forget or forgive. Of course she could do neither.

And he could not express his feelings for her.

He also looked at the barn from the window, and back at her, but her eyes were still trained upon it, lacking expression, as if it would always be part of her life. He knew that the scene would haunt her for ever. How great would his devotion need to be to irradicate that ghastly sight and, at least partially, replace it with the redeeming virtue of his love?

Now was not the time to express such feelings.

Now he felt he could merely give some gesture of comfort. But he did not do so. She could not be comforted. Not now. Later perhaps but not now.

Subsequently Walter walked the footpath every day. Somehow he knew that, as well as trespassing on her land, he was trespassing on her feelings. She did not look up and he kept his distance. He viewed her only twice, from the edge of the field. But, after the second occasion, he did not see her working in the field.

Walter waited for two weeks; surely she could not object to his presence? Again she was not in the field. Again he made his way to the farmhouse and past the barn.

As he passed the barn, he looked in – and around – it. She was not there and no ghosts haunted it. Then a male voice stopped him.

'Ghoul are you? Ghoul? Coming to see the scene of the…'

Walter held up his hand:

'No, no, not that. Certainly not that; I have come to see…'

'Yes?'

He looked at his feet. Absurdly, for the moment, he could not recall her name and, anyway, he did not propose to speak to a stranger of anything which would reveal his and her intimacy.

'I have come to see Miss Henderson.' It was as if he had dredged the surname up from his memory.

'Miss who Henderson?'

Walter became angry:

'I do not propose to stand here answering your questions. If you work for her…'

'I work for no one.'

'Then you are trespassing.'

The man approached Walter, who – with the image of the girl in his mind – feared for her if the approaching figure had somehow become part of her life.

At last the man laughed:

'Well, you don't seem to know her very well, and it is you who are the trespasser. This is *my* land, my house, my…' He stopped suddenly.

'But, if you have come to see her, I should tell you that I have bought the house, bought the land. I did not arrange it with her – but I did buy this property. Its reputation meant that I got it at a good price; I needed to be quick.'

He laughed again, more loudly. He seemed to find it very funny.

Walter heard it as a booming raucous noise, alien to the place in which they stood, in which she had stood.

'And, as for your girlfriend, whose name you appear not to know, I can't tell you where she has gone.'

Walter stared in astonishment:

'But surely you know?'

'I know nothing. My only interest was to acquire this property and she was in a hurry to sell and I was in a hurry to buy. She did not seem to wish to stay around to see you.'

He heard news of the outcome of the trial of the man who had drawn Callum into his aegis and to his dreadful fate. And the long gaol term brought some – if very little – comfort.

For some months, Walter searched for Amelia. His search proved fruitless. He approached everyone who might have known her; everyone they had known at school, anyone who had dealt with the land sale: but he could discover nothing which would lead him to Amelia.

Eventually he abandoned his search and took to walking the old tracks by the farm field. As he expected, he did not see her, but he imagined her figure, standing in the field as he had always seen her. He would return from these walks distraught. His life was empty. He would never see her again.

The Castle of Discomfort

The castle stood gaunt among wild hills. The brooding darkness gathered against its walls and seemed to assault its defences. Rain lashed against the ancient stone as if presaging attack by a rampant army.

Inside was no comfort. Darkness prevailed. One arrow slit was the only potential for light in the room; but none penetrated. Its occupant could see no brightness, nothing to relieve the gloom.

He lay, feeling fading consciousness as he felt for support from the cold stone walls. His body hurt from the rough treatment he had received when he had been thrown into the small cell by men with negligible consideration for his welfare.

Sources of comfort in the bare room were absent. He had imagined as he had been led along the corridor that there might be a bed but, if it were intended as such, the stone ledge running the length of one wall of the cell was the only place to lie.

Other, that is, than the floor. In the darkness, what was dimly seen could bring no alleviation of his misery. His foot slipped on the slime on the floor; the source of this he could not identify.

What needed no identification was the stench which emanated from the adjacent room. Or the well, intended to cater for the final days of prisoners without hope.

The oubliette.

The vile odours assailed his nostrils. He could only imagine the suffering of those who had been thrown down this pit of horror from which men rarely emerged. In which its occupants spent their days, deprived of food, sickened further by the evil stench of their own excrement, and additional layers of accumulated filth.

In his tight cell, he could have regarded himself as lucky, having avoided this fate although, even if his hopes might have been on release, he knew that freedom would be short-lived and his life uncertain. What he faced was unlikely to be pleasant.

The motion of his attempts to rise made him sick and, finally, his legs gave way and his head cracked on the stone bench. His visions of coming hell dimmed and he sank into unconsciousness. Unable to control his body, it slid to the floor where he remained as the odours seeped into his brain.

Had he been able to think, he could have reflected on the fate of kings, of the never ending uncertainty which accompanied the wearing of the crown. He now wore no crown; he had been treated as a common felon; he had paid for the joy he had experienced while travelling along a road without other comfort.

His body shook. His fate, could he anticipate it, would be the stuff of history books long after he had ceased to care. His means of execution, if such lay ahead, would be disputed by historians.

But he did not think about that. He did not think at all.

Until the fog in his head began to clear so that he was aware of the pain in his head.

He had awoken to the moment he had long dreaded.

The massive key was turning in the lock.

A rugged hand pushed the heavy door and its owner towered above him.

'We hope you have enjoyed the Incarceration Experience, sir. Are you ready for the Execution Experience?'

The questioner hesitated; his colleague brushed him aside:

'He's not playing along. He's not putting it on. He's… he's bad.'

Looking up, the prisoner trembled on the edge of consciousness. Instead of the expected rough hands, he experienced a gentle movement as his head was cradled in comforting arms.

Those moving him looked with horror at the vivid gash on his forehead.

'Get the nurse; get the nurse!'

Arms lifted him, not onto a stone ledge but a soft surface. He sank back.

He could dimly hear as someone above him spoke:

'You've paid for the Execution Experience; did you want to defer that until another day?'

Again, the speaker was brushed aside.

'Get him to the first aid bay. This man needs hospital help.'

The nurse supervised his movement in the first aid room and offered assistance to the paramedics who had been summoned. She sat in the ambulance, his head in her arms, while the men looked on with concern.

Slowly he regained full consciousness And stared up at the face of the nurse. A reassuring face.

A beautiful face.

She smiled.

He attempted to talk, but she silenced him, laying a well-manicured finger on his lips.

The smile on her face did not waver. She held his head, and stroked his hair with gentle motions.

He too smiled. He felt better.

He looked around the ambulance and at the two paramedics who had supervised his admission to the vehicle.

They smiled too. Knowing the nurse well and trusting to her experience, they knew she would do no harm by her tender caresses.

He sighed, smiled again and spoke:

'I am beginning to think the £10 for the Castle of Discomfort Experience was value for money after all.'

'And you will be responsible for a milestone in the castle's history.'

He was unable to understand why he should be the cause of such a momentous event.

'Well, I think this will be the last 'Experience'. It may have been a good money spinner in the past but it will hardly be allowed to continue after today. My employers will not risk it.'

He nodded. He clenched his teeth at the pain this engendered.

'Keep still,' the nurse said, 'keep your head still.'

He did so and watched those beautiful lips moving.

'I will wait at the hospital; I have an idea you will not be detained long.'

'But then I will have to return to my flat, where nothing happens. It was because of that dingy flat that I signed up for the Castle of Discomfort Experience. I thought, if I could throw myself into it, imagining that I was a king destined for execution, or someone bound for…'

'I think I can imagine a better experience.'

The man who has hitherto been described as 'the prisoner' looked unconvinced.

'Well, I,' continued the nurse, 'could offer you a more interesting experience, a flat more conducive to your comfort, and… well – just for a period of convalescence you understand - you could…'

Careful to move his head as little as possible, he raised his eyes in astonishment.

'Just for…'

'Yes - just for a period of convalescence.

'Or perhaps…'

'The prisoner dwelt on that "perhaps".'

Meanwhile, as the ambulance doors had closed and the castle staff had watched its progress down the winding roads through the hills, one spoke:

'He'll be alright. Nurse said he'd be alright.'

The other man looked dubiously as his colleague who continued:

'But we do need to look carefully at our health and safety policy.'

'Our…?'

The other smiled.

'Oh, you're joking.'

'Yes, I'm joking.'

'But it's not funny; it's serious. What about the "prisoner" who fell down the spiral stairs when we had the Swordplay Experience?'

'Well, what about him? Did he sue us?'

'No, but that was only because of Nurse Buckley.'

'And who is in the ambulance with our "prisoner"?'

His colleague nodded knowingly. And smiled:

'Oh, yes,' he said. 'Oh, yes.'

Reincarnation

It is little known that flies can communicate. It is even less well known that the communication to which I refer is conducted in a language known only to flies.

Because I am unique in knowing this language, which is not spoken and therefore cannot be heard, I will have to record the following changes in human speech – in the English tongue.

Therefore there is no question of humans disputing what follows: I am alone in being able to enter a world to which all others are barred. For I am a flyman.

It would not be likely, and my reader will not expect it, that flies can communicate on subjects which humans would consider a highly intelligent exchange. Flies do not discuss philosophy; they do not create great art or literature. Apart from the fact that flies seem to – the reader must admit – have little practical use, it is only that they do not have the implements by which to create them.

Everything that flies do is practical. It benefits flies. It may be surprising that what flies do also benefits the world – and human kind. So let us be under no illusions. We (and I am referring to myself, at the moment, as a fly) are an essential part of the food chain – although I prefer not to think about that because we are *very* near the bottom of it.

I am not only unique in comprehending fly language. But, also, I am a man and therefore capable of recording the present account which requires practical fly understanding but also writing skills (such as mine are). It is hoped that it will result in sympathy, understanding and – perhaps – affection for the poor beleaguered fly.

I will begin by recording a conversation with my fellow fly – for I appear to flies as a fly, and, to humans, as a human. The most common topic of conversation among flies is reincarnation. That might surprise humans but it does not surprise flies.

I should explain that I am a strange creation. I know about reincarnation because, having suffered an accident which would normally have ended my human existence, I was beginning the journey to reincarnation as a fly. But the mechanism of reincarnation stalled and became somehow wedged between my existence as a human – and the completion of the process, my metamorphosis into a fly. Since the reader will, by now, have understood my unique position, I must test his or her credulity just a little more.

Not only humans are reincarnated as flies.

And here I must turn to a conversation I had just yesterday with a dog who had undergone this process.

He is a fine fellow. A fly in a million. And my conversation with him will be rewarding to the reader.

'I was a dog in a lovely family,' he told me. 'They patted me, took me for walks, and made my life comfortable and enjoyable.

'But, as I approached the Rainbow Bridge, I realised that my next stage of life was to be as a creature universally detested.'

I sympathised. In purgatory I had experienced similar.

I enquired his name, this being our first meeting.

'I am not sure that flies have names.'

'Then use your dog name. Did you have a dog name?'

'Well, that was Fido but, as I go through life as a fly, I find it difficult to think of myself as Fido.'

I let the matter lie and resisted the temptation to question his family's lack of imagination in naming him Fido. And I resolved to call him by this name and let him continue telling me about his present existence.

'Well, the worst thing was that I found myself in the house of the family who had given me so much love and attention. Although my appearance might have changed considerably, I felt I could rely on them for kindness and understanding. Such was not the case.

'I needed only to land within their reach for the children – known to me previously as delightful humans – to reach for a newspaper, roll it up and attempt to end my existence. I was shocked. But then humans think differently. Imagine being reincarnated as a slug?'

'Oh don't,' I said, 'I couldn't be a slug.'

'Well, I must admit I respect them. Do you know they have over two thousand teeth and can bite - which we flies cannot? We flies cannot chew; we have to convert food into liquid and suck it up. Not that I have a problem with that. It's just humans that do. Yes, OK, I have eaten a dead slug – and very tasty it was too. But humans love lambs and still eat them.'

'True,' I replied, 'and I think – as flies – we have a much more balanced diet and it's a very useful one to humans.'

'Indeed,' said Fido, 'yes, we love all the things humans love – and most of what dogs love. But we have a wider diet: dead creatures, filth…'

I could imagine him licking his lips – since although not recognisable as such to humans, flies do have both tongues and lips.

'And,' he continued, 'we clear away things that humans don't like – from dog poo (I used to like that as a dog) to road kill.' Again he showed his delight in imagining it.

Had I been able, I should have nodded. But I continued:

'Absolutely right; I can remember, when I was merely a human, being disgusted at a pile of excrescence outside my front door – and pleased that, in just a matter of hours, it had disappeared.'

Fido had been a fly very much longer than I had and so had met a large number of flies with different backgrounds – different past lives. There was the Professor…

'Oh, yes, the Professor, a lovely fly and very clever. Most humans do not realise that flies take off backwards and swat them as if they made a more expected trajectory. He works things out that I, as an ex-dog, just can't understand. He holds lecture meetings because, of course, he can't write things down but, at the end of them, I'm none the wiser. I must admit I tend to do things that flies are better known for doing - having sex, eating and tramping over human food – but I leave the really complicated stuff to the Professor and make sure I'm near him if there's any danger.'

I was amazed to hear about the Professor and how he had used his knowledge of fly take-off and other previous experiences to further defend the species against those who would do them harm.

However, there were limits to what he was prepared to do for his fellow creatures: if flies were silly enough to become stuck on fly paper he would turn away with a shrug (I have never seen him so I am unable to confirm that a fly can shrug) as if to say: 'Well, if you fall for that one…'

There is also the menace of spiders. One of the benefits of spiders – humans don't like them either – is that they kill flies. Well, you can't expect us to sympathise and it's a horrible death. Being claustrophobic, it's the being trapped in a web that I fear most although, if I survive that, being eaten alive does not appeal either. The Professor had, apparently, invented a device which warned flies of the existence of a web. I don't know how that could work or how he could make it – since I've never seen one. But what this told me was that previous lives before reincarnation could influence fly life and lessons learned were useful even in our present existence.

But, moving on from the Professor, Fido had met a wide range of flies from diverse backgrounds. Ex buffalo, cats, even giraffe. I imagine it has been a sharp learning curve for many of them. But all have methods of beating the traps.

I remember swatting flies (that statement now sticks in my throat and I blench with shame) when they just flew away – and I *was* aware that they took off backwards. So those flies must have used such methods.

Fido directed my attention to a fly who had taken up residence in the kitchen favoured by us both. Also he pointed out the approach of a human with a rolled up magazine. It looked a fearsome weapon but both he and I felt we could survive an assault.

Reincarnation

We watched as the human, as if sensing our lack of vulnerability, approached our comrade.

'He should avoid this,' Fido said.

But, as the human moved forward, Fido noticed that he was lining up his attack – and that he was clearly aware that flies took off backwards. We looked at each other with some concern.

Then there was a mighty noise and the magazine landed on its target. We waited but – with a grinning face – the human lifted the magazine, on which was the squashed body of the fly.

It was a few moments before we were able to come to terms with the loss of one of our number. Then I said:

'Do you know what his background was? What was he before he died and became a fly?'

He hesitated for a moment, then he said:

'He was a fly.'

But You Never Can Tell

Mr McFarlane did have a forename although few people ever heard it. This was not entirely because he hated it – although he did – but because it was a matter of form. If he had been obliged to contact a company and its representative addressed him as 'Manfred', he would not be slow to correct such familiarity with a hissed 'Misssster' McFarlane, which he spat out with great venom. And, if any of his pupils ever dared to use that name, they would be corrected in such a way that they never made the mistake again.

Mr McFarlane ploughed through life like a snow plough. He was constantly on the edge of an aggressive retort, detested lateness, disrespectful behaviour, stupidity, carelessness – and most of all those who, usually unintentionally, misunderstood or made mistakes. It might be said that such were human failings although Mr McFarlane did not accept that human failing should be pardoned or forgiven. His students knew this and it might be said that fear of crossing their teacher made them more likely to commit them.

Needless to say Mr McFarlane was unhappy, unfulfilled and discontented. The world should have run on lines of which he approved, not on those others found acceptable. Indeed his happiest time was when he could shrug off the imperfections of the day and relax into his bed. 'Sleep it is a gentle thing,' he would quote – perhaps not out loud but at least in his mind.

Which is what made the events of this night so painful to him.

The quotation was on his mind as his eyelids closed and he put his book sleepily onto the bedside cabinet.

The noise was surprising. He did not know exactly where he was – presumably in a dream about his authoritarian regime at school.

What he heard was a thump. He could not identify it further. It had a surreal quality as if his dream persisted. But it was not a dream. He flicked on the bedside light and continued to speculate, but still considered his rude awakening to have been an object falling. Had he been asked – which, of course, he had not – he should have had to admit to being a little scared.

It was then that he heard a light footfall on the stairs. And his fright became something altogether stronger. He listened without seeming to be able to breathe. He half rose and then gathered the sheets around him as if to protect him against the source of that measured tread.

Again he admitted his fear to himself. He was aware that the logical course would be to investigate. But he did not do so. He continued to listen. He felt a horror he had never before experienced as the sound of the footsteps continued to approach his room. It was not like him; he was master of every situation. Even to himself he could not confess that here was one over which he had no control.

He rose as confidently as he could and began to move to the door. He listened but was too fearful of the consequences of investigating further. He stood, dreading the turning of the bedroom door handle. Stared at the handle. But it did not happen. Then he heard the footsteps descend. He waited for some time until he heard the front door open, and shut. It was some time before he could advance further towards the bedroom door, and – eventually - to the stairs, and down them to the kitchen. But he constantly looked around as he walked. He was sure that the intruder – if such it was - had now left the house but he could not be certain.

He put on the kettle and made a drink – something he rarely needed as an aid to sleep. And it did not have the soporific effect he had demanded of it.

He lay awake but, each time he felt himself drifting off to sleep, his recollection of the noise – that soft threat, those muffled steps – prevented his eyelids closing fully.

And then it was morning.

What was essential to Mr McFarlane was that this absurd event should not affect his life. But it did. If anything his dictatorial style worsened; his attitude became more strict, some would have said more brutal.

His ability to sleep remained to comfort him. However, having slept soundly on the following nights, he was not allowed to retain that satisfactory somnolence. And for this he blamed the happenings that are about to be recalled.

One night he awoke, perhaps now more prone to fear and sudden wakefulness, and immediately turned on the light. Not because he was prepared to face the spectre which was confronting him but because he feared it so much. This was the result, not of confidence, nor of bravado. Indeed it resulted from the lack of each – it was in hope that there might be some simple explanation for the event which had so affected his confidence.

Again he heard those steps ascending the stairs, a soft pad, pad, pad. His heart pounded. His eyes (the light now on) were trained on the door. The handle was turning. Gradually the handle was turning. He could not get out of the bed. He was transfixed.

Slowly the door opened. Very slowly.

A hand appeared. Then a cloaked figure.

He feared what he would see in the eyes of his tormentor. But there were no eyes. There was no face.

He stared in horror at a hood inside which there was no face. The figure did not enter the room, simply stood at the door, seemingly staring. He could not comprehend a faceless figure which could give the impression of sight, that could stare at him. His eyes were trained upon it. He was convinced it was an other-worldly figure.

He could not move. The figure held menace – and a threat.

He did not move to follow as the figure gently closed the door. He could hear it descending the stairs in a succession of light footsteps. He listened for the front door, heard it open and shut.

He still did not move; the figure had gone but its presence – and menace – somehow remained.

He had, as he congratulated himself, slept after the 'visitation' but he had suffered nightmares, night terrors which led to his suddenly awakening and screaming, convinced the figure had returned. He looked around. It had not; it was a dream. But a dream which recurred.

Night after night nightmares plagued him. Always he was looking into the eyes of a hooded figure. For, in his dreams, the eyes which had not been discernible, appeared to be boring into him out of a blank visage. A face – he buried his face in his hands – but not a face.

It was not to be expected that Mr McFarlane's days would be untroubled. He had never before lacked confidence in his own ability to meet and cope with every situation. His power over people was affected. His manner had always been quiet but, such was its authority, that his orders, his directions, had never been questioned. There had never been any necessity for a violent tongue; his influence over others had been total. There had never been any need for anger.

This situation was changing. He still believed in the rightness of his jurisdiction. He knew that he was still a figure of authority but, if he had once believed himself to be omnipotent, that belief had been sorely tested. Indeed it was disappearing. And it needed to be restored. The violence of his verbal attacks when students committed the cardinal sins of error, lack of diligence and lack of ability became greater.

Mr McFarlane had almost recovered from the earlier 'hauntings' as he chose to call them. It was rare that anything affected him sufficiently to cause his self-possession and self-belief to desert him. But now he had become used to the thought that some strange emotion had possessed him. And he felt himself to be recovering, to be fighting back.

He had even begun to sleep: to sleep soundly.

He had begun, again, to look forward to the night and dreams in which he became again the powerful, even god-like figure in which others responded to his wishes, to his whims.

It was some weeks later that the hooded figure appeared again.

He had slept soundly. He was not discomforted by the slight pressure on his side. He reached out his hand and encountered something that forced him awake with a start and made him swiftly withdraw his hand.

There was no question that someone, something, was moving by his bed, was touching him. He knew he should try to confront it, but his terror was such that he was unable to move.

What he had felt was like a slither, snake-like. It moved from his shoulder to his feet. He recovered sufficiently to turn on the light but all he was able to see was the familiar figure moving towards the door of the bedroom. A dark figure, a dark hooded figure.

The door opened and the figure moved through it. He was unable to see its 'face' but knew, if he could, he would be aware of that black emptiness where a face should have been. He still could not move.

He listened to the soft padding steps on the stairs, the opening of the front door. Its closing brought no respite.

He could sleep no more. There was no question of that.

Morning broke and the rising sun brought no comfort. He started to pack his brief case but his efficiency appeared to have deserted him.

Of course he had considered the meaning and nature of the hooded figure since its first appearance and what it might be. His fear of a supernatural being was absurd. He did not believe, even if he had wavered during the early visitations, in unearthly beings. He was too logical for that.

And he had considered the steps on the stairs, the opening

doors. As far as he was aware from what little he knew of them, that ghosts were merely spirits. They passed through objects: they did not open doors; they definitely did not brush against a person so that their body could be felt.

Somehow it did not comfort him, this growing realisation that he was not haunted by spirits. And his life was based on his ability to impose fear and dread on others; perhaps for the first time in his life he had become subject to such emotions himself.

He continued to pack his case, cursed – as he rarely did – and haphazardly completed the operation, determined to reject this visitation as he had the others.

He strode to the front door, opened and closed it. The noise reminded him of the noises of the night, of the figure who had departed through the same door – and could, perhaps, be lying in wait for him. His students were the victims of his mood: his anger erupted; his style, normally cold and contemptuous, had become spiteful and vicious. He began to consider every student a potential enemy, every associate an adversary. While fearful of the outcome, he was determined, since supernatural cause had been ruled out, to defeat his foe. But, like similarly combative men, he was unaware of the hatred he inspired. He did not know where to start looking, but he would find the perpetrator.

Melanie Everitt sat silently, her mind turning over the events of the night just passed. She had not intended this. She could hardly comprehend that one so self-assured and omniscient as he believed himself to be could succumb to her machinations.

Could that stony-faced, resilient man have hidden a weakness? A heart condition perhaps? One of which even he was unaware?

Over recent weeks the means by which she had inflicted her special brand of quiet haunting during her sporadic visits had increased in sophistication.

But it was on the previous night that she had found him lying, his face white, his body stiff. She had not waited to confirm what in her mind she knew. It was unnecessary.

She knew that he was dead.

She had intended to inflict upon him the sort of unhappiness and worry to which his students had been subject for too many years. She thought that doing so would provoke him and, perhaps, resilient as he appeared, cause him to consider his future as a lecturer.

But it had caused him to turn his venom more strongly upon those she had hoped would benefit. She had realised that loathing and contempt were intrinsic to him, and she had never believed that she could effect a change in his character.

All she had done was to drive him into a world in which so many of his victims had dwelt (which was her aim), but without doing anything to change their world.

Although she had not intended to drive him to his death, she questioned whether she was sorry.

She was not. She had hated him.

She had hated him sufficiently to inflict, and enjoy inflicting upon him, a period of terror. She had planned it so carefully: the theft of his keys had been a welcome result of an unusual piece of casualness on Mr McFarlane's part: his leaving them on his desk.

She had not expected that of Mr McFarlane. He did have weaknesses. She had heard him complaining that he had had to have another set cut from his spares. She smiled to think that such a man had not changed the locks. It had buoyed her, suggesting that her campaign might work, that he might suffer as they had suffered –and that his obdurate efficiency would begin to further shatter.

She put away her cloak, removed the gauze mask from the hood and smiled again.

No one would miss him. He was unloved and would be unmourned. He would be replaced but no one could inflict what Mr McFarlane had inflicted.

And what would happen to her? Would her part in his death by discovered? Even after she had destroyed the cloak and hood? She thought not. She had never seen anyone during her nocturnal forays. He would be found to have had a weak heart or some other condition which would have caused his death. Apart from the night she had brushed against his body, she had never touched him and there seemed no reason for suspicious circumstances to be considered.

No student who had witnessed her surreptitiously sweeping the keys off his desk would consider it in his or her interest to report it.

He was dead and, despite it not having been her intention to cause his death, she was glad. She continued for some time to wonder whether anything could point to her part in the affair. She thought not.

But you never can tell.

The Final Victory

Dapper could hear the front door opening. He rose slowly from his armchair and walked out into the hall.

Joe stood in the doorway. He had let the door swing back on its hinges and a mark on the wallpaper indicated where it had crashed against the wall. If Dapper had not already known the reason for his friend's errand, it was clearly written on Joe's face, for that expression showed the disappointment of their football team's relegation.

Dapper took his friend's arm and, together, they walked into the lounge.

'Is Mabel around?' asked Joe.

Mabel was not around. She had heard the front door open and had left the men to themselves; Mabel could never bear post mortems.

Dapper had married Mabel when most people had thought him set for a lifetime bachelorhood. His whirlwind courtship had surprised no one more than himself, and his hasty marriage had brought to an end a friendship with Joe which had begun when, as eighteen year olds, they had joined the local football club; for Mabel was not a soccer fan. Neither did she intend to allow the game to claim her husband on Saturday afternoons - a time of the week which, in her well-regulated past, had been allocated to shopping.

So, for fifteen years, Joe had gone to the matches on his own and little of the team's performance reached Dapper's ears until he was able to see a report in the local newspaper. But, after fifteen years of meek subservience, Dapper succumbed to a serious illness and found himself in the local hospital. Joe rallied round and, for all Mabel's faults, she had no intention of letting her husband die. So Joe's assistance was permitted and even encouraged.

That was when Joe's after match visits began. He would take news of the game to his friend's hospital bedside and Dapper often said afterwards that these visits eventually pulled him round.

When Dapper was taken home again, Mabel was in no position to forbid further visits, although she realised the harm involvement in football could do to one in her husband's delicate state of health. She argued to herself, however, that Dapper's chances of ever again attending football matches were slight and that encouragement, or perhaps acceptance, of Joe's visits could only reflect credit on herself. But if she thought every account would bring joy, she was mistaken. The recent season had been one of the most disastrous in the club's history and the final match had brought relegation for only the third time, and the ignominy of third division football for the first time since the early thirties.

Now Joe sat before his friend and watched the sorrow disappear from his face and a new expression replace it.

'Do you know Joe; we're going to do it!'

'We haven't done it,' Joe replied, 'we're down.'

'But what goes down must come up!'

Joe reflected on his friend's misquoted optimism.

'It isn't that Dapper. The third division is…'

But Dapper was not listening. He was remembering a warm spring day in the mid-thirties when their team had just failed to pull off the first division championship.

'Remember '37?' he asked. 'We were in the third in '35 and look what happened then!'

Joe was in no mood to share this optimism but had no wish to spoil Dapper's.

'Maybe,' he said, 'it could be.'

'It will be,' said Dapper, 'and what's more we'll drink to it.' Joe looked at him astonished.

'Drink! In this house?'

'In this house you say? Why it's my bloody house isn't it? I paid for the bloody rotten house didn't I?'

Joe had never heard his friend talk like this. He wondered if Mabel had heard. Dapper noticed his furtive glance towards the door.

'I know what you're thinking,' he said, 'and I don't care if the old bitch splits her knickers with shock. Do you hear that Mabel? I don't care if....'

Suddenly his voice disappeared into a croak and Joe rushed to his side.

Dapper's face was pale and his hand was pressed against his chest.

'Nothing to worry about,' he said quietly, 'Just a turn. I'll be alright.'

And, when Joe prepared to leave the house, Dapper had recovered enough to see him to the door.

The following August saw a resurgence of spirit. Both Dapper and Joe had forgotten the disappointments of relegation and concentrated all their efforts on ensuring their club's speedy return to the second division.

For the first time Joe met Dapper, as requested, before the match was due to start. Mabel showed some surprise at the unwonted independence which such an invitation implied, and stayed on hand to ensure that her authority prevailed.

When her husband disappeared up the stairs at an unprecedented speed, her surprise turned to alarm, but when he came down again, pulling his red and white scarf proudly around his neck, her expression clearly showed that alarm had turned the final corner into dismay.

'You're not wearing that thing this afternoon?' she said, her tone mid-way between question and order.

'I most certainly am,' Dapper replied.

'But I've never heard of such a thing. A fully grown man wearing a coloured scarf indoors.'

'Outdoors,' he corrected, 'I'm wearing it outdoors.'

Mabel searched desperately for words. She had never considered the possibility of a rebellion and, when it came, she found herself unprepared. When she recovered from her shock, the rebellion was over; Dapper and Joe had walked out of the front door and were already making tracks for the bus stop.

The season started well. Ten of the first fourteen games were won and, when the season reached its halfway point, Dapper and Joe were celebrating a top of the table position. What is more, the celebrations were becoming as joyous as in the old days when they had raised their beer mugs in the local hostelry. Now they always made for the same public house and the times at which Dapper returned home pushed further and further into the night. Indeed the two friends were regularly singing their farewells on Mabel's doorstep in the early, and sometimes not so early, hours of the morning.

Every ruse that Mabel tried failed. She could not win Dapper from the matches with threats that the excitement would be too much for him; nor could she appeal to the loyalty of a husband who was always ready to disclaim that he loved her and who further insisted that he never had. So Mabel just prayed for the end of the season and, when it came, she was unprepared for the rounds of celebrations which greeted the team's promotion back to the second division. Neighbours were invited in - a thing never dreamt of in the days of her supremacy, and friends were requested to toast the team and its future; the club flag fluttered from the chimney stack and newspaper cuttings of the after-match celebrations adorned the dining room walls.

But after three weeks of unparalleled gaiety, Dapper began to feel again the ominous pains in his chest, and Joe counselled him to take things more easily.

For a time he did this but, when the opportunity was seized by his wife to reinstate herself as the home's despot, he dragged himself off his bed for one last fling.

It was midsummer when Joe visited his friend for the last time. The sun was so hot that Joe found even a thin cotton shirt and light flannels excessive clothing. Dapper, too, was feeling the heat and it was perhaps for this reason that he threw back his bedclothes and walked to the wardrobe in search of his summer clothes. Joe could only watch as he slipped on a shirt and trousers, picked up his red and white scarf, and strode out of the room with the apparent health of a completely fit man. Then Joe heard his voice in the street and rushed to the window. Dapper was in the midst of a group of small boys, launching himself at a tin can, which acted as a ball, and being congratulated for the save by his scruffy team mates.

By October the weather was bitterly cold. Joe could not remember snow falling so early in the season. He pulled his coat collar up around him and walked out of the ground's main gates. Then he turned up a concrete path towards the church, as had become his habit, and pushed open the wrought iron gates of the cemetery, closing them silently behind him. He always felt differently once they were shut, as if he had really shut away the outside world. He walked down one of the well-ordered rows of stones and stopped at the end.

'One all,' he said as if addressing one particular stone.

Then he stared intently at the tomb and at the lines which never ceased to make him smile. For this epitaph was no wordy commendation by a loving wife; it merely read:

'Dapper. A supporter of The Reds.'

And that was Dapper's final victory.

Those to whom football is a way of life may recognise that the 'divisions' to which reference is made above have, these days, given way to new names which will no doubt change yet again in the future. But the Premier League and Championship were foreign to Dapper and Joe whose days are now, sadly, long past.

One Day While Out Walking

Morning autumnal sunlight enhanced my walks. Early ventures into the rugged hills were scented by freshness and a damp hint of morning dew. Those walks were the ideal antidote to the scurrying of the city and pressures and stresses of a world many miles away. Solitude enhanced my feelings of contentment.

But, after a few mornings of this solitary walking, there came to the Netherdene Guest House a girl who made me feel that sharing my walks would be an ideal enhancement of them.

It happened that, on her first morning, she was directed to my table as the only one offering a spare seat. I was asked if I should be prepared to share my table; the girl smiled and apologised for disturbing my breakfast.

I mumbled a polite response although, inside, I rejoiced in the company. Mundane conversation there may have been – but we were clearly both enjoying the company and when, a few days later, the girl was offered a table of her own, she declined it, pointing to the place at which she had shared her meals with me.

Did I mind?

I did not mind.

By this time we had discussed our walks – for she, too, was taking a morning hike over the hills, although not the routes which I had taken. And our mutual enjoyment of the country led us, one bright morning, to embark on walks together.

I required no solitude now; her company was my only desire. And, every morning, we finished our breakfasts before meeting outside her room and setting off across country.

But there came one morning an event which shattered my idyllic world. We took a now usual climb among the rocks, my way led by Isabelle, until we reached a cleft in the boulders at the top of a steep climb.

I passed through this gap expecting to see the girl ahead of me. But she was not there.

Although it was a narrow passageway through which we had passed, the way ahead of it offered a number of prospective routes. Still, I could not understand how she could have disappeared completely. I hurried along the path to a point where the passages opened out into a wider vista. I scanned the view in every direction. My companion was not to be seen.

I returned the way I had come and ventured along each of the divergent pathways, even plunging down to where a cave terminated my route. I sat down on a boulder to think.

The suggestion that she had been attacked, or at least forcefully led away was absurd. There had been no noise and, in this terrain, any violence would have been heard. At very least there would have been scuffling although I thought Isabelle would have screamed – or called for my help. She had not. There had been no sound after her footsteps had faded into the rock.

I walked back the way I had come and investigated every twist and turn. Having explored, as I thought, every way she might have taken, I looked for reasons for her disappearance.

Although the way to the cave was steep, it was not a way she would have taken voluntarily. We had used this route many times and always met the other side of the cleft in the rock.

If she had decided to explore, something on which I doubted she would embark, she would surely have awaited my appearance before doing so. I could not escape the idea that her disappearance had been deliberate. I was unable to see how her seizure would have happened without my awareness of it. And returned to the thought that she had avoided me on my reappearance.

Why should she do that? Had she decided not to walk with me she could easily have told me so. The suggestion that she might have taken this method of terminating our walks seemed absurd. Why had she not simply told me she did not want to take a walk that morning?

Having almost satisfied myself that she was not now in the area, I abandoned my search and started back for the Netherdene Guest House. But, on my way, I stumbled on an area of loose chalk. On picking myself up, for I had fallen, I saw before me a green light glinting in the sun. I picked it up – a pendant with a green stone which Isabelle had worn as we set out for our morning's walk. I turned it over in my hand, worried that it might be the last reminder of a girl I had begun to feel a deep regard for. A girl I had come to love.

On placing the pendant in my pocket I continued my journey to the guest house. Any hopes I had had that I should see her there and that the incident would be explained were dashed when I knocked on the door of her room. There was no reply.

I thought I should leave another day before reporting Isabelle missing and, before this, spoke to the owner of the guest house. Not only had the girl not retuned but the proprietor was concerned that she had expressed no intention of leaving, that her clothes – other than those she had worn on our aborted excursion – remained in her room.

The owner of Netherdene Guest House allowed me to accompany her to Isabelle's room. It appeared as the room would have done had its erstwhile occupant intended to return.

It was the proprietor who approached the police – who visited the guest house and asked to speak to me. I became uncomfortably aware that, in seeking information about the girl, and our walk, the police were showing signs of suspecting me of having played a part in her 'abduction', or even, possibly, her murder.

Having spoken to most of the guests, they appeared satisfied that there was no necessity to extend the interviews. The two elderly ladies who occupied the table next to ours were out on a walk when the police called but were unlikely, the police considered, to have information relevant to the disappearance. But, at the next meal, I broached the subject of Isabelle with them, and, clearly, they were certain that I was not responsible for the girl's disappearance.

Indeed Miss Brannon made it easy for me by smiling and sympathising when I spoke to her. Miss Vernon, her companion, was effusive. We were obviously very much in love and my loss was their main concern.

'I thought,' I suggested, 'that you might have seen her return.'

Receiving the expected reply that they had not, I asked further whether any other guests had talked about her.

'Well, my dear,' offered Miss Vernon, 'you will know about the young man?'

I replied that I did not know about any young man – it being unlikely that any resident, other than Isabelle and I, was under sixty.

On hearing about my ignorance of this person, Miss Vernon showed surprise:

'Well, he seemed to know you. But he also knew Isabelle.'

I urged her to elaborate:

'He knew her well apparently. He had come from Midthorpe to see her.'

I enquired about Midthorpe and was told that it was a village nearby.

'And he,' Miss Vernon continued, 'was going to go out to see her. I told him she was on a walk with her "gentleman friend" but he didn't seem to bother about that.'

If this man really had known Isabelle, and meant her no harm, I was surprised he had not awaited her return to renew their acquaintance.

The puzzlement of the ladies that, after his lunch, he had not returned matched my own. And, on seeking out the proprietor of the guest house, she told me that the establishment offered meals to non-residents and, although she had not remembered the man who had taken advantage of this arrangement, she would have no record of him.

'We just see them for the meal and that is it,' she said to my disappointment, 'and, if he had come in on that Tuesday, I should not have seen him anyway. I was in Midthorpe.'

I was convinced that the mysterious diner held the solution to Isabelle's disappearance. But the police were not convinced; I obtained the impression that, when I visited the police station to provide them with information about him, they believed the story to be an invention of mine to convince them I had played no part in Isabelle's disappearance.

The obvious solution would have been to speak to Miss Brannon and Miss Vernon and I suggested this to the police.

'Oh, the "silly old dears",' was the response, 'Miss Gilbert, the proprietor, told me about them.'

'They are not "silly old dears", they are perfectly sensible people.'

'They were,' I was told in a tired voice, 'inventing a story for your benefit.'

My suggestion that, their impression of the elderly ladies being incorrect, another visit to Netherdene should be made received a lukewarm response. I was therefore surprised when they did make such a visit, apparently in a search for the "silly old dears".

But, to my chagrin, Miss Brannon and Miss Vernon had checked out on the morning of their visit. I found the proprietor, asking her for their addresses, so that I could obtain more information, although I was unsurprised when the information was withheld. The police would not have accepted a similar refusal, but I never discovered whether they had asked and, if they had, whether they had taken advantage of the information they had been given.

And their visit led, to my great annoyance, to a request to search my room.

Refusal would have been pointless and, although annoyed, I had no real objection, believing they would find nothing connected with Isabelle.

In that I was mistaken.

And what *was* found was held up in front of my nose:

'And who does this pendant belong to? Not you I assume?'

I told them where and how I had found it and why I had kept it.

'Wouldn't have been because it was valuable and you wrenched it from the girl's neck? Something like this would be worth killing someone for, wouldn't it?'

Now my anger was aroused, having been prompted by the suggestion that I should have forcibly taken – wrenched it – from Isabelle's neck. But I hesitated at his next question:

'And you did not think to report it to us? When did you find it?'

I told them where I had discovered it, denied stealing it, but was unable to explain why, since it was located where Isabelle had disappeared, I had not informed the police. Had not told anyone.

'Did you know it was valuable?'

'I have no idea whether it is worth anything. Had I done so, I should hardly have left it on the dresser so that anyone, from the cleaner to a room guest could find it.'

As to why I had kept it, I could only explain that this was the only thing by which I could remember Isabelle.

The policeman stared. No such explanation could satisfy him.

I expected to be arrested, but was not asked, even, to return with him. And, although the pendant was taken, it was later returned. Why I could, and still cannot, explain.

I could only walk the walks that Isabelle and I had taken and hope against hope that I could discover something which would explain what I was incapable of explaining. But I was aware that, during these new walks, I was being followed. I took that as a sign that the police had not lost interest in me or my actions subsequent to the finding of the pendant.

And my period of leave was coming to an end. I should have to return to my normal existence. My life had been enlivened by my meeting Isabelle and I could hardly contemplate returning without her. It was very fortunate that I decided to extend my stay at the Netherdene Guest House until I was obliged to return.

For the proprietor of the guest house called me on the following morning as I was taking breakfast. She indicated the phone in the hall. For a few moments before she had identified the caller, I had entertained the absurd idea that it was Isabelle who would give me an explanation of the mystery.

'It is Miss Vernon for you,' the proprietor said to disillusion me of that exciting idea.

I took the phone, pleased at least that the lady who had seen the man, whom I increasingly believed to be the key to the whole matter, was about to provide me with further information.

She had seen the man again. And, like the proprietor, and unlike the police, she believed in my innocence and strongly believed in the stranger's implication in the matter.

Miss Vernon told me that she lived not far from the seaside location of the guest house and that, as she was shopping one morning, she had seen the man I sought.

It was fortunate that the house to which she followed him was in the centre of the village. For she could not have followed him had he walked far. Miss Vernon was not built for speed.

I asked where Miss Vernon lived, and her telephone number in case I should need to contact her again. But, most importantly asked – and was provided with - the address of the man we now both strongly believed had killed, or abducted, Isabelle.

Approaching the address to which Miss Vernon had directed me, I began to worry how I should be able to enter the house. It was not until I reached it that I realised that I had formulated no plan. Entry into the house of a possible murderer without his knowledge seemed to be a highly risky undertaking

I simply rang the doorbell.

I was prepared for violence. To say that I had come armed would have been an exaggeration although I felt I could do sufficient damage with the gimlet in my pocket – and a knuckle duster which I had acquired many years ago in an antiques shop but never thought would be required as a possible weapon.

As the door opened, however, I was amazed to see a smiling and

– I might almost say – welcoming man's face. He quickly assessed the situation, laughed, and opened the door wider so that I could enter.

'Isabelle,' he called as he did so, 'the boyfriend is here to see you.'

My surprise increased as my erstwhile lover came out of a room off the entrance hall. She came slowly towards me and took my hand.

'Oh, John,' she said sheepishly, 'I have a lot to explain to you.'

And then she came closer and gave me a peck on the cheek.

'We must,' she began, the man beside her taking her arm and pulling her towards the lounge – so firmly that I could see marks on her arm where his hands had gripped her.

'Yes, we must, as you say Isabelle, and I think we can discuss the matter in a comfortable chair. Perhaps you would make us tea?'

His tone suggested this to be an order rather than a question. He released her and, instead, took *my* arm, leading me into the room in which our discussion was clearly to be held.

His attitude to me continued to be friendly and almost ingratiating. He motioned me to a seat.

'Unless you would like coffee, or a drink?' he asked.

'Tea is fine,' I replied.

'Good, then we need to alter any misapprehensions you may have formed.'

'I am not sure about misapprehensions, I was…'

'You were out for a walk with a lady and she suddenly disappeared and you blame me – perhaps quite rightly – the man whose name and description were given to you by two old spinsters to whom I had rashly spoken to establish Isabelle's whereabouts.'

'But you came looking for her…'

'Oh, I knew that Isabelle had gone to that old people's rest home.'

'The Netherdene Guest House,' I supplied.

He nodded: 'Yes, I don't know why she liked the place so much but I had intended to surprise her and discovered from Miss, ah, from one of the old biddies that she was out with "her gentleman".

I was rather shocked and - well, let's be honest – rather annoyed.'

'But you abducted her.'

'Abducted? I don't like that word and it is hardly appropriate. I had some fun with her at your expense and she was quite willing to join in my little game.'

'But the police…'

'Unfortunate that the police got involved. Maybe they, too, thought she had been abducted. But I got the impression – not without reason – that they had decided you were responsible for her "disappearance". Such a pity that they did not put out a missing persons appeal.'

'But they did.'

'Well, I can believe they perhaps might have done that but Isabelle doesn't watch much news.'

'But, for goodness sake,' I stormed, 'you were willing to let them believe that I had killed her?'

'Oh no, my dear chap, that was only an assumption of mine since Isabelle had never actually disappeared. They could have investigated and found that she had merely returned home – without you. I will certainly visit them and explain the situation and put their minds – and yours I imagine – at rest.'

I muttered some words of annoyance, turning towards Isabelle as she came into the room with a tray of tea cups.

'Ah, lovely,' the man who identified himself merely as Dermot said to her, taking the tea. 'Shall we tell your "boyfriend" about us?'

Isabelle, looking uncomfortable, nodded.

'Now, I have known Isabelle a very long time. We met at school. Is that not true my dear?'

Again Isabelle nodded.

'So – John, isn't it? I think I heard Isabelle call you John – you should not be surprised that I was rather upset that you had become Isabelle's "gentleman".'

This was spoken in a harsher tone than before – but Isabelle nodded again and looked at me.

'Shall we tell John about our little game, Iz?'

She looked at the floor.

'OK, Iz, I've got a better idea. *You* tell him about it.'

She turned round, a look of reluctance on her face.

'No, you…'

'No, you can tell him about our inoffensive little game.'

With a sigh, Isabelle began:

'When we went out for our walk, I had no idea…'

'Oh, he doesn't want to hear every little thing. You walked ahead at the cleft in the rock. Now, what happened then?'

'I saw you Dermot.'

'And?'

'Oh, John.'

'Forget the "Oh John", What did you do when you saw me?'

'I was so surprised.'

'What did you *do*?'

'Well, Dermot grabbed my…'

'I helped you down. Quickly, so that we would be gone by the time your "gentleman" – sorry, by the time John came through the cleft…'

Isabelle appeared to wish to relinquish the telling of the tale. Dermot pressed her to proceed but found it necessary to continue the tale himself:

'I helped you to the upper rock, didn't I? And we waited.'

Isabelle was silent but, seeing Dermot's expression, hastily said:

'We waited, yes.'

'Yes, yes. And we watched you, John.

'It was very funny. It was as if you'd witnessed a magic trick – the trick of the disappearing woman. Anyway I'd told Iz it was a big joke and that we could meet "your gentleman" later. But we didn't. We waited and then came back here.'

Isabelle sat down, saying:

'I'd told you that you didn't own me. Yes, you'd bought a house for both of us – a very nice house – and I did have a great affection for you.'

'Did have?'

'Still do,' she said hastily. 'And I joined in your game because you said how much John would laugh. But, I now know the police thought that John had murdered me. I only just discovered that from you when I was in the kitchen. If I had known that and…'

I was more shocked than I could express. I looked at them both.

'You were both prepared to let me be apprehended…'

'Were you apprehended?'

'Well no, but she has been here all the time. You could have told them.'

'We didn't *know* the police suspected you. Perhaps they didn't; I suspect that was *your* assumption. They usually *arrest* people they think guilty of murder, or abduction.'

'But you could have told them.'

'Well we can do that now; we have been so busy you know and we have only at this moment had the opportunity to put it right.'

Dermot answered my puzzled look by opening the front door.

'I believed there to be a policeman at the door and here he is.'

The policeman appeared to believe an excuse for his – as he put it – 'intrusion' was necessary.

'We have,' the policeman explained, 'followed the gentleman here; well, we have been following him for some time. We thought he would lead us somewhere.'

'Well he has,' Dermot said politely.

Omitting to tell the policeman about the 'trick' he and Isabelle had played on me, Dermot introduced Isabelle.

'As you can see, although I don't think you have seen her before, this is the lady you have sought and I think you will agree that she is perfectly well. And happy.'

Although the policeman clearly believed that the girl, herself, could have reported herself to be alive – and, as Dermot had said, perfectly unharmed, he accepted that she was unaware of the furore she had caused. However, he looked sternly at Isabelle, increasing her discomfort:

'So,' said the policeman, 'she was never abducted.'

Dermot nodded and apologised that the police had been inconvenienced.

'I must admit that I was not aware that Isabelle, who returned I believe, rather earlier than she had intended, should have failed to tell anyone the reason. There was, of course, never anything untoward about it. She simply tired of the holiday and wished to return to me.'

While the policeman believed there was more to it than that, and muttered something about a charge of 'wasting police time', he picked up his hat and moved towards the door.

I said nothing.

I was anxious merely to leave the house as soon as possible. But, before doing so, I removed from my pocket, Isabelle's pendant.

As she took it, she said:

'Oh, you didn't need to bother. The "stone" is glass. It's of no value at all.'

I looked at her, and then at the policeman who had turned back from the door:

'Ah, yes, not all of us are great with an assessment of the value of jewellery. We thought, perhaps, it might be of value but had it valued and, well, as you say madam, it didn't have any.'

Again I said nothing although my anger was mounting. They had taken it because it was the only motive I could have had for killing Isabelle. They returned it without an apology and without informing me about the 'valuation'.

I should have felt relieved that all was over. But I didn't. I had been duped and I did not relish looking a fool. I considered Isabelle's feeling for me was not genuine, and only gradually began to see her in the light of a woman desperately seeking refuge from a bully.

So, as the days at home passed, my feelings for Isabelle changed. I entertained the thought that, however long her relationship with Dermot had lasted and however deeply she once felt about him, that feeling was no longer as strong. Why else would she holiday at The Netherdene Guest House and accept my friendship? Why had she given me every impression that my evident love for her was returned? And why had it needed the 'little trick' for her to return to Dermot?

I was aware, too, that Dermot treated her roughly. I had not forgotten the marks of his fingers on her arm, and the way he had bullied her at their house. But I was also prepared to accept that women could live contentedly with men who treated them badly. No doubt he satisfied her in many areas of their relationship. And maybe her 'holiday' was a rest from his overbearing nature, although she could not have expected to meet someone, like myself, who was prepared to offer her kindness and true affection.

Was I a relief from the intensity of her relationship with Dermot?

It was weeks later that I read about the assault – and, when I viewed the newspaper report on the incident, there was little doubt that the perpetrator was the man I had visited. I only needed to know that Dermot had received a custodial sentence and that – to my immense relief – the victim had not been Isabelle. I suspected that, following his release, they would return to their old relationship.

But then I reconsidered. A man who had done that? Could she ever return to their – I imagine his – house? I suspected that she perhaps would not, and the way might become open for our reconciliation. On the other hand, was I prepared to return to a woman who had treated me with such little respect?

And the cold winter passed and she made no attempt to get in touch.

When I arranged a short break at the Netherdene Guest House, it was with two motives. On the one hand it was to relive a time in my life that, with all its disappointment, had shown me that I could love and love deeply, and enjoy the rugged scenery with a girl who was, and was becoming again, the girl of my dreams. But, secondly, there was a motive that I could hardly admit to myself. Could Isabelle have sufficient tenderness (similar to that she had shown me on our walks) to arrange a similar holiday on the same week, at the same place, in a desperate hope that I might do the same and that we could become lovers again? For I had talked to her of my romantic spirit and she had admitted to a similar nature.

I dismissed this as soon as it had entered my mind. It was not only unlikely, it was not, I believed, something for which I really wished. A girl who had apparently loved two men and shown no willingness to renew her acquaintance with me.

No, my plan was to take those rocky walks on my own and remember.

Yes, remember.

The autumn days were similar to those on which I had walked with Isabelle. And to pretend that my walks were solitary – deliberately solitary – was absurd. Isabelle walked with me every step of the way. I found myself talking to her as if she really were at my side.

It was on the second day that I saw the girl. She was uncannily similar in appearance to Isabelle. There were differences of course, but her appearance began to have a similar affect on me as Isabelle's had done.

I almost began to feel that I was being disloyal to Isabelle although she had hardly shown herself faithful to me. If this girl could show me true devotion, there was no reason why I should not engineer a meeting.

Of course it was not as easy a matter as had been the case with Isabelle, who had been seated at my table. But I did make the effort to go to her table and it was by no means as easy to strike up an acquaintance as it had been to encourage Isabelle to take walks with me.

But I did make progress and, eventually, with every sign of reluctance the girl, who had given her name as Geraldine, finally agreed that we might take a walk together.

And, having taken this step, Geraldine showed herself very interested in the events of the previous autumn which I was obliged to relate after the proprietor, Miss Gilbert, had mentioned them to her. My annoyance at Miss Gilbert's disclosure was increased by the interest Geraldine showed, particularly in my last walk with

Isabelle. I wondered if she were trying to determine whether I had forgotten Isabelle, whether she still meant anything to me, and whether our friendship could flourish into something more lasting than a holiday romance. I sympathised and even admitted that my feelings were not as strong as those I had entertained for Isabelle.

So, when I invited her to visit me in London, I was anxious that our affection could mature into something stronger. I was unconvinced that Geraldine wished to turn our friendship into anything more either.

But, as the weeks passed before I met Geraldine at Victoria Station, my recollections had turned a lovely girl into a vision. And, surprisingly, as she stepped off the train, her appearance was not a disappointment to me. Had the memory of Isabelle dimmed so much? And, if it had, as Isabelle's features receded, had Geraldine moved forward to take her place? How could I not believe myself in love with this beautiful girl. And how could I consider her lukewarm in her response to me?

We toured the sights of London, and Geraldine became separated from my memory of Isabelle as the background to our relationship altered.

And then, one day, she suggested that I might meet her sister and I was not reluctant to do so.

When Isabelle entered it was as if my world had shifted. I sat down. I put my head in my hands. I felt on the edge of tears.

The girls explained to me how Isabelle had wondered if her 'romantic gentleman' might be driven by the past to spend that particular hallowed week in the place where his love for her had blossomed. She determined that Geraldine should engineer a meeting if that should happen. Her sister was not to make this too obvious but to make my acquaintance to discover what my present feelings for her were.

Was I so angry that she had not returned to me? Was I surprised that, after Dermot's arrest, she had not tried to renew contact?

'I could never have gone back to him after what he had done. Any love I had had for him was gone. There was little affection left after I had returned to him from "our" holiday and his temper had deteriorated, and he sometimes hit me, which he had never done before. When I left on that holiday it was intended to show him that I could live without him, and I never intended to return. But, after it, I became afraid of him and my staying with him was only intended to be temporary while I found a way to leave him without his finding me and – well – I was very afraid of what might happen.

'I believed that what you had found out about me might not have led to your welcoming me on your doorstep.

'So, I let the time pass, asking Geraldine to do my detective work on the basis that you – you silly old romantic - would return to Netherdene.

'If you had not, it would not have mattered to my sister; I had paid for Geraldine's holiday. But it would have mattered to me. I would have known – or at least strongly believed - that there was no chance for me.'

I sat bewildered and looked from Geraldine (thinking how lovely she looked) to Isabelle (thinking how lovely *she* looked). I could now see why the sister reminded me of Isabelle.

I was conscious of Geraldine's kindness to her sister. I did not believe, as Isabelle clearly did, that it was of no matter to Geraldine. And I could see the difficulty she probably had in bringing Isabelle to London when, perhaps, her feelings for me were stronger than those of her sister.

For some time we sat in silence. I was in love with two sisters and I had to make a decision.

I had a feeling that, as awkward as making that decision would be, I might relish the process by which I made it. I suspected, too, that both girls would understand my situation.

I ventured to say:

'So, I am unsure what to say to you both: one who tricked me and another who… um… tricked me.'

Both girls smiled.

And I smiled too.

The Wiles of Women

The morning presented a white vista. For the first time that year, a white blanket covered the ground. I planted my feet on the crunchy snow, marvelling at the clear outline of my shoes. The air, breathed with such pleasure, was exhaled in clouds of white – clean and pure. How could Christmas Day have started any better?

A great deal more pleasure was to follow, for the day was to be spent at my cousin's house and two of my other cousins had been invited to share it with us. All three cousins were female and all – to my twelve year old self – beautiful. The photographs I have of them, taken at this time, suggest my assessment to have been fully justified.

I viewed them in awe, reverence and with devotion. I would receive from them a kiss on the cheek which would thrill me as much as any romantic moment later in life.

But, first, the trek through the snow (we were merely a mile from our destination) was to be undertaken – an exciting journey where I could believe myself emulating my Antarctic expedition heroes as they made their way to the South Pole. When you are twelve, one is able to ignore differences as minor as the lack of sleds, huskies and, in the case of my greatest hero, horses.

You are able to suffer the dressing by your parents in triple layers of clothes, a woolly scarf which scratched the neck, and thick mittens. This was not the wear of an undertaker of expeditions and neither was it the appearance with which I wished to be presented to my three cousins.

All of them were older than I was and, during the trek across country – or along the snow-bound roads of east London, I could think, not only of the spectacle of the white panorama, but indulge in the pleasure that the prospect of seeing these mature, lovely examples of female charm would bring.

I regretted the end of our snow-bound walk but better things beckoned. We were met at the door where I was quick to dispense with my unmanly outer garments in the hope that I should be seen as a picture of male fortitude in the light of an epic journey.

And then it came. The 'how is my darling cousin' greeting and the gentle kiss on the cheek which I hoped to savour for a while until it was repeated by my other cousins. As if this were not enough, there was the anticipation of seeing the Christmas decorations, of indulging in present giving – and receiving, and the strong possibility of another walk – this time in even more delightful company.

As I gazed at the snow accumulating on the window cills, the wind began to blow it in drifts across the garden. I envisaged our making a snowman, in the company of my three cousins, while my parents assisted in the preparation of tea. The windows darkened as the snow piled on ledges and the garden walls grew several inches higher thanks to its covering, its flower beds and lawn increasingly taking on the undulating curves of a white desert.

But my attention turned back to my cousins, my beautiful cousins – and the presents they had brought. Each one offered me the opportunity for a chaste kiss, until… I cannot remember now who had decided – accurately - that I should appreciate a walkie talkie set but, whoever it was, had pleased me more than they could know. Primitive, perhaps, by today's standards, it was, however, as unexpected as it was delightful.

The suggestion followed: 'Why not sing to us?' and I obliged with not a little nervousness.

I cannot remember who had this idea, but I suspect it would have been my mother, who increased my pleasure by suggesting –

after the song had finished - that I should go up into one of the bedrooms, take the walkie talkie and sing some other songs. Either she had noticed my embarrassment at performing in front of such august company - or she believed the audience would appreciate the concert to be staged at a greater distance. Either way the thrill of singing to my cousins – and of using the best Christmas present I had ever received - filled me with such delight that even the prospect of snowman building could not match it. I took the 'receiver' – I learned that both units could act as transmitter and receiver – and provided my prospective audience with instructions on how to hear what I was about to deliver. A task so simple, although one I believed to be my responsibility as a man.

From just outside the room I spoke into 'my' end and, on returning, received the information that all was working perfectly. I took my 'transmitter' upstairs and began to think.

This process resulted in my decision on an opening number. Max Bygraves had recently recorded a song entitled *Jingle Bell Rock*. My three cousins were eighteen, twenty and twenty two – so were, while young by my parents' standards, still – as I termed it – getting on in life. So the introduction to the programme seemed suitable: seasonal, rocking, jolly and best known as sung by a singer popular with older people.

Having completed this number, I began to think that perhaps I could venture further into the realms of rock 'n' roll which was my great music love at the time. I could remember a friend's mother asking me which type of music I enjoyed – a question answered by a firm 'rock 'n' roll'.

'But you must like other types of music too?'

This question was answered by a shake of the head. And, for the rest of the day, we listened to music on the record player which satisfied the somewhat exclusive taste of her guest.

And I had performed this type of music before – albeit without the benefit of an audience. My 'guitar' was a tennis racquet; my hair was brushed into the biggest quiff my hair could manage and my performance – while needing to please no one was, I felt, satisfactory.

And so I began and, after that first song, I turned the 'transmitter' to 'receive' and could have sworn that what I heard was applause from the appreciative audience downstairs. While it might have been crackling – the walkie talkie was presumably not an expensive toy – I was sure that the sound indicated their satisfaction.

My thoughts returned to a day when visiting the home of one of these three cousins when she had played a record by Little Richard and took from me one – by Duffy Power – which I had brought, and put it on the turntable. While not to my uncle's taste – he wondered why 'my' record had to be sung with an American accent although I had admitted the singer to be English – it was a useful recollection. I had a wide repertoire of songs with which to delight those listening below.

I could smell the enticing odour of turkey and decided that, however much the end of the performance might disappoint my listeners, I should conclude the concert with a newly recorded favourite. I collected my walkie talkie and proceeded downstairs, trying to divine who would be currently holding the receiver. I moved stealthily and at speed so that I could interrupt them before they had realised the entertainment had finished.

As I entered the room, I beheld the group engaged in conversation. But, on their realisation that I was standing at the door, the talking suddenly stopped. I saw the 'receiver', and a hand diving to the cushion under which it had been placed. I realised that the cushion would have had the effect of muffling any sound but, worse still, I then perceived that its switch had been turned to 'off'.

It was hard – given that my three cousins were loved with a feeling which only a twelve year old boy could feel. As I scanned their guilty faces, I realised that – at such a tender age – I had experienced for the first time what I should later come to recognise as the 'wiles of women'.

The Lord of Caeragan Castle

The thirtieth Earl of Caeragan sat moodily over the fire, warming his hands against the cold December air. He rose, caught sight of his image in the only mirror in the castle, and reflected. His face, he considered, was handsome. Sullen and cruel perhaps. But, in the quest for a countess to share his castle, it would do, and the title that came with it should attract a suitable bride. He rested his hand on the crumbling stonework and looked again. He needed to extend the line; his was a noble family, one of the oldest in the land.

But then there was a shudder which was reflected in his features as he stared at his reflection.

Behind him was a face.

He looked again. He had often before seen that evil face. Quickly he turned. There was no one there as he knew there would not be. He looked back into the mirror but there was no face.

If his reaction to this phenomenon would surprise others in its comparative calmness, he felt little of which to be afraid. He had come to accept it. Yes, it was an evil face; yes, he was haunted by the past, by his forebears – or one particular ancestor. So while, as always, he felt initial fear, the sight was not unwelcome. He had accepted a situation which he was unable to control. He even smiled.

The face bore a resemblance to his. A great resemblance. He could even believe the twenty third Earl bore him no ill will. Indeed he felt that he could harness this ancestor's power; that he could assist his endeavours with his evil. He believed that he was obsessed and possessed by him: their united malignity pleased him.

He resumed his seat and fell to musing.

The peasantry, he considered, were an ungrateful breed. They had rebelled too often against the benevolent rule of their masters and, by the century in which he lived, had reduced them to penury. Their homes had been sold to pay iniquitous taxes; many of their greatest buildings had been reduced to playgrounds for the common man – or left to sink into disrepair.

The great lords of this land had been reduced to uniting their blood with that of common stock in order to maintain the few homes that remained in their hands. He, the present representative of one of the oldest families, was obliged to do the same.

And his thoughts turned to the bride he had chosen to further his line. Petronella was an appropriate name for his Countess. And, if her lowly origins were to be regretted, their progeny would bear suitable features. And her duty towards her parents and, unusual in this age, obedience to their wishes, would ensure her acceptance.

But she would have no idea of the prospective misery her marriage would bring. The Earl offered her no clue as to the harsh treatment she would receive after she had come into his possession.

If her family's offering of their daughter might appear heartless, she, at present entertaining the prospect of life with a devoted husband, had no idea of the transformation which was to come.

Her father had built his business empire without considering the welfare of others – of his family, nor of his workforce. His unscrupulous practices were signs of his determination to make a great name for himself and, in uniting his family with Caeragan's, he believed for his family too. His daughter had little choice but to dutifully assist him to fulfil his ambitions.

Her pliancy and timidity owed more to her mother who had shown these traits in meekly acquiescing with her husband's wishes and tolerating what few women would have accepted with forbearance.

In turn, the future Countess would be an asset to her husband:

she would bring him the beauty which he craved and the prospect, he believed, of suitably attractive children. She would also bring wealth.

The Earl of Caeragan awaited his bride.

A dark and gloomy castle awaited her.

The tower would provide her with her living quarters – these having been built in the eighteenth century by the Earl to whom we have already been introduced, and had replaced the most ruinous part of the castle. It had provided royalist forces with a defence during the Civil War but had been slighted following their defeat to prevent its use by subsequent defenders.

The rebuilt structure resembled the tower it replaced but sundry buildings and the curtain wall attached to it had continued to crumble and moulder over the intervening years. The fortification had originated as a means by which Edward I could pacify the Welsh. But it was hated by the population of the village as a symbol of their subjugation.

While the building had provided the twenty third Earl with luxuries undreamt of during his day, even the central keep had received little care during the years between his occupation and that of its current owner. And the self-professed penury of the Earl had not allowed the major building work that could now be achieved with the wealth his bride would bring to him.

The marriage of the Earl and his Petronella took place in the ancient church of St Julius and was attended by many villagers who were attracted by curiosity and the rumoured beauty of the bride. Petronella's appearance disappointed no one and the Earl was, with difficulty, able to hide his contempt of those who admired her.

The new Countess entered Caeragan Castle with a degree of ceremony similar to that she had enjoyed at St Julius' and during the procession up the hill to her husband's ancestral home. Her happiness was initially undimmed by the forbidding walls of her new abode and the severity of his demeanour.

It was not to last.

Everyday existence with the Earl after the union did not compare with the kindness and consideration with which he had wooed her. His mission accomplished, his cruel nature asserted itself. His efforts to produce an heir were inconsiderate of her welfare and she began to dread his approach. The wealth she had brought to the marriage did not enhance her comfort or detract from the gloomy surroundings in which she was obliged to live.

And, increasingly, she succumbed to the harshness with which she was treated, and the Earl's taciturn behaviour became so pronounced that he hardly bothered to recognise her existence. The coldness of the castle and its air of despondency increased her depression.

In his turn, Lord Caeragan had become increasingly disappointed in his Countess. As the years progressed, there was no sign of the heir for whom he had hoped. He blamed her. With justification, he thought, since village women who had given in to the charm of which he was capable had produced children. He had not considered that these children might have been fathered by others. They were *his* children. His evident fertility proved the barrenness of his wife and his treatment of her deteriorated still further.

Climbing the staircase by which the Countess approached her room had become a torment to her. On one side of her were the portraits of the earls of which her lord was the latest. And one particular portrait seemed to her more frightening than the others. That of the twenty third Earl.

Each day it became more difficult for her to pass his likeness without a feeling of horror, and she had begun to press herself against the stair rail to distance herself from his threatening stare.

And each day his menace seemed greater, until, one day, his aura projected itself towards her. She could see his hand grasping her, although she could physically feel nothing.

She looked, in terror, at the man who tormented her each evening and, one evening, he seemed to emerge entirely from his picture and confront her.

Suddenly she heard a sound behind her.

She screamed. And now she could feel hands grasping her.

She turned sharply – to stare into the eyes of the Lord of Caeragan Castle. Knowing that this threat, at least, was not a spectral one might have calmed her.

But it did not.

She stared in horror at his evil eyes.

'My dear,' he said, 'you have met the Black Earl.'

Petronella continued to stare.

'Would you like to hear about his life? You would find it very interesting.'

Convinced that she could never find information about the twenty third Earl of interest, she violently shook her head:

'No, no, leave me alone.'

'You do not wish to hear about my illustrious forebear?' the Earl asked.

'No, leave me. Please, please leave me.'

'You have to thank him for building your home. The home in which you have been able to live in comfort. You show no gratitude.

'His Countess,' he continued, 'showed him little gratitude. Perhaps that is why the stories circulated at the time and, in the village, still do.'

Petronella stood transfixed. 'You do not wish to hear the stories?' he asked. 'After all stories are only stories and the suggestion that he killed his Countess are absurd. He was a kind man; like me he was a kind man. How could anyone believe it of him? I am sure you don't.'

He laughed, and, as she slumped against him, let her fall to the floor.

'You will not give me an heir. You,' he shouted more loudly, his anger rising, 'will not *give me an heir*. You do not deserve to live. You are a peasant, but peasants breed. You had to be one who does not.'

He left her now unconscious body on the floor and glanced toward the portrait, now smiling.

'She does not deserve to live,' he said to it.

And he believed the man in the picture nodded.

'Acquiescence, you see?' he said to no one.

As the months passed and, he permitted Petronella to take up her own room, his visits to his wife became increasingly violent. Allowing her her own quarters was not an act of kindness – there was no reason why he should try to please her – but because he had become tired of her company, because the very sight of her angered him.

But the room into which she had moved had no lock, and his visits were unannounced. As she heard his hand on the door and, as he announced his presence by flinging wide the door, her heart would fail her.

'You do not wish me to take you? Well, that is all the better.'

And these assaults became more regular while Petronella encountered the Black Earl in every corner of the castle. Often the appearance of her husband seemed to be associated with these visitations and he would watch her while she would kneel, helpless, her head in her arms in hopeless misery.

With each incident, his wife's strength drained. She would lie unheeded as he returned to his quarters. His disinterest in her welfare suggested that he would leave her until death took her.

Although the Earl of Caeragan's associates were few, he tolerated the company of the village doctor who, when calling one day, witnessed the outcome of one of the spectral events. He clearly had not seen the vision which had caused her distress, having entered the house after its manifestation, but he hurried to assist the victim of the attack.

He was astonished that this was the same woman whose beauty and comeliness had so impressed those who had seen her at her wedding. Her beauty had faded and her appearance had become that of an old woman.

To his immense – but hidden – anger, the Earl had had to assist his wife's transportation to hospital where he resumed the aspect of a caring husband. Although, as she lay in the hospital bed, she welcomed this change, she was under no illusions. She had little hope that the alteration would survive their return to the castle.

While she lay alone, she considered her future. Escape, she thought, was impossible. She feared the forms of retribution her husband's revenge would take. And she was uncertain of the attitude of her father, upon whom her elevation to the peerage had conferred such benefits. An escape to her parents was not an option. An appeal to the police was unlikely to benefit her, so careful had the Earl been to maintain good relations with the local constabulary. And, without feeling able to rid herself of her husband, she saw ahead only the torment of the ghost of the Black Earl, the harsh treatment of her lord, and the lack of respite to her misery.

She knew her stay in a hospital bed would soon come to an end – although tests suggested her heart had been weakened. But she tried to prolong her stay.

Meanwhile her Lord seethed at the delay in her return – not because he felt anything other than contempt for this woman who no longer bore the looks he had beaten out of her, but because his assumed tenderness and consideration were becoming increasingly difficult to maintain. And he wished her in his power and not in the care of the hospital staff under whom he could not reach her.

He knew that toleration of the situation and a continued show of gentle affection were essential to her returning to him. And he wanted her dead. He wanted the continued pressure on her constitution to exacerbate the condition from which he had discovered she suffered. He wished to be left a widower and to rid himself of this now useless female.

He wanted to marry again. He needed, more than anything, to sire an heir.

So the return of Petronella, Countess of Caeragan, to her husband's seat was welcomed by him.

But it was not the present earl who began the process by which the Countess would, he believed, meet her end.

As Petronella entered the Long Gallery of the castle she saw, as she so often did, a spectral shape. She recognised, in this wraith, the features of the Black Earl, and sank to the floor, her hands to her head, her breath coming erratically and with difficulty.

'No, no. God no,' she moaned.

She tried to shape herself into a ball and cried as she had never cried before.

She looked down at the floor, not at the spectre. But its influence was all around her. Her breath now came in huge choking sobs and she could feel the shape approaching her without seeing it.

Finally, becalmed, she looked up to see, not one evil, grinning face but two. The grins of the Black Earl, and her husband turned to twisted looks of hatred, their black eyes matching their black hearts.

She looked straight at them, compelled to do so.

Then, with a choking sound, she sank backwards.

The thirtieth Earl of Caeragan continued to live in his castle of ghosts with only the doctor, although on noticeably fewer occasions, for human company. Others might have noticed the doctor's change in attitude: a reduction in the respect he showed. Caeragan, being Caeragan, did not.

And still he acted in fiendish partnership with his forebear: the man and the phantom. Still the Earl felt inspired and stimulated by the ancestor he so closely resembled. The Lord of Caeragan Castle felt the hand of the Black Earl in everything he did.

Lord Caeragan emphasised his tragedy – the loss of his weakly wife despite his gentleness with her, his compassion and his desperate efforts to prolong her life. For the moment he delayed his search for a replacement.

However, it did not affect the plan that he was preparing and, absurd as it may seem, the unorthodox alliance with his unnatural partner seemed to encourage and assist him in his quest. Following his previous failure, his new plan was to select a widow, a woman who had mothered children already; but a woman of beauty and of whom the Black Earl would approve. He needed to return to conjugal activity and possession of a human being for his own purposes.

When the mists gathered and a cold clammy atmosphere pervaded the castle, he welcomed it.

It was on a stormy day which further blackened the gloomy darkness of the castle that we find the thirtieth Earl of Caeragan seated in the chair in which we first found him. And we witness him staring into the mirror, assessing again whether his features would attract a suitably appealing prospective countess, when the familiar evil face appeared beside his in the reflection.

But, this time, the face began to fade before he turned. A cold blast hit his body and the face of the Black Earl began to be replaced by another. Another manifestation. The face of a woman. Caeragan's eyes widened as the swirling mist emphasised the second figure, a second spectre. He stared – unbelieving – until the face strengthened its appearance – its eyes full of hatred.

As it continued to manifest itself, his shock was mixed with horror. It was a woman of whom he did not recognise the features. He had begun to fear his wife had returned but this was not his wife. This wraith was of a woman unknown to him.

Behind him he felt a sensation that almost touched him but he could not take his eyes off the harpy before him. And he noticed that she did not stare at *him* but behind him. And, at this, he did spin round to witness the withering of his deathly companion. Slowly the spirit of the twenty third Earl behind him faded and its features showed its agony – until the vision was no more.

But, to his utter terror, the woman before him did not disappear. And her glowering hatred was now directed at him.

As his strength ebbed, another figure appeared. Another woman. He sank to the ground in horror, his hands clasped before him as if in supplication. His subjection to these figures was now complete. He cried out against their persecution. He begged for forgiveness.

As he cringed in fear, he stared in disbelief at the face of his

Countess. But she merely watched him.

'You…' he muttered as the breath ebbed from his body.

'Lived…' she completed. 'I lived. Just lived, and those who saved me preserved my secret.'

The Countess turned to the apparition beside her. Her Lord similarly turned and, although he did not recognise the face of the spirit, the truth dawned upon him that here was the manifestation of the twenty third Countess.

His wife simply stared and watched as he struggled to breathe, his head slid to the side and his soul joined all other such souls in hideous and eternal torment.

Life With My Father

We ensured the front seats on the bus and my father pulled down the blind behind the driver. I felt warm and secure. The conductor pulled the wire with a ding which indicated the driver could move again. Out of the side windows we were able to see the bright lights of London. It was late; I had been allowed to go with my father to a football match in north London. The lateness made it a rare occasion and that much more special. But also a little frightening and my hand often stole into my father's.

It was exciting to travel on the new petrol buses, so modern in comparison with the trolley buses, on which I travelled to my grandfather's house, and which were more familiar.

Thrilling as were these, now more frequent, forays into the night, the day that I was allowed to accompany my father to his office in Moorgate holds a special place in my memory. I had always waited at home for him to return from his work, waiting for him to finish his dinner and sit down on a comfortable chair so that I could regale him with the events of my day, events perhaps less exciting than my memory paints them today.

But this was something new. The office was a strange – and a remote – place. I was unsure where it was although I knew it was in the centre of London. The thought that I was to accompany him on that mysterious journey thrilled me. And I could hardly wait for the day to come.

I knew that he travelled in to work on the underground – I was not unfamiliar with this because many in our London suburb used that method of transport so conveniently running through our town, not only to London but to other east London suburbs.

The first shock was the number of people boarding the train. I had no idea my father was just one traveller among so many. We waited for our turn, having spent ten minutes looking down at the football ground which ran alongside the platform. I regularly did this while a match was in progress. My father had had a disagreement with the chairman of the club and so regularly bought two platform tickets and we watched matches from the station platform. I cannot remember who the chairman was, nor the issue which caused my father to abandon his place on the terraces and take up this new vantage point. Whatever the 'argument', I was convinced that opposing my father made the chairman a very bad person indeed.

So the first part of our journey was familiar to me. But everything that subsequently happened was enwrapped in the type of mystery that its lack of familiarity brought, including the different hums of the train and the exodus of passengers.

My father took out his newspaper, pausing only to ask me if I was 'alright'. Yes, I was alright; I was overwhelmed, but immensely enjoying the day. I had been tempted to slip my hand into my father's, but the necessity to maintain the fiction that I was a seasoned traveller was too strong. And such an action would involve my father letting go of his paper. Above our heads was a mystifying map of railway lines. The long central red line represented our route, and I was exhorted to look out carefully for Bank station. I did so; I kept my eyes on the red line and at every sign, at every station, peered round our fellow passengers to ensure that we had not reached it. I had a job to do and I was determined not to fail. My father told me that passengers were disembarking to follow lines of other colours, but we stayed on the red Central Line for almost all of our journey.

And, when it was our turn to get off, it was onto a black line. My father informed me it would take only a minute to reach our destination, so I must be ready to leap up.

My father's office was in a street named Moorgate; I felt that having a station named after it enhanced the street's importance. My first impression of all the office buildings was of the black coating each displayed, although I was unaware then that it was a coating. This gave them a status not shared by buildings in our area of east London. Indeed it was many years later that I learned that this black coating was the result of years of grime laid down before legislation reduced the pollution which had caused it. I certainly did not associate it with the smogs which necessitated the wearing of scarves around our faces when walking to school and being able to see only a few feet in front of us.

As I ascended the stairs from the foyer, the stairway and the pictures on the wall of the eminent figures of the company's past seemed to boast an ancient structure, although, again some years later, I was to learn that it had been built in Victorian times: long after London had acquired its reputation as the financial centre of the world.

I wondered why the lift began its journey on the first floor: my father told me it was so that visitors could be impressed by the grandeur of the foyer with its polished wood panels and impressive documents housed in glass cases.

The lift operator held his lever firmly until all his passengers had boarded, when he pushed it forward to begin its elevation. I expected him to announce the functions performed on each floor, similar to the responsibility of a lift man in large department stores. But he remained silent, other than to bid good morning to each passenger in the lift.

Several passengers smiled at me and I returned what I hoped was a mature greeting. I had not forgotten the previous Saturday when my father had taken me to a local football match – and a group of teenage girls had similarly smiled although one had said: 'Isn't he cute?' Since I was with my father – and taking a serious interest in the match – I had strongly resented any suggestion of cuteness. I had therefore adopted a stern and serious exterior on all subsequent occasions when encountering people – particularly ladies who were most likely to discern an element of cuteness, and see through my rugged and manly exterior.

We travelled several floors before exiting into wood-panelled corridors where my father directed me to 'his' office. I had heard that he was manager of a 'section', although I needed to be told what a 'section' comprised. I learnt that it was not as large as a department and dealt with very specialised areas of work. The 'section' we entered was managed by my father and another man who, because of the initial letters of their surnames, were generally known as Mr B and Mr K. I understood that these names were derived from the two men who ruled Russia, Mr Bulganin and Mr Khrushchev. Later employees would not have understood the reference since, while Mr Khrushchev had subsequently firmly written his name in history, Mr Bulganin had faded from the international stage. But all that was well into the future – and my father and Mr K seemed on more amicable terms, which extended to our once visiting his house.

Entry into the 'section' tested my resolve but I was determined to make a nonchalant entrance. I was pleased that the section turned out to be quite a small one, a room with only eight people sitting at desks. My father's desk, as befitted his eminence, was separately situated from the others, as was the similarly divorced desk of Mr K.

My father had assured me that I was to 'work' and I intended to take my duties seriously. The first was to use the company's rubber stamps on a number of pieces of company notepaper. The paper was piled before me and I was – joy of joys – permitted to open the drawer (with a key) in which the stamps were held. I was given an ink pad onto which I pressed them before making an image on the first piece of paper.

The fulfilment this task gave me, and the impressive designs and fascination of the rubber stamps, enhanced what I felt to be important work.

It was only after two attempts that a young lady approached my desk, and showed me that, since my first effort had resulted in a smudged image and my second was upside down, there was – as she told me – a 'knack' involved, which she would show me. It was clear that this was not as easy a task as I had imagined – and she showed me a raised part on the stamp which indicated that this edge was the top. She had come over only when my father had become involved in a clearly important conversation. Although she was very serious, I liked her smile. She obviously found me a serious person and would certainly not consider me cute.

My father continued to watch me with a benevolent eye. I loved my jobs; I loved the impressive stamps, and I was truly happy. I was unsure what would be the results of my labour. I was certainly unaware of what would happen to the sheets of paper and it only occurred to me many years later that I had been allocated a task which I would enjoy and that the sheets of paper, after I had left, might join the crumpled sheets in my father's waste paper basket.

Much as I enjoyed my time in the office – doing this and other work – I could hardly wait for lunch to come, because my father had promised that we would see the gardens with the 'spitting lions'. And, as we unwrapped our sandwiches, carefully prepared by my mother, I was greeted by my first sight of the lion faces spitting water into a trough running the width of the gardens. There were subsequent visits to my father's office and not all of them coincided with sunny days. On wet days, we went instead to The Royal Exchange, a gloomy building which suited the day's darkening skies, but which added a grim beauty and atmosphere to our lunch. Our other 'rainy day' building for eating lunch was The Guildhall, another imposing and dark building in keeping with my view of what the city should look like. Here I was introduced to two grim monsters of a dark and forbidding nature, Gog and Magog. A dark, dusty and almost funereal atmosphere prevailed, and the monsters seemed disapproving of our levity in daring to consume sandwiches in their presence. I relished it. It was an important part of my father's routine. I was unaware of the story of Gog and Magog because they were – like the spitting lions – a part of a strange world in which I felt myself an outsider – and I never subsequently researched their story.

When we returned to the office, my father, while giving me another task to perform, whispered 'Lambourne End on Saturday' as if I needed something to keep the enjoyment alive. It was not necessary, but it did make me think, while I worked, of the cycle rides we would undertake, the visits to the café where we would eat savoury biscuits and drink tea – in my case the 'milky one' that my father had ordered. A wink to the waitress ensured my milky one and, had I but known, it was largely milk with only a splash of tea to colour it.

We might go on to Dick Turpin's Cave, the stocks at Havering-atte-Bower and the secret depths of Epping Forest: other spots which thrilled and tantalised me.

The summer spread out before me, with so many delights ahead. For instance, when my father would take me to The Oval to watch Surrey play. I knew that, when the play became a little slow for one of my tender years, he would ask me (as he always did) to tell him when the gas holders associated with that cricket ground went up – or down – assuring me that, when they went down (which I was unaware was not so easily discernible) it was the result of someone putting the kettle on for a cup of tea.

Nothing my father told me was ever to be questioned. And no one was permitted to do so in my hearing.

And, as I sit here now, I remember him and the magic world in which, for a time, we both lived. While that time is as vivid now as then, it has gone and, when I am not here to remember it, that vital, vibrant world will disappear and never be replaced. Nor will any future world eclipse it. Such memories are part of ourselves; they are always with us. No one will ever experience their like again.

I sit here now; my poignant memories evoking pleasure but sadness too. I wait for the next mundanity to temporarily replace them.

The phone rings.

'Hello Grandpa.'

No mundanity this: one of my greatest present pleasures is to talk to my grand-daughter, a girl with whom I have a rare affinity.

She was excited:

'I have had such a great day. I went to work with Mummy, and I used this computer program, and do you know what it did?'

She told me what this amazing piece of software did.

'And Mummy introduced me to the people there. Do you know that, at Mummy's work, there is…?'

I didn't know anything about that, but I enjoyed hearing my grand-daughter's excited voice and about the wonders she had beheld. The sun streamed through the window as she chattered on. These were, I realised, the new enchanted days, the new world of wonder and, to my grand-daughter, their magic would last for ever.

A Tale By Ann Radcliffe?

Ann Radcliffe was the mistress of the Gothic novel. It was a genre whose devotees included impressionable young ladies of the eighteenth and nineteenth centuries, and one which was satirised by Jane Austen in Northanger Abbey. *The writer of five novels, it has hitherto been believed that Ann Radcliffe wrote no short stories. That could mean that the following draft, discovered in recent times, might be the work of another writer, a forgery, or a piece of writing that Ann did not acknowledge, or considered not worthy of publication. Although the story line is a familiar one to Radcliffe admirers, its crude writing style perhaps suggests the last mentioned. The handwriting closely resembles that of the author and to replicate it would have required considerable skill, expertise and knowledge of Ann's personal correspondence. Why, one wonders, would a forger take such pains to produce a work for, one assumes, little return?*

Thunder rumbled far off, a grumbling noise suggesting the approach of a storm. Forlorn hopes were driven by its distance from the place which sheltered her but the night summoned an increasingly black sky which did not allow such optimism to persist. This encroaching menace advanced directly towards her refuge. Ahead of it rolled in a lighter vanguard with arrow shafts that presaged the coming of heavier rain. This began to eddy like furious whirlpools until it was subsumed in the black unbroken cloud which began to join hands with the encircling black ring of sky.

When the lightning came it was simultaneous with the rolling thunder that became louder as it let loose a deluge of rain, which drove on the wind over the crumbling ruin in which she cowered.

Were she not preparing, for she was a pursued woman, to leave her temporary shelter, she might have marvelled at the grandeur and might of nature; at the dazzling flashes of lightning and the crashing thunder which seemed now to encompass the earth.

And she would certainly not have ventured out. But she had no choice.

As uncaring was the storm, so was the compulsion that drove her out of the comparative safety of the ruin.

The protection she sought from her garments provided little defence and she was driven by the furious wind, often from the path upon which she struggled to walk.

Ahead of Isadora was the Castle Valdina; behind the pursuit led by the Signor Brosco and the Mother Superior.

She had found her refuge from the weather and, apparently unaware of the vision she presented to those who greeted her, sank, unconscious, to the cold stone ground. The misty dampness seemed to have entered with her, and her swoon was evidence of her exhaustion. For some minutes she lay before the Count Vincentio before he lifted her and carried her to a place where she could rest. As he watched her, marvelling at her familiar looks, she awoke with a start and looked up, reaching towards him. She did not think that her pursuers were far behind her but here was the man she sought – her refuge from the storm and pursuit.

'Isadora?' he said, his memory revealing the identity of the companion of his youth and the love of his adolescent years. He called for assistance, a female servant appearing at his call.

'Help her,' he said. 'Get her clean, dry clothes. I will wait outside the room.'

As Isadora was supported away, she called to him:

'I am in danger. They are…'

Count Vincentio, appalled at her appearance and the empty look in her eyes, tried to console her. He would soon discover to whom she referred. He summoned another to bring food to the hall and waited for her re-appearance. The clothes in which she appeared were those of his lady, Matilda. He moved his arm so that it encompassed Isadora's waist and he guided her to the hall, where a banquet had been laid.

Vincentio pleaded with her to eat. And soon she did so without the need for encouragement. The Contessa Matilda followed her lord and Isadora into the hall and sat without expression while Vincentio turned towards his wife:

'Isadora has known me for many years. We were as brother and sister. We parted when the Signor Brosco carried her to Tuscany where she married him. It was an arrangement with which I was not entirely content, but I felt his feelings for her were genuine and his expression of love for her convincing.

'Isadora's uncle was decisive – he was happy with the match and I was willing to give Isadora my blessing since I could offer her little while Brosco, so I understood, could offer her fortune. My action was also the result of my affection for Isadora, that I should give up her friendship for a future more secure than I could ever offer her. Those,' he said to Matilda, 'were my feelings.'

'Your brotherly feelings?' she replied.

Count Vincentio barely heard her softly spoken riposte. 'My brotherly feelings; of course, my brotherly feelings. And it was, my dear lady, years later that I met you and my life seemed complete. But I always wondered what had happened to Isadora – and now I find that she is in danger.'

The Contessa turned her attention to Isadora as that lady finished her meal and wondered what form his protection would take. Isadora returned Vincentio's lady's look.

It was at this point that Isadora commenced her tale - at the point where Vincentio had yielded her to Signor Brosco:

She had, she informed them, followed where Brosco had led and, in a ceremony which was attended only by her uncle and the groom, was married in the Church of the Holy Sepulchre in a small Tuscan town.

Very quickly the spurious affection which Brosco had initially shown her and which had convinced Vincentio of the authenticity of his feelings, was dropped and his true nature revealed to Isadora. He did not, and never had, loved her. He viewed her merely as a source of wealth. And, having secured this, he took his unwilling wife, as he had planned all along, to the neighbouring convent. The Prioress, with whom he had been in collusion since his plan had fermented on meeting Isadora, had received a significant donation in recognition of her part in the plot to accept Isadora as a novice.

To what purpose she intended to use that donation Brosco neither knew nor cared.

But the girl was horrified at what was planned for her and her heart rebelled.

Days passed.

Weeks passed.

Mild as was her nature, Isadora found it impossible to hide her resentment, and her misery influenced the nuns against her. Her hatred (her feelings cannot otherwise be described) of the life she had been forced to endure was accentuated by the treatment of the Prioress who had inducted her. If this were the result of Prioress Brigid's disappointment that Isadora did not succumb to her blandishments and meekly accept her future, the girl was unable to say, although she doubted that Brigid possessed any feelings of kindness.

Isadora had one hope only – and that was to contact her uncle. And, one day, her hope was realised as she was granted her wish. He made her an offer of freedom from the chains of her servitude and assured her he would approach the Prioress accordingly. And it appeared, much to Isadora's surprise, that the matter was progressing.

Days passed before she was summoned to Prioress Brigid in hope of a successful outcome to her uncle's pleading.

But the expected kindness was not afforded her. Instead Brigid vented her fury upon the girl. That her father's brother was complicit in her husband's plan had become apparent and, now, the reason for her uncle's visit to that lady took on a different aspect. He had reported to her that the girl's desire was to be released from the hated incarceration.

Her attempt to secure her release from a life into which she had been forced against her will not only failed but increased the hatred Brigid felt towards her. And, besides destroying her belief in her uncle's support and affection, she felt now completely alone in the world. That her uncle could have so betrayed her…

But she began to find that her isolation was not complete. One nun not only showed compassion and befriended her, but afforded sympathy for a young girl in her misery and offered her a means of escape.

Isadora and Ingrid (for it was she who had shown the novice sympathy) convened one morning at four o'clock, an hour before the nuns were expected to embark upon their day of devotion with an hour of morning prayer and Bible reading. Already some nuns in the dormitory were preparing for the day but Isadora and Ingrid avoided those whose duties took such an early turn.

Walking the corridors of the convent was a chilling experience, even cloisters which were occasionally used at early hours. While traversing the narrow corridors from the dormitory, the nuns encountered no one except the shadows of past occupants of this dismal house. Isadora even fancied their habits could be seen and their veils floated against her face.

The terrifying passage through the early morning led to Ingrid's planned destination, the outer courtyard, where the guardian of the gate confronted them.

Ingrid knew the guardian and the lapses to which Sister Barthold had been subject when apparently doing the work of the Prioress outside the convent. It was sufficient for the guardian to pretend to be engaged elsewhere, and unable to see her when Isadora made her escape from the convent gates, acquiring her freedom.

It was not long before Isadora's absence became apparent, and Prioress Brigid's investigation discovered the part that Ingrid had played in the affair when Sister Barthold (with her story ready when she was approached for an explanation) implicated her. The guardian's version provided an account of violence upon her person to explain her inability to prevent the escape.

Ingrid was led to the Prioress' room. The loss of Isadora showed Brigid to have been defied and defeated. The meeting between Brigid and Ingrid was not a pleasant one. She had, Ingrid was informed, jeopardised her immortal soul and, also, incurred the wrath of the Prioress. She would face her future enmity.

Ingrid could not regret the part she had played, which she could easily justify as an act suited to the compassion with which she believed those in her order should show. And the outcome resolved the issues she had experienced while living under the Prioress. The nunnery was under the ultimate rule of the Abbess Serena and it was to her that Ingrid was sent, ostensibly in disgrace. However her tale confirmed rumours that the newly appointed Abbess had heard of Brigid's rule, and facilitated an investigation into Brigid's treatment of her nuns.

Meanwhile Isadora began to find that the liberty for which she had so long craved was not without its difficulties. She knew only the way to the town in which her husband and, she later discovered, her uncle had taken up residence. And this town was not a suitable destination. However it was the only place from which to embark on the long journey to the Castle Valdina – the only place where she could find safety.

And so she started a journey which was fraught with danger, encompassing narrow passes, weather which ranged from hot sun to bitter winds and, most frightening, strangers she met but whom, by inclination, she did not trust.

Her costume ensured that few queried her right to be traversing the mountain passes and barren lands through which she passed. A nun might go where she pleased.

But her greatest concern, as she moved on, became hunger. For three days she had eaten only what she could find at the roadside and her weakness threatened her ability to progress. Such was her weakness that she stumbled and fell.

The man who found her in this state provided the only source of kindness since that shown by Ingrid when she had assisted her escape. And, when she awoke, it was to the pleasant surroundings of the bedroom in a small villa and a gathering around her of smiling faces. Their smiles and encouragement alleviated her distress and, during the days that passed, she began to recover her strength and respond to the hospitality with which she was provided.

Her rescuer continued to treat her with tenderness, his wife satisfying her needs. His curiosity for a young girl's need to traverse country where brigands were rife was unspoken; his partner's care and provision of sustaining food required no justification on her part.

She was reassured that she was safe under this roof and, although the man needed – as he said – to work in a town not far distant, the family provided her with reassurance and raised her spirits.

She was able to explore the villa without hindrance. But, after a period of contentment in the family's care, an event occurred which renewed her anxiety. The head of the household had been away for two days when she heard the sound of voices. They brought her to the window and to a sight which filled her with horror. She saw her rescuer, with two men and a woman, approach the dwelling. The first man was her husband, the second her uncle. The woman wore the habit of a nun.

She lightly descended the stairs and left the villa.

She had no time to consider the reasons for such treachery as she opened the gate and made haste for the fields and the comparative safety of the woods.

Had she been able to witness the meeting which was taking place within the villa with the family who had harboured and sustained her, she might have dismissed thoughts of treachery and her opinion of those who had protected her. She might have considered that the family had saved her life and future.

But here she finished her tale.

Signor Brosco and her uncle, and the now cowering figure of the head of the household she had just departed, were holding the meeting which would have dispelled her thoughts of betrayal. He was telling Brosco the motive which had caused him to find those who, he believed, would ensure Isadora's permanent safety.

'I had seen Lady Brosco,' he said. 'I saw her being led by my lord Brosco on the day of the marriage at the Church of the Holy Sepulchre. I am sure I meant your Lordship no harm. I realised your Lordship would be worried to know that your…'

'And you did not speak to her about coming to me?'

'No, I knew her joy would be greater if…'

Brosco cut the man short:

'You are speaking to no purpose and you are wasting my time… *my* time. I must follow my wife and set out quickly. I need only to know the direction she took.'

The man began to speak but his wife interrupted him:

'You need to know quickly,' she said. 'Come with me.'

Brosco followed the woman:

'Why you did not ensure that she could not escape I do not know. But, at last, you seem to realise her safety depends upon me. I know what is best for her.'

The woman could not equate imprisonment with benevolence. Nor had she, since her husband had informed her of his plan to bring Brosco to the villa, believed that her poor charge would benefit from being reunited with him. Now, she showed him the route she told him she had taken.

The route was not the one by which the girl had left.

The wife had watched her and realised that it had not been Isadora's desire to meet or be taken again by Brosco. She had, as the party approached the villa, taken notice of the girl's route until she disappeared into the woods, and determined the best course to advise Brosco to take was the opposite to the one which the girl had actually taken.

It was a ruse which had gained the fugitive an hour's respite, and given her an hour in which to make haste towards Castle Valdina.

Although she was unaware of the deception served upon Brosco, and believed him to be closer than he was, Isadora had known that he would attempt to follow and made the best haste she could.

Vincentio planned to keep her at the castle where, he believed, he could easily defend her against Brosco, however apparent his brutality had become. While numbers were on their side, he could, he knew, defend her against, in addition to Brosco, a middle aged man and a mother superior. Especially as he believed he could count on the loyalty of his servants.

A room was prepared for Isadora next to his own, where she could spend her days in relative comfort, and peace.

As a result she spent her first night of relief from anxiety.

But this was not to last.

Count Vincentio assured her that her days would be spent without fear of an uncertain future. Contessa Matilda offered no such solace. Indeed, on the rare occasions their paths crossed, she would either ignore her guest – or meet her with rudeness. Matilda, and indeed Isadora, could see that the Count was beginning to remember too well the halcyon days before Brosco had entered Isadora's life.

It would be inaccurate to report that Lady Matilda's attitude towards her lord had changed. Their marriage had been a union of convenience, engineered by her father to add nobility to the riches his family had acquired. Vincentio realised that love would play no part in his union.

And Matilda, although she felt no love for Vincentio, suffered a jealousy unsurprising in the circumstances.

About this – although she was aware of Lady Matilda's hatred for her - Isadora knew nothing. However she was soon to find that the lady's hatred was greater than she could ever have expected. It followed a period during which the Contessa's attitude towards her seemed to change. She was more amenable, even shared her pleasures, assisting Isadora with her embroidery at which she excelled.

During one of these amicable conversations, when Isadora had been led to a room where Matilda had begun to embroider a large panel, Isadora once more saw a figure she had hoped never to see again:

Brosco.

Isadora screamed and called for Vincentio.

'He will not hear you,' said Brosco, 'and he is in my power.

'He is in a room which his ancestors created as a prison for their enemies. He is securely manacled, and he will be so constrained while I remove you from this place. I am grateful – very grateful – for the assistance of your new friend, the Contessa, in admitting me to the castle, for showing me the layout of the building – and for advising me of the servants who might be willing to join our cause. They have shown their loyalty to my Lady, and were willing to receive, I admit it, considerable sums in order to maintain that loyalty to their mistress.

'By governing my wife's actions, I have never acted unlawfully. And I have no intention of putting your lover to death… oh, yes, I believe him to have been your lover, however much you may protest. He is more useful to me alive.

'I am very angry with you, my wife. You have rejected the life of service to your God with which I presented you. And, after a period in shackles, you will be admitted, regrettably, to an institution far less amenable than a house of God, the convent I selected for your contentment.

'You have given me much trouble and expense, and, if I allowed you to remain with your lover, I can anticipate that your nuisance would be far greater. You could have planned to wreak your revenge – totally unjustifiable revenge – upon my person.'

Isadora turned astonished eyes towards him.

'I planned nothing. I am not his lover. I did not mean you any harm…'

'No harm!' Brosco thundered. 'No harm! I have had to follow you over many miles to find you with your… No greater inconvenience could I have suffered.'

Tears had no affect on this monster. Indeed he enjoyed her discomfiture.

'And now,' he said, his rage abating and a smile appearing on his face, 'we will introduce you to *your* new quarters. I am sorry that they are not as comfortable as those you have hitherto enjoyed in this castle. But how else can we prepare you for the institution which is arranging a place for you? A place which will make the life you have led at the convent seem such a comfortable one.'

Isadora knew no more. How she had left the comparative comfort of the Contessa's room she had no idea.

She felt a pain in her head as she emerged from a troubled sleep. She looked around her, unaware how she had become incarcerated in this gloomy cell. She tried to lift her hands and, as she did no, felt the constricting metal of her bonds. Already her wrists were marked by the force with which her captor had pinioned her, the manacles being connected by a short chain to the wall, giving her little chance of movement.

She looked around with a feeling of terror. Her brain would not interpret events; her head ached and her body had already become stiff and painful, despite the short time during which she had been imprisoned. But she had no idea how long her sojourn in this vile place had already lasted. She leant back against the cold damp wall; such was her general discomfort that she welcomed its solidity.

And, despite all that had happened to her, her discomfort, her pain, she again slept.

But sleep did not come without a cost. Her dreams tormented her; faces appeared before her, mocking her, laughing, their laughter echoing through the small room.

And, suddenly, she awoke to find that the mocking laughter was all around her, in her conscious state as well as in her dreams. She watched in terror as a creature, whether human or spirit she could not tell, crept its way round the wall of her prison. In a moment it was gone with a noise like the clanging of a gate.

Shivering, and cringing with horror, she sank back from the furthest extent of her chains. But consciousness evaporated and her mental torment continued.

And, for two nights, the hauntings continued. She flitted between consciousness and the blackness of unblessed sleep. The nature of the visitations varied as, with dread, her mind awaited the next. And the next was a vision of a black cloak and the sweeping sound of its hem on the stone floor. She watched in horror, knowing that, this time, the vision was not ephemeral but that its shape was approaching where she lay. She turned her head away from the figure and sank down awaiting a blow. But, since none came, she raised her eyes towards the black shape and, in the near darkness, could discern the white flash of a headdress. She closed her eyes again in desolation, awaiting the face of Sister Brigid. For this was no wraith, although a visit from the Prioress was scarcely less terrifying than the appearance of a spectre.

But all she could feel was a gentle hand touching her, lifting her face from where it had sunk in misery.

The hands lifted her head and gently stroked her cheek. She looked up – at a face she did not recognise.

It was not Brigid.

And the visitor smiled. Brigid had never smiled.

Isadora, despite her weakness, strained to stand, although she was unable to do so.

Her visitor motioned for her to remain seated. And then started to release her from her chains.

'I am not a ghost,' she said with a smile, 'and neither were the "hauntings" to which you have been subject. I am sorry that I could not prevent Brosco's plans to further terrify you by schooling your uncle into a very believable supernatural performance. Yes, it was your uncle who acted as a very plausible spirit. Even I was frightened by his rehearsals. I imagine you were *convinced* that you were being visited by a series of spectral visitations.

'But your uncle has been very useful. Inadvertently he supplied me with the means by which I could obtain the keys to your manacles and to your dungeon. And it was when he visited you to torment you that I was able to follow and discover this information.'

'But I still cannot believe my uncle would…'

The Mother Superior, for it was the Abbess Serena, looked at the girl with sympathy and kindness in her eyes:

'I am sorry. Your uncle is an evil man. And he has carried out Brosco's attempts to ensure that no servant of Vincentio could openly show their loyalty to him. Some had been well rewarded for their perfidy, although, as they had witnessed what had happened to those who remained loyal to their master, I suspect their courage was tested to the limit. It is also true that many showed loyalty, not to him, but to his lady.

'I was trusted by Brosco and your uncle and this made them less likely to concern themselves with my wanderings which led me to your prison, to the room in which its key was stored – and the key to your manacles.'

'And Vincentio?'

'And of Vincentio's cell. He is waiting ready for me to bring you to him so that we might escape to the mountain pass and gain time on those who are bound to pursue us.'

Isadora was now free of her chains since Serena had wasted little time in explanations while freeing her. She followed where the Abbess led, to the arms of Vincentio and freedom.

And, as they walked, Serena explained what had happened during her journey from the villa to the castle:

'Your uncle, I believe, is your only living relative?'

Isadora, to whom the question had been directed, nodded.

'I learned on the journey,' continued Sister Serena, 'that your uncle believed that the inheritance from your father had been wasted on a young girl – yourself – instead of coming to the brother who had hoped to succeed. The girl, he believed, would take her fortune to the man to whom she had shown a great liking, Vincentio.'

Vincentio here interjected that he had not believed this feeling was equal to his at the time, and that his admiration for her should not prevent her from accepting the offer about which her uncle had informed her.

Signor Brosco's offer of marriage, he told them, appeared to be an escape from a penniless aristocrat who could offer her only his love and a gaunt crumbling castle. Vincentio, having misinterpreted the willing obedience of Isadora towards her uncle as love for Brosco, had acquiesced in the plan.

'I would not take a fortune this way because it did not accord with my love for her. So I gave up my hopes and, believing Brosco to be able to offer similar riches to those which Isadora would bring, and a love and affection equal to my own, relinquished my dream of a happy union.

'While I was not prepared to enrich myself at Isadora's expense, I must admit that my eventual marriage was made in the hope of acquiring prosperity that would renovate my decaying castle and secure my place in the world. Since Matilda, too, had married only to acquire a title, this new affluence came at the cost of a loveless marriage and one which had led to the acquisition of a wife who was prepared to betray Isadora and me to our enemies.'

In her weakness, Isadora accepted Vincentio's help up the mountain pass until he found that it was necessary to carry her. Serena now continued her explanation of her supposed alliance with her two evil companions. It was her Prioress, Brigid, who had engineered, with them, the scheme to bring Isadora to her convent and to enrich – not the nunnery – but herself in the process.

Serena's concern was that Brigid's administration was not as beneficial to her nuns as it should have been. Serena, whose overall administration meant that her powers were greater than those of her Prioress, was determined to investigate - and the news that was brought by the nun, Ingrid, of her treatment of Isadora confirmed her fears.

It prompted a search for Isadora which the Abbess Serena hoped could result in her providing a suitable convent for her, similar to that which had provided a settled future for Ingrid.

But, instead, it had led her to the villa in which Isadora had temporarily found respite and from which Serena had accompanied Isadora's rescuer on his mission to Brosco. By this means she had hoped to discover what had caused Isadora's escape. Neither Brosco, nor Isadora's uncle, had seen, or known of Serena, Brigid's Abbess, but accepted that she would have been privy to the agreement made by her with Brosco.

And Brosco had suggested the plan which had taken her on her long journey to the Castle Valdina. She had the comfort of supposing that Brosco and Isadora's uncle did not intend the deaths of Vincentio, nor of Isadora. Neither, despite their evil intentions, had committed any crime with which the Tuscan authorities would concern themselves, especially since theirs was a family dispute between a master and his wife. Serena believed that their future plans depended on retaining their good name. Whatever malevolence governed their plans for Isadora, they did not include murder as Serena had discovered. Indeed she became privy to their intention of entrapping Vincentio into releasing his present wealth. She added that, with the Contessa Matilda now part of their scheme, this would become easier.

As Ann Radcliffe can be imagined setting down her pen from this unfinished draft, she can also be envisaged ruminating on the fate of Brosco, Isadora's uncle and the Contessa Matilda. That it would involve their demise we can have no doubt.

We will not attempt to predict how the author would have dealt with Brosco's end - for his role had been fulfilled. Such as he existed in eighteenth and nineteenth century Gothic novels merely for the purpose of hunting innocent young ladies across the continent and inflicting the maximum pain and suffering upon them, usually involving incarceration in some gloomy institution.

So we will assume that she would have eventually adequately dealt with the predators and provided Vincentio and Isadora with the happiness which, until the very last, had seemed unlikely.

If anything in the tale appears unclear or poorly expressed, we must speculate that those rough edges might later have been smoothed out, and that the final version of the story – had it been completed - made wor-

thy of her other writing. For devotees of Ann – such as the editor of this fragment – will not tolerate a sub-standard tale.

The Cricket Match

The rain in the night had seen the worms on the move. They were making their way – although their movement was imperceptible – across the pavement on a suicidal course towards the road. Human feet or road traffic would curtail that journey. I watched them with an absurd sadness and sympathy. I wondered why they were leaving the safety of the grass for such an end. I could not save all of them; there were too many. And I was convinced that if I had they would once more embark upon their fruitless journey.

I was early; my study of worms, snails and other tiny creatures embarking on their dangerous treks was the result of having time on my hands. I always arrived early; I had a fear of being late. And today, of all days, I could not be late. My mother had received the call on the previous evening. Would John be available to play for the school cricket team the next day? John would, my mother replied, knowing my love of cricket.

But loving the game did not imply skill in playing it. When I was told, I quickly dismissed my initial joy in wondering why I, a much younger schoolboy than those who normally constituted the school team, should have been chosen. There were others – I had to admit – much more adept. In informing my mother of my selection, the captain had told her that new blood was needed, that someone enthusiastic should be given a chance to show his skill.

I was not convinced by this explanation. More likely, I thought,

The Cricket Match

he had tried several others to make up a team and none were available. I knew that, at the height of summer, many at the school were away on holiday and that the depressing trend of having found more interesting occupations for their weekends had become a real problem for selectors.

So I waited without high expectation. I waited for the rest of the team. The captain arrived first, surprised that his early arrival had not ensured that he was the only one there to rally his troops. However, typically, he used the situation to strengthen the resolve of his team or, at least, the weakest member of it.

He told me he had heard of an incident in a house match a little while ago in which a team of my own age had been involved. This had been the high point of my cricket career at the time since I had been selected, or – considering my well-known love of keeping wicket - given a chance to prove myself. The school master who ensured that a group of eleven schoolboys behaved and played the game correctly also umpired it. He had been positioned at square leg, about ten yards behind the right handed batsman, when a young messenger approached him with a note. Clearly it was important and caused him to leave the field.

We all stopped – until the captain of our side suggested a resumption of play. Objections were expressed that only one umpire remained – and he a member of the batting side and therefore not totally reliable when it came to close decisions.

But the game resumed. The bowler bowled and the batsman, reaching to his right, clipped the ball with the edge of his bat. I threw myself to my right and then stared at the ball as I, lying prone on the ground, saw it nestling in my gloved hand. There was no need for an appeal; it was quite clearly out – and the best catch I had ever made.

The school master-umpire returned.

'Right,' he said, 'we will resume.'

The batsman hesitated in his walk towards the pavilion. I protested that I had caught the ball, that he was out.

'Never mind; I didn't see it. We'll start again from where I left.'

The batsman returned to his crease with a grin.

It was the last time I played wicket keeper for my house – mainly because, in my disappointment, my game deteriorated from that point.

But now I was encouraged to know that the captain had heard of the incident. Someone had witnessed it and reported to him my biggest moment in sport.

I nodded, smiling. Yes, that had happened. I even wondered whether I might be keeping wicket today. That would, however, have to wait until the positions, and the batting order, was announced.

The captain filled the time until the arrival of the rest of the team by expressing a conviction – so he said – that I would make the difference today. Without believing it to be true, I nodded, smiled, and expressed a hope that this might be the case.

Choosing the captain was a carefully considered task. I knew that our captain was not the best cricketer by some way. But he could marshal his troops; he could encourage where encouragement was needed, and discipline those who required a firm hand. He was also – and this was significant – older than the other members of the team.

As the other players arrived and entered the minibus, it was noticeable that they paid me no attention. In a way I was glad of this, and I took a seat on my own while my team mates selected seats next to their friends. I had no friends in the team; no one was in my year.

I was grateful that the captain came to sit on the vacant seat next to mine, although a little apprehensive that he might discuss cricketing matters of which I had had no experience. But this he did not do.

Arriving at Fletchlands School, I looked around at the classical frontage with some awe. Fletchlands was a public school and it was easy to think that they regarded the players from a mere state school with some disdain. It was – my team mates assured each other - unusual for a team to be greeted by the opposition's headmaster; only a junior master represented us, and he had travelled, not in the minibus, but in his own car. There was clearly no desire on his part to be discomfited by the lack of space – and inane chatter of a group of schoolboys. Especially on a Saturday. I felt, in so travelling, that he had abnegated his responsibility for the team on their journey unless, of course, his faith in our captain was such that he was confident in his ability to accept that responsibility.

As we issued from the minibus, the headmaster of Fletchlands approached us, shaking each boy by the hand. Strangely this instilled in me a feeling a self-worth. He was, apparently, unaware that I was younger and of little importance.

In the changing room, our school master issued not a word of encouragement, nor any advice. Although, as a geography teacher unconnected with sports in any way, I imagine that he felt unqualified to do so and, since he was clearly only accompanying us because he had drawn the shortest straw, our captain fulfilled his role.

He took out a sheet of paper.

'I have the batting order here. I am sorry you have not been able to study it, as you normally can on the notice board at school, but there was some question as to whom we would select for the match. That didn't happen until the last moment.'

I interpreted that to mean that the captain had been scratching around to find eleven players, a belief which had already occurred to me in receiving my late 'call up'.

Instead of reading the list, he pinned it up on the wall and we were obliged to gather round to see how our batting abilities had been recognised. I noticed that a cross indicating who would take wicket was set against the name of Nathaniel Bleaker. I was unsurprised and showed no disappointment. The amazing catch, of which my captain had been aware, had not qualified me for such an exalted role. Bleaker had kept wicket for the school for some years.

Where I did feel a little disappointment was when my eye scanned the batting order to find myself at the bottom of it. As a closed-eyes cross-bat swiper, could I really expect much else? Probably not but, not being a bowler (a task I was only too willing to admit I should have been unable and unwilling to tackle), it meant that I was regarded as the only member of the team performing no useful function. I had to admit that such doubts had assailed me from the moment my mother had excitedly informed me that I was 'in the team'. Of course I was the only one they could find. As such, I should feel no disappointment – and no resentment.

I eventually decided that this was not entirely fair to myself since I could think of a number of my school mates who, while available, had not been 'called'. They had even less talent than I and, if I were honest, no interest in the game. But I had. And I soon consoled myself with a new thought – that I had been selected for my ability in the field. I did not need to stand behind the wicket to take catches, nor to stretch for balls flying my way.

I stood at deep point. This was a position on the boundary at right angles to the batsman. Had he played his favourite stroke, then I was ideally placed to thwart him.

The fact that few of the first batsmen chose to play that shot was more down to the bowlers' skill in keeping the run rate down. Always a tight game, Fletchlands had struggled to forty two runs with the loss of eight wickets. A tail-ender prodded the ball to point and I ran forward to collect it. Although I say so myself, my quick movement and throw to the wicket keeper were as efficient as any member of the side would have accomplished.

Indeed Nathaniel Bleacher gave my efforts a clap as he grasped the ball over the stumps, partly no doubt to give the young fielder some encouragement but also – I was under no illusions – to demonstrate that he could catch the ball and clap in the same movement.

With only one wicket to fall, I was to see the ball again. With a lucky slog in my direction, the tail-ender was embarking on a run. With surprising speed he had almost reached the other wicket while I ran rapidly towards the ball. I reached it some way inside the boundary and was determined to again earn my wicket keeper's praise by hurling in accurately over the stumps. A further distance than on the previous occasion, I summoned greater power and threw the ball with great gusto.

But, as a result of my extreme effort, the ball went not towards the wicket keeper, who had a good chance of running out the desperate batsman, but out of the back of my hand. I launched myself at the boundary rope but the ball had long since gone over it. I stared in disbelief – not only at the realisation that I had donated the batting side four runs but also that I had missed the opportunity to help take another wicket – the wicket of a boy who went on to score enough runs to boost our opponents' score to sixty.

During tea, I was no more part of the general conversation than I had been on the minibus, but I was clearly the subject of it. What I was now subjected to were icy stares. Those hateful glances suggested a bigger total may well be beyond us. My donation to our opponents of those four runs was bad enough because, psychologically, sixty was a reasonable total – but, without the incident in which I had been involved, the opposition would, probably, have posted a score in the mid-forties. Far more attainable.

I watched as our batsmen made a reasonable attempt to reach our opponents' score. Having reached fifty nine, we were eight wickets down. Then, to my horror, one of two very fast bowlers took the ninth wicket. We were afraid – or at least I was - of these very fast bowlers, partly because they were also *very* good, but also because, in those days, we were unused to seeing such cricketers at all. They reminded me of the dominant West Indian team which had recently defeated England with consummate ease. During that game it had been the fast bowlers who had decimated England's batting line up.

Not only had I now the task of facing these fearsome bowlers, but I had to either score, or assist my fellow batsman (new to the crease) to score the vital run to tie, or two runs to win. I left the pavilion knowing that, initially at least, I could not be considered in a supporting role. I was facing the bowler. If I were clean bowled – I could envisage no other outcome – the anger of my teammates would escalate to a degree that made my journey home a frightening prospect.

I have admitted that I was not, and am not even now, a batsman. I placed my bat in what I considered to be a reasonable place.

'What guard?' shouted the umpire.

'Middle and leg,' I shouted impressively, remembering one of the best players at the school having taken such a guard, but without any firm understanding of its meaning. Once the umpire had lifted his hand to indicate that I had reached the required place with my bat, I began to make a mark on the ground. This took some time but I could delay no longer. Sooner or later I should have to face the terrifying experience of standing in front of my wicket as the bowler took his long run-up at frightening speed.

As he approached the other wicket, I could stand the experience no longer. I held my bat as firmly as my fear allowed me, and closed my eyes.

I heard a crack. I was pleased to note that it was the noise of ball on willow rather than on the wicket behind me. But, given that there were three more balls of the over to face, I had no sense of relief.

Then I heard it. The other batsman:

'Yes.'

I hesitated.

'Yes,' he repeated as he approached.

I began to run as fast as my legs would carry me and – on reaching the other wicket – I could see that he had turned, and similarly set out for another run.

As I firmly earthed my bat, the ball flew past my face. The wicket keeper took it in his hands but did not bother to remove the bails. I was in. I had scored two runs. I did not know where the ball had gone but it did not matter. Our opponents' score had not only been reached, but surpassed. We had won.

Having left the field, I was aware of a feeling of happiness in the camp. It had not been forgotten that I had forfeited four runs and there were still comments - and yes stares – that reminded me that, had I not committed that sin, my last minute heroics would not have been necessary. But the general joy of achieving victory – and my admittedly fortunate – part in it, led to a lighter mood on our journey home.

Again the captain sat next to me; again he made the journey a more pleasant experience, although he was the only team member to recognise my part in the victory. Whether or not he was aware of the part played by luck in dealing with the only ball I had faced I never knew. His praise was enough, and I was able, on my arrival home, to recall the day's play in the role of hero, of the man who had rescued my team and prevented a galling defeat. I saw no reason to elaborate on my fielding experiences, and I could therefore bathe in my parents' warm reception of my tale. But, to myself, I was always the boy who threw the ball over the boundary rope.

I was never selected to play for the school team again.

The Battle of Lewes

The Battle of Lewes was fought on 14 May 1264 between King Henry III and the rebel baron, Simon de Montfort, 6th Earl of Leicester. Henry's son, Prince Edward (later King Edward I), drove back part of the baronial force but pursued them from the battlefield leaving his father's forces vulnerable. As a result Edward, in returning to his father's defence, was taken hostage. He escaped, eventually defeating Montfort at the Battle of Evesham.

It was the evening air on the coming soft summer days to which she looked forward. Living on the edge of the South Downs, already the freshness of the air was accentuated by the scent of cowslips, and the last of the spring orchids.

It was on the Downs that she took her walks, aware that she was walking the paths trodden by those who fought and died on the battlefield of Lewes so long ago.

But it was difficult to people these peaceful slopes with the turmoil of war, with danger, violence and death. She smiled. Although some would say that it was too long ago that this area had been a killing field to be affected by it, her move to this part of Lewes had been influenced by a fascination – and, indeed, a feeling of association with - the battlefield and those who fought upon it.

Only recently had she purchased a house in this area; only in the last few weeks had the ground become suitable for walking, and the serenity of the coming dusk was such that her walks became longer and her pleasure in them increased.

May was approaching and the days were growing longer. The sweet smell of glistening downland was giving way to the scent of summer flowers: days on the Downs stretched before her.

Into this tranquillity came, one morning, a reminder of a less peaceful past. It was while tending her garden that her trowel hit metal in the soil. She scraped round the object she had discovered with the care of an archaeologist extracting her find from the earth. And, further fuelling her interest, she realised that this was, indeed, an artefact: something not from the current age but from one many centuries ago, an age with which she felt a strange affinity.

Unwilling to make a judgement on this fragile piece of steel, she lifted it from the ground. It could have been a sword but insufficient remained for her to be sure. She exercised great care in its excavation, sliding a spade carefully underneath it – a task not assisted by the hard chalky soil.

The sword, if it were truly a sword, was very broad and, even now, very heavy – but only a short length of it was discovered. Despite extending her search many feet around it, nothing more could be found.

It was something to be treasured and carefully stored before being taken to the curator of the museum – a visit from which she returned without the sword but with great satisfaction since her assessment had been correct.

'A long sword – probably thirteenth century.'

Discovering where she had found it, the curator had admitted the likelihood of its having been used during the Battle of Lewes in 1264. Somehow she had known that - because she had been drawn to the sword, drawn to an object and an age in which she felt she was well acquainted.

Days progressed through the season. May had arrived with similar shimmering days to those with which the spring had blessed her.

And, more often now during the day, she was drawn to the gate of her garden and out for walks on the sweep of downland beyond it. It was going to be a hot summer, and already she would wear no more than her sleeveless, short dresses, and the lightness of her attire added a further pleasure to her walks. The sun kissed her arms and legs so that they became lightly tanned. She could not remember a summer like it. May was continuing to bring the sun without the strong heat and humidity which, later in the year, would possibly make her walks less comfortable.

But it was one evening, as the sun was setting, that she first experienced what she initially believed to be a 'tremor in the earth'. She was shaken with a movement which made her stumble, although she soon regained her stability and, planting her feet securely apart, looked at the earth around her. There were no signs of a quake – not that she now supposed such an unlikely event to have occurred. She attributed the momentary unsteadiness, not to the earth itself, but to her own giddiness. She smiled, shrugged off the feeling, and started out on a longer walk during which no repetition of her sensation was experienced.

Her walks were, indeed, becoming longer, but always she passed through an area where she felt an unsettling but, at the same time, strangely uplifting feeling. Each day the experience was repeated and, indeed, affected her more strongly. She would be bombarded with a rapid movement of light; her head would spin – and her body would quiver in a fashion which began to cause her concern. What was happening to her? And why did she encourage feelings which caused distress and pain?

As soon as she passed a certain place, little more than a hundred yards from her garden gate onto the Downs, the feeling passed, and she did not experience it on the remainder of her walk.

She tried to locate the exact spot at which she was affected by these sensations. It was not easy because she believed she had experienced them in more than one place. One evening, she varied her walk by keeping parallel to her back fence when accessing the Downs from her garden, taking a wide sweep and avoiding the area she had identified. She felt nothing. She did not know whether to feel relieved, or disappointed.

On her return, she realised that her disappointment was the predominant emotion and so she deliberately took her previous route, suffering similar feelings of unsteadiness. But, disorientated as she became, she seemed to long for it, as if for a place and a century to which she was destined to return.

But, soon, the violence of the attack took her by surprise. She fell to the ground where she heard the whistling of the wind and the sound of horses and the cries of men. Slowly her head cleared, her peace returned. These had been moments of excitement, as if she had witnessed – although she had not seen – a battle.

The wind subsided and, as she stood, a gentle breeze blew. She returned to the point outside her gate where the intensity of her experiences was always strongest. Although she could feel nothing of the overpowering sensations experienced on previous days, she believed that there was a reason why this location was the point at which her emotions were at their highest – and her excitement greatest.

She looked around her; no one was moving on a wide sweep of Downs. She felt an urge to explore this area and, as if walking in her sleep, she followed an unseen guide and dug where she was bidden. The earth was hard, the digging difficult. But compulsion drove her. She *knew* she would find something and her determination to do so outweighed the difficulty of her task. She struck metal. Lifting the object she had located, she sat on the grass to rest. Sweat ran into her eyes and, although lightly clad, her dress was drenched. She lifted the object.

She believed that what she had found, and the sword fragment she had previously discovered, belonged to the same weapon. But there was more. The next item she gently lifted surprised her greatly. Ragged though it was, she was able, sliding her hand gently into the soil beneath it, to carefully remove some cloth which had lain under the sword. It was more extensive than she had originally thought. In all the material she held was a considerable size. Although its colours had suffered the fading of nine hundred years under downland soil, she knew that she could identify it. The Royal Standard. The large fragment displayed a golden lion on a red background.

She smiled; no one else, she believed, would have been able to identify it as such. Only someone who had dreamed of a man riding and carrying this banner aloft could have been confident enough to have done so.

She took the cloth into the house and, with the sword hilt, stored them in the chest in which the other sword fragment had rested.

On the following day, she unlocked the chest and removed both artefacts but, without quite knowing her reason for doing so, replaced the 'banner' in the chest. She prepared the sword for its journey to the town where it would join her previous find – possibly to be reunited with it to form a near complete medieval weapon.

On her return, she again took the banner fragment from its chest. She folded it gently, fearing it would disintegrate in her hands. The buttoned pocket at her breast was, however, ideal to hold it, and no damage occurred. She could not understand how something so fragile could fold without crumbling to dust. But she had seen it before; she knew it and who had borne it. And she realised that this association outweighed the effects of its age. Thus prepared, she embarked upon a journey which was to have major consequences for the remainder of her life.

She had travelled half a mile when a familiar sensation affected her. Her head felt as if it were exploding; her vision split so that areas of her sight overlay each other and, eventually, the placid Downs were replaced. Gradually pin-points of light settled into a picture of dust and low sunlight. Her eyes strained to see, although her senses were ablaze with noise and furious, deadly activity. She was aware of lying in the midst of carnage as arrows flew and horses panicked in the midst of sword wielding men.

If battle strategy were such as she had been led to believe, all would have been organised, reflecting a commander's plan. An army's flank would have proceeded towards the enemy. There would have been noticeable progression and falling back. There was none. There was only chaos.

The girl's senses were assailed with the tumult of battle. She looked up in terror. Above her a horse reared and its rider, a man in chain mail, lifted a mace above her, and brought it down with electric speed.

She felt no pain. She felt nothing. Shouting and ferocity abounded but she was touched by nothing. To the side of her a man fell to a heavy sword cut, his assailant completing the attack by running his victim through. She looked at the vanquished. He was unprotected by armour and his only weapon was a pitch fork.

She watched as the knight continued to move forward, not in line with his fellows but ahead of some, behind others, all of them engaged in separate combat. Horses' hooves landed around her; men fell and advanced. Dust swirled, making it difficult to see. And one man, avoiding a blow from an axe, fell towards her.

Her attempt to protect her head was unnecessary; she felt nothing, but all around were hatred, fear and carnage. Her terror grew. She curled into a foetal position although she knew that the threats around were not meant for – and did not physically affect – her. But her panic grew; no one could witness this scene without wishing desperately to escape it.

And then, emerging from this maelstrom, a familiar sensation assailed her; she began to emerge into the twenty first century and the placid Downs. She unbuttoned and felt inside the pocket at her breast. The banner fragment remained. The sun shone, a fresh breeze blew, and her head began to clear. But, just as she felt that she was returning to normality, a swift and stronger wind blew by her and the dim shape of a man appeared, passing her, looking at her with more than interest. She followed his progress, noting his interest in her. *This* figure from the distant past was aware of her. And then he was gone.

The look he had cast at her, however, remained in her mind and, as she curled on the ground, unmoving, she knew that she had seen him before. Where she had seen that face she could not say, but it was a face of significance and, recalling the look he cast in her direction, she felt that, absurd as it might seem, *he* recognised *her*. And that look held more than recognition; it was a look of adoration – a quality difficult to explain in a man separated from her by over nine hundred years.

It was that look and that affinity which guided her in the coming days, that permeated her dreams, leaving her with an affection, with a love for, a man seemingly so remote from her both in time and experience. A man whose name – by what means she could not understand – was known to her.

Her reluctance to re-live participation in the scene of the battle was great but her growing obsession with the man on the horse, Mortain, meant that she could not let the experience go.

And her recollection of that terrifying day was vivid, vivid enough to recall the standard bearer who proudly rode into the confusion of battle. For she knew who that standard bearer was – and, although he was but dimly seen, she was convinced that it was he who had passed her as she was emerging through the curtain into the modern day. The man who was beginning to haunt not only her dreams but her waking moments.

It was with some trepidation that she would venture out on her walks, but she recognised the inevitability of the next episode in her encounter with the past. And soon it came. She began to feel sensations, familiar, and yet strangely different.

She imagined that she rose, ascending to enter a gate into another place. Climbing, climbing. And then she felt herself falling.

At last she felt solid earth beneath her. Again she curled her body as if it could offer protection against any violence which might present itself.

She remained in the position for some time, venturing only to lift her head. It was a warm May day; the Downs looked familiar to her, although there were more trees. However, on looking back the way she had come, she could see no houses, no signs, indeed, of the town in which she had lived.

There were hoof beats around her. Soldiers returning to a town in the distance – a huddle of huts around a castle with a priory dimly seen.

She looked up into the sad eyes of her standard bearer, whose look at her held surprise and – it could not be hidden – recollection. He dismounted and stood over her. She continued to lie at his feet but her eyes were trained on his face.

He began to speak and she struggled to hear. Both pronunciation and his words were unfamiliar, but she was surprised that she understood him. He lifted his hand and said something which sounded to her like: 'Hail lady'.

She did not – could not – speak but continued to stare. She was perhaps aware that her dress was very unfamiliar to him – that this added to his astonishment.

She understood him to say that he remembered her. That she could comprehend was now no longer a surprise to her: that she could understand the speech of someone who had lived in the thirteenth century. Realising that, around her, were solid men and not the visions of before, she feared that they were men who perhaps would not respect her as Mortain had done. She needed to rise but could not do so. He bent to the ground and lifted her onto his horse, mounting himself and encouraging her to wrap her arms around him. He then urged his steed forward.

She listened; he seemed to believe that she would understand details of the battle that had occurred; that she would know that the man he called Longshanks, his Prince, Edward had pursued his enemy and that this was the remains of his desperate force, struggling to the aid of the remainder of the royal army.

She rested her head on his shoulder, seeking the comfort of contact with him. She was loath to speak, fearing that she might not be understood but, when she did, her words sounded strange but oddly familiar, as if the words she spoke were being translated into a tongue which was once hers. To her great surprise, she was understood, and she understood *him* as he told her of the disaster which had followed Edward's pursuit of his quarry to the River Ouse, where many of those pursued had had to attempt a crossing – and had perished in its waters.

Edward's realisation that he had abandoned his father, King Henry, had urged his return - as she was only too aware. As the horsemen travelled, the man around whose body she was so closely pressed, spoke of their return to Lewes and their fear of what would be found there.

The day was still hot but, within the stone walls, the coolness was welcome. Ahead of her was an elderly man, seated on what could well have been a throne of state. Neither he nor the assembled group paid attention to her. But there was an air of fear, faces apprehensive of any move the soldiers, who constantly moved in and out, made.

Mortain lifted her from his horse, summoning to him one of a group of women gathered round the king (for she realised it must be he). While Henry paid no attention to the movement, seemingly sunk in gloom and fear, she was taken away to a darker part of the building where her clothes were removed and replaced.

As she reappeared, she did so in similar garb to those around her, in a long dress of thin material and a sleeveless mantle. Her hair was now covered with a white headdress, her feet, unlike those around her, uncovered. She waited as they all waited, now painfully aware of the smoke of burning buildings which surrounded them. They had lost their prince, who had been taken under guard, and she was able to understand them as they murmured their fear and hatred of 'Leicester'.

Her horseman, Mortain, the standard bearer of the royal army, turned towards her and took her arm, staring at her bare feet and the woman who had brought her back to him unshod.

'Rebel Leicester,' he explained to her, wondering if she were aware, 'is Simon de Montfort.'

She stared in wonder although she felt strangely familiar with her new dress, and the speech, and actions of those around her. She gazed at Mortain, and the intense look could not be mistaken. He was more than her horseman and devoted follower of Prince

Edward. He was her knight. And, although his prince had been taken by Montfort, Mortain explained that he was confident of his escape. And his look reflected that his compensation was in the woman before him, a lost love whom he had found.

Before her dress had been removed, she had unbuttoned the pocket at her breast. The fragment of the standard had disappeared.

These were dark days. The early summer, the bright days of May and June, had not fulfilled their promise. The year was sliding into autumn with grey skies and the all too familiar pattern of misty rain and high winds.

In addition, the people of the county town of Lewes had a greater concern. The girl had been known in Lewes and admired by all. She would speak to strangers and brighten their days. Her beauty was appreciated as much as her free nature. It was as if her disappearance had taken the sun.

Her house had been searched and, although a lockable metal chest had been found, with a key in its lock and with its lid standing open, there appeared to be no other item disturbed in the house. Indeed the house appeared as it should have been had its occupant merely left it to take one of her normal walks. All confirmed that she had been happy – and contented with her new life on The Downs. She had seemed more than that – she had a radiance which those who knew her believed might be symptomatic of a newly found relationship – although no one conceived its origin. Suicide had definitely been discounted, although abduction had not. The Ouse, and the small areas of woodland had been searched. A combing of the surrounding Downs had revealed no trace. The town, and the police, were mystified. There seemed absolutely no clue to her disappearance, nor reason for it.

And it remained a mystery, for she was never found.

The Beautiful Songbird

Flies kept buzzing across my face. I moved out of the shade but still they came. The whole garden seemed hot to the touch; the concrete (of which there was much) and the parched soil (of which there was only a small patch) were cracked and dry.

I noticed parsley incongruously growing amongst the rows marked by ice cream sticks and a broad bean seed packet. I wondered idly, as a non-gardener, how long the strawberry plants would take to bear fruit. But it was only an idle thought. I reached for my glass of ice cool 'beer' and sipped. One sipped and nibbled things at grandfather's; otherwise he would rush to fill your glass or plate with more drink and food with which he could ill afford to part.

I looked up at the tall characterless building which overlooked the small patch of garden and wondered, not for the first time, that the sun, like the snow, can make the ugly acceptable. No day could render Grandfather's house beautiful but, as I sat in its shade with the hot sun beating down on the neighbourhood's only green patch, I was certainly willing to agree that it was agreeable.

I wondered how long Grandfather would be, and watched the fluffy specks of wind-born seed floating across the garden in their fruitless quest for a patch to make their home. Even those, I reflected, that found what Grandfather modestly called his cabbage patch would not survive. Grandfather was too thorough a gardener for that. It was surprising that the seeds were able to make their journey at all, so still seemed the air.

When Grandfather reappeared he found me asleep in the sunshine, my 'beer' still unfinished at my side. When he tapped my shoulder I came to with a start.

'You'll frizzle boy.'

I nodded sleepily.

'Take your chair in the shade. Sun's too hot to lie in for long. And sup your "beer"; there's another inside.'

I strongly suspected that my 'beer' was not beer at all but I had never let on to Grandfather. It certainly never tasted like the beer I had sipped from my father's glass when he had left it unattended. It had none of the bitter taste. I imagined it was a fruit drink with a little drop of beer to justify my grandfather's description.

However I drank it up and smiled. I was beginning to feel uncomfortably hot and, as I wrinkled my brow, my skin stung, warning me that I should burn later.

The peace of the summer's day in my grandfather's garden was soon brought into sharp contrast by the tale he began to relate. The story brought back to me stories my aunt had told me about the East End of London, in which she, my grandfather and my mother had grown up and where our family had lived for many generations.

My aunt had told me – my mother would never speak about the East End, of which she was ashamed - about her sister sitting crying, looking from the window of their Warley Street slum at the men issuing from the public houses at closing time, and returning to their homes. It had explained my mother's feeling about alcohol, although the cause of her tears was that the cost of the men's evenings was money desperately needed in the homes to which they were wending their unsteady way. My mother, it appeared to me, bore the guilt for the whole of the East End.

Not that her – our – family had not striven to 'better themselves'. My great grandfather had opened a sweet shop whose speciality was home-made ice creams – this trade fading as enterprising Italian immigrants began making and selling a similar product without what would have previously been regarded as the essential ingredient of cream. It became a rivalry with which my great grandfather could not compete. But still he made a 'go' of the shop and became known as one of the East End's aristocrats. It was not to last. When the 'headaches' began, his temper suffered and his trade with it. As an adult, many years later, I saw the report of the inquest after he had been found hanging from a beam in his shop, and also a list of the inmates of a 'lunatic asylum' where my great grandmother ended her days.

While the reason for my great grandfather's headaches has been explained in recent times as an illness unconnected with the worry of working all hours in his shop; the reason for my great grandmother's incarceration had been provided on her admission record as 'fainting'. On her death certificate, this was described as 'syncope', a condition of little consequence in modern times but one, in those hard times and without medical understanding, which caused temporary loss of consciousness. It was no cause for her to end her life in a home for the insane.

The shop came into in my grandmother's ownership but, on her marriage to my grandfather, its profits declined, and my grandparents sank back into the poverty prevalent among their neighbours.

While beginning his tale, my grandfather looked behind him at the Victorian house in which he and my grandmother had lived since it was acquired by their children (who had all become successful after small beginnings). The rent was – befitting the facilities – low. My father had arranged for the outside toilet to be joined to the house by a covered walkway which could be used, not only by my grandparents but also by the joint tenants of the house, who lived on the upper storey which had no toilet. This couple could often be seen walking through the kitchen (which served also as a lounge and dining room) to use it – often when my grandparents were at dinner.

It was not a comfortable residence, contrasting greatly with the semi-detached house in which I lived, a house very small, but palatial in comparison with Grandfather's. Extending the comparisons, Grandfather's house was luxurious accommodation if contrasted with the house in Warley Street in which, not only my mother's family, but also her aunt and other relatives lived out their lives.

My grandfather lifted his cup of tea, smiled a rare smile, and – with a second glance at the back door – began his tale. He sipped his tea as if requiring refreshment to begin a story which was clearly one close to his heart. He began slowly to tell of events which he obviously vividly remembered but of which, I suspected, he had not recently spoken.

He eased himself back in his chair and it was as if I had been forgotten as he became immersed in the past, when he was a young man of seventeen. It was before the Great War, he said, that events occurred which needed now to be recalled, and which, he admitted, dealt with young love.

The East End was a tight community and it was almost as if, initially, he was reluctant to mention the name of his young love. But he did so. Mary Ann.

She was a year younger than my grandfather and lived but a few doors away from his own home in Warley Street, Bethnal Green. And, as I suspected, she was in my grandfather's eyes, a girl of great beauty and modest charm. But he was unable – perhaps unwilling - to express his feelings for this young lady. And there had been a good reason for remaining silent then. She was, although so young, and in the term commonly used at the time, already courting.

While this was not a situation likely to meet my grandfather's approval, it was not – either – an alliance approved by her family. Grandfather suspected that Mary Ann was not in love with Edgar Bream but that she had agreed to his advances simply because of his name and reputation. Edgar Bream was a music hall star. The singer of songs which circulated the East End, and the teller of jokes which did the rounds of the district – although they were rarely aired in polite society. And music hall itself was yet to shrug off its reputation and dissolve into the post-war 'variety' scene with which families were happier to associate.

Not that my grandfather was familiar with the music hall – he could neither afford to go, nor was his family willing to expose him to the vulgarity they believed he would witness there.

Mary Ann did go. Edgar insisted. But her presence was the result of neither willingness nor even acquiescence. Mary Ann hated the mean streets of the East End and saw in Edgar Bream a route out of it. The Hoxton Playhouse was one of the last music halls to permit drinking at tables and did not provide rows of seats where the audience could witness the show without the distractions of the drunken behaviour of others. Indeed it had grown out of a public house which had always provided entertainment and had changed very little since its metamorphosis.

When Edgar Bream appeared on stage, the audience rewarded his introduction with the rapturous applause his celebrity warranted. And, after his act of songs, jokes and a few acrobatic tricks, appreciation was signalled by applause which, in the words of his compère, 'brought the house down'.

The only audience member who did not show her appreciation was Mary Ann. She sat silently, wishing the show were over and that she could return home. But this, she soon discovered, was not to be allowed. Edgar Bream approached the front of the stage and held up his hands for silence.

As more applause and raucous shouts greeted him, he held up his hands again.

'I wish, for a moment, to be serious,' he shouted.

The noise, while not dying away completely, did allow him to continue:

'I wish to introduce you to a songbird.'

Members of the audience could not recall an act on the playbills scheduled to follow his. Edgar Bream was top of the bill and could not be 'followed' by anyone.

But Edgar Bream had launched himself into the audience, had taken Mary Ann by the arm and was dragging her towards the stage. She stood before the audience in a state of terror.

'Sing,' Edgar Bream told her.

She stared at him.

'If you do not sing, I will make it my business to…'

His threat was drowned by a chorus from the inebriated audience.

'Sing, sing, sing.'

Edgar Bream gripped her arm again, tightly:

'If you do not sing, you will not get out of here alive,' and then, turning to the audience, he unnecessarily asked:

'Do you want her to sing? She says she won't sing.'

Bottles began to rain onto the stage.

'Now,' said Edgar Bream, 'is that nice? Just because she is a modest little miss and is frightened of you. Look, you have made her cry.'

He turned towards her and whispered:

'And if they don't kill you, I will.'

She tried to stem her tears and looked fearfully at the man who was beginning to encourage the audience as the small orchestra struck up. It had clearly been arranged; they knew her favourite song and were prepared for her to be slow in beginning to sing it.

But she did. Looking back, she could not believe that she was able to do it. It was, in some ways, a chance for her to make her name but this was not the over-riding emotion; she was so frightened, she knew she *had* to sing. She tried to ignore the sound of the crowd, and the vicious grip in which Edgar Bream held her arm. She sang. To her own astonishment, she sang beautifully. The tremor in her voice which was evident when she began disappeared slowly as she performed in a world of her own. She was performing without thinking and almost without awareness that she was doing so. As they reacted to the final line of her song, Hoxton Playhouse's patrons erupted. But the cries of 'More' were ignored. Edgar Bream knew he could not risk an encore.

'And now,' he said, 'I am able to take my beautiful songbird home.

He leered: 'Don't you wish you were me?'

The audience's expression of envy was not unexpected. Edgar Bream left the playhouse by the stage door, almost dragging his protégé along the street and evading any of the audience who might wish to make the acquaintance of Edgar Bream.

Or his beautiful songbird.

It was several days before Edgar Bream came calling. And, on this occasion, the reluctance of her family to admit him was equalled by the determination of his beautiful songbird not to renew his acquaintance.

As always, he treated Mary Ann's family with respect and used the charm which had so enhanced his popularity.

They could be charmed; they were not unaware that the income the music hall star would bring would raise them from the poverty in which they struggled. And they were aware of her determination to leave the confines of the East End.

They shared it.

But Edgar Bream was not to be her route away from London's grimmest area. While Mary Ann had mentioned nothing about her 'performance' at the Hoxton Playhouse, the story of it had reached her parents' ears. While the terror she had experienced had not been part of the news circulating the East End (the audience, anyway, had considered it part of the act) the beauty of her voice – even if a little tremulous at the beginning of the song – was evident from these reports.

And Edgar Bream had, of course, been very careful to hide from his audience the threats and coercion he had used to force her to sing. In the tale of the 'beautiful songbird's' première, it was a carefully stage managed performance which, he believed, was merely a foretaste of a brilliant singing career – perhaps of a double act which would further enhance Bream's reputation.

Edgar had no intention of letting this opportunity slip by further antagonising her family. He removed his hat, smiled, and made no attempt to enter the house.

'I am not sure,' he said, 'whether you would have approved of

Mary Ann's singing. I am sure you will have heard about it – and I apologise.'

Her mother nodded, wondering what was to come.

'It was not initially in my plans that she was going to sing either,' he said. 'It was on the spur of the moment, knowing what a beautiful voice she has, that I gave her her chance. She has always said to me how much she has wished to sing at music hall and I had always discouraged her. I was reluctant to introduce her at such a young age – and at such a venue. But I could see her looking up at me, and so wanting to sing, that I decided to go, against my better judgement, down into the audience. She was very nervous and so her slowness in coming on stage enhanced the stage act – the pretty young girl taking her first chance of stardom.'

In telling this story, Edgar Bream was relying on Mary Ann's reticence. He was convinced she would not have told of the angry words, the hurtful grip and the threats. He, rightly, believed that she had not told her family of the incident. He was certain, however, that news would have circulated the area and was comfortable that that story would present him and his songbird in the best possible light.

However it was presented, Mary Ann's mother and father were quite determined that it should not happen again. This, he feared, would be their reaction and, not wishing to jeopardise his future plans, apologised for any worries he had inadvertently caused them. He did not ask after their daughter, other than to convey to her, through them, his good wishes. He reached into the hallway as far as a hall table, however, and placed upon it a number of banknotes, saying 'She has earned that for her act'.

And left.

My grandfather paused in his tale; I wondered if he was involved in his story or whether he was remembering a young woman whom he greatly admired but had never personally known. He sipped his tea – I was certain it must now be cold – and glanced again at the back door. He returned to his tale:

'I am sure you are wondering why I am telling you all this,' he said. 'I have never,' he continued, confirming my growing belief, 'told anyone before.'

He then told of Edgar Bream's pursuit of Mary Ann. Bream's belief that the girl would be a sensation had been confirmed by her one, enforced, performance, and he further believed that, with training, her voice would develop so that he and she would become one of the greatest music hall acts of all time.

My grandfather turned with a guilty look at the back door as my grandmother came out.

'Here's a hot cup,' she said, taking his cold tea and smiling at me.

'What silly stories is he telling you?' she asked.

I knew better than to give details of the tale. One thing I strongly believed was that it was not a 'silly story', that it was true, and that it might be wise to keep it to myself.

I cannot now remember what I told my grandmother, but she had appeared satisfied and re-entered the house.

'I will be brief,' Grandfather said – to my great disappointment.

But he did continue and told me further about Bream's attempt to force Mary Ann into stardom. His harassment had not been successful; his promise of riches far greater than those he had left on the hall table – which had been returned by her parents - had not achieved his aims.

His pursuit was relentless; his charm, however, was wasted. Although he never again employed them, his threats and physical intimidation had not been forgotten and Mary Ann correctly believed that his polite gentle manner would change as soon as he had secured her as an artist.

And she began to hear about previous encounters he had had with young women, fearing that she, like them, would not achieve the fame with which he had enticed them. And the promise of marriage was, she knew, not one he intended to keep.

My grandfather did, at this stage, become part of his own story. It was my firm belief at this time that his efforts to protect his young friend resulted in great hardship for him and that he had, somehow, protected her against the wiles of the music hall star. He did not detail this part – his part – of the story but his depth of feeling – his increased nervousness in imparting the generality of his story – convinced me that he successfully, as he said, saved her from Bream's clutches.

But the story was never completed, my grandmother coming into the garden to summon us to tea. As he passed me, Grandfather raised his eyebrows in an expression which informed me that, for whatever reason, his story was to go no further.

Having eaten the usual tea of bread and jam, Grandfather excused himself and made himself busy with 'jobs' about which I was to know little.

I was left with Grandmother as she cleared the plates and put them into the sink.

'He never talks so much normally,' she said. 'He never talks so much to me.'

She smiled again. But, this time, she did not ask the substance of my grandfather's conversation. Instead she retrieved my coat from the cupboard and went with me to the side gate. I walked on that path, making those strange metallic steps as I opened the side gate and continued towards the bus stop.

I could just hear what I had not often heard before: my grandmother singing. A sweet, tuneful sound:

The song of a beautiful songbird.

Tammy

One September morning, I prepared for my new life. I looked out at the sunshine, sitting at the bottom of the stairs with my mother, receiving instructions for my first day at work. I was to listen carefully to everything I was told and do my best. That was all I could do – my best. The nagging little voice at the back of my head asked me if my best would be enough. This was a big new world. It would not be like school.

My mother straightened my tie. She knew that the man that I had become would not welcome a public hug outside and so I received my embrace in the house, there on the stairs. And I welcomed it and wished that I could stay there, enveloped in my mother's arms, and not make my entry into the big new world at all. I only needed to say that I felt unwell – I believed that not to be untrue at that moment. Or I could walk round the corner and go, not towards the high street, but in the other direction.

And it was only because I knew the trouble that would cause that my legs took me where they knew I must go. I turned the corner, round by the State Cinema, where I was tempted to linger and look at the stills on display outside. I passed the corner shop where, on my way to school, I had stopped to buy sweets, and on across the road instead of down it to where, for so many years now, I had made my way to school.

A general provisions shop would not have been my first choice of somewhere to work. Far from it. My first employment choice had been something which involved reading or writing. I had – or my father had – approached the local newspaper and I had had an interview. Would many interviewees, I wondered, be unable to answer their first question – one deliberately designed to ease them into the more difficult interrogation to follow. I knew the name of the prime minister. Of course I did but, at that moment, I did not. I knew nothing. If my mind were a rich source of interesting and vital facts, the staff at *The Recorder* would never know it.

To my relief, I could answer the next question. Which books had I read? Unfortunately, some devil in my mind produced an answer inappropriate to the circumstances. Why did I say Balzac? Because I thought him a very adult author? And why, of all the works of that writer did that same devil force my lips to utter: *Droll Stories*.

I can remember to this day the response of the questioner to my unwise selection: 'Yes, we've all read that haven't we?'

I was unconvinced that we had all read the book but the waspish response clearly indicated that, even if we had, we should not have done. In his expression was no semblance of a smile. His face showed only contempt, probably for my choice of answer rather than for my crime in reading the book.

At least my stunned look – I assume it was my stunned look – evoked pity in another of the interviewing panel who not only took over the questioning but ensured that the following questions were ones which I could easily and suitably answer.

It was only as we approached the end of the interview that the reader of Balzac returned to the fray.

'And if you were asked to go and tell someone that their son had been killed in a motor bike accident, would you be able to do that?'

I hesitated and opted for honesty.

'I don't think I should be able to do that,' I said.

'But, in order to get a story, you sometimes need to do that. To describe the shock of their reaction, to…'

I would write different types of stories I told him. My uncle had been a writer of the Star Man's Diary which appeared every evening in the *Evening Star*, I said, and he had used stories from history to bring alive current events. People's feelings I *could* deal with but not...

'But not their feelings when a story needs to be written and you had been sent to cover it?'

I sat without responding. I didn't think I could do that and my expression must have shown it.

My father was waiting outside – my father who had bought me Butler's *Introduction to Journalism* – the recognised authority of the time – and had encouraged me in researching my chosen occupation. What would he think of my being unable to answer easy questions?

He thought nothing of it. It did not matter. There were plenty of jobs. I could work in his insurance company with him.

While I did not want to work at a desk, the thought of having my father to guide and help me greatly appealed to me at that moment. That was better than telling someone who would become a grieving relation of his, or her, loss.

It was at this point, as we made our way to the bus stop, that I determined I was going to banish the sort of fears that had prevented my informing my interrogators the name of our prime minister - and strike out. Since the premier's name had soon, in the company of my father, returned to me, I knew it was my confidence and not my knowledge that needed boosting.

And so, the next week, I entered the largest shop in the high street. Small by the standards of what was already a major company, and now one of the major supermarket chains. But the biggest shop in our little town and massive to my young eyes – and sufficiently daunting to satisfy my wish for a major challenge.

It was many years before supermarkets would appear for the first time in England; it was some time before I became acquainted with the alien concept of customers helping themselves without hindrance. In America this way of shopping would have been known at the time – but not here. Presumably, in America, the idea of designing one's own refrigeration unit would be considered odd. To me, my father's digging a hole in the garden, lining it with short planks and covering it with a hinged lid was a common method of storage. And we would take out our milk, cheese and butter to store it. It did not appear strange to me. But Americans were using machines to wash their clothes as well as to store food. They were also employing machines to dry clothes - which was a method my friends and I considered a task only performed by our mothers - and with a ringer.

As I approached the shop the thoughts of working there had begun to excite me. But, as I went through the door, my fears returned and I looked anxiously at the other members of staff who were similarly filing in. Where would I go? To whom would I report?

I steeled myself; where was my dynamic self who had walked into these same premises to ask the first assistant I encountered whether any jobs were available? Where was the boy who had followed her directions to an office at the end of the shop where a kindly man had asked him to sit down? Where was that boy and how had he answered all the questions asked? After all he knew that he would not be asked for the name of the prime minister, or charged with the task of informing parents of the loss of their progeny in an accident.

And the memory of that self-confident boy urged me to approach that same office and report to the manager.

The manager then surprised me by asking to inspect my hands.

'We do it to all staff every morning,' he said. 'Anyone with nicotine on their fingers will be told to rub it off with pumice.'

I was reassured since no nicotine was found and I was not, therefore, required to find the pumice or to know what it was.

I was relieved that it was the same man to whom I had spoken on the day I enquired about employment, particularly as he had told me I was the type of employee his employer admired – someone who would not wait to be approached but would proactively select 'the company'. It was why, he had told me, he had promptly given me a form to complete and send to head office. And it was why both of us were happy that they had responded so quickly.

When they had done so, the offer was made by telephone. The caller – it was exciting to have a call on the newly installed telephone but even more thrilling to hear that it was for me that the caller was asking. Yes, I had visited the local store and, yes, I had spoken to the manager and – again – yes he had said there were vacancies in the store.

That last was not quite true. Indeed it was not true at all. I had been given no such assurance and, looking back, I was astonished that I had answered in the affirmative. But, given his anxiety for the company to employ me, the manager surely would have been willing for me to work in his store.

At this distance in time, I think back to an organisation which was unsure where its vacancies existed. However, I later received a very important looking letter confirming that I had become an employee at the local branch and instructing me what plans they had made for me.

This included the provision of a course in London and training in my local store. But I should initially be enabled to meet the staff and familiarise myself with their methods.

As I walked back to the main part of the shop, I passed two rows of workers having their hands inspected. I appreciated that the task of hand inspection indicated that the staff member undertaking it must be of some seniority. After all my own hands had been inspected by the most powerful man – the chosen representative of a company which, I was beginning to realise, took their responsibility to the public very seriously.

I had seen, when I had visited the shop with my mother, how sales were made. The customer would queue at each counter at which their requirements would be met. Each counter had a manager and that manager was ultimately responsible for purchases made. But some staff had more mundane tasks to perform before they moved behind the counter at which they had been directed to help. This included the spreading of sawdust on the floor once the sweeping up of yesterday's layer had been completed. I felt quite glad that this task had already been performed since I should have had no idea where to obtain sawdust.

I took my place at a counter and began, very slowly, to learn the ropes, but it was not until the afternoon, when the manager left, that I met Tammy. Like most of the female staff, Tammy wore a white coat and hat, the latter intended to keep hair out of the unwrapped food. Through this unflattering garb, though, shone the glory of Tammy.

She led me to the dairy counter where inexperienced staff, I had been told, were not permitted to serve. There were tasks performed there that were unsuitable for the uninitiated. I had watched staff 'patting' butter to meet the weight requirement of the customer – and cutting cheese placed on a board to which a wire was attached. I had often, particularly when small, watched this with wonder. I did not, of course, compare this meticulous effort of serving the customer's needs with the pre-packaged provision of the supermarket which was to replace the store in which I was working.

Tammy winked at me as she introduced me to these skilful procedures. That wink made the day come alive. I had no idea working in a shop would introduce me to delights such as this. As Tammy.

'You will not be able to do this straight away,' she told me, 'but you can prepare yourself now for the months ahead when it *will* be allowed.'

Until that moment I had not seen such work as my life-long vocation. Now I was eager to progress.

And, for many days, I would be eager, after the working day, for the next to start. I am certain my parents, while gratified by my enjoyment of the job and reluctance to leave every evening, could not understand the vehemence of my devotion to it. Until, that is, I told my father about Tammy. He understood.

And I thought of Tammy while at home, to such an extent that I could be caught in day-dreams of her. I am sure that my mother was surprised at my success at work given that I was unable to concentrate on the more mundane activities of my life at home.

I knew nothing about Tammy; I was unable to establish whether she was married, in a long-term relationship… I could not believe that a man had not devoted his life to caring for her. And I had several times, when working late, seen her in her normal clothes – in which she displayed her unalloyed beauty. I increased the occasions when my work would take up more than its normally allotted time, and this convinced my manager that I was utterly committed to my work.

All I knew about Tammy was that she was very much older than I was. That didn't matter; my friends were beginning to go out with girls younger or of a similar age to themselves. They could keep them. I had Tammy although, were I honest, I could not claim to have Tammy, and weekends were beginning to stretch out without her. I never heard a cross word from Tammy and she seemed to be determined to work with me if she could. While, looking back, I consider that this might have been her determination to help the new member of staff who had shown such dedication to working at the shop, I did not consider that then. I was sure that her kindness came from a great liking for me since she rarely showed it to others.

I made no attempt to deny it to myself. I was in love with Tammy.

So, when my training course in London came around, although I was eager to participate and it would mean only a week away from Tammy, I knew I should desperately miss her. However, I was willing to learn the skills necessary to serve the company and thereby to cement my relationship with her.

Filing into a room like the schoolroom I had not long left, I took my place with other students from all over the south east. Our education in the butchering of meat was to be supplied by Mr Willis. Unfortunately, Mr Willis' face, with its upturned nose and fleshy cheeks, closely resembled that of a pig. I do not think that I was alone in considering his occupation as a butcher an ironic choice.

While I absorbed Mr Willis' lessons to the best of my ability,

I felt that I should not be undertaking this work for some time if patting butter and cutting cheese were considered skills beyond my capacity.

Mr Campbell taught us cleanliness. I had heard that 'cleanliness was next to godliness' but I little thought that I should hear the expression so often, indeed more in Mr Campbell's hour than in the rest of my life.

My confidence did not permit me, during his and other lectures, to raise my hand, no matter how little my understanding had been of the matter being addressed. I looked at my, mostly much older, fellow students with awe as their questioning hands were frequently raised. But I was able to benefit from their willingness to do so, particularly when one asked whether we should be concerned that, being unable to wash our hands throughout the day, we risked spreading disease. Mr Campbell's answer was that bacteria was necessary in our lives, particularly to boost the immune system. It was a fine balancing act too, he said, between good and bad bacteria or, at least, that was my recollection of his words. The exchange on this subject was prolonged and I soon found myself, during it, thinking of Tammy and not the matter in hand.

Not that this was the only occasion when visions of the woman swirled across the classroom and eclipsed the words of wisdom on which we were supposed to have been concentrating. And, on the course's completion, I was unable to control my emotions as I anticipated seeing Tammy again.

On my first working day back, Tammy approached me. Would I like to have lunch with her at the restaurant along the high street and discuss the content of the course? On regaining speech, I emphatically accepted.

Our lunches together continued. We talked. And we ate. Nothing passed between us but opinions about the job, the passing on of her experience in it and everyday gossip about our fellow workers and happenings at work.

And my parents began to notice that my late nights became later as Tammy walked the first part of my journey home – short as it was – before turning off to her own home. She would say that we were friends but my affection for her was deeper than that: there was no question that I was deeply in love.

But, while the strength of my feelings could not be denied, I was also able to treat her as a friend as she obviously regarded me. We would talk about the shop and its clientele – the fact that customers were prepared to complete their purchases at one counter and then join perhaps five or six other queues. This had not really occurred to me but was one of the things about our customers (and indeed those at other similar establishments) which Tammy respected. She called it 'typical Englishness'. We talked too about the things the customers would tell us, Tammy again emphasising the patience and respect shown by them. Many of those stories fed our conversations. There were never any words to which objection could be made. Although I should have liked to talk words of love, Tammy never expressed any such sentiments. Ever.

The bombshell dropped several weeks later. I received a telephone call but, this time, the pleasure in being summoned to this fascinating new instrument soon vanished.

'Checking our records… No vacancy at your local store… Not sure why you had got that impression…'

Well, I thought Mr Tompkins had said…

'Spoken to him… Apparently not… Be prepared to take up duties at… (a large town at some distance from my home was mentioned) … Monday. Go there Monday.'

It appeared that the company did *not* take the word of new recruits. Or, at least, eventually such claims were checked. So, while this might have shown *some* efficiency at head office, the logic behind the following decision made little sense. While, every minute of every day was fully utilised at the local branch, the one to which I now took the underground each day was unable to use my skills.

I would be told to unload a lorry and wait sometimes for nearly an hour before that lorry arrived; only once did I serve on a counter. The pleasures of the dairy counter and others which required skilful

Tammy

work were barred from me.

As I set out round the State Cinema, and the sweet shop, as I had that September morning, the cool wind chilled me and my hands felt the bitter cold of December air. I thought, as I walked, about how much I had let people down. No, no, I didn't stay there; I didn't feel that my vocation was as a shop worker. No, I hadn't tired of the mundane round – it was that there was insufficient work for me to do. No, I can see what you mean, but I wasn't bored; I just wanted more of a challenge.

My mother had not charged me, as others did, with lack of perseverance; my father was already looking at other suitable employment for me but perhaps, he suggested, I should like to extend my schooling, take advanced level exams, go to university. That would increase my job opportunities.

I had, of course, left the big store without a reference - what I was later to realise was an important document. But that was unsurprising: I had achieved nothing other than helping to unload lorries and – given that I was supernumerary through no fault of my own – provided no benefit to the store.

Now I was about to see Tammy, which was reason enough for braving the cold at soon after five o'clock. And that would have been enough. That would have brightened my life… considerably.

But I had another motivation. If I could speak to her, and I was sure she would be extremely happy to engage, I could ask her to intercede for me. Ask the manager to consider re-employing me by convincing the powers that sat on high in the company that I would be invaluable to the local store. I should have to leave if I resumed my education but, I thought, continued employment there might make such a move unnecessary. Such, I only realised subsequently, was a forlorn hope. Companies did not admit their errors, nor bow to the views of their junior employees

As I crossed the small road on my way to the main part of the high street, I could see staff already issuing from the doors of the store. I could not see Tammy but I knew that she was usually one of the last to leave, such was her dedication to the job.

So I stood, waiting, seeing many familiar faces. But eventually I was faced with the sight of the manager locking the doors and summoned the courage to speak to him. He was, I thought, unwilling to talk to me.

'Tammy?' he said. 'No Tammy has left.'

I stared.

'She has gone, I think to another job.'

I continued to stare.

'Er, I don't know why she left, except, well, you know, sometimes things happen. Sometimes it's better if people leave. You know.'

This was not an explanation I could accept, but I could see that I would receive no other.

The manager smiled, I think realising for the first time the extent of my disappointment.

'You liked her didn't you?'

Yes, I had liked her very much.

'And I think she liked you too. She often said she was so disappointed at your having to leave.'

This, although it was very welcome to know that my affection was returned, could not cheer me for long.

And the manager was picking up his briefcase and raising one hand in dismissal as he departed.

I stayed there for some time. I did not notice how cold I was becoming, nor did I see the shopkeepers along the high street pulling down their shutters, marking the end of the working day. I was staring at the shop in which Tammy and I had worked. At the place hallowed by her presence. Now it was a shell.

After some time I emerged from a mist of reminiscence and started back towards home.

I would never forget Tammy.

My Brother Bob

It wasn't a nice experience – that motor cyclist coming straight at me (deliberately I thought) on a country lane. I didn't think he was out of control. It looked as if he made a beeline for me. What really annoyed me, even more than the shock, was that he didn't stop to see whether I was alright. Maybe he didn't want to be done for dangerous driving (or perhaps he'd been drinking) and, knowing that I had landed up on my back and was unlikely to have seen, let alone taken a note of, his number, he had left the scene as quickly as possible.

There had been a number of incidents besides that one. Do you feel a hand in your back on a virtually deserted station platform before being pushed forward and treat it as just one of those things? Particularly if the few people that were there scuttle off and don't get on the train? There was no need to push. No crowds. No rush. I suppose I should have followed those people, but you know how it is. And this incident was followed the next day by that falling rock during a walk I often take along the path under the cliffs. The cliffs were subject to rock falls. Just rather bad luck I thought. But there had been lots of bad luck.

My brother thought it was bad luck too. Not that he knew much about bad luck. He got into every kind of scrape and always came out smiling. And what scrapes! He wasn't known to the police. That was more luck than judgement I felt. But perhaps that's not quite right. Bob was no fool; there was a lot of judgement involved. He got away with murder – well, not murder perhaps but his wealth didn't come from law-abiding clean living. You didn't know how much he made from his wild, and rarely above board, investments and how much from other criminal activity. I didn't know that he had committed any robberies at that time. That knowledge came later.

I admired him in a way. As long as no one got hurt – and I didn't know, but was pretty sure, that he had never hurt anyone - and, when he told me great stories of how some of his wealth had been accumulated, I thought he was someone to look up to. I would never have had the nerve to do things like that.

We met for a beer quite frequently. As I say, he was good company, and I enjoyed his chat. On one of these occasions, I had been able to report another 'attack'. I was beginning to think of them as attacks because so many 'accidents' in such a short time didn't seem likely. I told Bob about the poisonous snake in my brief case. Now encounters with poisonous snakes in a small south coast town weren't common. Downright uncommon. What did Bob think?

As usual he took a light-hearted view but even *he* thought a snake making an appearance in my case was pretty surprising. He even began to consider I was right to worry. I asked him who would do that to me. His answer surprised me. Melvin Drabble. Melvin Drabble? Yes, he said, Melvin had been pretty annoyed when I'd got the job at Merthyr's. He had gone for it too, but I beat him all ends up. He didn't have my style.

And there was Lily, Bob had said. I had to think hard to remember Lily. But then I did. Nice looking girl. Very nice looking. She'd been going out with Melvin and there'd even been talk about engagement. But I didn't care about that; she was damned good looking, and I fancied her rotten. But she was one of many. The girls seem to like me and, when I met Ruth, Lily was old news. What happened to Ruth? Don't remember now; can't even call her face to my mind. I don't worry about the past; if I see a girl I tend to give her a go if she's up for it. I'm pretty honest about things; I don't promise them a cottage in the country with roses round the door. So I began to try to remember more about Lily. She was the 'roses round the door' type. That's really, I think, what put me off.

I don't know what happened to her, can't remember. Thinking back, though, she never went back to Melvin. Who would after a time with me? I don't want to sound arrogant, but I did begin to think, when Bob mentioned it, that he may have a point. Especially as I had done so well at Merthyr's. I know he thought he'd be good at the job but then he thought a lot of himself. I just tend to accept life as it is – I know my qualities and work to them. I just play to my strengths. And one of my strengths is my skill with the ladies although I suppose I spoil them for other men; other men just can't compete.

Anyway, back to Bob. He thought I was in a bit of danger, so I listened. I would be careful. Yes, Bob, I'd be careful. He even invited me round to his place. No harm in talking it over. It wasn't a good idea to do it in a crowded pub.

The day I went, the sun was shining brightly. The woods round his house were bathed in sunshine. Looking up at the sky gave a view of scattered lights. I almost walked into a tree; I was so fascinated by the dream-like scene. But I was still twitchy; I had begun to doubt whether the 'attacks' were genuine attempt to kill me. Just to scare me perhaps, after all none had succeeded in hurting me at all. But I still felt a little vulnerable, waiting for another 'accident'. Enjoying life in all its beauty – while I could.

Oh! Come on. That's not like me. I pulled myself together and stopped looked upward. I began to look around me. In my position I should be more observant. There wouldn't be another motor bike in the wood, or a car - and any snakes would be going about their normal business, but…

The bullet whizzed past my nose.

It wasn't a random shot; it wasn't being fired at some unfortunate bird or rabbit. It was being fired at me. I threw myself to the ground. A bit late you might think, but the person who fired that shot was still around and he (I really didn't think it might be a woman) knew where I was. I took shelter behind a tree. Then I heard a rustling. He was nearby. Of course he was; he couldn't have been that accurate if he'd been firing from a distance.

This time I knew it was no accident. Really I knew that the other incidents hadn't been accidents. Then I saw a flash of red in the trees. And felt a feeling of relief. I saw that flash again, and now I was certain. Whoever had tried to kill me wasn't waiting around to take another shot. I didn't blame him. He'd blown his cover. And, if he was only trying to frighten me, he was accurate enough to fire a bullet under my nose without harming me. Likely? No, not likely.

But I still waited there for some time – until I was convinced that he had left the scene. Then I began to move towards the road. There were usually people around there. But I did carry on thinking. All the other attempts – and yes, they had been attempts on my life – could have been put down to accidental death if they had achieved their aim. Even a stray shot – as it no doubt would have been painted – could have been aimed at a rabbit. Alright not many rabbits are six foot tall, but it may have been a shot at a bird in a tree, or...

It was then that I tripped.

I was still in the wood and I was trying to get out of it as quickly as possible. That's why I tripped – should have been more careful. But, as I fell, I caught my hand on something metal. I looked around. Despite my hurry I had to take the risk of finding out what had hindered my progress.

A metal box. A big metal box. I had to scrabble for ages in the dirt. Then I forgot my caution - old 'Red Coat' must have been miles away by now, the speed he was going when I last saw him. Just as well it had been so wet before this lovely – well it had begun as a lovely – day. I still didn't want to hang around too long though, and there was no way I was going to get the box out of the ground. It had been there for a while.

I looked at my watch. I had been early to meet Bob and, although I was only a hundred yards or so away from his house, I had the time to get a shovel. Which I did.

I did not know what the box contained; it wasn't going to be flimsy enough for anyone passing to wrench it open and investigate. And, if it had a lock of some sort, I wasn't going to be able to unlock it in the wood. I guessed the metal box contained money – lots of it. It wasn't a safe deposit box but I suppose it could have been a safe of some sort. I hadn't seen enough of it to know, and I certainly couldn't lift it out of the ground.

I re-buried what little I had excavated, and I wondered whether someone had already done that. Perhaps that was why a small part of it was protruding. And why I fell over it. Even so, I shouldn't have seen it if it hadn't made me fall.

However it had come there, I didn't want to investigate any further. My investigation was pure curiosity and it wasn't any of my business. I thought that it was something to do with Bob. I didn't want to make life difficult for Bob. Come on, it was within a hundred yards of his home.

So I covered up the whole area. Since I hadn't taken the box out, that wasn't very difficult. Then I hid the shovel in the ferns and continued to Bob's house.

Bob lived alone. We both lived alone. He was a ladies' man too. He didn't have the success that I did but few men did. A partner, or a wife would have cramped his style as it would have done mine. And, in his case, he had other skeletons to hide.

Perhaps I had been longer than I thought, digging round that spot in the wood, because it wasn't long before I saw Bob coming out of his house.

'I thought you were never coming.'

I looked up and what I saw worried me. His coat.

A red coat.

As he approached, I was already putting two and two together. I could see what he might have thought. Why was I coming from the spot at which – I now convinced – he had hidden the proceeds of some robbery.

I provided monosyllabic answers to his questions while my mind whirred. I was beginning to think the unthinkable.

The incidents had occurred over a relatively short period. But, since I'd only discovered the box today, why had he been trying to kill me before then – even before I actually *had* discovered it?

That question was quickly answered. He thought I had known of the metal box long before. I wasn't taking a pleasant walk in the woods; I was returning to a spot which I knew only too well hid a box of very great interest.

And, again, my mind was churning over this new situation. Would he want to kill me because I was aware of his crime, assuming he had committed one. I thought it unlikely; we got on fairly well and – as I had – I would have let him get on with it. I rather admired his lifestyle. And I wouldn't have reported it. Of course I wouldn't.

But would I have expected a share, perhaps even a half share?

No, of course I wouldn't. Come on, he was my brother.

The thing was, would *he* have thought that? Known that I wanted him to get away with it? You just couldn't tell.

'You seem preoccupied,' he said, jolting me back from the conjectural world of my worried mind.

'Oh, yes, a little bit. Things haven't been going so well. Been losing money lately and…'

I could have kicked myself. Losing money. Needing it badly. Prepared to do almost anything to obtain it. I was a fool sometimes. Well, not often, but this time I'd really said the wrong thing.

And he looked at me with a strange expression I hadn't seen before. Had I confirmed a worry, a belief, he had long entertained – a worry that had led him to…?

No, I still didn't think so. But, the red coat. Well, lots of people wore red coats. Didn't they? Well, some did.

That was a lot of thinking I'd been doing, and we'd by then reached his front door. He threw it open and smiled. What I did know was that someone had been making attempts to kill me.

The thing that concerned me was that I was about to spend an afternoon talking about those attempts with a person who could, and I was still emphasising *could*, have committed them.

My Brother Bob

It was going to be a long afternoon.

As I left the house, and having had no very convincing clues that my brother was trying to kill me, I took to the most public thoroughfares. No woods for me.

And what happened on my way home left no room for argument. Not for me anyway.

It was a white car – I knew Bob had a white car – that screeched into my path. It was the second time that day that I had found myself prone on the ground.

And, when Bob shot out of the car, I flinched away from him. I was unhurt but it was just another brick in the wall. And I had no wish to give him another chance. Even in my now fevered state, I thought back to the 'accidents'. They could all be explained as such. OK, it was a series of coincidences – and some, I thought, might have been witnessed by others – but, if he'd killed me there and then, that could not have been explained as anything unintentional: that would be murder. No disguising it.

So I leapt up. No injuries. Just a bit shaken up.

He tried to put his arm round me – I didn't want any of that. I shook him off.

'I can understand your feeling like that. It was stupid. Skidded on the ice and of all people to…'

'Yes,' I said. 'Of all people.'

He tried the loving brother bit again, and – again – I shrugged him off.

He looked as if a coin had suddenly dropped.

'But you surely… you didn't think?'

I interrupted him because I *did* think. And now I was convinced that I *knew*.

'I know exactly why all those "accidents" happened.'

'But you can't believe that. You can't.'

Suddenly I just felt so angry. You know when they say a red mist descends. Well I didn't see a red mist but I suppose the result was just the same. I couldn't look at him. I hated him. I couldn't look at him. I could only hit him, Hard. Very hard.

What happened then, I certainly hadn't intended. He fell heavily onto the side of his car. That's when the blood started flowing from his head.

Suddenly I didn't care whether he'd been trying to kill me or not. I just wanted him to live. But I didn't think he was going to.

I held his head. He looked up at me. I believe he wasn't sure what had happened.

'I was going to give you a big surprise,' he said.

I just got closer to his ear to hear what he was saying to me.

'I have made my biggest haul.'

I told him I knew.

'You knew?'

Of course he would say that.

'I was going to share that money with you. Ano…'

I listened closely as his voice became weaker.

I dialled 999 while I held him.

It needed to come quickly.

I listened again.

'And now,' I heard him say as I put my ear to his mouth, 'I know that you are so hard up…'

His head slumped against my hand.

I knew it was silly. I didn't do things like that normally – but I kissed his cheek.

Then I heard the ambulance.

I had spent the whole night at the hospital but, for much of it, I had to sit outside the room into which he'd been moved, not allowed to see him.

I saw they had a TV in the corner. I watched it without interest. The local news was never of any interest anyway but, tonight, it was. I jerked forward. Because it told the story of the arrest of Melvin Drabble. How he had been accused of several attempts on the life of…

Why hadn't the police wanted to see me?

Well, they had. They were waiting too. I could see the man at the end of the corridor and realised now who he must be. You don't crash in on man who is waiting to see if his brother had pulled through.

But, when the nurse came out of Bob's room, I knew what she was going to say.

I looked at the ground.

'Would you like to see him?'

I nodded, unsure that I did.

When I came out I could see the policeman approaching me.

'I'm sorry,' he said. Sorry for my loss.

I just stared at him and he said all the things he would say. But what he said next I wasn't expecting.

'I am sorry, but he was so unlucky. He died as a result of the skid.'

How could that be? If they'd found the wound which had bled so profusely, they would also find the mark on the *outside* of the car where he hit his head. And what about the bruise from my fist? That had hit him hard although I supposed that he could have sustained it as he fell out of the car. Not that he had of course.

'I'll leave you a few moments,' the policeman said kindly. And he did, going back to his post at the end of the corridor.

And I watched that local news. You know how it always goes round and round and, if you missed it first time, you'd catch up with it next time round.

And we were back to the arrest. And, despite my feelings of grief, I was able to concentrate on it. Especially because there was a surprising statement. Melvin Drabble had been brought in accused of attempted murder (I wonder who'd reported that because I hadn't) but he'd been *charged* with murder. The murder of Victor Lanning. Victor Lanning had appointed me at Merthyr's.

It made me think of Bob, careering across the road. Of course that *was* an accident. That corner was always treacherous, whether it was ice as he thought, or wet on the road. The sun wouldn't have dried it out.

When I went back to the police station to 'help them with their enquiries' I learned that those charges of attempted murder related to two of the attempts on *my* life (Bob must have been right) and *two* on that of Victor Lanning. I still didn't know where Lily came into it or if, indeed, she did at all.

Bob's funeral was difficult for me. Very difficult. I knew I hadn't meant to kill him but, equally, he wouldn't have died if I hadn't hit him. As to whether the police suspected anything I couldn't find out. But, if they ever came back with any accusations, I could defend the case with the best lawyer in the land.

Well, you don't think I was going to leave that metal box to rust in the wood did you?

Stella Verity's Pendant

The dust blew in clouds on the wind as he walked on the parched earth of the track. Ahead was a small cottage; further ahead was a large mansion to which he made his way.

He stopped and brushed his sleeve across his forehead. But the sweat still ran down his face. To his annoyance, as he passed, a girl emerged from the cottage. She looked up and he decided it was wise to move on. But, since her purpose did not keep her long, and she had turned back towards her house, he was able to study her more closely.

She was wearing a sleeveless blouse and a skirt of thin cotton. His eyes travelled down her long brown legs to her bare feet. Her arms, too, had been kissed by the sun. Despite his need for caution, he experienced a stirring of interest.

Edward Snelling planned his 'jobs' with great care. When he heard that a house – usually a large one – would be vacated for a period, he would investigate the ease with which he could enter it. The most sophisticated of defences were rarely proof against his ability to disable them but diligent planning was nevertheless required. The mansion towards which he walked had been occupied by a man of substance whose name had appeared in the births marriages and deaths – in this case significantly deaths – column. Whoever had placed the notice had been unwise enough to refer to where the wake would be held, informing Edward that the house he was approaching would be unoccupied on the day of the funeral, and perhaps until the 'for sale' board went up.

He had carefully studied the man's life: he had merited an obituary which offered information that would be helpful in his pursuit of valuable pieces.

His de-activation of the alarm system had been surprisingly easy; his search of the house had been unhindered.

Caution had carried Edward through his career of crime without the necessity of visiting any of the country's penal institutions. Hence he was unknown to the police and was – he believed – without a recorded stain on his character. That caution had become so ingrained that he avoided even the slightest risk – and was the reason for his careful preparation.

Feeling that every risk could be avoided, he looked back, through the window, at the cottage in which the girl lived. However much he desired to see her again, his intentions required that he should not be distracted by her – the girl he later identified as Stella Verity. He was now able to concentrate on the valuables, the choice of items depending largely upon their portability, and a lack of identifiable provenance, even by the greatest expert. For he was not greedy; as a burglar he made a steady if unspectacular living.

He began his careful selection. The ideal items he moved, with plastic gloved hands, into the inner garment he had worn for this purpose. His task would next be to move them to a place of safety for later collection. This, too, would be arranged so that the goods would never be found in his possession.

But, at this point, his whole body froze. A sound had caused him to move, noiselessly, to a place of cover. His perfect hearing had been a great aid in his avoidance of capture many times, and he was depending upon it now.

Again he heard a noise, barely a noise, almost the suspicion of a noise. Then he heard a movement, a stealthy movement. He remained in his place of safety although his heart was beating fiercely. There was a soft footfall on the stairs. He would naturally do nothing until the source of that movement could be identified.

And, so, he waited, remaining concealed.

He knew that the person was climbing the stairs and that he had only to await their arrival in the room in which he crouched.

And then he saw her. From his vantage point he could see a pair of long brown legs and, as they moved further into the room, he – while still invisible to her – began to ease his body. He had recognised those legs and was able to imagine the girl as she moved across the room.

Believing herself to be unobserved, she went, without hesitation, to a box on the dressing table. Edward knew what it contained and, having a name engraved upon it, he had rejected it, despite its obvious value.

She opened the lid of the box and withdrew a pendant. Edward remained concealed and watched her slip the jewellery into the pocket of her blouse, waiting for her to carefully close the box – and walk towards the door.

However, the relief that he felt caused an incautious movement and she spun round. He sprang, and it was the work of a moment to clap his hand over her mouth. He motioned her to silence:

'If I take my hand away, will you scream?'

Her terrified look suggested to him that she had no more wish to advertise her presence in the house than he did. He slowly took away the hand which covered her mouth. Her looked reflected the continued fear she felt at the angry look on his face. They stared at each other for some time.

He spoke only one word: 'Why?'

She tried to conquer her fear and said:

'I saw you come past my house. There is only one reason why you would be coming to this empty house.'

'And what made you follow me?'

'I can explain; I believed that you must have disabled the alarms. I should not have been able to do that.'

'And thought you would take anything I had left?'

'No, I haven't taken anything else.'

There was little chance for her to conceal anything in her short skirt, and she was still barefooted, only the outline of the pendant showing against her breast in the pocket of her blouse.

He sighed:

'I could have been caught because of you – and now you are a danger to me.'

'But I...' she stammered.

And it took little thought for him to consider the absurdity of his last statement. Her admission that she had been in the house to witness his actions would also reveal *her* crime. He looked into her pale blue eyes:

'Why the pendant?'

'It is mine.'

He again showed annoyance.

'No,' she said, more emphatically, 'it *is* mine.'

He looked into her eyes again. He wished to believe her. No one could turn eyes so innocent upon their accuser and not be believed. At last he smiled:

'Tell me about it.'

It was a strange story. For seven years she had lived in her cottage next to the large house. The occupant of *that* house, Giles Hanson, was her brother-in-law who had acquired the cottage, and had sold it to her for re-payment by instalments. He said that he had taken a liking to her pendant and would accept it as collateral to guarantee her repayments. The pendant had been willed to her by her mother: it was her most treasured and her only valuable possession. Edward was surprised that Hanson would demand (Stella felt that she had little option but to comply) such a re-payment from a relative, albeit a relative by marriage.

'And you didn't think you would get the pendant back?'

'I have since paid off the loan so that he could return it, and he has refused to do so.'

'He can't do that. What about the paperwork?'

She looked abashed and he realised there had been no paperwork, no official arrangement.

'My sister died young; it had been an unhappy marriage,' Stella told him, 'and the house which had been occupied by my in-laws by that marriage passed, after her death, to his father. My brother in law moved to a house in Tipley.

'Only my brother-in-law knew of the arrangement which allowed my occupation of the cottage. As for the pendant, he said that he had developed a fondness for it and that, if I forestalled, he would be glad to keep it. But I heard that he had had it valued and…'

'And it was valuable. Yes, it's very valuable.'

'*Very* valuable.'

'So you retrieved what is yours. And you have it now.'

Stella looked up at him with some concern.

'Oh, come now; you don't think I am going to take it from you?'

She continued to stare at him, her innocent blue eyes looking into his. He was more and more aware of her body, her bare legs, her pretty face…

'This has turned out well,' he said. 'You have your pendant and your brother-in-law is unlikely to believe you responsible. There was a – very carefully planned – burglary and the pendant went with the other stolen items. And I am going to help you secrete it away – just in case he does see you as a modern Raffles. You will be able to look at it for as long and as often as you wish.'

Stella was still unable to understand that a burglar would give up such a valuable item, but Edward explained his reluctance to steal the piece because of the dangers of its disposal. Did she but know it, he now had a more potent reason.

'And, now… ?'

She looked again and, as his arm reluctantly released her, he took her hand.

'And, now we depart.'

'Have you everything you need?'

A request to a burglar as to whether he was satisfied with his takings was a first in his experience.

'I have everything I need,' he said, looking at the outline of the pendant in her shirt pocket and at the girl in front of him:

'Everything.'

The days passed and Edward secured the items stolen from the big house. As the news of the burglary justified fewer column inches in the press, the police had to confess to being baffled. And this event became consigned to the vaults with other crimes which were categorised as unsolvable.

He wondered if Stella's brother-in-law had told anyone of his possession of the pendant; given the circumstances, he doubted it. It was after all worth more – as it transpired, and as Hanson knew perfectly well – than the entire purchase price of the cottage. He would be angry certainly, and, presumably since it would not have been included on any inventory, he would be unable to claim on the insurance – as he could on the other stolen items. Edward began to believe that all had benefitted from his 'job' except, perhaps, for the insurance company and its clients who would face higher renewal premiums the following year. He also felt satisfaction that a relationship had developed between himself and Stella.

He had promised to make the pendant secure and had done it. He brought a safe to the cottage which, with his experience, he was able to guarantee would resist any future attempts to remove the pendant from Stella's possession. His kindness was not entirely altruistic. The couple's friendship was blossoming and, by now, they felt able to meet more frequently and talk at length.

The weather had turned; it had done so soon after the burglary and been part of Edward Snelling's planning. No signs of his approach to the house were evident from the parched paths which had lately turned into quagmires.

But the heat had returned and Stella had begun again to wear the type of clothes in which he had originally seen her on that hot summer's morning. She deliberately did so, believing that they were garments that had pleased Edward. And they had – and continued to do so.

Conversations between the couple often centred on Stella's

brother-in-law, on the abuse suffered by her sister during her period of marriage to Hanson, on his continued hounding of Stella and his claim that full repayment on his loan had not been made.

What they later learned of Giles Hanson's activities were, however, a surprise to Stella although Edward had been aware of his reputation and therefore experienced less surprise. Stella could not believe that, unpleasant as he had been to her, and to her sister, his other activities had resulted in his arrest for international fraud. And, having read the article in the local newspaper, she was even more interested in a paragraph in its report of his crimes:

'He was also responsible for the burglary of his father's house?'

Edward took the newspaper with a smile. Stella Verity looked at him:

'Why should he burgle his own house?'

'Well,' he laughed, 'it wasn't his own house – he was a joint beneficiary.'

'But, surely...'

'And he stood to gain from the insurance company; the policy was in his name.'

'How do you *know* that?'

Stella did not wait for an answer:

'And how was it that the jewellery that *you* stole was found in Giles' house at Tipley village?'

Edward adopted an expression of innocence.

'You...'

For a moment Stella stared:

'Did you...?'

He looked hurt:

'Well, if you thought I would keep it, I should have been a criminal - and how could you marry a burglar?'

'I haven't been asked to.'

'And,' Edward said, 'you won't be.'

Stella's disappointment was evident.

'Marry a burglar I mean.'

'I haven't been asked to marry anyone.'

Snelling smiled.
Did he need to say more?

In Bessie and Arthur's Garden

It was the same as always: overgrown, exciting and a hiding place where could be found innumerable discoveries. Always there were kittens, feral but responsive to our overtures. Always there were treasures, such as long disused agricultural equipment, of which our favourites were the tractors which, after our manful attempts to release them from the grip of a year's growth, afforded us the pleasure of 'riding' them and pretending to return the wilderness of weeds and bushes to fields acceptable to the farmer.

Just what farmer had once tended this area we had no idea. It had been overgrown all through our annual visits to Bessie and Arthur, kindly friends of our mother referred to as Aunt and Uncle, although we were aware that they were in no way related to us.

The area had been our playground during our yearly visits for as long as we could remember and, being always thus, we could never imagine it becoming any different.

Bessie and Arthur enjoyed their remoteness, and the wide acres of neglected country which, since they had not the ability nor willingness to clear it, simply existed to enrich our lives – or so we believed.

This year was no different. Our mother had stayed for tea on the day she had delivered us into Bessie's care for this week of our summer holidays. Then she left us, knowing that, for a period, we would love to ramble and explore country which the environs of our east London home could never afford.

And Bessie and Arthur – who had been my mother's neighbours at our previous home – enhanced the experience. In short we loved them and they provided a freedom which our mother would not have done and about which, perhaps, she did not know.

Each morning consisted of an early rise – we had no wish to waste any part of the day in sleep – and a breakfast of egg, bacon – and as many other delights as Bessie could heap upon our plates. Then Bessie – or Arthur – would usher us out into the jungle which acted as their garden and had, long before, been their predecessors' farm.

Despite our familiarity with most of it, the overgrown vegetation was sufficiently dense to hide all the area's treasures and it was these we sought, having inspected the barns, the air raid shelter – and, of course, the tractors.

The afternoon found me in my favourite seat on one of the tractors on which the faintly legible name 'Massey-Harris' indicated its origins. Clearance of the area around it was a two man task and the assistance of my brother, four years older than my eleven years, was essential. The country air and exercise would increase our appetite for Bessie's dinners. But there was much more to unearth.

The greatest surprise came when we turned our attention to the air raid shelter. For efforts had already been made to clear some of the bushes on the track approaching it, although, strangely, the entrance had become hidden by bushes that had been placed in front of it, and were probably the plants that had resulted from the clearance.

The shelter had always been fascinating but could not delay our search for too long, and we turned our attention to the barns. These required us to exercise caution because years of neglect had caused areas of decay which, had this been a public place, would have displayed notices warning of the danger of entering them. We knew, but we ignored the possibility of the collapse of these structures.

And it was in one of the barns that we had begun to support sagging timbers, when I glimpsed a movement in the grass near the tractor and shelter which we had just left.

My silent warning to my brother was unnecessary. He had seen it too.

My brother exercised his authority by motioning me to remain silent and to follow him.

Quickly.

I did so, scarcely breathing in case it warned whoever had attracted our attention of our approach.

Our caution was rewarded. We had expected an animal but, as we stood over a patch of uncleared grass, we heard a gasp.

We drew the grass aside and, invisible though she must have been to all but two inquisitive and eagle eyed boys, the object of our search was revealed.

My eleven year old self found it difficult to assess her age although my brother assured me later that she must have been about eighteen – three years older than him but at an age which made her a woman to me.

For a few moments we just stared. The girl sat hugging her knees, her bare legs drawn tightly in to her body. To me she was the most fascinating find that we had encountered in Bessie and Arthur's garden. My brother's reaction was similar although he determined to discover her reason for being there.

She could have been a relative of Bessie and Arthur although we felt sure that they would have told us that we might encounter her during our exploration.

Clearly my brother did not accept the right of anyone except us to be in their garden.

The girl had seen me first. Although she flinched, she seemed slightly to relax seeing what she would regard as a small boy. My brother provoked a greater response and a frightened look appeared on her face.

'I was doing no harm.'

Her melodious voice intrigued me. She had a noticeable accent. My reaction was to reassure her, although my brother exhibited his maturity in questioning her existence in a place to which only we should have had access.

'This is private land,' he said.

'I didn't know; I really didn't know. If you don't tell anyone else, I will just go. I won't come back.'

This response saddened me. I wished her to come back. Indeed I was already planning for her to play a part in our games. A maiden to be rescued perhaps.

'I am sorry but I will have to ask you to leave,' my brother insisted.

'Yes, I said I would. I *will* go.'

I suspected that my brother was exercising the authority he considered invested in him by Bessie and Arthur in informing her of her trespass. The kindness in his tone suggested, however, that he would be as reluctant to lose her as I.

She slowly arose, pulling her skirt's hem down to its normal level just above her knees.

She continued to look at my brother and, as she began to walk away, she peered back at him as if wondering whether he would take the matter further. To me she directed only one darted glance. As she walked, she continued to look behind her to ensure that we meant her no harm.

And, as my brother began to follow her to see where she had entered the field, she increased her speed.

Pathetically she said:

'I am going; I am going.'

But my brother told me to follow her:

'She isn't as afraid of you. You can tell her we won't take the matter any further if you like.'

Clearly he had seen the look of adoration in my eyes, and I welcomed his words which, I was sure, emphasised my belief that he, too, would welcome her return.

I hurried on and, at first, she increased her speed. Then she allowed me to catch up, seeing that my brother was not accompanying me.

But, for some time, she did not speak. I could see that we were walking towards a remote part of Bessie and Arthur's field and, when we arrived at a gate, I knew that this was a limit for me, not having their permission to pass through it.

Now I noted that, as the girl passed through the gate, she was entering a wooded area, through which ran a lane.

She stopped on dropping the gate's latch and looked at me, speaking to me for the first time:

'I was hiding from… I was trying to get away from him.'

I was unable to enquire from whom she was hiding. I wished to know but I could not speak to her.

She pushed away from the gate and said nothing more.

I watched as she walked through the small, wooded area, turning along the lane at its end.

I was angry with myself. Why could I not speak?

But I knew why. She was a creature from another world to mine. I simply watched her, captivated by a heavenly creature, by her graceful motion and the beauty of her body, bewitched by a being to whom I meant nothing. But I did continue to wonder who it was she wished to avoid and whether her flight had been successful.

Increasingly I contemplated her plight. If we had not found her, would she have been safe and escaped her tormentor? Would her exposure lead to her capture? I wondered if my brother would feel similarly guilty about the fate to which our expulsion might lead her.

Having told him what she had said, his expression showed me that he did. Would it really have been wrong to encourage her trespass, or, indeed, deliberately ignore her, so that she could find a more suitable hiding place than the long grass?

For the rest of the day, the tractors, the barns, the feral cats and the air raid shelter failed to draw us to them. What my thoughts dwelt upon was the figure of the girl as she passed through the gate. Young as I was, I was smitten. I believed myself to be in love with her.

And our low spirits were noticed by Bessie and Arthur. Always we had returned from our adventures brimming with the excitement of exploration and adventure, chattering about our doings in the area to which they had generously given us free rein.

Again I wondered whether my brother's feelings were similar to my own. Would he dream of her as I suspected I would? In the event I did not dream of her; I could not sleep thinking about her.

The sun shone brightly the following morning and bathed the fields behind Bessie and Arthur's house in a radiant glow. Small clouds hurried across a blue sky as the slight breeze which propelled them rippled the long grass.

As I walked out into what had become our adventure playground, my spirits began to rise again. There were several days of our holiday at Bessie and Arthur's left and we must make good use of them. For this morning, though, I was alone, and our best adventures happened when my brother was able to add his ingenuity to my imaginative plans. The main dampener this morning, though, was that I was certain I should not see again the girl for whom I had developed a passion unique in my young life. But I could never really know her: she would never be within my reach. I could at least think of her, however: imagine she was with me in my solitary moments.

So my walk on that bright morning was with her. She was by my side, her hand in mine.

But, as I wandered towards one of the barns I saw a motion which made my heart leap; however it was not her. And my excitement turned to fear: there *was* someone in the barn. Not the girl. Definitely not the girl. I looked with horror at a man who, having not seen me, was stacking plastic bags in piles. I quietly eased myself to the ground, not ten feet from him, fearful that he might have been aware of my approach. It seemed, though, that he had not heard me and was unaware of my presence.

As I lay behind an extension of the barn, my heart beating notes of thunder in my breast, I could see, through a gap in the boarding, that he was gathering the bags, which contained a white sugar-like substance, and taking them out of the barn.

My eyes followed his progress towards the air raid shelter where he pulled back the bushes which my brother and I had noticed and re-appeared, moments later, without his load.

I made no attempt to move since, even in my frightened state, I realised that it was a place of safety. To move now would certainly lead to my discovery as I could see the man was returning to the barn.

As he began to stack more bags from what I assumed (since we had not seen them in the barn the previous day) were nooks and crannies in the dilapidated structure sufficiently carefully chosen to hide them from sight. I was near enough to hear his voice. And see him roughly handle another person who had clearly been bringing the bags to a convenient place for him to move them to the shelter.

The shelter was clearly a better place for storage than a leaky barn and I assumed the barn had not been used for their storage for any extended period. But my attention was focused on the person whom I had quickly labelled his accomplice. Whatever their relationship, the man's role was clearly to direct the operation. And I sensed that the as yet unseen confederate was reluctant to obey his commands.

Then he grabbed by the arm what I could now adduce to be a woman and flung her to the ground. She scrambled to her feet and, in turning, presented me with a view of her face.

To my astonishment and disappointment, it was the face of yesterday's visitor to our 'garden'. Although she was obviously an unwilling assistant, she took a batch of the bags and walked, in front of the man, along the path that led to the air raid shelter.

Between them they quickly disposed of the bags in their new home. Quite why they had been initially kept in a place I regarded as inappropriate for such storage, and one which necessitated their removal, I could not fathom. But it might not have been apparent to anyone unfamiliar with Bessie and Arthur's garden, until a proper search was made, that there was more suitable storage available. Perhaps this explained the girl's presence yesterday morning. Maybe she had discovered the shelter in the overgrown area in which it had been concealed. And, as these thoughts revolved around my mind, the conspirators completed their operation.

Clearly the girl, though mortally afraid of her associate, was unwilling to co-operate fully in the operation and was now increasingly angering the man with whom she had accomplished it. And this idea was emphasised by his hitting her round the face, an action which made a resounding thwack and echoed around the barn.

I moved forward to defend the girl but quickly re-assumed my place of safety, realising that no interference on my part would protect her and would probably worsen the situation. So I watched them, he striding, she stumbling, towards the gate through which she had yesterday made her exit.

As they did so, I could hear their surprisingly loud conversation:
'Yes, you *will* come tomorrow,' he said, his stare threatening further violence.

She clearly would not chance answering back and risk being hit again, but she obviously did not relish another visit.

'I will need to keep the car engine running; you will come in and help 'A' move the stuff. Then our part will be over and you can stop worrying because you do my head in with your worrying.'

Although he continued to talk, he was, by now, out of earshot. I remained in my place of concealment for some time before daring to carefully look round the barn to ensure that no one else had been involved in the operation.

There was no one and I proceeded to the air raid shelter to find the bags stacked up as I had expected to see them. My course was obvious. Again with extreme caution and looking carefully about me, I walked back to the house. Bessie was in the kitchen and listened to my story with great concern. Fortunately she accepted the story as true and not the result of a boy's feverish imagination.

But, knowing that Bessie would inform the police, I worried about the consequences for the girl. A discussion with my brother, with whom I could not wait to share my experiences when he returned from the task on which Arthur had dispatched him, did not set my mind at rest. He insisted that what I had witnessed was an illegal trade which would harm many and for which the malefactors should be soundly punished. That was understandable but I was convinced that the girl was an unwilling participant.

We were instructed, the following day, to keep out of the garden. The police were apparently mounting an operation and our presence would jeopardise its success. But what youths would not be tempted to witness an event in whose discovery they had been instrumental?

And I think we both wished to ensure that the girl did not suffer a similar fate to the men who did indeed richly deserve it. I could offer my story of the man striking her in her defence perhaps. But we kept out of sight of the police as they, too, hid themselves and waited.

Eventually a man I was seeing for the first time entered the field and, with the utmost caution, approached the air raid shelter. I did not, however, see the girl. My spirits rose. Perhaps her accomplice had decided not to risk bringing her in case she would prove a liability on such an occasion.

It was quickly done. And, the bags having been moved into the awaiting car, the police moved into action. I realised that they needed proof of the two men's complicity in the operation and that they now considered they could surround the car.

Had the dealers escaped, they would have been prevented from making further progress by a road block a little way up the lane. But they made no attempt to flee; there was little point.

My hiding place gave me a poor view of the arrests and I suspected that the girl had been in the car. Had she been there, there could be no doubt that she, too, would now be in the hands of the police. I began to move back towards the house, realising that my brother had not followed me. Indeed I could not find him when I returned.

It was several hours before my brother appeared, during which I had to suffer Bessie's admonition concerning my disobeying of her orders.

I felt foolish tears well up in my eyes. For I had lost the girl who had made our stay so memorable.

Putting his arm around me, my brother smiled comfortingly:
'She's in the barn.'
'She's…?'
'In the barn.'

I looked at him with astonishment, unable to speak:

'When you came out into the field this morning, I made my way round to where you said the car would be waiting.

'She came out to wait for the man with whom she had been detailed to move the drugs.

'As soon as she was out of sight of the car, I came out of the barn and put my hand over her mouth, dragging her in. I explained that the police would be waiting and kept her in the barn with me until they had left with the two men.

'Everything played into my hands. She was obviously going ahead to the shelter and he, I imagined, was helping to prepare the car for the reception of the bags. I assumed they would need to have been carefully concealed. But, anyway, the man waited before he came to find her and, by the time he did, she was with me in the barn.'

'So she's still in the barn?'

'I think we can go there now; I told her to wait until I had thoroughly searched the area. But she's probably made her escape by now.'

But she had not. We found her lying where my brother had left her.

In the only expression of emotion I had seen her make, she rushed to my brother and embraced him.

How I wished I could have been him. But I felt no bitterness towards my brother: he had saved her. Her accomplices had been arrested and could no longer trouble her.

When we – the girl and my brother, with me trailing behind - came to the house, she started to explain how she had become part of an operation with which she clearly had no sympathy.

Her accomplice, she explained, was an evil man who had taken advantage of her vulnerability in being an immigrant, without legal right to be in the country, to use her. She knew she could not go to the police and looked in vain for ways to escape what was virtually imprisonment.

My brother asked her where she would go now.

There was, she explained, nowhere to go.

Looking back on that day, I think of Bessie and Arthur and their subsequent complicity in the girl's eventual escape. I think of the police – and their failure to arrest the whole gang. And I think of Anna. I envy my brother who, years later, made her his wife. And I love her still.

I wonder yet how he was able to make her stay in this country legitimate. And I still wonder at his achieving her rescue in Bessie and Arthur's garden.

But, then, my brother can accomplish anything.

The Ruined Cottage

Living at Beacon Edge provided the needed contrast to the stresses experienced in London: a peaceful respite from the bustle of the capital and the tension of my life in the business world, the hectic ever-present pressure to meet each deadline and satisfy those whose use of the company was essential to our future.

My marriage to Marina had enabled a move to the wild country refuge in which we settled. The necessity for a high salary to maintain my lifestyle was reduced by our combined salaries – and by Marina's willingness to settle for a life of calm contemplation of the beauty of the area which we had found together.

I could not say that our union was one engendered by passion but, after the years of living – as Marina put it – 'on the edge', passion could not have been further from our thoughts. We were content, if not jubilantly happy; satisfied while not living on a wave of ecstasy. With this I was content, genuinely loving the tranquillity of my new home – and fulfilled by the companionship which Marina provided.

I could work from home in a stress-free environment, and Marina could – and did – the same. It gave me the flexibility to enjoy my solitary walks in country which provided dramatic scenery nd a spectacular panorama, but it also allowed perambulations in ᴐded areas into which few people ventured. Marina was happy 'ease me, not needing to partake in my energetic pleasures, but perfectly content to await my return, and enjoy the scenery in a more sedate way.

It was on the third morning of my new life that I discovered the ruined cottage. It was appropriate that I should find it on a day when the black skies had emptied their rain upon the parched earth. The wind seemed to blow me towards it as if offering the source of shelter against the coming deluge. I walked into what I assumed had been the parlour of a Victorian home and found in it surprising protection from the elements. I was even able to seat myself in the corner of the room, imagining a family contentedly seated around me.

Visions of the past invariably suggest domestic tranquillity although perhaps that reflected a view of our world rather than theirs.

I could watch the sky from my perch – as if through a window but actually through a section of jagged stonework which had replaced the original aperture. Although the cottage had clearly been derelict for many years, I did wonder just how long it had been since it had been inhabited and by whom.

Perhaps the solid grey, local stonework had protected the interior and therefore suggested a more modern evacuation than I had envisaged.

The sun made a welcome return and I left – I have to say with some reluctance – my refuge from the storm. And it was as I looked back that an image appeared in front of me that held me spellbound.

The cottage was no longer a ruin but a vision of country domesticity – a dwelling similar to those seen in numerous Victorian paintings depicting a rural idyl perhaps very different from the lives experienced by dwellers in such properties.

Around the cottage appeared before me a well-tended garden, with larkspur, Canterbury bells, campanula, marigolds, irises, hyacinths arranged in a multitudinous array, and with honeysuckle trained up the walls.

That idyllic image was soon to fade. As I continued to view the garden, only few of those flowers remained amongst weeds and the small trees which had surrounded the cottage when I had first seen it. And the charming cottage was largely gone, my ruined refuge returning, filling me with a feeling of disappointment but curiosity.

I made my way home, determined soon to return to a place which had fascinated me. And try to establish just what it was that had caused that fascination – a disintegrating dwelling appearing, again, as a picturesque cottage.

For the next few days, as well as visiting the cottage in the brighter days that followed, I made use of the facilities provided in the map section of Christminster's reference library, and it was revealing to find that the cottage – or a dwelling in its place – had existed for over one hundred and eighty years.

It was in the 1840s that a dwelling began to appear on the Ordnance Survey maps and the latest still showed the cottage despite its ruined state. The maps did not show the date of the cottage's construction, nor, if it happened, its re-building. There may have been justification for its original construction in the growing economic prosperity of nearby Christminster, already at that time a thriving town.

While a number of cottages had been built around the town, and some remained, the one in which my interest lay was the most remote and was evidence that Christminster's influence was greater than today. I believed, without being able to prove it, that the cottage I saw was the original construction.

While I had shared my strange experience with Marina, she had shown only mild interest. Few events disturbed the even tenor of her ways.

Possessing a certain amount of skill at writing and a belief that I could write an account of my inexplicable vision at the ruined cottage, I submitted a 'story' to *The Recorder*.

The 'story' and a subsequent letter was sent with the hope that ˑl newspapers (particularly in these times) would print any letif not the more substantial piece. Neither appeared in *The*

Recorder.

My puzzlement at the reluctance of a local newspaper to use any of my writings caused me, next time I was in Christminster, to view their offices. The Victorian building in which the publisher had disseminated news to the area since, as the sign over the door revealed, 1839, seemed to invite me in. The sign read further: Proprietors: Stiffwald and Sons. I decided, since I was there, to go in, and, seeing a young woman at the desk, approached her:

'I sent a story recently but it never appeared in the paper,' I said.

'Not everything can go in, I'm afraid,' she replied.

I told her that I appreciated that, but elaborated on the story and suggested that it was not just *any* story. That it was something quite remarkable.

The girl smiled and held up her hand for me to wait and, bending forward, apparently to ensure that her departure was not discovered, left the desk. She returned a few minutes later with a dusty book. Handing it to me, she again checked that her visit to a store had not been witnessed. She quickly wrote a very short note and placed it in a page which she clearly knew to contain something of interest.

I did not open the book but thanked her and asked its price. She shook her head and waved her hand to indicate that, to me, there would be no charge.

'I have put a book mark in the book,' she said. 'You can never have too many book marks.'

So, with Marina's encouragement, but not participation (she preferred to engage in her work and solitary pleasures) I had made more headway than I expected. I began to read the book I had been handed at *The Recorder* offices, having been discouraged from reading it there. In this, written in the 1920s, I read a fascinating but, in many ways, tragic story. I was even able to discover from it the name of one of the cottage's occupants:

Annabelle Lincoln.

The name intrigued me but I was saddened by her story. According to the history, Annabelle, then a girl of eighteen, had murdered her husband.

'It is believed,' I read, 'that the occupier of the cottage had, all those years ago, caused the death of her husband, possibly by the administration of arsenic.'

It might well have been 'believed' but it might not have occurred. *My* belief was that it had not, although I had no more justification for my disbelief of the claim than the author apparently had for making it. With a judiciary only too willing to find against women in that age, it is significant that the author was unable to justify his statement by the production of proof.

And I became increasingly fascinated with the name of the lady and the visions that it conjured up. She had apparently suffered ostracism inflicted by neighbours (so the book recorded with emphasis, although there seemed not to be many dwellings near hers). I felt I could add an account of Annabelle Lincoln refuting the claims in the book (*A History of Christminster and its Surrounds*), without the slightest evidence to support my argument.

As I put the book down, I removed the 'book mark' which the young receptionist had placed in it. It read: 'Stiffwald, not Lincoln'. I shrugged, not understanding to what this referred.

I returned to the cottage frequently after I had obtained shelter from it. One visit, some weeks afterwards was particularly memorable. The ruin appeared as it had when I had first seen it. I entered through the frame of wood which had once supported the front door. The significance of this occasion was that, when I did so, it was with a strange feeling that I was entering at the invitation of the occupant.

The night had seen rain and the interior had a strange odour of damp wood and earthiness which permeated the building. From inside I viewed the garden which had undergone such a transformation on my first visit.

If I had been transported back to the age when an eighteen year old Annabelle Lincoln occupied the cottage, I felt I could become absorbed in her life and times. I was beginning to feel already that I had leapt back through the years. Although thoughts of the mystery of the resurrected cottage and its garden occupied me for long periods and apparently amused my wife, I did not revisit the cottage for a few days after this. When I did so, it was to find that the mystery had deepened.

I looked outside to see if I could find any solution to the mystery, finding none, although my entry again seemed to be welcomed. Unseen and feeling absurd, I greeted any inhabitants that might be at home. It was this play-acting that led me later to suppose that I could have imagined what followed.

The golden reflections of the sun cast an ethereal glow upon the interior of the cottage.

But, all at once the sky darkened. The dramatic change could not have been more sudden.

Spots of rain began to fall and the wind, negligible before, picked up and began to howl around the cottage. It made little sense to venture out and I prepared myself for a lengthy stay in what had again become my refuge.

The noises I began to hear were not unexpected in a house which had existed for so long. I entered again the room I had surmised was the parlour. From it I was able, despite the stairs having partially fallen a victim to the ravages of time, to lift myself into an upper room, almost certainly a bedroom. I seated myself on a low collection of beams.

As I waited for the bad weather to pass, I felt my head whirling and my eyesight affected as if I were experiencing a migraine. I continued to sit, unable to stand but slowly finding my 'seat' to be more substantial than the planks on which I had originally perched. I strained my eyes to see and what I saw amazed me. In the corner of the room – a normal room with no signs of the ruination with which time had demeaned the cottage – was a light. The light gradually metamorphosed into a shape. And into a figure.

The figure of a woman.

It was as if I could recognise her as Annabelle. It was as if I had known her and that this was a familiar figure. She stared ahead seemingly unseeing.

The blankness in her eyes created the impression of someone mistily staring from a distance. I was unable to resist the impression that she was staring through time, and that, eventually, she might see me.

Her eyes became more animated. Her head moved and began to view her surroundings as if they were familiar to her but not seen for some time. Recognition was followed by astonishment.

I had caused that.

I tried to remain still. I did not wish her to go.

She was Annabelle and she was beautiful.

But, perhaps, I was to her as indistinct as she had been to me. Maybe I was slowly emerging from a vapid form into an animated being. I should not have been surprised if she had been unable to see me; I expected her to be unaware of my presence. But she clearly could discern at least my shape.

And she looked afraid.

The transformed garden had, however, prepared me for something like this. I had somehow expected it, hoped for it.

I moved my hand and she flinched.

I tried to make my motion one of reassurance.

But the fear was obvious in her eyes, which had just moments before lacked intensity of any kind.

I smiled, hoping that would reassure her.

Slowly my attempt to calm her appeared to succeed.

Her features, her body, relaxed, strange as that might seem for a sprite.

Again I smiled and there was a flicker in her own features.

I spoke.

But she could not hear me. And, although I saw her lips move, I was unable to hear, understand or react.

And then *she* smiled.

I slowly stood, attempting to make my movement unthreatening. Her eyes followed me but she did not move.

I began to look around the cottage. We were a couple in a room which had once been hers. I looked out onto the garden through a window which I had only hitherto seen as a dark hole in the brickwork.

I then looked back.

The girl had gone.

My walks in future all took the same direction. Sometimes I would see her; sometimes not.

But, as time progressed, my feelings began to change. I found myself becoming irritated by the prosaic and largely sedentary life led by Marina and, more worryingly, fascinated by Annabelle. I could not wait to take my walks and my anxiety to leave the house was noted. It was not that Marina wished to share my walks, only that she suspected their purpose to be more sinister than she had previously imagined. Or perhaps she could imagine my slipping away from her and that my love – little as it had ever been for her – was being transferred.

In that – I had to admit – she was correct.

I did leave in hope of seeing Annabelle. And, when I did, I had to admit that I was falling in love with her.

It was all too strange to admit. I was enamoured of a girl who lived over a hundred and eighty years ago – to whom I could not speak, whom I could not touch and with whom I seemed to be unable to share those feelings. Most absurd of all I imagined that she was falling in love with me. And for that I could present no justification other than her apparent pleasure in my presence.

She had begun to follow me down from the upper room, the stairs of course reinstated during my visits, but she would stand at the door. She did not wave or move when she stood there – but I took her presence as a farewell – and perhaps sadness that I was leaving.

I *had* to find out more about her. And perhaps right the wrongs done to her, correct the mistaken impressions of her which had been created by a book written eighty years after the events they had recorded.

I had little doubt that, however the author had obtained his information, the belief in the crime, perhaps shared by a few contemporaries, had faded away with time.

My attempts to research the girl's past and the events surrounding the publication of the book were enlivened by a second visit to *The Recorder* offices. This was where I had expected to find the publisher and editor whose reaction to my story and my letter had been so unwelcoming.

The family who had issued *The Recorder* from a time before Annabelle had moved into her cottage was not represented when I called. Instead I found the proprietor of the South West News and Media Group – a chance and welcome encounter – and his new editor.

Like most local news groups, the Recorder Group had fallen victim to the changes in the public's methods of obtaining local information. However, South West News wished to capture the existing – but dwindling – readership, whose determination to continue their subscriptions perhaps owed more to loyalty than pleasure in reading the printed word.

To Samuel Hayden that audience was part of the reason he had added the Recorder Group of newspapers to the already numerous newssheets and online media which were part of his massive – and forward-looking – empire.

For the incumbent editor on his arrival he had no time. He was a relict, unable to embrace the present let alone the future. Hayden had no respect for such fossils; his intention was to rebuild *The Recorder's* readership with exciting news, perhaps scandal and certainly crime. Basil Derwent was the incoming editor and one who had already made personnel changes, which had weeded out many who had worked for the paper for many years, these becoming redundant. New, young, ambitious journalists replaced them.

Derwent was the type of person I instinctively disliked – a feeling I had also for the new publisher who had installed him in his post. But I soon found that their attitude to the industry could serve my purpose. The correspondence and submissions, which, of course, had been stored in paper form in bulging filing cabinets, were ruthlessly pruned. Reports of fêtes and church gatherings were consigned to recycling bins while the few – the very few – items of interest (most of which had been rejected by the previous editor) were studied carefully.

Fortunately for me, for the current editor, and unfortunately for the previous regime, my 'story' and my letter had been retained by them – and I was able to update the narrative, my excitement and feelings for Annabelle animating the story for the new editor. Indeed he had shown such interest and enthusiasm that my initial impression of him was changing rapidly. I found myself liking him.

I was also able to explain the background in a way that increased – if that were possible – that enthusiasm. Clearly this story was the one to get *The New Recorder* off on the right foot, and Basil Derwent felt there was nothing in it to antagonise the existing readership.

His thirst for details engendered a foray into all aspects of the tale and resulted in his taking his mobile phone from his pocket:

'Griff!'

At the other end was a response – presumably from the unseen Griff.

'I want background on the Stiffwalds… yes the old publishers… Yes and I want to know about Gervase Stiffwald.' He was unable to stifle a snigger which clearly had been prompted by a similar response from the ubiquitous Griff.

'He was a member of the owners' family… may even have been a publisher himself.'

I sat forward on my seat:

'I don't think so,' I interrupted. 'But the cottage on the 1842 Ordnance Survey map was called Stiffwald Cottage.'

Basil Derwent reflected my enthusiasm by sitting forward on *his* chair.

'So, there is a connection,' he said, taking a leap from my information on the grounds that Stiffwald is not the most common of names. 'So he was the husband she is supposed to have murdered.

Do we know anything about him?'

To my shame I was unable to claim any knowledge about him, having not made the connection, nor fully understood the receptionist's cryptic bookmark.

'Griff!' he shouted, hoping that he had stayed on his phone. He clearly had.

'Check everything: censuses, births, marriages, deaths, everything. Should be easy; there are few Stiffwalds about and Gervase Stiffwald must be even rarer!'

Griff would check everything.

'From the marriage records, we can trace Annabelle's maiden name (we're assuming it's going to be Lincoln but Griff will check) and we can go backwards in her records. We can also check newspaper reports and court cases.'

'Oh, Griff!' he shouted, but Griff had gone.

But there was time to put him, or another of his new henchmen, onto newspaper reports. 'There will be plenty that still exists.

'All that will confirm whether your Annabelle [I smiled; I liked her being so described] really did kill her husband and, if not, the other sources may well reveal what *did* happen to him.'

His phone played the tune *Fat Bottomed Girls*. He rapidly removed it from his pocket.

'Bloody hell, Griff, already?

'She was Annabelle Lincoln!' Derwent said as he turned to me. 'God, she must have hated acquiring her husband's name – enough reason to kill him I should think. Yes? Yes? [this to Griff]. Married in 1840? OK, more for you Griff.'

Derwent asked for the research to be done that he had outlined to me.

'And don't forget the…' Griff had clearly not forgotten.

'And you,' he said as he again turned to me, clearly forgetting that I was not one of his employees to receive orders, 'come in tomorrow. We should have most of the background by then and you can give me more atmosphere – your thoughts, your feelings for the girl. You're obviously in love with her.'

His orders bothered me not one bit. I was so caught up by his enthusiasm.

My return, the following day, found me full of expectation.

'Well,' Derwent said as I entered the office. 'We have the answer.'

'The complete explanation?' I said, astonished.

'Almost complete. Where there is no evidence we can make a pretty shrewd guess.'

I smiled since I imagined most journalists worked upon 'pretty shrewd guesses'. However I was too anxious to hear the news to question that.

'Firstly, I have confirmed that there was no report of a murder in the area in 1841. The 1841 census shows Gervase Stiffwald living at the cottage that bore his name.'

'In 1841?'

'In 1841, yes,' he said hurriedly, apparently annoyed by the interruption.

'But, by 1851, there was only one occupant – Annabelle Lincoln. So she had reverted to her maiden name.'

I was about to comment but, remembering his desire to report in full, held myself back.

'Annabelle Lincoln,' he repeated, 'and, although she's not there in 1861, she might have died…'

He noted the look of disappointment on my face and continued:

'Or of course moved, or re-married, or not been there on census night, or…'

I sat back in my chair as if in agreement that I should not interrupt, or even show *signs* of interrupting his flow again.

'So she could still have murdered her husband except that there was no report of any case in *The Recorder* – or any other newspaper,' he said emphasising the thoroughness of his, or Griff's, research.

'Besides, there was no inquest. Nothing.

'And there was nothing in any other records, nothing to even indicate that such an event had ever happened.'

'But local gossip?' I ventured.

'There could have been some but that's all it would have been. However, that would explain your Annabelle. Ghosts don't hang around unless there's a reason – like a desperation to prove that a wrong needs to be rectified. There could be no major wrong in her life as important as accusations that she killed her husband.'

'But you believe in ghosts?' I queried, amazed.

'Of course; you obviously do.'

'But I've seen one. I've…'

'Well I do because it makes sense, in this case, to do so. Put yourself,' Derwent said, 'in your Annabelle's position. She couldn't have read the book; she was reacting to the situation at the time.'

'Yes, I know that she is a worried girl.'

'Of course you do.'

And, whether Derwent really did believe, he certainly made a convincing case – and it would be good for his paper's circulation.

'But local gossip,' I continued, 'must have fuelled the story which was remembered for eighty years.'

'It doesn't need to be remembered: people pass it on.'

'But why did the book talk of murder; it's only a small passage?'

'To increase sales. There may have been a belief that it had happened and there was no recourse to the Internet to prove it wrong. It didn't happen.'

'But, what about Annabelle's family? They…'

'No family. Annabelle appeared on her birth certificate as the daughter of Mary Lincoln, but the father's column is blank.'

'Illegitimate?'

'Plainly – and that might have put people against her if they knew it. And it may, in turn, have fuelled gossip. The death certificate of her mother shows a date which indicates her death was soon after the birth – and almost certainly a result of it.'

'And Gervase Stiffwald?'

'Ah! The clinching evidence that he was not murdered.'

I waited expectantly.

'He appears again in the next census in a village beyond Christminster – with another partner – and children. I imagine the situation did not suit our philanderer for the next census finds him in Newquay – with another woman. For all we know he was a serial bigamist, if he bothered to marry Annabelle's successors. We don't know and – as far as Annabelle's story is concerned – we can leave him in Newquay.'

'But why did the Stiffwalds publish the book when the evils of their errant ancestor might be exposed?'

'Because it wasn't published by the Stiffwalds; it was published by a company (we'll use that grand name) who seemed not to have existed before and who disappeared afterwards. We have tried to track them down but they seem to have disappeared. The publishing seems to have been the work of the book's unknown author – an early twentieth century forerunner of self-publishing!'

'But the Stiffwalds were powerful people; wouldn't they have objected to its publication?'

'Well, at first we thought that possibly the family did not object because it gave their family history an interesting character.'

I nodded, knowing that genealogists love to find a skeleton in their family cupboard.

'But we dismissed that.'

'So the Stiffwalds would have…?'

'Have you met the previous publisher of *The Recorder?*'

I had to admit that I hadn't.

'No, I thought not. "Respectability" sums him up. He would not have countenanced such a revelation and nor would any of his ancestors judging from our survey of the family.'

'Then I return to my question. The Stiffwalds seem to have had considerable power. Why did they permit publication?'

'Well, it may have been that they were unable to prevent it. But they may, as you say, have had some influence. As you have seen, Annabelle's name is recorded as Annabelle Lincoln, not Annabelle Stiffwald. Again, the girl did revert to her maiden name so it depends where the author got his information.'

'We just don't know then?'

The editor darted a glance at me to show his displeasure at this.

'So, where do we go from here?' Derwent asked.

I felt that he knew exactly where we – or he – went from here and that he was about to tell me. Confirming this, he said:

'Now, we have your "story" and we have your letter. Those are interesting as a starting point but you had not met your lady at the time you wrote them. This story can run and run. It will exonerate her – even create a beautiful myth. The cottage may become a tourist destination.'

I was unsure that I liked the idea of encouraging this – especially as Annabelle was 'my lady'. I emphasised to Derwent that the story would not run and run if I did not have exclusive access to her and she was unable to communicate in a way I felt she was beginning to do to me.

And, on leaving the *New Recorder* offices, I made my way to the ruined cottage, hoping its resident would be, as she usually now was, awaiting me.

My heart raced as I approached the cottage and entered her home, witnessing as I did so, the process of its transformation into a home of the early Victorian age.

I had only to wait seconds before a light appeared before me – a light which, unlike during its earliest appearance, caused me no discomfort but infinite expectation.

The vague form readily transformed itself into The Beloved – a word for Annabelle which I was no longer ashamed to use.

It was as if we commenced a conversation although neither could hear the other. I was convinced that my love was reciprocated. Annabelle loved me. I almost sang it on the way to my home. Without shame I must admit, I *did* sing it.

Although my days at home had been mundane – they had always lacked excitement – now my life did not lack enchantment. And Marina appeared less responsive to what I felt was my normal behaviour. Despite my kindness to her – I could pretend to affection – she did not respond. Her manner had become cold towards me and I never mentioned Annabelle although, I suppose, returning from my walks, my demeanour was evidence enough of my feelings. On the rare occasion that Annabelle did not appear, I was more morose – and that was when friction led to argument. Marina was not one easily stirred, but, for the first time, our marriage had begun to show cracks.

I put aside my concerns and continued to visit *The New Recorder* offices. My story appeared – similar (although without the expressions of my 'feelings' for Annabelle) to the account which I am now putting before the public. It was serialised in the newspaper, along with editorial comment and the promise of future revelations. Just what those revelations would be were unknown to me and – I suspect – to the editor who promised them.

When the series of articles appeared, I realised that they would be seen by Marina. I had disguised my obsession with Annabelle. But I cared little about that now. Instead I collected the three relevant newspapers and set off for Annabelle's cottage. I was unsure whether she would be able to read them, and suspected she would not. But we had in the past shown objects to each other and neither had looked directly at them. I was, however, certain that she – and I – understood their purport.

Such was the case on this day. I *knew* that Annabelle understood what the report was about. The success of our exchange was evidenced by the emotions which stirred in my breast and, I believe, in hers.

I placed the newspapers on a low table.

And I felt a shock – fear gripped me as the papers fell to the floor. The cottage slowly returned to its ruined state. I could not bear to watch it.

I hurried to the door and out into the garden, the wraith of Annabelle having dissolved.

And there she stood, clearer than I had ever seen her.

Upon her face was a look of affection, of love, of kindness. But also I was given the impression of her sadness. I could not understand that look.

But the garden, too, was slowly returning to its wild state, the cultured plants and flowers becoming strangled by the weeds that had engulfed them.

I looked at Annabelle in horror.

She was dissolving into the indefinable shape which always heralded her coming – and her going. And her expression bore the heartbreak that I knew she was suffering, until it, too, became part of the bright light that gradually dimmed.

I cannot deny that, when she was gone and the cottage and garden were as I had first seen them on that walk (which now seemed so long ago) I cried.

I cried.

And I made my way home.

The thought that Marina would be there and would be ready with harsh words enhanced my despondency.

But I did not encounter Marina and I did not try to explain to myself why someone who was always at home, initially to welcome me, and now to greet me with angry words, should have vanished.

I soon discovered the reason for my wife's absence, contained in a note propped against the clock.

I hardly needed to read that note. She had left me. The reason was of course understandable. To me Marina was nothing. My attitude towards her had changed. I could not dispute any of the words she had written. I could not defend my behaviour. I could not explain my obsession with another woman – albeit one who had lived one hundred and eighty years ago. Such behaviour had stirred even such an unemotional spirit as my wife's. Even though the account had not included the truth of my love for Annabelle, my daily walks and my early admission that I had seen her ghost must have said something of the fascination she held for me.

As I should have expected, Marina's note included the practicalities of our separation – and eventual divorce. She claimed that she should be entitled to our cottage although she had temporarily vacated it. And a discussion she had had with her solicitor had resulted in a second sheet which would ensure, I felt, an acrimonious and, to her, beneficial split.

Certainly, at that moment, and subsequently, I hardly cared.

Annabelle had provided an excitement, an elation which Marina could never have approached. My loss of Marina was no longer important. I did not crave the cut and thrust of city life; I could live without Marina's contribution to my financial welfare. All I would live for was Annabelle.

Further revelations about our story did not appear in *The New Recorder*. Because there was no basis for any.

I often walked to the ruined cottage – every day included it in my walk – but it remained as I had seen it for the first time, ruined and forlorn. But it was a hallowed place – even though I never saw Annabelle there again.

Renowned author and major prize winner, Peter Lovesey, said of the author:
'John F Bennett has a rare talent for short-story writing.'

Also by John F Bennett & published by The JoFra Press:

Lights in the Wood (ISBN 978-1-5272-6858-6)

A collection of 28 short stories with subjects ranging from suspense, mystery, crime and the supernatural to humour and nostalgia. A few are a blend of some or all these.

Reactions to this book:
'John F Bennett is such an acute observer that everything rings true. Strongly recommended.'
- *Peter Lovesey*

'John F Bennett deserves our congratulations. He has a remarkable talent for the short story! The idea of a barrow wight's phantom skull appearing in a clothes drawer! Then hauling an archaeologist into his grave! And the twist at the end of "I Knew You Would Come". They are all a really good read, and there's some seriously weird stuff in there. And a very nice twist in "A Long Texas Road". "The Record Shop" fills one with nostalgia for a long gone world.'
- *Loose Cannon Press*

Girl on the Seventh Floor (ISBN 978-1-5272-2033-1)

A set of 33 short stories with subjects ranging from the awakening of a young man's desire to evocative and nostalgic stories with an emotional edge; suspense and the supernatural; crime and mystery with a twist. It's all here.

Peter Lovesey wrote of this book:
'Superbly crafted stories that touch on experiences common to most of us in our imaginations and probably in real life, but served up with surprising twists. I enjoyed them all and can recommend them.'
- *Peter Lovesey*

HORSES TO FOLLOW
2011/12 JUMPS SEASON

THE HOME OF WINNERS SINCE 1948

© **PORTWAY PRESS LIMITED 2011**

COPYRIGHT AND LIABILITY

Copyright in all Timeform Publications is strictly reserved by the Publishers and no material therein may be reproduced stored in a retrieval system or transmitted in any form or by any means electronic mechanical photocopying recording or otherwise without written permission of Portway Press Ltd.

Timeform Horses To Follow is published by Portway Press Ltd, Halifax, West Yorkshire HX1 1XF (Tel: 01422 330330 Fax: 01422 398017; e-mail: timeform@timeform.com). It is supplied to the purchaser for his personal use and on the understanding that its contents are not disclosed. Except where the purchaser is dealing as a consumer (as defined in the Unfair Contract Terms Act 1977 Section 12) all conditions warranties or terms relating to fitness for purpose merchantability or condition of the goods and whether implied by Statute Common Law or otherwise are excluded and no responsibility is accepted by the Publishers for any loss whatsoever caused by any acts errors or omissions whether negligent or otherwise of the Publishers their Servants Agents or otherwise.

ISBN 978 1 901570 83 0   Price £8.95

Printed and bound by
Charlesworth Press,
Wakefield, UK 01924 204830

TIMEFORM
HORSES TO FOLLOW
2011/12 JUMPS SEASON

CONTENTS

FIFTY TO FOLLOW 2011/12	5
HORSES TO FOLLOW FROM IRELAND	49
THE BIG-NAME INTERVIEWS Philip Hobbs & Charlie Longsdon	63
FUTURE STARS Brian Ellison, David O'Meara, Anthony Honeyball, Michael Byrne & Kielan Woods	79
TIMEFORM RADIO TEAM	85
ANTE-POST BETTING	91
THE BIG RACES IN PERSPECTIVE	96
TIMEFORM'S 'TOP HUNDRED'	127
RACECOURSE CHARACTERISTICS	129

Timeform's Fifty To Follow

Timeform's Fifty To Follow, carefully chosen by members of Timeform's editorial staff, are listed below with their respective page numbers. A selection of ten (**marked in bold with a pink ★**) is made for those who prefer a smaller list.

Aikman	5	Paintball	26
Amaury de Lusignan	6	**Penny Max ★**	**27**
Bally Legend	7	Quel Elite	27
Barbatos ★	**8**	Rock of Deauville	28
Bears Affair ★	**8**	Rose of The Moon	29
Bubbly Breeze	9	Royal Guardsman	29
Cedre Bleu	10	Salubrious	30
Champion Court	11	Seren Rouge	31
Chartreux	12	Simonsig	32
Dark Glacier	13	**Sprinter Sacre ★**	**32**
Diocles	14	Storm Brig	34
Fishoutofwater	14	**Strongbows Legend ★**	**34**
Flying Award	15	Sunley Peace	35
For Non Stop	16	**Swincombe Flame ★**	**36**
Freddie Brown	17	Sybarite	37
Global Power	18	Tarn Hows	38
Havingotascoobydo	18	**Tenor Nivernais ★**	**39**
Jetnova	19	Tornado Bob	40
Kilcrea Kim	20	Trustan Times	41
Lovey Dovey	21	Veiled	43
Milo Milan	22	Victor Lynch	44
Molly Round	22	**Victor's Serenade ★**	**45**
Montbazon ★	**23**	Water Garden	45
Moscow Chancer ★	**24**	Whoops A Daisy	46
Next To Nowhere	25	Yurok	47

Timeform's Fifty To Follow 2011/12

The form summary for each horse is shown after its age, colour, sex and pedigree. The summary shows the distance, the state of the going and where the horse finished in each of its races since the start of the 2010/11 season. Performances are in chronological sequence with the date of its last race shown at the end.

The distance of each race is given in furlongs. Steeplechase form figures are prefixed by the letter 'c' and NH Flat race or bumper form figures by the letter 'F', the others relating to form over hurdles.

The going is symbolised as follows: f=firm, m=good to firm, g=good, d=good to soft, dead, s=soft, v=heavy.

Placings are indicated, up to the sixth place, by use of superior figures, an asterisk being used to denote a win; and superior letters are used to convey what happened to a horse during the race: F-fell, pu-pulled up, ur-unseated rider, bd-brought down, su-slipped up, ro-ran out.

The Timeform Rating of a horse is simply the merit of the horse expressed in pounds and is arrived at by careful examination of its running against other horses. The ratings range from 175+ for the champions down to a figure of around 55 for the meanest selling platers. Symbols attached to the ratings: 'p'–likely to improve; 'P'–capable of much better form; '+' –the horse may be better than we have rated it.

Aikman (Ire) h137
7 b.g Rudimentary (USA) – Omas Lady (Ire) (Be My Native (USA))
2010/11 F16g* 16d^F 16g^2 20s* 20s* 21g 24g^6 Apr 8

It wasn't so long ago that Dumfries & Galloway was one of the hotbeds of northern racing, housing as it did the seemingly all-conquering yard of Len Lungo. Lungo eventually succumbed to the harsh economic climate and handed in his licence in 2009, but since then James Ewart, based twenty or so miles away in Langholm, has steadily climbed the training ranks to become top dog in Scotland's South West. What's more, it seems that the public at large are yet to cotton on to Ewart's abilities, as he regularly turns a profit with his bumper performers and chasers, while in 2010/11 he completed the hat-trick with his hurdlers also coming out in the black to level stakes.

One of the main contributors to Ewart's success in 2010/11 was Aikman, who joined the yard after winning all three of his starts in points in 2010. A bumper winner on his debut for Ewart in May, Aikman wasn't seen again until the New Year, when he took three attempts to get off the mark over hurdles. There were extenuating circumstances, however, not least the fact that those first two runs were over two miles at Musselburgh, far from ideal conditions for an ex-pointer. A step up to two and a half miles at the same venue saw Aikman open his account, after which he was sent to take on a select field of promising novices, including Tolworth Hurdle winner Minella Class, at Huntingdon in February. Aikman admittedly enjoyed the run of things that day, gifted a twelve-length lead by his rivals, but there was plenty to like about the way he went about things as he caused a 16/1 shock. He was essentially beaten on merit in the Baring Bingham next time, and was arguably feeling the effects of a busy few months when flopping in another Grade 1 at Aintree on his final start, but that's not to be held against him considering it's unlikely that he'll be seen to best advantage until tackling fences. We think Aikman's been underrated so far, just like his trainer, and we expect him to enjoy a fruitful campaign in staying novice chases this winter. **James Ewart**

Amaury de Lusignan (Ire)   h103p
5 b.g Dushyantor (USA) – Celtic Sails (Ire) (M Double M (USA))
2010/11 19s⁵ 20s⁵ 21d³ Mar 14

The Gary Moore handicapper is fast becoming a staple of Horses To Follow, at least over jumps, and rightly so as Moore has time and again demonstrated his skill in bringing horses along slowly. Last season's offering Via Galilei was, in terms of level-stakes profit, one of the stars of the show with a couple of wins at Newbury, returning at odds of 16/1 and 8/1 respectively. He would also go on to finish second in the Imperial Cup and third in a competitive race at the Grand National meeting. Impressive stuff we're sure you'll agree, and it's fair to say we'd be delighted if Amaury de Lusignan's season in 2011/12 proves half as lucrative.

In terms of his background, Amaury de Lusignan doesn't exactly fit the usual Gary Moore mould. Having joined the yard after finishing runner-up in an Irish maiden point last autumn, he was sent straight into novice hurdles and shaped with promise on each of his three runs, seemingly not fully wound up for his debut in a decent race at Newbury and outpaced on both subsequent starts, nevertheless achieving fair form when fifth at Fakenham on the first of those. On what's been seen to date alone, Amaury de Lusignan should have no trouble defying an initial BHA mark of 107 once he tackles longer trips, and after that it's all about what his trainer can draw from him; history suggests that could amount to plenty. **Gary Moore**

Bally Legend   h129
6 b.g Midnight Legend – Bally Lira (Lir)
2010/11 17d⁴ 16s 19d² 17d³ 22d 16s* 16g 16d⁵ Apr 2

Since taking out a full licence in 2008, Caroline Keevil has been going about her business with a fair degree of success given the limited ammunition at her disposal. A string of just three horses in 2006/7 had increased to twenty-seven in the latest season, with the yard turning a level-stakes profit thanks to the likes of Arctic Flow and Cornish Sett. With her background being in points, it's with staying chasers that Keevil has enjoyed most success with to date, and it's promising to say the least that Bally Legend, who's bred to fit into that category, has shown so much around two miles over hurdles.

After a couple of encouraging bumper runs in 2009/10, Bally Legend made a fairly quiet start to his hurdling career before shaping well behind Nicene Creed at Taunton on his third start, caught only close home having looked set to win before his greenness showed. It was also on his third start in handicaps that Bally Legend showed his true colours, taking a two-mile event at Ludlow stylishly

Bally Legend (yellow) looks one to follow over hurdles or fences

by thirteen lengths from Tom O'Tara. That Bally Legend was able to create such an impression around a track as sharp as Ludlow clearly says plenty about his long-term potential, so for all he was unable to build on that at either Newbury or Chepstow subsequently it shouldn't detract from the fact that more handicaps are bound to come his way over longer trips. In addition, he'll also be worth following if connections opt to send him novice chasing. **Caroline Keevil**

Barbatos (Fr) ★   h122
5 gr.g Martaline – Peace Bay (Fr) (Alamo Bay (USA))
2010/11 18s^3 20d^5 20s^5 22d^5 19m^2 Apr 10

Barbatos had just a single start in the country of his birth, but achieved a feat that only two horses were to equal during the latest National Hunt season when finishing within three lengths of subsequent Mersey Novices' winner Spirit Son in a hurdle race at Auteuil. Just over three months later, Barbatos found himself at Cheltenham having left Christophe Aubert and joined his current trainer, and a yard that also houses the same owner's Invisible Man and Othermix (both of whom, coincidentally, began their careers in France).

Following two promising efforts in novice hurdles, Barbatos fared creditably on what was his only outing in handicap company, strongly supported when fifth to Golden Chieftain at Uttoxeter, where next-time-out winners Basford Bob and Sir Kezbaah finished second and fourth respectively. However, Barbatos was to save his best till last, when a short-head clear second to Invictus in a maiden hurdle at Ascot, a performance that quickly banished the notion that he was going to need a thorough test of stamina to show his best. A tall gelding who, like his two aforementioned ex-French stable-companions, is sure to go chasing sooner rather than later, Barbatos' immediate future may lie in handicaps over the smaller obstacles and it's unlikely that an official rating of 121 sums up his ability. **Ian Williams**

Bear's Affair (Ire) ★   h124p
5 b.g Presenting – Gladtogetit (Green Shoon)
2010/11 F16d* 16d* 17g* Mar 26

Owner and former trainer George Barlow hasn't been so active on the racecourse in recent years, presumably focusing instead on his role as chairman of the North West Hunts Club. Barlow might have thought that he'd reached his zenith in racing when Big Brown Bear outran his unflattering odds in the 1987 Grand National, but Bear's Affair, the first horse to run under Rules in the Barlow colours since 2007/8, could well reach greater heights.

The fact that Bear's Affair was put in training with Nicky Henderson and sent straight into bumpers suggests his owner held him in fairly high regard, and he wasted no time in justifying that faith, getting the better of Champion Court at Uttoxeter despite palpable inexperience. If that wasn't promising enough, Bear's Affair was to create an even bigger impression on his hurdling debut when bossing the likes of Basford Bob and Ashammar over two miles at Southwell, needing just a shake of the reins to assert having jumped with an assurance so often evident in Henderson novice hurdlers. His final start at Bangor wasn't quite so awe-inspiring, but he did maintain his unbeaten record and would have done so even if the fairly useful Our Mick hadn't fallen at the last.

All of the above is encouraging enough, but what's really exciting is the fact that Bear's Affair has a background more in line with one of his owner's pointers than a two-mile hurdler. By Presenting, his family is chock-full of staying chasers, including Free Gift and Little Brown Bear, the latter of which was also owned, as you might have guessed, by George Barlow. The fact he missed the big spring festivals means that Bear's Affair may sneak under the radar somewhat, but expect him to take high order among his trainer's team of novice chasers in 2011/12.
Nicky Henderson

Bubbly Breeze (Ire)   h86 c–p
6 br.g Hubbly Bubbly (USA) – Belon Breeze (Ire) (Strong Gale)
2010/11 22v^5 24v^{ur} 24s^3 c25d^F :: 2011/12 22m^2 22g^4 May 30

As far as small Northern yards go, Pauline Robson's operation just outside of Newcastle takes fairly high order, partly but not wholly thanks to the patronage of Raymond Anderson Green. We've already given endorsements to Robson in this very publication, with Humbie and Locked Inthepocket featuring in last season's 'fifty', both holding their own in terms of level-stakes profit/loss. This year's selection from the Robson yard, Bubbly Breeze, may not be in the ownership of Anderson Green, but his profile is pretty similar to many of the horses supplied to Robson by her principal owner.

As one who has had seven tries in handicaps without success, Bubbly Breeze's appeal isn't immediately obvious, and it's only upon digging deeper into his pedigree and profile that the full picture begins to emerge. A full-brother to Scottish National fourth Idle Talk and Northumberland National winner Belon Gale, Bubbly Breeze's future clearly lies in staying chases if breeding is any guide. That impression has only been bolstered by what he's shown on the track, once again shaping as though anything less than three miles is inadequate when finishing fourth behind two subsequent winners at Cartmel when last seen in May. Still with plenty of untapped potential over fences (jumped at least adequately before falling at the thirteenth on his chasing debut), it'd be a surprise if Bubbly Breeze couldn't make light of a BHA mark in the 80s over fences this winter. **Pauline Robson**

Cedre Bleu (Fr) h128
4 b.g Le Fou (Ire) – Arvoire (Ire) (Exit To Nowhere (USA))
2010/11 18s³ 16s* 17v² Feb 13

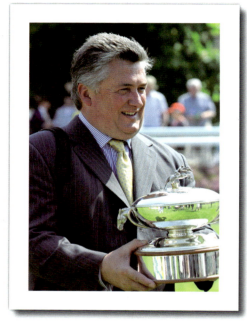

Paul Nicholls

What links Voy Por Ustedes, Well Chief, Flagship Uberalles and Champleve? The answer is that they all won the Arkle in receipt of a weight allowance given to five-year-olds. That quartet all took the two-mile novice championship within a nine-year spell, a run of results which ultimately brought an end to the concession. It's probably no coincidence that only three five-year-olds have even contested the race in the four renewals since the rules were changed, two of those supplied by Paul Nicholls who could well have another in 2011, namely Cedre Bleu.

The chief appeal of Cedre Bleu comes from promise rather than achievement, his imposing build easy to pick out among the juveniles he came up against over hurdles last season. It's not as though his form is in any way substandard, however, as he made a very pleasing British debut in January, handing Titan de Sarti a ten-length beating at Newbury. Cedre Bleu's only other outing in Britain came in a listed novice in very testing ground at Exeter, where he proved no match for subsequent Supreme runner-up Spirit Son. Nicholls' skill in handling chasers is second to none, so you can rest assured that Cedre Bleu will be placed to best effect this season. Should he take to fences as well as his physique implies, then he could be the one to show that five-year-olds don't need a weight allowance to come out on top in the Arkle. **Paul Nicholls**

Champion Court (Ire)   h138p c–p

6 b.g Court Cave (Ire) – Mooneys Hill (Ire) (Supreme Leader)
2010/11 F16g* F16d² 21s* 20d 24g⁴ :: 2011/12 c20d^{ur} Sep 22

Located deep in the heart of the Cotswolds, Condicote Stables is home to a trainer who is really starting to make his mark on the British National Hunt scene. After having just fourteen winners to show for his first seven years with a licence, Martin Keighley has saddled forty-six winners over the last two seasons. A mid-season lull meant that his 2010/11 haul didn't quite match the twenty-seven successes attained in the previous campaign, but Keighley's achievements haven't gone unnoticed and quality as well as quantity is ever-increasing at his yard. It's surely only a matter of time before one of its inmates really provides the breakthrough for this upwardly-mobile stable, and we reckon that Champion Court is the prime candidate to deliver that big-race success in the coming season.

Bought for £130,000 after winning a Kilbeggan bumper in May 2010, Champion Court finished a good second in a similar race at Uttoxeter before making an

Champion Court storms to victory in the Hyde Novices' Hurdle at Cheltenham

impressive debut over hurdles in a Grade 2 novice at Cheltenham's Open Meeting, where he swept to a seven-length victory over Sybarite. Having shaped as though amiss on his only run in between, Champion Court was sent off at 16/1 for the Spa back at Cheltenham in March and redeemed himself in no uncertain terms, shaping better than the result in finishing fourth to Bobs Worth, conceding the initiative to the first three with a mistake two out.

His recent debut over fences mightn't have gone to plan, unseating three out in a novice at Perth when looking the likeliest winner, but everything about Champion Court, including his build, suggests he's a useful staying chaser in the making. Expect to see him back at the Festival come March, either in the RSA or the four-miler, the latter route the one taken by his yard's Any Currency in 2010.
Martin Keighley

Chartreux (Fr) h128+
6 ro.g Colonel Collins (USA) – Ruaha River (Fr) (Villez (USA))
2010/11 24d³ 24g Mar 17

David Pipe

Chartreux is a breed of cat native to France, but you won't find many in Britain as the Governing Council of the Cat Fancy refuses to recognise the breed on account of its close similarity to the more popular British Shorthair. Conversely, fans of National Hunt racing are implored to discriminate between a six-year-old gelding named Chartreux and the numerous other unexposed handicappers in the Pipe yard, as he looks one who could well land a big prize before 2011/12 is out.

Chartreux boasted the sort of profile in his novice season that would have made him a viable candidate for this list in 2010/11, with a win in a bumper and a maiden hurdle quickly followed by a run in a Grade 1 at Cheltenham, such ambitious campaigning worthy of note where Pipe runners are concerned. As it was, he didn't make his return until New Year's Day, when he shaped notably well in a three-mile handicap at Cheltenham, travelling best and just paying for pressing on too soon with stablemate Junior in the end, another Pipe inmate in Ashkazar eventually taking the pair's measure. The effort was enough to ensure that Chartreux was sent off favourite for the

Pertemps Final back at Prestbury Park on what would be his final start, but he was ultimately disappointing behind another stablemate in Buena Vista.

Although raced over three miles on both starts in 2010/11, the feeling is that Chartreux will prove at least as adept over shorter trips, while fences are likely to be on his agenda eventually given both his stature and winning point form. There are clearly plenty of options, and David Pipe is better than most at picking the right ones, so expect to see Chartreux in the winner's circle well before his nine lives are up. **David Pipe**

Dark Glacier (Ire)   F110
6 b.g Flemensfirth (USA) – Glacier Lily (Ire) (Glacial Storm (USA))
2010/11 F16v* F16v^2 F16s* F16g Mar 16

In the most recent edition of this publication's Flat-oriented counterpart, Jamie Lynch wrote a memorable ode to obscure nicknames in a piece on Hurricane Higgins. This feels like a good point to touch on the subject again as many racing fans, especially those under thirty, will be unfamiliar with the precise origins of jockey-turned-trainer Chris Grant's epithet, 'Rambo'. Grant attributes the name to Steve Smith-Eccles, who proposed it following an incident in which he was involved in a heavy fall only to dust himself down and ride the next winner. Although the man himself would probably never say as much, Grant's strength in the saddle presumably also contributed to the name being adopted so widely. Grant is now enjoying his best spell as a trainer, with the likes of Jeu de Roseau, Star Player and Dark Glacier all contributing multiple wins in 2010/11, and we think the last-named is capable of elevating his yard's standing even further over the coming season.

Expensive at three but not seen on a racecourse until he was rising six, Dark Glacier immediately set about making up for lost time when winning a Kelso bumper in November by four lengths from Fourjacks, the pair finishing well clear in testing conditions. He was to finish clear again, with Triptico, at Newcastle two months later, passing the post first but later demoted for causing interference as he hung left. The memory of that was soon erased as Dark Glacier accounted for subsequent winner Bygones Sovereign at Ayr, but his season would end on something of a low note when he finished mid-field away from the mud in Cheltenham's Champion Bumper. That's likely to prove no more than a blip, however, and with longer trips sure to suit Dark Glacier all the more he's well worth following in novice hurdles through the coming winter. **Chris Grant**

Diocles (Ire) F106p
5 b.g Bob Back (USA) – Ardrina (Ardross)
2010/11 aF16d* Dec 6

All told, we at Timeform weren't particularly enamoured with the programme of 'jumpers' bumpers' that took place during the height of the cold snap last winter. Obviously horses need to be kept fit even during inclement weather, but racecourse gallops are always an option, while the argument that it swells betting turnover was diluted somewhat by the general lack of competitiveness of the races. We are, however, willing to concede that they weren't a complete waste of time: totesport Trophy Hurdle winner Recession Proof had been successful in a jumpers' bumper at Southwell on his previous start, while a Donald McCain newcomer named Diocles created a deep impression in a similar event at the same course in December.

As a product of a meeting between Bob Back and Ardrina, whose finest hour came when she was fourth to Istabraq in a Grade 1 novice at Punchestown in 1997 but who eventually ended up a stout stayer, two miles on the all-weather seemed unlikely to bring out the best in Diocles. However, he was prominent in the betting for his debut and suggested that he's a smart performer in the making by sweeping to an easy eight-length win over Bunclody (who would also end the season with McCain, incidentally), travelling strongly and leading over a furlong out; what's more, the time compares favourably with others on the same card. Although not seen after, that doesn't really erode Diocles' potential any and you can expect him to really hit an upward curve once facing longer trips over hurdles this winter. **Donald McCain**

Fishoutofwater (Ire) h126p
7 ch.g Old Vic – Frost Bound (Hawaiian Return (USA))
2010/11 22v^6 16d^5 17v^5 16d^6 16g :: 2011/12 24m* 20m* May 14

Rebecca Curtis will be hoping that 2011/12 can be the season that she translates her fine record in the summer months to success in the season proper. Her strike-rate of more than one in three for the current campaign at the time of writing certainly bodes well, and with the strength of her string increasing all the while, there's every reason to think that her yard will also be a force to reckon with from autumn through to spring.

With that said, it's actually a Curtis horse who has registered on the radar during the summer months that we've earmarked as the one to follow. Fishoutofwater was a useful sort in bumpers, winning at Hereford on his debut before finishing

fourth in a Grade 2 at Aintree behind Megastar, on both occasions leaving the impression that further would suit. He would live up to his name somewhat in novice and maiden hurdles during 2010/11, persevered with over inadequate trips and rarely subjected to a hard time, but it was a different story once switched to handicaps. Having come in for support, Fishoutofwater landed a quick-fire brace at Worcester and Bangor in May, really impressing with how he travelled and on both occasions beating a next-time-out winner into second. It's fair to say that the BHA handicapper has been equally impressed (or wounded) by those wins, raising Fishoutofwater to a mark of 120, 31 lb higher than at Worcester. Nevertheless, his bumper form strongly suggests there's more to come and it would be no surprise at all to see Fishoutofwater in some of the top handicaps before the season is out.
Rebecca Curtis

Flying Award (Ire) h112p
7 b.g Oscar (Ire) – Kates Machine (Ire) (Farhaan)
2010/11 F16s 19d 20d 19v 22d* 22g* Apr 10

Whilst the triumvirate of Nicholls, Pipe and Hobbs are synonymous with racing in the South West of England, the small yard of Susan Gardner in deepest Devon should not be overlooked and further success is predicted with her progressive handicap hurdler Flying Award.

Although a winner of a maiden point in 2010, Flying Award took a while to find his feet under Rules, well held in a bumper and in three novice/maiden hurdles. However, the way Flying Award travelled in the last of those races suggested that, once assessed, he could well find his level in handicaps, and that was certainly the case. An opening BHA mark of 84 proved a gross underestimation of Flying Award when he made his handicap bow at Newton Abbot in March, running out a well-backed winner by six lengths from Boosha, who was in turn clear of the remainder and would win himself next time. The handicapper clearly took a dim view and raised Flying Award 16 lb, but he was well up to the task when next seen in what looked a warm race at Wincanton, beating King Kasyapa by two lengths.

That run goes to show how rapidly Flying Award is improving, so it's not difficult to foresee more improvement once he returns this winter. The handicapper hasn't been so draconian this time, raising Flying Award just 6 lb to a mark which, in truth, now looks pretty lenient. What's more, the chances are the depths of his stamina haven't been reached yet, while his pointing background suggests a switch to chasing will afford him more options down the line. **Susan Gardner**

For Non Stop (Ire) h140
6 b.g Alderbrook – Lost Link (Ire) (Shernazar)
2010/11 20d* 21s² 21d⁴ 21g^F 24g Apr 8

You wouldn't necessarily know it from a record of one win from five starts, but there weren't many better handicapped hurdlers starting out in 2010/11 than Nick Williams' (*pictured right*) For Non Stop. It was his misfortune that two of the three times he ran in handicaps he bumped into horses with even more in hand than him. The individuals in question were Grands Crus, who was about as far ahead of his mark as it is possible to be when the pair met at Cheltenham's Open Meeting, and Carlito Brigante, behind whom For Non Stop would have finished a clear second in the Coral Cup but for a last-flight fall. Things didn't really go For Non Stop's way the two occasions he ran in graded company last season either, so all that he had to show for a year of relentless progress was a win in a handicap hurdle at Chepstow in October, his sole career success to date.

By the very fact you're reading about him now, it's pretty clear we're hoping that For Non Stop can improve that win record in 2011/12, chiefly with an eye on a novice chase campaign, and there are plenty of good reasons to think he'll thrive in that sphere. He has the pedigree (related to loads of good chasers, notably

For Non Stop (red/epaulets) just before his last-flight exit in the Coral Cup

the smart mare Fiddling The Facts), the physique (big, strong), the trainer (pound-for-pound, there aren't many better than Nick Williams) and, most importantly of all, plenty of rock-solid handicap form over hurdles. It's reasonable to assume that For Non Stop is going to be at least as good over fences as he was over timber, in which case he could well be competing with the best novice chasers in 2011/12. **Nick Williams**

Freddie Brown h107
7 b.g Missed Flight – Some Shiela (Remainder Man)
2010/11 F16m* 16g^5 16d^4 18s^3 16g^5 :: 2011/12 18g^3 May 22

Given his stature, Freddie Brown's owners might well have had the former England cricketer F R Brown on their minds when they named him. Brown was an all-rounder who played mostly in the 1930s and '40s and was famed for his build, standing over six feet tall and weighing over fifteen stone in his prime. Freddie Brown the horse is no weed, either. He's very much a chasing type in fact, one who looks sure to do well when tackling fences.

Prominent in the betting on all three starts in bumpers, Freddie Brown got off the mark at Kelso early in 2010/11 and subsequently promised plenty in novice hurdles, his inexperience (often pulled hard) seeming to prevent him from having a bigger say in some pretty competitive heats. Although Freddie Brown seemed to have a better grasp of his job by the time he tackled handicaps, there are still reasons to view his efforts favourably. He was rather pitched in at the deep end on the first occasion at Ayr's Scottish National meeting and emerged a creditable fifth to Remember Now. Back at Kelso the following month, Freddie Brown was to shape even more encouragingly in finishing third to the unexposed pair What A Steel and Cool Baranca. There are races to be won with Freddie Brown over hurdles, but it's his potential as a chaser that makes him of greater interest.
George Charlton

Global Power (Ire) h131
5 b.g Subtle Power (Ire) – Bartelko (Ire) (The Bart (USA))
2010/11 F18s* 22s* 22v^F 20s^2 20d^4 20g^4 Apr 13

Eric's Charm was one of those chasers who really built up an affinity with the racing public, particularly Sandown Park racegoers who would have seen many a gallant front-running display around the Esher track during the gelding's eight-year career. His jumping was by no means always perfect, resulting in more disappointments than not in his last couple of seasons, but his twelfth and final success saw him put all his qualities together for one last time at his favourite track, before sadly being fatally injured at Newbury.

Eric's Charm's trainer Oliver Sherwood won't find replacing his stable stalwart easy. But in Global Power he has a horse with not just handicapping potential over hurdles, but also longer-term chasing aspirations, so the 2011/12 campaign could well prove a fruitful one as Global Power builds on the foundations laid during his first six starts under Rules.

Global Power won a bumper at Plumpton and a maiden hurdle at Folkestone on his first two outings, but it was his fourth to Skint in the EBF Novices' Handicap Hurdle Final at Sandown on his penultimate 2010/11 appearance that really left the impression he was a horse to follow seriously. Held up in a race which suited prominent runners, Global Power did well to get as close as he did, staying on as if sure to appreciate at least three miles before too long, very much leaving the impression his current mark of 130 is exploitable. Even when his handicapping scope evaporates, the fact he's an Irish point winner suggests that Global Power will be able to make a smooth transition to chasing. **Oliver Sherwood**

Havingotascoobydo (Ire) h121
6 b.g Witness Box (USA) – In Blue (Ire) (Executive Perk)
2010/11 F17d*20v^4 24v^3 21d* 22d^2 21d* 20m^5 Apr 23

Such is the wide-ranging appeal of Hanna-Barbera cartoons that there are several instances of horses being named after characters from their productions: Pebbles is a given, while Yogi showed useful form over hurdles in Ireland and Jetson proved to be a fairly useful (but sadly not a winning) novice hurdler in 2010/11 having been selected as part of our Irish Horses To Follow. A couple of horses to bear the name of Scooby-Doo, one of Hanna-Barbera's most famous creations, proved no great shakes, but Havingotascoobydo has shown himself fairly useful already and we fully expect to be hearing a lot more of him this season.

Trained by up-and-coming handler Martin Keighley, Havingotascoobydo arrived with something of a reputation, sent off at odds on in an admittedly weak Newton Abbot bumper which he won by fourteen lengths. He was quickly switched to hurdles, but it wasn't until handicaps that he hit an upward curve, winning twice over twenty-one furlongs at Ludlow despite still showing signs of inexperience. Possibly unsuited by firmish ground when below form on his final start, Havingotascoobydo should resume his progress when he returns in 2011/12 and is capable of winning more races over hurdles. However, as a chasing type in appearance and with a win in a point in Ireland under his belt, it is over fences that we expect Havingotascoobydo to really come into his own. Three miles should suit him well. **Martin Keighley**

Jetnova (Ire) h130
6 b.g Luso – Yamashina (Ire) (Kahyasi)
2010/11 22g^3 24g^6 21s* 21d* 21s^6 22s* 24g^F 24g Apr 8

It's testament to how far Alan King has come in his twelve-year training career that a return of seventy-six winners in the 2009/10 season was seen as a lull in form. The latest season was certainly an improvement in terms of the fortunes of the yard as a whole, while the likes of Mille Chief and Medermit promise to keep King with a hand in the top races. Jetnova isn't certain to reach such dizzy heights, but he's certainly a horse with untapped potential and one who may have escaped the gaze of many despite running at both Cheltenham and Aintree in the spring.

Jetnova was bought for £45,000 in May 2009 having won an Irish maiden point the month before, but it would be another year before he made his hurdling debut, when he shaped as though in need of the experience. It would be a similar story at Towcester another five months on, but Jetnova soon got the hang of things, winning twice at Plumpton before the year was out; on the second such occasion, he beat subsequent EBF Final winner Skint, as well as several other subsequent improvers. An unsuccessful foray into graded company next time was soon put to one side as Jetnova won a handicap at Wincanton in February, shaping as though ready for a return to three miles. He was granted that on his last two starts, albeit pitched into Grade 1 company, and he was seemingly in the process of running a fine race in the Spa on the first of those occasions, still just behind the leaders when coming down two out.

A rangy sort, it's anticipated that fences will be the making of Jetnova, and with him still being unexposed at three miles to boot we can see him building on the useful form he showed over hurdles in 2010/11 and, hopefully, playing a part in the continued resurgence of his yard. **Alan King**

Kilcrea Kim (Ire) h139
6 ch.g Snurge – Kilcrea Deer (Ire) (Brush Aside (USA))
2010/11 20g* 20v* 22s* 24d⁵ 22d* 24g⁵ 24g Apr 8

It's unusual to see a horse in the well-known James and Jean Potter colours that doesn't boast a name featuring a reference to the couple's surname. Potts of Magic was one notable servant for the pairing in the care of Richard Lee, while that one's half-sister Missis Potts landed a chase and reached a useful level over hurdles in her time on the track for Philip Hobbs.

And in a further departure from the norm, this year's Potter-owned member of the 'fifty' isn't even from the family that has served the Potters so well. Both Potts of Magic and Missis Potts were out of Potter's Gale, a useful hurdler in her own right and a daughter of that fine racemare Polly Puttens, whose other offspring have been headed by Gold Cup winner Denman.

Happily, the theme of success for the Potters is one thing that hasn't altered judging by the exploits of their Kilcrea Kim during his novice season over hurdles. His transition to timber on the back of his win in an Irish maiden point was little short of seamless, opening with three consecutive wins, and the remainder of his

Kilcrea Kim (centre) looks a smart prospect for novice chases

campaign wasn't too shabby either; Kilcrea Kim added another handicap success to his name in a good-quality race at Sandown in February, and signed off with respectable efforts in big fields at Cheltenham and Aintree.

All the while, though, Kilcrea Kim was shaping like the sort to do even better as a chaser, and it's in that sphere in which he's expected to excel in 2011/12. Early staying novices should prove a formality, and beyond that he appeals as likely to make his mark in good handicaps later in the campaign, most likely when the mud is flying (raced on good going or softer to date). ***Philip Hobbs***

Lovey Dovey (Ire)   h115p F112
7 b.m Winged Love (Ire) – Dansana (Ire) (Insan (USA))
2010/11 F16d* F16d* 20g^2 20s* :: 2011/12 24s^5 May 11

After spending eighteen months as assistant to Kate Milligan prior to taking over the licence from her in February 2009, Simon West has made a fine start to his training career, and for those punters who spotted the early potential of the Middleham trainer, the period has been very profitable. Indeed, if you excluded his runners in bumpers you would be showing a very healthy level-stakes profit of more than £30 to a £1 stake. Further progress this term looks likely from the yard, and a horse capable of thrusting West's name further into the spotlight is Lovey Dovey.

A daughter of Irish Derby winner Winged Love, whose ability to sire top-class jumps performers has been highlighted in recent years by the likes of Twist Magic, Lovey Dovey made her debut under Rules in a bumper at Sedgefield back in March 2010 when in the care of Irish handler Stuart Crawford. Having landed a point-to-point the previous month, Lovey Dovey attracted market support before running out a clear-cut winner. Lovey Dovey went on to show useful form when winning similar events at Perth and Hexham, after which she was given a seven-month break and switched from Crawford to West, making her debut for the latter in a mares novice hurdle at Musselburgh. A promising second there, Lovely Dovey went one better in a novice at Newcastle next time and then shaped better than the result suggests when fifth in a handicap over three miles at Perth, racing freely and travelling best of all before her early exertions took their toll. Lovey Dovey's performance suggested strongly that she's capable of winning races off her current mark, while chasing will be another viable option for her further down the line. ***Simon West***

Milo Milan (Ire)   h106p
6 b.g Milan – Simply Divine (Ire) (Be My Native (USA))
2010/11 17v^2 17v^3 17s* 20d^4 Apr 2

As would be expected in these times of austerity, fewer owners maintain a large string and those that do tend to focus on the big-name yards. It follows that many trainers have had to adapt or suffer, and one of the success stories has been Herefordshire-based Richard Lee. In recent seasons, Lee has found success mostly with purchases from other yards, with Heathcliff, Cadoudalas and Victory Gunner all ready-to-hand examples. Milo Milan, who had one start for Steve Wynne before switching to Lee, remains a relatively unexposed horse who's sure to win handicaps over the coming season.

Placed in a couple of heavy-ground events at Hereford after the turn of the year, Milo Milan was soon switched from novice company to handicaps and made light of an opening BHA mark of 103 when beating Calico Rose by three and three quarter lengths at Newton Abbot, underlining his potential for longer trips with how he responded having come under pressure a long way out. As a result, it was no surprise to see Milo Man upped in trip next time, though the fact he was returned to novice company was rather more unexpected, his penalty leaving him with a stiff task. As it happened, the steady pace and a mistake two out were more pressing reasons for Milo Milan faring no better than fourth, though in form terms his run was up to scratch. It's highly likely that Milo Milan has a good deal more to offer as his stamina is drawn out and he could well be the latest handicapper to highlight the skill of his trainer. **Richard Lee**

Molly Round (Ire)   h107 c–p
7 b.m Old Vic – Mondeo Rose (Ire) (Roselier (Fr))
2010/11 17v 19d 19v* c16s^{ur} 24d* 22s* 24g^2 21g^6 Mar 26

For many, Grant Cann will just be starting to register on the radar following a bright start to the 2011/12 campaign, but he's been around for some time and can't be said to have gained overnight success. His skills have been advertised in recent seasons by the likes of Molly Round, Dennis The Legend and Arctic Watch, all improved having been bought from other yards. It's the first-named of the three that we see having the greatest potential for the season ahead and she's been earmarked as a handicapper to follow.

Having joined Cann from her owner/breeder Andrew Kavanagh before her belated return, it took until Molly Round's third run before she showed her first form of any kind, winning a Towcester handicap from a BHA mark of 71. Molly

Round was then switched to chasing in a race at the same track in order to avoid a penalty, but it backfired with her unseating at the fourth after three bold jumps at the preceding fences. She was then returned to hurdles and completed a hat-trick in that sphere, over three miles at Taunton (did well to hold on having been more forcefully ridden than the placed horses) and Wincanton, with subsequent winner Whispering Jack a length and a half behind at the second-named course. On both subsequent starts, Molly Round shaped as though her recent exertions were catching up with her, but neither effort could be termed a disaster; she finished runner-up at Taunton on the first occasion and sixth in a much warmer contest at Newbury on her final start. The chances are that Molly Round can pick up the thread again afforded a break, while in time there are likely to be options back over fences for this good-topped mare. **Grant Cann**

Montbazon (Fr) ★  F122
4 b.g Alberto Giacometti (Ire) – Duchesse Pierji (Fr) (Cadoudal (Fr))
2010/11 F16d² F16g* F17g² Apr 9

With Champion Bumper winner Cheltenian reportedly out for the season, no bumper graduates are being talked about in the same terms as Cue Card was twelve months ago. Granted, Cue Card was an exceptional bumper performer,

Montbazon (spots) impresses in landing a valuable bumper at Doncaster

one of the best in Timeform's experience, but the last two champion novice hurdlers have both been among the top bumper horses from the previous season and, from the class of 2010/11, we think Montbazon could be the one to go to the top of the novice tree this winter.

The fact is that, under most circumstances, Montbazon would be unbeaten in three starts. On his debut, he came within a length of Cheltenian at Kempton, despite that one hanging left across him two furlongs out, arguably costing him the race. Sent off favourite for a valuable sales race at Doncaster on the back of that, Montbazon made no mistake in accounting for Close House by three and a half lengths, impressing with how he travelled before sprinting clear once he eventually got the hang of things under pressure. Montbazon sidestepped Cheltenham for a tilt at the Grade 2 prize at Aintree's Grand National meeting, but he came up short against Steps To Freedom, two lengths back in second and clear of the rest. Steps To Freedom has shown smart form on the Flat since, underlining what Montbazon achieved in getting so close to him. He may have skipped Cheltenham last season, but we see Montbazon lining up at the Festival in March, with the stamina on the dam's side of his pedigree suggesting that the Baring Bingham could be equally as viable a target as the Supreme. **Alan King**

Moscow Chancer (Ire) ★ h92p
5 b.g Moscow Society (USA) – I'll See You Again (Ire) (Presenting)
2010/11 19g^5 19g 16d^4 Mar 11

Tom George

When Galileo (the other one) took what is now the Baring Bingham in 2002, not many would have predicted that his up-and-coming trainer Tom George would have to wait another nine years for his second Grade 1 success. That wait was ended in April when Nacarat landed the Bowl at Aintree by six lengths from Carole's Legacy under a fine ride from Paddy Brennan. Now a freelance jockey after his split from Nigel Twiston-Davies, Brennan will presumably be riding regularly for George, and we reckon Moscow Chancer will provide him with a few victories over the coming season.

The path of Moscow Chancer's career to date is a well-worn one. Brought over from Ireland after finishing fifth in a maiden point there, he shaped with abundant promise over nineteen furlongs at Doncaster on his hurdling debut, travelling well until greenness and a couple of mistakes told. Moscow Chancer wouldn't quite match that form on either start after, again travelling well before being badly hampered at Market Rasen then faced with an inadequate trip at Sandown. Clearly, none of those runs get anywhere near to the bottom of Moscow Chancer's ability and, for all he's unlikely to deliver Tom George his third Grade 1 victory anytime soon, it would be a surprise if he couldn't overcome an initial BHA mark of 103. **Tom George**

Next To Nowhere (Ire) h87p
6 ch.g Exit To Nowhere (USA) – Zarote (Ire) (Mandalus)
2010/11 16s³ 16s⁴ Mar 8

With only eighteen winners in each of the last two seasons, it's fair to say that the Nicky Richards stable has been in something of a lull. The signs have been promising so far in 2011/12, however, with eight victories already on the board at a strike-rate comparable with what the yard was returning in its pomp. Things will obviously get tougher once the season gets into full swing, but with the likes of Next To Nowhere still to reappear the omens are that the winner count at Greystoke should keep ticking over.

Not to say that he's slow, but it's clear that Next To Nowhere is very much in need of a greater test of stamina than he's been afforded so far. Off almost a year after shaping quite well in a bumper at Carlisle in March 2010, it was at Ayr that Next To Nowhere made his hurdling debut. That outing was primarily about experience, Next To Nowhere not given a hard time as the first two, which included stablemate Flinty Bay, shot clear. His next and final run at Newcastle was also merely a hint at what's to come, though this time it was a lack of speed that was apparent above all in a slowly-run race. There's no disgrace in that considering Next To Nowhere's pedigree (both his dam and winning half-brother stayed well), and on the evidence so far his current BHA rating of 104 should prove to be well within his reach when going handicapping over longer trips. With that route seemingly the plan all along, expect Next To Nowhere to start contributing to his trainer's tally this season. **Nicky Richards**

Paintball (Ire) h128+
4 b.g Le Vie dei Colori – Camassina (Ire) (Taufan (USA))
2010/11 16d² 16s⁶ 16s* 16g 17g* Apr 13

Those of you who've skipped to our trainer interviews (or indeed, those who simply read the contents page) will know we're already singing Charlie Longsdon's praises elsewhere in this publication, so in order to prevent duplicating the message that Longsdon is a trainer destined for big things, it suffices to say he has a few horses of particular interest this season.

Among those we've singled out is the four-year-old Paintball. A fairly useful handicapper on the Flat for William Muir, Paintball joined the Longsdon yard for 70,000 guineas at the Autumn Sales. He went on to make his hurdling debut in a juvenile at Huntingdon, in which he finished second to Tony Star, a mistake two out seemingly crucial. Jumping was again a thorn in Paintball's side on his next outing at Warwick, but he allayed fears over his hurdling at Ludlow in February when accounting for King's Realm by twelve lengths. Presumably mindful of his previous Flat experience, connections decided to pitch Paintball straight into the Fred Winter where he finished ninth, hindered by a mistake four out and being

Paintball (white face) gets the better of Salontyre at Cheltenham in April

squeezed for room turning in. Returned to Cheltenham a month later, Paintball cemented his promise when taking a less-competitive heat from the same mark, not enjoying the clearest of runs but comfortably on top on the run-in. Paintball's new mark of 130 doesn't look insurmountable and he looks the type to do well in decent handicaps; potential early-season targets would be the four-year-old handicap held at Chepstow in October or the Gerry Feilden at Newbury in November, the latter of which was won last year by one of the stars of our 'fifty', Tocca Ferro. **Charlie Longsdon**

Penny Max (Ire) ★   h118+
5 b.g Flemensfirth (USA) – Ballymartin Trix (Ire) (Buckskin (Fr))
2010/11 F17s* 19s^3 21d^4 Feb 12

Regular readers should know the drill by now: here we have a strapping, lightly-raced hurdler trained by Emma Lavelle who has created a positive impression over timber following a single bumper run. Kangaroo Court and Court In Motion are horses with a very similar profile who've made it into our 'fifty' in recent seasons, and Penny Max is the latest off the production line at Lavelle's Hampshire base to pique our interest.

Runner-up in an Irish maiden on his only start in points, Penny Max was clearly showing the right signs at home to be sent off at 4/1-on for a Folkestone bumper and he duly made short work of his seven rivals in spite of greenness. The impression left on Penny Max's hurdling debut was even more positive for all he met with defeat, clearly still lacking in experience as he raced freely before keeping on in vain pursuit of a couple of useful sorts in the form of Pride In Battle and Radetsky March. His final run of the season, in a race at Warwick won by Radetsky March, was no more than a minor hiccup on what's likely to be a steep rise up the ranks for Penny Max, the manner in which he travelled a stark reminder of his promise even if he did tire in the end having got to the front easily three out. As a son of Flemensfirth out of a Buckskin mare, there are no prizes for guessing that Penny Max's long-term future is likely to lie over longer trips, but in the meantime there are surely races to be won with him, either in novices or from a seemingly-lenient initial opening handicap mark of 118. **Emma Lavelle**

Quel Elite (Fr)   h113p
7 b.g Subotica (Fr) – Jeenly (Fr) (Kadalko (Fr))
2010/11 16v^6 19d^5 18s^2 :: 2011/12 20s^3 May 11

Jimmy Moffatt endured a season to forget in 2010/11, when he saddled just two winners and, more worryingly, had a major health scare due to a serious blood infection which laid him low for much of the winter. Happily, both Moffatt and his horses have been in rude health so far in 2011/12, and we think Quel Elite will be adding to the stable's tally yet further over the coming months, Indeed, Quel Elite will be one of the few horses selected here that probably doesn't need to improve to win a race and, with natural progression plus a step up to three miles sure to bring out the best in him, the chances are he'll be picking up more than one prize.

Making his debut in a novice hurdle at Kelso, Quel Elite shaped with promise, deserving more credit than his finishing position (sixth) suggests as he came from a long way back in a race in which few got involved. He was to catch the eye in all three of his subsequent starts, too. Upped to two and a half miles for the last of those, Quel Elite still looked in need of a stiffer test in finishing third to Fiddlers Reel in a maiden at Perth but showed form bordering on fairly useful even so. There is no doubt that Quel Elite already is up to winning a maiden or novice event, and well capable of exploiting a current rating of 110 in handicaps; and the icing on the cake is that he is the type who should go on improving for a little while yet. **James Moffatt**

Rock of Deauville (Ire) h123+
4 b.g Rock of Gibraltar (Ire) – Ruff Shod (USA) (Storm Boot (USA))
2010/11 17s^3 17d^3 16s^5 16g^6 16m^F Apr 10

Both trainer Paul Nicholls (American Trilogy, Desert Quest and Sporazene) and owner Terry Warner (Rooster Booster) have recent history in winning the County Hurdle, and the pair are involved with a horse we see as likely to feature in some of the biggest two-mile handicaps over the coming winter in Rock of Deauville.

Recruited from the Flat in France, where he won two of his three starts up to thirteen furlongs for Stephane Wattel, Rock of Deauville made his hurdling debut at Hereford in November, where he shaped as though he'd be better for the run. Another promising effort, albeit with another less-than-convincing finish, followed at Taunton before it was decided to switch Rock of Deauville to handicaps. Sent off favourite at Ludlow, it was a similar story in terms of finding little off the bridle, to the point that concerns had to be raised. The fact that Rock of Deauville was tongue tied when next seen in the Fred Winter furthered the idea that he was amiss at Ludlow, and his performance at Cheltenham went some way to confirming previous promise, finishing sixth behind What A Charm despite scrappy jumping. He looked set to build on that promise in no uncertain terms on his final start at Ascot, but it was again jumping that let him down, still on the bridle and in a narrow lead when falling two out. If the tongue tie has the desired effect and the bugs can be ironed out in his jumping, there's no question

that Rock of Deauville can climb the handicap ranks from a starting mark of 116.
Paul Nicholls

Rose of The Moon (Ire)   h125
6 gr.g Moonax (Ire) – Little Rose (Ire) (Roselier (Fr))
2010/11 F16v* F16s⁴ 20d² 20d 24v⁵ 20g Mar 18

Milton Harris' record over jumps in his last few seasons with a licence couldn't be deemed a bad one, but it's worth noting that even though he's been out of racing only 4 months some have already been able to draw improvement from his former charges. Gulf Punch bounced back to form on her very first start for Donald McCain to win at Cartmel in August, while both Snake Charmer and Tri Nations have seen their fortunes improve of late for Martin Keighley. It's interesting, then, that Rose of The Moon, who was unexposed for Harris anyway, has joined David Pipe, and he's surely one to side with in the coming months.

A bumper winner on his debut for Harris, Rose of The Moon was persistently highly tried in subsequent runs, firstly in a listed bumper at Cheltenham's Open meeting. He would return to Prestbury Park for his next two starts, finishing second to Bobs Worth in a novice on New Year's Day despite a less-than-fluent round of jumping before again being let down by his hurdling in a Grade 2 won by the same horse on Festival Trials Day. Rose of The Moon failed to go with much fluency on either of his last two outings, in another Grade 2 novice at Haydock (heavy ground) and back at Cheltenham in the Martin Pipe at the Festival. It'd be spurious to say those runs aren't a concern, but even so David Pipe is a dab hand at getting the best out of horses who aren't always the most enthusiastic and everything points to Rose of The Moon proving better than his current BHA mark of 125 suggests. ***David Pipe***

Royal Guardsman (Ire)   F111p
4 b.g King's Theatre (Ire) – Lisa du Chenet (Fr) (Garde Royale)
2010/11 F18g* Apr 19

As a Colin Tizzard-trained son of King's Theatre making his debut in a Fontwell bumper, it's fair to say that followers of trends would have been all over Royal Guardsman on his successful first visit to a racecourse back in April, with Cue Card very much on their minds. At Timeform, we don't really pay much heed to trends and prefer to take each case on its merits, and in the instance of Royal Guardsman the impression left could barely have been more positive.

Much like on Cue Card's debut, the market didn't exactly predict what was to come at Fontwell, with Royal Guardsman eventually going off at 15/2. Everything

Colin Tizzard

in the race itself was overwhelmingly positive, however, as he cruised through the field to take over on the bridle turning in before streaking clear for minimal pressure from the saddle. Runner-up Grabtheglory would go on to win a weak race next time, but in relative terms that's no real boost to the stellar impression left by Royal Guardsman himself and he looks an exciting prospect for novice hurdles this season. What's more, the balance of his breeding points to longer trips suiting in time, even if his sister Chocolat showed her best form around two miles. Cue Card may have fluffed his lines somewhat last spring, but expect Royal Guardsman to give the Tizzard stable another crack at good novice hurdling prizes this time around. **Colin Tizzard**

Salubrious (Ire) F110
4 b.g Beneficial – Who Tells Jan (Royal Fountain)
2011/12 F16g* Sep 3

Including a horse whose name means 'health-giving' in our list of horses to follow is almost certainly tempting fate, but it was hard not to be impressed by Salubrious' successful debut at Stratford in September. Early indications are that he will more than likely pay his way this season in novice hurdles and, what's more, he's trained by Pam Sly who, despite a classic win on her CV, isn't one of the more fashionable names in the training ranks.

Upon looking at Salubrious' stout pedigree (by Beneficial out of a sister to fairly useful staying chaser Norman Conqueror) you would think that a two-mile bumper around a sharp track like Stratford wouldn't play to his strengths. However, not only did Salubrious win, he created a most favourable impression in beating a heavily-backed debutant from the Rebecca Curtis yard in The Romford Pele by twenty-one lengths, showing plenty of speed and drawing right away in the straight.

It's fair to say that, at this stage, Salubrious provides something of a blank canvas. The option of supplementing his debut success under a penalty in bumpers is entirely plausible, but the bottom line is that he's more than likely to prove a stayer in the long run, with fences sure to appear on the radar at some point if his pedigree's any guide. For our purposes, we hope Salubrious is switched to hurdles and upped in trip as soon as possible, and we advise you not to underestimate him, as some are bound to. **Pam Sly**

Seren Rouge h125
6 b.g Old Vic – Bayrouge (Ire) (Gorytus (USA))
2010/11 20s³ 20v⁴ 24d³ :: 2011/12 20g² May 17

Keith Reveley

The trainers' championship standings won't tell you this, but the Reveley stable is back on the up. The reason for the deceptive numbers is pretty simple: as yet, nothing has emerged to fill the gaps left by the injury to Tazbar and the departure of Ungaro and Rambling Minster (now retired). However, the strike-rate over the last couple of seasons has never been higher since Keith took over from his mother Mary in 2004 and the amount of promising horses housed at Groundhill is as healthy as ever. Enter Seren Rouge, who made a highly-encouraging start over hurdles in 2010/11 and almost certainly hasn't peaked yet.

A fairly useful bumper winner in 2009/10, Seren Rouge made his hurdling debut at Carlisle last October, finishing third in a very strong novice won by Yurok (who will crop up elsewhere in this publication). Seren Rouge would again shape as though just short of a run when finishing fourth in testing ground at Newcastle three months later. Despite more than likely possessing the ability to win a novice, it was decided to switch Seren Rouge to handicaps straight away, and on both starts in that sphere he shaped like one well ahead of his mark. On the first occasion at Doncaster, he pulled well clear with Al Co and Ackertac despite coming from much further back than that pair, and three months later he again finished well ahead of anything else when runner-up to the highly progressive Red Not Blue at Southwell. Raised just 2 lb to a BHA mark of 117 for that second performance, there's no doubt that Seren Rouge is up to winning handicaps in 2011/12. Chasing may also be an option down the line, but it's worth noting that most of his immediate family have made better hurdlers.
Keith Reveley

Simonsig   F121p
5 gr.g Fair Mix (Ire) – Dusty Too (Terimon)
2010/11 NR :: 2011/12 F18g* Apr 25

The Champion Point-to-Point bumper over two and a quarter miles at Fairyhouse's Easter Festival is never an easy race to pin down in terms of form and the 2010/11 renewal looked no different, with only one horse in the field having run under Rules previously. It does tend to throw up some talented sorts though, with Horses To Follow emerging from the race in three of the last four seasons, Simonsig being the latest to catch our eye.

Simonsig won both completed starts in points, the second by a wide margin, and took the Fairyhouse race in the manner suggested by his position at the head of the market, cruising into contention from the rear before settling the issue in a matter of strides, beating Kandinski by thirteen lengths. It looks worth taking a positive view about such an effort, acknowledging that there is an element of guesswork involved, and a rating of 121 puts him right in the upper echelons of last season's Irish bumper horses.

Simonsig possesses plenty of physical scope and looks just the type to do well in novice hurdles at two and a half miles and beyond next season, certainly bred that way. He'd be one to keep on the right side wherever he was trained, though it's significant that since Fairyhouse he's been moved to the Nicky Henderson yard from Ian Ferguson (the same owner's Zemsky, winner of the Foxhunter at Cheltenham, made the opposite move last summer), and if any British handler can get the most out of him over hurdles it's the man based at Seven Barrows. **Nicky Henderson**

Sprinter Sacre (Fr) ★   h150p
5 b.g Network (Ger) – Fatima III (Fr) (Bayolidaan (Fr))
2010/11 19g^2 16d* 16s* 16g^3 Mar 15

As a rule, we use the overall level-stakes profit as a gauge to the success of Horses To Follow, but it's always nice to land winners of big races. There were three Grade 1 winners buried in last year's 'fifty', namely Oscar Whisky (Aintree Hurdle), Finian's Rainbow (Maghull Novices' Chase) and, probably most significantly, Captain Chris in the Arkle. We're nominating Sprinter Sacre as our best chance of following up the last-named of those successes.

Admittedly, it's not as though Nicky Henderson's gelding has snuck in under the radar. Unbeaten in a couple of bumpers in 2009/10, he started his hurdling career in a good race at Ascot where he finished second to the much more experienced

Sprinter Sacre (red) very much appeals as the type to take to chasing

Frascati Park. A couple of wins were to follow in lesser company at Ffos Las and then back at Ascot, with Sprinter Sacre having plenty in hand on both occasions. Experience gained, Sprinter Sacre was thrown into the Supreme Novices' on his final start, where he really impressed with how he travelled, last off the bridle by some way and likely to have finished even closer to the winner Al Ferof but for flattening the last, eventually coming home in third.

What's really exciting about Sprinter Sacre is that it's sure to be over fences that he comes into his own, having the size to make into a top performer over the larger obstacles. Winning the Arkle may be a big ask if Peddlers Cross takes to fences as well as anticipated, but even if that does transpire, Sprinter Sacre could always win the Maghull like his stable-companion Finian's Rainbow (who was runner-up to Captain Chris in the Arkle). **Nicky Henderson**

Storm Brig   h128
6 b.g Heron Island (Ire) – The Storm Bell (Ire) (Glacial Storm (USA))
2010/11 16s* 16v* 18d 20g⁵ Apr 9

Storm Brig was a major contributor to what was a good season in 2010/11 for Alistair Whillans, the Borders trainer in better form in recent seasons than he's ever been. Whillans was represented in this publication last year by Storm Kirk, a brother to Storm Brig, who sadly died before he even made the track last season. Let's hope nothing prevents Storm Brig from returning to action in 2011/12, for he looks sure to win his share of races, be it over hurdles or fences.

Successful on two of his three starts in bumpers, Storm Brig made a winning debut over hurdles at Newcastle in November and followed up at the same track three months later. The form of those races more than stacks up, with several subsequent winners emerging and the runner-up on each occasion (Flinty Bay and Bunclody respectively) almost working their way into our 'fifty'. Unsurprisingly, these impressive successes meant that Storm Brig went off well fancied for a Grade 2 novice at Kelso in March, but he was disappointing to say the least, surely under the weather so poorly did he run. He was then sent to Aintree to tackle another Grade 2, where he had plenty on his plate up against the likes of Spirit Son and Cue Card but ran respectably in finishing fifth, seeing out the two-and-a-half-mile trip well and, if anything, suggesting that further may suit in time.

Regarding the season ahead, Storm Brig has plenty of untapped potential and boasts the size to suggest he'll take to fences should connections decide on that route. There is a possibility, however, that he could contest a handicap hurdle before going chasing; his mark of 132 would not be beyond him on last season's evidence, and if his hurdling has sharpened up over the summer then there's every reason to think Storm Brig can start paying his way immediately. ***Alistair Whillans***

Strongbows Legend ★   h100p c108
6 b.g Midnight Legend – Miss Crabapple (Sunyboy)
2010/11 16d² c18d c21s² c24m³ c26sᶠ c24d² Mar 24

In physical terms, Strongbows Legend doesn't fit the profile of one we expect to do well over fences, being a sparely-made gelding. Yet he has shown enough in five starts over fences to date to make us think that he's a young handicap chaser to follow in the coming months.

It was notable just how well he took to fences on his chasing debut at Newbury back in December, especially considering the rough passage he came in for. He was to encounter a similarly rough time of it at Hereford the following month, but to his credit he still managed to finish a close second to Brenin Cwmtudu. A combination of bad luck and novicey jumping was to continue to prevent Strongbows Legend from getting off the mark over fences, most notably at Plumpton in late-February, in front and travelling best when he came to grief four out. That experience had the potential to dishearten him, but he showed no ill effects when finishing second to Oscar Prairie at Chepstow on his final start, with next-time winner Troy Tempest back in third. Provided he sharpens up his jumping, Strongbows Legend will surely be up to winning handicaps this winter for his up-and-coming trainer. **Charlie Longsdon**

Sunley Peace h127
7 ch.g Lomitas – Messila Rose (Darshaan)
2010/11 19s^{pu} 16d^2 16m* 16d^5 19m* Apr 23

Unlike stablemate Amaury de Lusignan, Sunley Peace has a background much more in line with what one would expect of a Gary Moore handicapper. Useful on the Flat at three for David Elsworth, for whom he finished fifth in the Queen's Vase and fourth in the Melrose, Sunley Peace spent more than three years on the sidelines before reappearing for Moore in a novice hurdle at Newbury in January.

Sunley Peace (green) sees off the strong-travelling Monetary Fund at Sandown

It was initially feared that Sunley Peace retained little or none of his old ability such was the paucity of promise in that run, but he would show at lot more on his next outing, finishing an admittedly well-beaten second to the useful Gibb River at Wincanton, though he wasn't given a hard time in doing so. With no such opposition in the field on his return to Somerset, Sunley Peace got off the mark at the third time of asking, sweeping to a six-length success over Mawsem. It was back to Newbury for Sunley Peace's handicap debut, but he flopped in more testing conditions than when successful, his jumping not helping his cause as he weakened from two out. Progress resumed back on firmer ground at Sandown in April, when Sunley Peace took a nineteen-furlong handicap by three lengths from Occasionally Yours, seeing things out well despite mistakes at the last two flights. With his useful form over staying trips on the Flat and the fact that his jumping still needs sharpening up, there's every reason to think that Gary Moore can continue to draw improvement from Sunley Peace and build on his own fine record in handicap hurdles. **Gary Moore**

Swincombe Flame ★ F116
5 b.m Exit To Nowhere (USA) – Lady Felix (Batshoof)
2010/11 F16v* F16d* Mar 12

Rangy in appearance; good form in bumpers despite a stout pedigree; trained by the excellent Nick Williams: it's fair to say that Swincombe Flame ticks just about all the boxes as far as Horses To Follow is concerned. Not only is she an obvious one for our list, but she also goes down as arguably the best novice hurdle prospect of the season, at least among the mares.

The above paragraph pretty much sums up our thinking on Swincombe Flame, but it is worth pointing out just how obvious her long-term potential was on her two runs in bumpers last season. Starting out in heavy ground at Warwick in February, she defied unflattering odds in style, palpably green when first pressured but going on very strongly once the penny dropped to win an above-average mares race by eleven lengths from Florafern. That run was good enough to justify connections sending Swincombe Flame into a listed similar event at Sandown just fifteen days later, and it proved to be a shrewd decision as she managed to account for Tante Sissi by just over two lengths. Although clearly much more professional that day, it was still plain to see that Swincombe Flame is going to be best suited by a lot further than two miles in time. That much is backed up by her pedigree; her dam Lady Felix recorded all four of her wins around three miles, while her full sister Lady Everywhere—also in training with Williams—is a promising novice hurdler who also shapes like a stayer in the making. It's to be hoped that Swincombe Flame can start winning novices straight away, even if

Swincombe Flame (red cap) looks one of the most exciting novice hurdling prospects for 2011/12

pitched in against the boys, and show that her selection was much more than just a box-ticking exercise. **Nick Williams**

Sybarite (Fr) h133
5 b.g Dark Moondancer – Haida III (Fr) (Video Rock (Fr))
2010/11 F16g* F16m³ 21s² 21d² 24g Mar 18

A tall individual with a good jumping pedigree and from a top yard, Sybarite has plenty going for him and remains a very smart prospect even if his wins-to-runs ratio arguably hasn't matched his connections' expectations so far. Sybarite made steady progress throughout 2010/11, but failed to add to his wide-margin debut win in a bumper at Uttoxeter in September so starts the new campaign still a novice over hurdles. He has shown above-average form in that sphere already, finishing runner-up to Champion Court and Chablais in hot novices at Cheltenham and Kempton respectively, and will have no trouble winning races if kept to the smaller obstacles. Admittedly, Sybarite failed to live up to expectations when well held in the Spa Hurdle at the Cheltenham Festival on his final start, but the Nigel

Twiston-Davies yard wasn't firing on all cylinders at that stage of the season, whilst the fact he was pitched into that company illustrates how highly this gelding is regarded.

Whilst Sybarite obviously still has some potential as a novice hurdler, it is more likely that he will make his mark in the staying novice chase division this season given his impressive physique. He's certainly bred for the chasing game too, his dam being a half-sister to the very smart staying chaser Eudipe, who was placed in a whole host of valuable handicaps during his short career. Twiston-Davies has enjoyed plenty of success in pitching his leading novice chasers into valuable handicap company down the years, so it wouldn't be a surprise to see Sybarite popping up in such races should he take to chasing as well as we expect. ***Nigel Twiston-Davies***

Tarn Hows (Ire)   h101p
5 ch.g Old Vic – Orchardstown Lady (Le Moss)
2010/11 F17s^2 F17s* :: 2011/12 17m^6 16g^2 Jun 2

There haven't been many hurdlers in the last couple of seasons more progressive or indeed prolific than the Jennie Candlish-trained Cross Kennon, who finished fourth in the World Hurdle just two years after winning his first handicap off an official mark of 72, his six wins in the intervening period including one in the Grade 2 Rendlesham Hurdle at Haydock. Sadly, for us at least, Cross Kennon has never been a Horse To Follow, but hopefully we can make amends for that by including his stablemate Tarn Hows this time around.

At this early stage of his career, Tarn Hows has plenty in common with his illustrious stablemate. First of all he is a stoutly-bred sort whose pedigree very much points to his being well suited by distances of two and a half miles and more; secondly, he has good winning bumper form; and, thirdly, his outings in novice hurdles have only scratched the surface of his ability. In fairness, Tarn Hows has already achieved more in a couple of two-mile novices than Cross Kennon did on his three qualifying runs. Indeed, he might even have got off the mark but for an awful blunder at Uttoxeter on his second outing, but essentially it remains the case that we won't see the best of Tarn Hows until he gets to tackle longer trips in handicaps. When that happens, we're hoping for a Cross Kennonesque rate of progress. ***Jennie Candlish***

Tenor Nivernais (Fr) ★   h129
4 b.g Shaanmer (Ire) –Hosanna II (Fr) (Marasali)
2010/11 17g* 17d* 16d³ 17d³ 16g Mar 16

There are few more agonising things in racing than a plan that nearly comes together. In March, several members of Timeform's editorial team were discussing the upcoming Cheltenham Festival in a local tavern (outside of working hours, of course!) when a couple of those present brought up a potentially well-handicapped Venetia Williams juvenile who was, at that stage, 25/1 for the Fred Winter. Enthusiasm built—in due course even the odd giddy tweet leaked from the room—and the next morning Tenor Nivernais was advised as an ante-post bet by the Timeform Jury.

We must have been on to something, as eight days later Tenor Nivernais was sent off 11/2 second-favourite for the Fred Winter and, most frustratingly, he finished an eye-catching seventh behind What A Charm, hampered around halfway before making up plenty of ground from two out.

Venetia Williams' Tenor Nivernais

Our reasons for getting behind Tenor Nivernais at Cheltenham remain relevant, to the extent that we think he's a handicapper worth following this season. Prior to the Fred Winter, which was his final start in 2010/11, he had won both outings in France (for Guillaume Macaire) before finishing third in handicaps at both Wincanton and Taunton. At Wincanton he was plain unlucky (hampered), but Taunton was a different story; the pair who finished in front of him were the ill-fated Karky Schultz and Via Galilei, who would win at Newbury next time before finishing second in the Imperial Cup. As for Tenor Nivernais, he's bound to be suited by longer trips and is booked to win handicaps from his BHA mark of 124. You can rest assured that when he does we'll be on. **Venetia Williams**

Tornado Bob (Ire) h144
6 b.g Bob Back (USA) – Double Glazed (Ire) (Glacial Storm (USA))
2010/11 F16m* 16d² 20v* 20s* 19s² 21g^{pu} Mar 16

If you plot a graph of Donald McCain's winners for the last four or five seasons you get something that looks a bit like the north face of the Eiger. It's remarkable to think that a yard now firmly entrenched as one of the best in the country had just eight winners in 2003/04 (when his late father Ginger still held the licence). Since

Tornado Bob (left) concedes the initiative to Sonofvic with a mistake at the last

then it has been a tale of inexorable progress, and 2010/11 was the first time that McCain cracked the 100-winner barrier. Only Paul Nicholls and Nicky Henderson trained more winners or won more prize money, and if anyone is going to break their dominance, then McCain is the obvious candidate. The key to upsetting that duopoly is the backing of big-spending owners and the ammunition to match, and that's exactly what McCain is starting to get, the Diana Whateley-owned Tornado Bob being a shining example.

Tornado Bob announced himself as a horse of some potential when winning a bumper at Cork in May 2010 for Eoin Doyle, after which he changed hands privately. The next time we saw him was in novice hurdle at the Hennessy meeting when he impressed our on-course reporter with his strong physique and did nothing to dispel that positive impression in the race, doing well to finish fifteen lengths second to Kid Cassidy given that he clearly found the two-mile trip on the sharp side. Upped in distance straight away, Tornado Bob had little trouble landing a maiden at Uttoxeter and novice at Leicester, and might have completed a hat-trick at Ascot but for a mistake at the last. He shaped as if amiss when a 10/1-shot for the Baring Bingham at the Festival on his only other start in 2010/11, but that doesn't diminish his potential for a campaign in staying novice chases in 2011/12. The list of positives is a long one; pedigree and physique both point to Tornado Bob making a better chaser than a hurdler, his form in the book is already decidedly above-average and he could hardly be in better hands. If everything goes to plan, Tornado Bob could be one major reason why Donald McCain will have Messrs Nicholls and Henderson looking over their shoulders in 2011/12. **Donald McCain**

Tim Easterby

Trustan Times (Ire)
h127p
5 b.g Heron Island (Ire) – Ballytrustan Maid (Ire) (Orchestra)
2010/11 20s* 22s^2 Feb 5

Tim Easterby may be more accustomed nowadays to contesting big sprint races at York with the likes of Captain Dunne and Hamish McGonagall, but he remains a dab hand over jumps and he looks to have an exciting novice chase prospect on his hands for the 2011/12 season in the shape of Trustan Times. A winner on his only

Trustan Times looks set to thrive as a staying novice chaser

start in points last October, this son of Heron Island made a striking impression on his hurdling debut at Wetherby in January. Expected to be in need of the run that day as a result of the stable's horses being held up by the inclement winter weather, he belied his market weakness (started 20/1) to beat Yurok comfortably by more than three lengths, that despite mistakes at the last two flights as he ran green in front.

Returned to Wetherby three weeks later and stepped up to two and three quarter miles, Trustan Times lost nothing in defeat under a penalty, exceeding the form of his debut when going down only to the promising Moonlight Drive, who would contest the Spa at the Cheltenham Festival on his next start. Trustan Times was arguably still green that day, inclined to race freely towards the head of affairs and arguably paying for that in the closing stages, for all he probably wouldn't have matched the winner in any case. Still only a five-year-old with just those two runs under Rules to his name thus far, Trustan Times is sure to be stronger with the summer under his belt and he looks the type to make a big impression over fences this season. **Tim Easterby**

Veiled   h132

5 b.m Sadler's Wells (USA) – Evasive Quality (Fr) (Highest Honor (Fr))
2010/11 16g⁶ 21m* 21g* :: 2011/12 18g⁴ May 7

Both Landing Light and Caracciola won the Cesarewitch for Nicky Henderson in the previous decade, with the latter also successful in the 2009 Queen Alexandra Stakes, so it was no surprise when the Lambourn-based trainer took another long-distance Flat prize with Veiled at Royal Ascot earlier this year. Ascot Stakes winner Veiled was better than ever on the Flat during 2011, and there is every reason to believe that the marked progression she has demonstrated on the level can be transferred to hurdles during the forthcoming jumps season.

Veiled remains a relatively lightly-raced hurdler, with just six starts over timber to her name. Although raced mostly in handicap company for her current yard, it does seem that the top mares races will soon be within her compass. Veiled started 2010/11 late, weakening tamely at Doncaster in March. That run was presumably needed, however, and Veiled created a much better impression when winning

Veiled (leader) continues her upward curve at Cheltenham

a mares handicap at Warwick less than three weeks later in ready fashion. That was to prove the springboard for a productive spring, with Veiled overcoming a mark 15 lb higher at Cheltenham in April before finishing a creditable fourth in a Grade 3 mares race at Punchestown.

With Carole's Legacy now retired to the paddocks, there is a space for a Henderson-trained mare to take in all the best sex-restricted races over hurdles. Given her progress in the spring and subsequent exploits on the Flat, we think Veiled is the prime candidate for the role and you can expect to see her taking high order among the mares this side of the Cheltenham Festival. **Nicky Henderson**

Victor Lynch (Ire) F96
5 b.g Old Vic – Jmember (Ire) (Jurado (USA))
2010/11 F17s³ Nov 14

Although she's been training for over twenty years with a reasonable degree of success, Kate Walton's career has an undoubted highlight, that being Sitting Tennant's shock 66/1-win in Aintree's Champion Bumper back in 2009. Walton has a comparatively good record in bumpers in recent seasons, with a strike-rate of 18% reflecting well against the yard's overall winning percentage of 11%. We've selected a bumper horse from Walton's stable to keep an eye on this season, albeit one who didn't contribute to his yard's winning record last term.

A look at Victor Lynch's pedigree should tell you that bumpers aren't going to bring out the best in him. By Old Vic and out of a half-sister to Fundamentalist among others, it's staying trips and, most likely, fences that will see him to best effect. With that considered, his effort in a bumper at Market Rasen in November becomes all the more encouraging. After drifting in the betting, Victor Lynch gave a strong hint towards what's to come, only really getting going late in the day after being outpaced and eventually finishing six and a half lengths third to Jukebox Melody.

The form of that race looks more than respectable, with the aforementioned winner going in again at Musselburgh next time, while since then he, runner-up Our Mick and fourth-placed Brunswick Gold have all won over hurdles. As for Victor Lynch, he wasn't seen subsequently, but that shouldn't be perceived as a particular negative given that he's very much a long-term prospect. In the meantime, expect to see improvement from Victor Lynch once he tackles hurdles and longer trips in 2011/12. **Kate Walton**

Victors Serenade (Ire) ★   h116 c96p

6 b.g Old Vic – Dantes Serenade (Ire) (Phardante (Fr))
2010/11 23s* 23v^3 22s^2 24v* c20s^2 Mar 20

Without meaning to spoil the surprise, you'll find out later in this publication just how highly we rate Anthony Honeyball's recent work. Barring a blip in 2009/10 it's been all up for the Dorset-based trainer, and with the start he's had to 2011/12 he could well be making his presence felt at big meetings before the season is out. Victors Serenade is already one of the stars of Honeyball's burgeoning string, but we think the best is yet to come from him.

Much like with his yard as a whole, 2010/11 was something of a breakthrough campaign for Victors Serenade, kicking off with a win in an Exeter handicap on his first try around three miles. That form had a strong look to it, so it was surprising that he couldn't follow up a week later, acknowledging that there were extenuating circumstances (raced on an unfavoured part of the track). There were more encouraging reasons for Victors Serenade failing to win at Hereford two months later, the fact he gave the highly-progressive Salpierre such a stern test very much to his credit. A simple task in a novice at Towcester was to follow, though it did serve to underline that he's all about stamina.

Off another two months prior to his final start, Victors Serenade made a chasing debut at Carlisle which was all about promise. Jumping accurately in the main, he travelled smoothly for a long way before shaping as though the run was just needed, eventually finishing second to Lord Villez. A rangy physique suggests Victors Serenade will thrive over fences granted more experience and, still fairly unexposed in general, he should be well worth following in 2011/12. ***Anthony Honeyball***

Water Garden (Fr)   h86p

5 gr.g Turgeon (USA) – Queenstown (Fr) (Cadoudal (Fr))
2010/11 F18s^2 21s^5 19v^4 17d Mar 20

Before opening this publication, you would have thought it unlikely that a horse that had left six-time champion trainer Paul Nicholls would be featured, but that doesn't concern us too much as Water Garden has joined David Pipe, who we're sure you'll agree isn't too shabby a replacement! What's more, he's owned by David Johnson, whose association with the Pipes shouldn't need reiterating to anyone who follows National Hunt racing.

Water Garden was all the rage in the betting before his debut in a Fontwell bumper, and for all he failed to overcome Camden (subsequently a fairly useful hurdler) the pair did pull well clear and, if anything, Water Garden looked the better prospect as his inexperience was more evident. Quickly switched to hurdles in a warm race at Plumpton, Water Garden looked for a long way as though set to play a part but wasn't knocked about once it was clear that he wasn't going to trouble the principals. Both subsequent starts didn't offer as much in terms of form, more about gaining experience and Water Garden left the impression on both occasions that he had plenty more to offer. We know what David Pipe can do with horses like Water Garden, the likes of E Street Boy underlining the point last season. Water Garden will be winning before long, most likely once switched to handicaps, and trips of two and a half miles plus will suit him ideally in time. *David Pipe*

Whoops A Daisy   h125+
5 b.m Definite Article – Bayarika (IRE) (Slip Anchor)
2010/11 F16d² 17s* 20s* 16v* 21g Mar 26

Let's Live Racing have previous history when it comes to prolific winning mares. Noun de La Thinte racked up six wins for Venetia Williams and her syndicate of owners during the 2009/10 season, including five consecutive victories in December and January. Hopes are high that history could repeat itself with the same owners' Whoops A Daisy, trained by Nicky Henderson, who already has four wins under her belt.

Successful on the first of her two bumper starts, Whoops A Daisy thrived once sent over hurdles last season, winning on her first three outings. After opening her account at Hereford in January, beating subsequent winners Charminster and Gurtacrue, she followed up at Bangor and Towcester. Those victories earned her a tilt at the valuable Mares' Novices' Hurdle Final at Newbury in March, where despite running off an official mark of 130 in her first handicap she featured among the market leaders. Ridden by stable conditional jockey Richie Killoran, Whoops A Daisy weakened quickly that day after travelling well to three out and was virtually pulled up after the last. Something was presumably amiss and she was not seen again.

Given a summer break, it would be a surprise were Whoops A Daisy not to resume her progress in 2011/12 and, being a half-sister to the winning staying chaser Chorizo, she looks sure to prove profitable to follow in mares novice chases this winter. Her sound jumping of hurdles will stand her in good stead over the larger obstacles and a return to Newbury for the Mares' Novices' Chase Final back at Newbury in March could well feature on the horizon. **Nicky Henderson**

Yurok (Ire)   h131+

7 b.g Alflora (Ire) – Wigwam Mam (Ire) (Commanche Run)
2010/11 20s* 20s² 22v² 24g^{pu} Apr 8

A half-sibling of a former champion is always welcomed with a certain buzz on their early visits to the racecourse, but the degrees of success can be mixed; to take the example of 2010/11 alone, we saw relatives of Kauto Star (Kauto Stone, won a Grade 1 chase at Auteuil), Florida Pearl (Rey Nacardo, progressive handicap chaser) and Best Mate (China Sky, struggled in a bumper and two novice hurdles) all come to the attention of the racing public. Yurok, trained by Sue Smith, is a half-brother to 2006 Champion Hurdle winner Brave Inca and, although he probably isn't going to reach such lofty heights, he remains with plenty of potential and should prove capable of upholding the family name.

Making his debut in a strong-looking Carlisle bumper back in March 2010, Yurok showed plenty until fitness and inexperience appeared to catch him out. Seemingly all the better for a summer break, he followed up that promise by winning a novice hurdle at the same track in October which appeals as one of the strongest of its type in the North last season, the likes of Rival d'Estruval, Seren Rouge and Blenheim Brook all in behind. That was to be Yurok's only win in 2010/11, but he did finish a good second on his next two starts, behind Trustan Times (also included in the 'fifty') and Battle Group (who would go on to win a Grade 3 handicap at Aintree in April) at Wetherby and Newcastle respectively. Yurok's season did end on a low note, pulled up lame in the Grade 1 Sefton Novices' at Aintree, but he should be back in action in 2011/12 when three miles or even further looks sure to bring out the best in him. It's pretty safe to assume there's more to come from Yurok, especially over fences given his yard's superior record over the larger obstacles. **Sue Smith**

HAVE YOU CALLED YET?

Over £1400 profit to £20 stakes
92 winners • 24% strike rate

The best verdict on the TV racing!

CALL 09062 653555

Every Saturday. All the big festivals. 8.00am.

Profits to level stakes at SP 05/02/11 – 01/10/11. Lines updated by 8.00 am, every day there is CH4 or BBC racing coverage. Calls cost £1.02 per minute from a BT landline. Cost of calls may be higher from mobiles and other networks. 18+ only. SP: Timeform, Halifax, HX1 1XF. Helpline: 0844 8246421

THE HOME OF WINNERS SINCE 1948

Horses To Follow From Ireland

Back In Focus (Ire) h143+
6 ch.g Bob Back (USA) – Dun Belle (Ire) (Over The River (Fr))
2010/11 24v* 24g Apr 8

Two of our fifteen to follow from Ireland have made the transition from Howard Johnson to Willie Mullins over the summer; you'll read about Prince de Beauchene later on (apologies for the spoiler), but first up is Back In Focus, who already looks custom-made for the switch.

Back In Focus, like so many Graham Wylie purchases, started his career in Ireland, winning a point there at the third attempt in January. He clearly showed the right signs from the off, as a month later he was entered in a Grade 2 at Haydock for his hurdling debut, for which Court In Motion was the odds-on favourite. Sent off at 16/1, Back In Focus created an excellent impression in sweeping to a six-length

Back In Focus appeals as the type to thrive in Ireland

victory over the admittedly non-staying market leader, challenging on the bridle three out and streaking clear after the next, already in control when making his only real mistake at the last. It was no great surprise to see Back In Focus well fancied for the Grade 1 Sefton at Aintree on his next start as a result of that, but he seemed unsuited by the much less testing conditions and could finish only eighth. That doesn't erode his potential at all, however, given he's a well-made gelding who should be suited by a switch to fences. Small-field novices in the mud are the order of the day in Ireland, something which should be right up Back In Focus' street, and it's not difficult to envisage him among the leaders of the Irish challenge come the big spring Festivals. **Willie Mullins**

Beautiful Sound (Ire) c134p
9 ch.g Presenting – Croom River (Ire) (Over The River (Fr))
2010/11 c20v* c24s c25v* c21g^3 :: 2011/12 c25d^2 May 7

2010/11 was something of a 'season mirabilis' for Gordon Elliott, whose rise through the training ranks has been meteoric. In 2010/11 he made two major breakthroughs, notching his first Grade 1 success with Jessies Dream and his first Cheltenham Festival winner with Chicago Grey. He is also beginning to enjoy the patronage of some of the top owners in the game and did well with a few who sport the Gigginstown House Stud silks last term, notably Cheltenham Festival winner Carlito Brigante and progressive chaser Beautiful Sound.

Following an absence of three and a half years Beautiful Sound returned to the fray in November in a Punchestown handicap, and quickly showed his troubles to be behind him with a convincing win. Not only that, he used that success as a springboard for greater things, much better than the bare result in the valuable Paddy Power Chase at Leopardstown over Christmas and then winning at Fairyhouse in January. Although not successful again in 2010/11, it's in defeat at the Cheltenham and Punchestown Festivals that Beautiful Sound really marked himself out as a horse to follow this time around, making a couple of early mistakes and then hampered at a crucial stage before rattling home to finish third in a Grade 3 handicap at the former, and then jumping brilliantly but taken very wide throughout when short-headed at the latter in a race that is already starting to work out well.

Although effective at around two and a half miles, Beautiful Sound's future basically lies in staying handicaps and, off just a 5 lb higher mark than when touched off at Punchestown, he looks sure to pick up a valuable prize or two this campaign, while further down the line a tilt at the Grand National could be in the offing, his bold-jumping, strong-travelling style ideal for the test provided by that famous race. **Gordon Elliott**

Bold Optimist (Ire)   F108P

5 b.g Oscar (Ire) – Massappeal Supreme (Ire) (Supreme Leader)
2010/11 F16s* Dec 30

Once the toast of the bookies after landing a shock 33/1 success in the 2007 Grand National with Silver Birch, Gordon Elliott's is now undoubtedly one of the most feared yards in Ireland when it comes to sending raiding parties to Britain. In 2010/11, Elliot managed a strike-rate of greater than one in four with his runners this side of the Irish Sea, duly showing a handsome profit to level stakes of almost fifty pounds. The Elliott onslaught is only likely to continue as his reputation swells, and the likes of Bold Optimist are the horses who can take the yard to the next level.

It was at Leopardstown over Christmas that Bold Optimist made his racecourse debut in a seemingly everyday bumper, and expectations were clearly high as he was a well-backed favourite. In event they crawled round and, none too surprising given his stout pedigree (by Oscar from a family of stayers), this worked against Bold Optimist who was still virtually last turning in. Despite his obvious greenness when first pressured, Bold Optimist picked up really well in time, storming home once switched wide to mow down subsequent winner Felix Yonger with plenty more to spare than the official two and a half lengths would suggest. The fact that he's being quoted for the Supreme Novices' Hurdle says it all about the regard Bold Optimist is held in, though it's more likely that the Baring Bingham or even the Spa may wind up being better options for him at the Cheltenham Festival.

Gordon Elliott

Caheronaun (Ire)   h91+

5 b.m Milan – Fair Present (Ire) (Presenting)
2010/11 20s F18s^3 F16s^5 20v^6 16d Mar 31

Milan, winner of the 2001 St Leger, is already making a name for himself as a jumps sire and has shown himself very much an influence for stamina. It's this influence that we're interested in with regards to Caheronaun, who is also out of a Presenting half-sister to useful staying hurdler/chaser Mount Clerigo. She certainly shaped in line with her pedigree last season.

Caheronaun was still mixing bumpers with hurdles in 2010/11, the test posed by the former almost certainly inadequate and her runs over timber chiefly about gaining experience. Nevertheless, she managed to achieve fair form on both of her starts in bumpers at Punchestown on the first occasion getting to within five lengths of Ceol Rua and Whatwillwecallher, both of whom would go on to prove themselves useful. In terms of her hurdling efforts, the clear pick in form terms came at the same course in February, where Caheronaun went in snatches somewhat but made up plenty of ground to finish sixth to Avondhu Lady.

The fact that she's finished no closer than sixth on three tries over hurdles suggests Caheronaun may well be given a low starting mark in handicaps, while her bumper form simply scratches the surface of what's to come once she tackles staying trips. All told, we'd be amazed if she doesn't prove up to winning handicaps this winter.
Dessie Hughes

For Bill (Ire) h137 c141+
8 b.m Presenting – Bobalena (Ire) (Bob Back (USA))
2010/11 c20v^3 20s^4 c22s* c20s* c20v* c22s^2 :: 2011/12 c20g^3 c20v^2 Sep 16

Naming horses after friends has brought mixed fortunes for octogenarian owner Donal Sheahan. Back in the early-1990s, For William developed into a useful staying chaser in Sheahan's white and purple colours, running one of his best races when fifth in the 1993 Irish Grand National. Other buys didn't hit the same heights; For Kevin's form tailed off after he picked up a couple of handicap chases the following year, while For Orla and For Amy failed to win outside points. It wasn't until more recently, when Sheahan picked up a daughter of Presenting out of a half-sister to For William, that the good times started to roll again.

Sheahan stuck with his formula by naming the mare For Bill (after a deceased friend), and she quickly made her mark, unbeaten in points, bumpers and hurdles on her first seven starts. For Bill took just as well to fences last season, surpassing For William's tally of eight wins under Rules when rattling off a hat-trick in mares events. She was particularly impressive when accounting for Blazing Tempo by five lengths in a well-contested Grade 3 at Thurles in January, finding plenty having led three out. That form has been well advertised since, with Blazing Tempo going on to finish second in a handicap at the Punchestown Festival, and, more recently, winning the Galway Plate.

For Bill, on the other hand, has met with defeat on her last three starts, but there have been excuses, seeming undone by a steady pace at Limerick, good ground at Fairyhouse, and the track at Listowel on her return from a break. For Bill was a shade hesitant in the jumping department at the last-named venue, but she's proved extremely sure-footed otherwise, and looks to be crying out for the chance to tackle three miles. She revels in testing ground and more graded contests should come her way, while a mark of 140 looks potentially lenient and gives her the opportunity to have a crack at some valuable staying handicaps.
Michael Winters

Hidden Cyclone (Ire) h146+
6 b.g Stowaway – Hurricane Debbie (Ire) (Shahanndeh)
2010/11 16d* 16v* 16s³ 20s* 20s* 23v* Mar 13

In the 2009/10 season Western Leader looked set to become a flag-bearer for the up-and-coming yard of John Joseph Hanlon, only to be forced into retirement through injury. Happily for the man known universally as 'Shark', he hasn't had to wait long for another top-notch prospect to come along in the shape of Hidden Cyclone, who met with defeat only once in six starts over hurdles in 2010/11. Following a maiden win at Tipperary last October, Hidden Cyclone was fast-tracked to Grade 3 company at Navan and took it all in his stride with another facile success, earning himself a tilt at the Grade 1 Future Champions Novices' at Leopardstown around Christmas. Hidden Cyclone lost his unbeaten record in that event, but in finishing a close third to future Cheltenham hero First Lieutenant and Zaidpour he lost no caste in defeat, especially as a last-flight mistake proved costly in what was a steadily-run contest.

Hidden Cyclone (noseband) is the type to do even better over fences

Subsequently upped in trip, Hidden Cyclone won Grade 2 events at Leopardstown and Thurles on his next two starts; and he then showed further improvement when signing off for the campaign with an effortless victory in a small-field novice over just short of three miles at Navan. A fine stamp of a horse who will stay even further, Hidden Cyclone is reportedly set to embark on a novice chasing campaign in 2011/12. He has the potential to go right to the top of the tree in that sphere, making the RSA Chase at Cheltenham an obvious long-term prospect, whilst he looks sure to mop up lesser races in Ireland along the way. Soft/heavy ground seems to suit Hidden Cyclone well, which will be an asset over the winter months, but he won his bumper on good and is a strong-travelling sort, so it would be folly to dismiss him as just a mudlark. ***John Joseph Hanlon***

Jetson (Ire) h117+
6 b.g Oscar (Ire) – La Noire (Ire) (Phardante (Fr))
2010/11 20v^{bd} 16v^5 18s^3 19v^2 16v^2 Feb 13

True to the spirit of Hanna-Barbera's animated sitcom, in which George Jetson was always reinstated in his 'full time' nine-hours-a-week job at the end of the episode, we're giving his equine namesake a second chance after a winless 2010/11. Jetson hasn't exactly been worked into the ground himself, with only seven runs behind him in two seasons, and we expect him to start reaping the benefits of the patient approach in the campaign ahead.

Jetson's hurdling career got off to an unfortunate start, brought down five out when yet to be asked for his effort in a maiden at Navan in November won by the useful Our Girl Salley, who Jetson had got to within three quarters of a length of in a strong bumper at Fairyhouse seven months earlier. His next outing suggested that experience had left a mark, but he soon regained his confidence, putting in his best work at the finish when placed in strong maidens on his three subsequent starts last winter, including when third to subsequent Grade 1 winner Shot From The Hip at Leopardstown, and when almost a distance clear of the remainder in second behind Lios A Choill back at Navan.

The dam La Noire showed just poor form in bumpers but has already produced a smart hurdler in the now-deceased Jered, a leading novice in 2007/8, while another of her foals, Jenari, is one to look out for over hurdles, having made great strides in three bumpers last term, finishing third to Lovethehigherlaw in a Grade 1 at Punchestown. Jetson's sole win remains his debut success in a bumper, but with handicaps and trips in excess of nineteen furlongs yet to be explored, he still has plenty of untapped potential himself. Winning a maiden will presumably be a first priority for Jetson before anything better comes under consideration. ***Noel Meade***

King Vuvuzela (Ire)   F109p
4 b.g Flemensfirth (USA) – Coolgavney Girl (Ire) (Good Thyne (USA))
2010/11 NR :: 2011/12 F16g* May 3

Anyone who watched the 2010 World Cup in South Africa will grimace when the word vuvuzela is mentioned, with the instrument known to produce a sound of around 120 decibels (a similar level to a rock concert) if you're unlucky enough to be stood within a metre of the insufferable person blowing it. The vuvuzela won't be heard at Cheltenham next March, but King Vuvuzela could raise cheers of a similar magnitude if he comes up the hill in front in one of the novice hurdles there.

By Flemensfirth out of an unraced half-sister to the 2008 Grand National winner Comply Or Die, King Vuvuzela seemed unlikely to have the speed to figure prominently when he made his debut in a two-mile four-year-old bumper on good ground at Punchestown in May and not surprisingly he was one of the outsiders in a twenty-four-runner field. However, that turned out to be far from the case. In a truly-run race, King Vuvuzela made smooth headway from mid-field to lead early in the straight and quickened clear impressively to win by five lengths from Morning Royalty. The form has been boosted since, notably by fourth-placed Morning Ireland who comfortably landed the odds in a maiden at Clonmel on his hurdling debut. King Vuvuzela himself will be making his mark over hurdles before too long. Sure to stay at least two and a half miles, he looks an exciting prospect.
Paul Nolan

Lovethehigherlaw (Ire)   F127
5 ch.g Presenting – Markiza (Ire) (Broken Hearted)
2010/11 F16v* F19s^2 :: 2011/12 F16g* May 4

The family of Champion Hurdle winners Morley Street and Granville Again is one of the most prominent in jumps racing, with relatives appearing on the racecourse with notable frequency. In the 2010/11, a Willie Mullins bumper horse named Lovethehigherlaw, whose dam is a half-sister to the aforementioned pair, made a deep impression and is one to follow in both the short and long term.

A winner of his only start in points back in February 2010, Lovethehigherlaw went off particularly well fancied on his Rules debut and had plenty in hand as he beat Caolaneoin by two lengths at Fairyhouse, the pair finishing well clear. He was to meet with defeat at Limerick next time, runner-up to Mount Benbulben, but that proved a mere blip as he secured Punchestown's Champion Bumper on his final start, travelling powerfully and just getting the better of a sustained tussle with

Lovethehigherlaw (maroon) could dominate the novice hurdling division in Ireland

favourite Waaheb. By Presenting, it's likely that longer trips and eventually fences will bring out the very best in Lovethehigherlaw, but in the meantime there's every reason to think he can develop into one of Ireland's top novice hurdlers over two and a half miles and beyond this winter. **Willie Mullins**

Nearest The Pin (Ire)   h131
6 b.g Court Cave (Ire) – Carnbelle (Ire) (Electric)
2010/11 16v 16s⁴ 20s³ :: 2011/12 16g* 16g² May 3

Those involved in what is currently known as the Sox Syndicate have already done well with the produce of the unraced Carnbelle. The mare's first foal Hold The Pin has enjoyed plenty of success as a staying hurdler/chaser over the years, and now her fourth foal Nearest The Pin looks set to scale even greater heights.

Surprisingly for one who is a close relation to Hold the Pin, Nearest The Pin has looked a very different sort in a handful of runs so far, and the progress he made in his debut season was impressive. Following three runs in maiden hurdles when Nearest The Pin showed clear signs of ability, he made a mockery of his opening mark in a two-mile contest at Fairyhouse over Easter, pulling hard in the early stages but still having enough in reserve to challenge on the bridle two out and gallop clear for a four-length success. He had next-time-out winners back in second and fourth that day, so it's an effort that looks even more meritorious now than it did at the time, and he did his bit for that form when second at Punchestown off a 13 lb higher mark the following month. That display represented another significant stride forward as he all but succeeded in defying the hike in the weights, really impressing with the way he moved into things around the outer but just unable to find a way past another unexposed sort on the run-in, the pair pulling clear of the remainder in a time that compares well with other races on the card.

All of this was achieved in less than six months which makes it all the more encouraging, so further progress looks assured when Nearest The Pin returns for his second full season, especially as he is probably only just starting to fill his frame. As his pedigree suggests, he will probably stay two and a half miles when he learns to settle a bit better and he has all the tools to be a force in valuable big-field handicaps, races such as the MCR at Leopardstown likely to be on the agenda, that a race that tends to place an emphasis on a high cruising speed and fluent jumping. **Tony Martin**

Oscars Well (Ire) h152
6 b.g Oscar (Ire) – Placid Willow (Ire) (Convinced)
2010/11 18s^2 20s* 20s* 18s* 21g^4 Mar 16

People have certain expectations of Timeform—and Horses To Follow in particular—to avoid the obvious and highlight those who've hitherto failed to register on the radar of the racing public at large. We find this is generally the best way to gain an edge and ultimately allow our selections to make a profit over the season, but sometimes even we'll plump for horses that have escaped the gaze of few so clear is their promise. Enter Oscars Well, who was campaigned on the biggest stage last season and already has two Grade 1s to his name, but is almost certainly destined for another big haul in 2011/12.

Oscars Well seemed to need his hurdling debut at Thurles in November, but he stepped up on that in no uncertain terms at Punchestown ten days later. Sent to tackle the Grade 1 Navan Novices' Hurdle the following month, Oscars Well confirmed himself useful in beating Sweet Shock by eight lengths with the minimum of fuss. The Deloitte Novices' Hurdle at Leopardstown in February was a much stronger Grade 1 and it required Oscars Well to step up again in order to beat Zaidpour comfortably by over five lengths. The run that has really caught most people's eye, however, was the one Oscars Well didn't win, the Baring

Oscars Well (pink with sash) beats smart novices Zaidpour (spots) and Shotfromthehip (hoops) in a Grade 1 at Leopardstown

Bingham at the Festival, when he looked the likeliest winner before a dreadful mistake at the last cost him all chance. Possessing more speed than his pedigree would imply and having the build to make an even better chaser, Oscars Well looks destined for the top whatever route connections decide to go with him.
Jessica Harrington

Pittoni (Ire)   h145+
5 b.g Peintre Celebre (USA) – Key Change (Ire) (Darshaan)
2010/11 16s* Feb 27

When Yorkshire Oaks winner Key Change was sent to visit 1997 Arc victor Peintre Celebre in 2005, great things on the Flat would presumably been expected from the resulting foal. True, Pittoni has developed into a borderline-smart performer on the level, but we're interested in his exploits over hurdles above all and see him competing with some of the leading lights in Ireland before long.

Well fancied for the 2010 Triumph Hurdle only to be found out by conditions less testing than he's used to, Pittoni made a couple of starts on the Flat (the first of which, incidentally, resulted in him being given a ban of forty-two days from racing under the non-triers rule) before returning to the jumping arena in February. Sent off a strong favourite for a competitive handicap at Leopardstown, Pittoni made a mockery of his opening mark of 130, needing only to be pushed out to win going away by two and a half lengths from Cass Bligh, once again shaping as though a try over further could prove worthwhile for all he clearly isn't short of speed.

As mentioned above, Pittoni has improved on the Flat since then, winning a minor event at Tipperary (in which he beat subsequent Kilternan Stakes winner Galileo's Choice) before landing the odds in an amateurs' race at Listowel. Both of those successes came over fourteen furlongs on testing ground, which further underlines Pittoni's abundant stamina, and he should be mixing it back in graded company over hurdles before long; his exalted pedigree demands nothing less.
Charles Byrnes

Prince de Beauchene (Fr) c141
8 b.g French Glory – Chipie d'Angron (Fr) (Grand Tresor (Fr))
2010/11 c24v^{ur} c20g^5 c19s^3 c20g^5 c25g* Apr 9

You won't find much sympathy for Howard Johnson around these parts given the severity of the offences that saw him warned off for four years by the BHA in August. As a final insult, his former principal owner Graham Wylie has dispersed a significant number of the Johnson string to the most powerful yards on both sides of the Irish Sea: Paul Nicholls has received thirteen of Wylie's string, while Willie Mullins will train a further seven in the now familiar black and beige silks.

The fact is that Prince de Beauchene would have been in the running for our 'fifty' even if he'd remained with Howard Johnson, so he was a natural choice now he's switched to Mullins. His season in 2010/11 looked set to be a frustrating one, with excuses being present for each of his first four runs; an unseat as his fitness gave way at Carlisle was followed by three runs over inadequate trips in handicaps, though he did shape well when fifth behind Fine Parchment in a Grade 3 event at Newbury in March. It wasn't until the Grand National meeting that Prince de Beauchene confirmed his status as a progressive staying handicapper when taking a listed event by one and a half lengths from Categorical. As well as proving himself away from the mud, that day Prince de Beauchene impressed greatly with his jumping around the very stern Mildmay Course, something which gives us the impression that he'd be an ideal type for the Grand National in 2012. Mullins obviously has previous in the National, saddling 2005 winner Hedgehunter and last year's favourite The Midnight Club, and you can expect to see Prince de Beauchene campaigned in fairly similar fashion to the latter with a view to a tilt at Aintree this time around. **Willie Mullins**

Samain (Ger) F121p
5 b.g Black Sam Bellamy (Ire) – Selva (Ire) (Darshaan)
2010/11 F16s* F16s* F16v* Apr 3

You wouldn't normally expect a bumper performer from a largely Flat-based family to make our 'Horses To Follow' list, but that's exactly what we've plumped for in Samain. Bear with us, though, as there's reason to think he's an above-average novice hurdler in the making despite his profile.

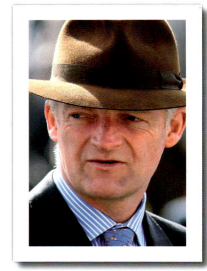

Willie Mullins

From the family of the likes of Doyoun and by Black Sam Bellamy, it's fair to say that Samain's breeding is far from prohibitive as far as a career over jumps goes, while his unbeaten record in bumpers for Willie Mullins in 2010/11 certainly promises a fruitful career when he tackles hurdles. Bought for £165,000 after a promising debut for Eddie Hales in late-2009/10, he improved with every subsequent outing, kicking off at Punchestown in January when he came clear with Cairdin despite greenness, leaving Espresso Lady (who would go on to prove useful) ten lengths back in third. The experience of that run clearly wasn't lost on Samain, as the following month he looked much more professional in dispatching a smaller field at Naas, cruising to the lead a furlong out and quickening clear.

It was at the Curragh that Samain would make his final start of the season, in a race his handler had won on two of the previous three renewals. Here Samain confirmed his promise for trips longer than two miles, hard ridden a furlong out but staying on strongly to collar Shadow Eile and win by six lengths going away. He ultimately wasn't sent to Punchestown a month later, none too surprisingly given his trainer won that Champion event with Lovethehigherlaw in any case, but Samain will surely be taking in some big races as a novice hurdler in 2011/12 and is likely to pay his way. **Willie Mullins**

Sir des Champs (Fr) h146p

5 b.g Robin des Champs (Fr) – Liste En Tete (Fr) (Video Rock (Fr))
2010/11 16s* 20g* Mar 18

A 'Horses To Follow' list wouldn't be complete without a Willie Mullins-trained French import, and few of his current string come to mind more readily than Sir des Champs, who is unbeaten over hurdles and looks one of the brightest prospects in the Mullins yard as a whole.

It might have been in a handicap that Sir des Champs really announced himself on the scene, but graded races look to be on the agenda sooner rather than later such was the impression left by his performance in the Martin Pipe at Cheltenham in March. Held up well in rear that day, Sir des Champs still had plenty to do turning in but stayed on strongly to nab Son of Flicka near the finish, clearly suited by the step up to two and a half mile. Whilst Sir des Champs' stamina capabilities were evident at Cheltenham, he certainly wasn't found wanting in terms of speed prior to that, as demonstrated when an impressive winner of a two-mile minor event at Navan on his debut for Mullins, having been successful at Auteuil on his only previous start over hurdles. At the time of writing, it is uncertain whether Sir des Champs will remain hurdling for the time being or whether connections will choose to send him novice chasing, but either way he's destined for the top.
Willie Mullins

Sir des Champs after his Festival win

OPEN ACCESS FROM £2.50 A DAY

Race Passes are the ultimate form guide, featuring ratings, In-Play symbols, live Betfair prices - plus unlimited 'Horse Search' career summaries and performance analysis.

Subscriptions give you open access to Timeform data for every meeting in Britain & Ireland, starting from just £10 for 24 hours, to £70 for 28 days. That's only £2.50 per day.

It's like a Form Book, Black Book & Race Card all in one!

Race Passes

Ratings. Form. In-Play symbols. Betfair prices. Search any horse, any time.

ONLY AVAILABLE AT
timeform.com

TIMEFORM
THE HOME OF WINNERS SINCE 1948

Interview
Philip Hobbs

Much is made of the criteria used to decide the Trainers' Championship; accepted wisdom points to the existing prize-money based system offering the fairest route, though some suggest simple number of winners is a more defining indicator of a trainer's success.

Consistency will never be used as the basis for deciding a title, but if it were then Philip Hobbs would almost certainly have pocketed his elusive first Championship by now.

While long-time stable jockey Richard Johnson has seemingly forever been in the shadow of a certain A. P. McCoy, Hobbs has had to contend with such powerhouses as Martin Pipe, Nicky Henderson and, latterly, Paul Nicholls, in his quest for his title breakthrough.

In terms of sheer reliability, though, very few other regular fixtures in the upper echelon of the National Hunt training ranks can compete with Hobbs, as ten successive seasons exceeding the £1m barrier in prize-money goes a long way to proving.

For all that success, not many campaigns have promised as much for Hobbs as the one currently in progress, with a host of notable up-and-coming types on his hands, especially in the chasing division, courtesy of major Festival winners Wishfull Thinking and Captain Chris. That consistency seems sure to continue, and Philip kindly spared time recently to run the rule over his team.

Chasers

Wishfull Thinking (Timeform Rating c165) 8 ch.g Alflora (Ire) – Poussetiere Deux (Fr) (Garde Royale) 2010/11 c20d^F c21m* c21g^2 c21d* c20g^2 c20d* :: 2011/12 c21g* May 6 He's a probable for the Old Roan Chase at Aintree, though we might struggle to get him ready by then, in which case he'd run in either the Paddy Power or the Amlin Chase. So we'll start at two and a half miles, and I'm not sure which trip we'll end up going; before Cheltenham he was entered in the three-mile novice chase, but as the season went on he ended up making the running and showing lots of pace, particularly at Aintree. If he's that enthusiastic, you'd wonder whether he'd really get home over the Gold Cup trip, and I think he's got the pace to drop back to two miles; I have a theory that the better a horse is, the less the distance matters.

Wishfull Thinking looks destined for the top

Planet of Sound (c157) 9 b.g Kayf Tara – Herald The Dawn (Dubassoff (USA)) 2010/11 c24s³ c24d⁵ Jan 15 He's all right. His first run at Haydock was good—we were well happy—but he ran in the King George and choked, so we gave him a breathing operation with the aim of getting him ready for the Gold Cup. Then he had a very peculiar problem with an infection in a hind leg, and his leg blew up enormously, which meant we couldn't get him back in time even for Punchestown. He's fine now, back in training, and he looks particularly well actually. He's unlikely at his age to be top conditions race material, but I'd like to hope we could get him ready in time for the Hennessy and, if Denman runs, there wouldn't be too many others in the handicap.

Captain Chris (Ire) (c156p) 7 b.g King's Theatre (Ire) – Function Dream (Ire) (Strong Gale) 2010/11 20s² c16s² c18d² c20d² c20s* c16g* :: 2011/12 c16g* May 5 He's in strong, serious work already, and is going very well. We have rather the same problem (as with Wishfull Thinking), as I don't think we're at all sure what his best trip will be, though I suppose, of the two, he's more likely to end up in the King George. I do think he's better right-handed, as he does have a tendency to go that way, so we're going to start in the Haldon Gold Cup. If either are going to be good enough to run in these conditions races, then they ought to win a handicap off

Captain Chris (left) could well be stepped up in trip

their marks, but if I had to have one or the other, I'd probably go for Captain Chris. In terms of ability, I certainly hope he's right up there.

Quinz (Fr) (c153) 7 b.g Robin des Champs (Fr) – Altesse du Mou (Fr) (Tin Soldier (Fr)) 2010/11 c24g* c24d* c25g³ c24s* c36g^{pu} Apr 9 He's in good nick and we're very happy with him. His first run is likely to be at the end of October, at either Ascot or in the Charlie Hall at Wetherby. He was staggering last season to be honest; when he won a novice chase at Exeter, I could never have thought he'd end up winning the Racing Post Chase. In fact, he doesn't have to improve that much more to be a contender for something like the King George. I think he's pretty versatile, but he probably doesn't want the ground too soft.

Fair Along (Ger) (h150 c144) 9 b.g Alkalde (Ger) – Fairy Tango (Fr) (Acatenango (Ger)) 2010/11 25g* 24d c24d³ c24g⁴ :: 2011/12 c30g^{ur} May 6 We'll aim Fair Along at Wetherby again for the staying hurdle race there; he's not going to be good enough for the three-mile conditions races as the season gets going, but he might just be good enough for that race as you don't usually get the top hurdlers there. He'll be going back chasing after that, and he did show promise again over

Stable stalwart Fair Along will continue to mix hurdling and chasing

fences last season—he ran well in the Aon Chase, and also at Punchestown until the softer ground and his breathing again caught him out at the end.

Balthazar King (Ire) (c136+) 7 b.g King's Theatre (Ire) – Afdala (Ire) (Hernando (Fr)) 2010/11 c23g* c24d* c24m⁴ c24d² c25g⁵ c25s* c25g* c29m^pu Apr 23 It won't be easy for him; he certainly won't be winning four this season! He's only a little horse, but his jumping has been very good, which has been his major plus. We'll have to run him in handicaps and allow him to find his level; I don't think you're ever happy running a second-season chaser in handicaps around Cheltenham and Newbury, because it's very hard, but unfortunately we have no option.

Cappagh (Ire) (h118+ c130p) 6 ch.g Presenting – Random Bless (Ire) (Montelimar (USA)) 2010/11 19m^ur 23m* c16s* c21m* 21s⁵ 24d⁵ :: 2011/12 c21m* Sep 5 He won well at Newton Abbot last time, and you'd like to hope there's a decent handicap chase for him somewhere. He doesn't want the ground too soft, and I think it was the going that stopped him getting home over three miles at Newbury. He's not the most consistent, and I don't know whether he's better fresh.

Menorah (centre) will go chasing in the autumn

Novice Chasers

Menorah (Ire) (h160) 6 b.g King's Theatre (Ire) – Maid For Adventure (Ire) (Strong Gale) 2010/11 16s* 17g* 16g^5 :: 2011/12 16g^4 May 6 Everything has gone well with him. The plan is very much for him to go novice chasing in late-October or early-November. He hasn't schooled over fences yet, but I'd be surprised if there was a problem and I'd be hoping that should be his job—that's what he's bred to do anyway. He might have run below par in Grade 1 races in the spring, but, realistically, I don't think he was quite in that league; he was probably in the top dozen hurdlers, but not the top four.

Duke of Lucca (Ire) (h142) 6 b.g Milan – Derravaragh Native (Ire) (Be My Native (USA)) 2010/11 20s 24d^4 24g^4 20d^5 24g Mar 17 It was probably a mistake last year keeping him over hurdles. Interestingly, at the beginning of the season, there was only about 4 lb between him and Menorah, and Menorah went the right way whereas Duke of Lucca blatantly couldn't win off his handicap mark. He's six now, the right age to go novice chasing, and I'd be surprised if there was a problem when we school him.

Kilcrea Kim (Ire) (h139) 6 ch.g Snurge – Kilcrea Deer (Ire) (Brush Aside (USA)) 2010/11 20g* 20v* 22s* 24d^5 22d* 24g^5 24g Apr 8 We had a great season with him last season; he's a really nice horse who we like a lot. He stays well—when he won at Sandown over two mile six furlongs, all he did was stay, and that was up that hill on very soft ground—and he'll start at two and half miles plus in novice chases. He could well be a better chaser.

Hurdlers

Nearby (h152 c125) 7 b.g King's Best (USA) – Contiguous (USA) (Danzig (USA)) 2010/11 17g 17g* 16d* 16m* 16d^5 16s 17g^3 16g^5 16g :: 2011/12 c16m^2 c16g^2 c16g^3 Sep 20 He's been rather disappointing really. I think we're going to have to go back over hurdles, but he's not going to be easy to place; he had those three fantastic runs in the autumn and went up to 150 plus. Ideally, he wants a big field and to be dropped in, but the problem of course is that he's a possibility for conditions hurdles now and they get only five or six runners which doesn't really suit him, as has been part of the problem in these novice chases. Whatever happens, we'll still have his mark over fences to go back to.

Arthurian Legend (h125p) 6 b.g Alflora (Ire) – Be My Adelina (Ire) (Be My Native (USA)) 2010/11 16s* 17s^6 16d 16d* Apr 2 He's a very stressed horse who gets worked up. He won his first and last races at Chepstow, but in between got rather keen and lost the plot a bit. I think it's a coincidence that he's shown his best form at

Chepstow, but because of his record there he might well run in the Silver Trophy, as two and a half miles is what he's going to want. He definitely has ability if we can keep his mind straight.

Dunraven Storm (Ire) (h136) 6 br.g Presenting – Foxfire (Lord Americo) 2010/11 17d* 16g* 16d² 16d⁴ 16g^pu Mar 15 He just lost his way a bit last season, though he had excuses on his final run. Some of his form is good, though, and I think he'll stay over hurdles. I'm sure he will stay further than two miles.

Dunraven Storm (red) could get back on track over longer trips

My Shamwari (h134+) 7 b.g Flemensfirth (USA) – Quilty Rose (Buckskin (Fr)) 2010/11 17g 17d 20d* 20g* Apr 13 He's a horse who doesn't hold his condition great—he's a bit of a worrier—but he progressed quickly in the spring. His first two runs were disastrous, and I don't know why he suddenly came right at Ffos Las, and Cheltenham was even better. He may run in a hurdle race at Newton Abbot, but I'd imagine he'd be novice chasing before very long. He's had a breathing operation during the summer.

Dare Me (Ire) (h126p) 7 b.g Bob Back (USA) – Gaye Chatelaine (Ire) (Castle Keep) 2010/11 17g* 17s* Nov 2 He's back now after his leg injury and he's going to have to go the handicap hurdle route to gain some experience before he goes chasing. He's always been a very good horse, though.

Filbert (Ire) (120p) 5 b.g Oscar (Ire) – Coca's Well (Ire) (Religiously (USA)) 2010/11 19s³ 19d* Jan 1 He had the same problem as Planet of Sound, and we tried to get him back before deciding it was best to call time on the season. He's in a similar boat to Dare Me in terms of experience, and he'll have one run in a handicap before going chasing; he's built for chasing, but I think he can be competitive over hurdles from his mark.

Novice Hurdlers

Dream Function (Ire) (118p) 6 b.m King's Theatre (Ire) – Function Dream (Ire) (Strong Gale) 2010/11 F16d³ F16v³ 22d² 21s :: 2011/12 19g* She won at Newton Abbot the other day and was impressive. She's a full sister to Captain Chris and, with her future as a broodmare in mind, she could well go chasing sooner rather than later. I'd like to think she could be a 125-plus mare, and the mares handicap at Newbury in the spring could be a possibility if she gets qualified.

Fingal Bay (Ire) (F113) 5 b.g King's Theatre (Ire) – Lady Marguerrite (Blakeney) 2010/11 F17v* Feb 13 I'm interested you've included him—he's a very, very nice horse. Not many came up to scratch in that Exeter race, but all he could do was to win impressively, and I don't think he needs that heavy ground, either. He'll probably go straight to hurdling.

Persian Snow (Ire) (F111) 5 b.g Anshan – Alpine Message (Tirol) 2010/11 F16g* F16s³ F17g Apr 9 :: 2011/12 NR We thought he was a very good horse, but he was disappointing after his win at Ascot in the autumn. He did have a bout of coughing before his next run, however, and he should win his races over hurdles. He'll want two and a half mile and beyond.

Interview
Charlie Longsdon

It's surely too soon in Charlie Longsdon's training career to describe his 2010/11 campaign as a renaissance, but there was certainly an element of the fledging handler restoring the faith.

Following a debut season that yielded nine winners from just fifty-nine runners, followed by a 2007/8 campaign that produced more than double the amount, Longsdon appeared to endure something of a stall—his next two terms mustered only thirty-four successes between them, with his strike-rate dropping to a mere 7% in 2009/10.

Statistics do throw up anomalies, however, and, evidently aided by a move from the Cotswolds to new premises in Chipping Norton, Oxfordshire, Longsdon went a long way to fully confirming initial promise during the latest term, handling the likes of Hidden Keel and Hildisvini with aplomb and signing off with forty-four wins in the bag, more than double the total he'd managed in that ever-so-impressive second campaign.

And what's more, 2011/12 is already threatening to produce further milestones, thanks to an early salvo that, at the time of writing, has placed Longsdon in thirteenth place in the trainers' table, just six places behind one of his many notable former mentors, Nicky Henderson.

It was with no hesitation, therefore, that Charlie was pursued as a potential interviewee for this year's publication, and he generously took time out towards the end of September to assess his burgeoning string.

Chasers

Hidden Keel (Timeform Rating c141p) 6 gr.g Kirkwall – Royal Keel (Long Leave) 2010/11 19g* 21s⁴ c19s² c20d* c20d c19d* c19g* Apr 5 He won three novice chases last season—all very easily—and he's rated 149, so it's an important year for him really. He goes to an intermediate chase at Carlisle on October 30 and where he heads after will depend on how he does; if he does badly there, then we'll have to go into handicaps, but it he wins we'll have to go against the big boys, in something like the Peterborough Chase. I'd like to think he can only improve from what he's done so far—he's only a six-year-old—and he's getting bigger and stronger every year. I've always thought he's the one with the potential to take us to the next level, and Paddy Brennan thinks the world of him.

Songe has long been a flag-bearer for the Longsdon yard

Songe (Fr) (c137?) 7 b.g Hernando (Fr) – Sierra (Fr) (Anabaa (USA)) 2010/11 c20d^ur c16m² c20g* c20d* 21d^F c20g^pu :: 2011/12 c20g Apr 28 He's always got a '?' alongside his rating! Songe is Songe, unfortunately. He's always had a talent but been quirky, though one thing we have done this summer is to give him a wind operation. He's always good first time out and fresh, and he runs in a couple of weeks at Huntingdon in the race he won last year. I think he's a 140-horse, and he seems to be thriving at the moment, but you never know how long that is going to last with Songe.

Ostland (Ger) (c134) 6 b.g Lando (Ger) – Ost Tycoon (Ger) (Last Tycoon) 2010/11 20s^{ur} 21s^4 21g^2 20g^4 :: 2011/12 c22g* c22m* c22g* c24g^2 c22g Sep 24 He's a good ground horse and he's been brilliant, winning his first three chases and then finishing a good second at Bangor. That showed he stays three miles, which gives us more options. He has got a funny head carriage, and we did start thinking of putting cheekpieces back on, but he's really battled in his chases this year prior to a below-par run last time.

Qhilimar (Fr) (c129+) 7 b.g Ragmar (Fr) – Fhilida (Fr) (Zelphi (USA)) 2010/11 c24d^5 c26d^{pu} c24s* c33d^R :: 2011/12 c26g* Sep 20 I think he's the most changed horse we've had this season—he's improved, grown and strengthened up. I'd have been very disappointed if he hadn't won at Newton Abbot the other day, as if he'd have got in the race at Listowel the week before he'd have had a great chance. He's thrived this year, and he's now improved into the 130s, which means he can get into some of the best staying handicaps in Ireland and in this country; there's the Munster National, and also the amateur handicap at Cheltenham in November to consider. I love the way he jumps, and he's travelling better this year as well, and I think he's far better than his mark.

Minella Boys (Ire) (c129) 9 br.g Bob's Return (Ire) – Ring-Em-All (Decent Fellow) 2010/11 c24s^4 c32s^3 c29s* c29s^2 c33v^{pu} :: 2011/12 c24s^{pu} Sep 14 He just didn't jump very well at Listowel (Kerry National) the other day, but three miles on that ground probably has him going a little faster than ideal; he's an out-and-out stayer who has to have soft ground, and over three and a half miles he's got a bit more time at his fences. He's a good staying handicapper, and he'll be looking at all those regional Nationals, if not a few slightly better.

Baseball Ted (Ire) (c118) 9 b.g Beneficial – Lishpower (Master Buck) 2010/11 c17s* c16s^3 c16d^3 c16d* c17d* Mar 4 He was a pleasant surprise last season, winning three out of five. He's a nine-year-old now, and whether he can improve again I don't know, but the biggest thing in his favour is the weakness of the two-mile division. It's going to be hard for him this season off a career-high mark, but he can certainly pick up prize money here and there.

Rey Nacarado (Ire) (c118) 6 b.g. Posidonas – Ice Pearl (Flatbush) 2010/11 26g* 24d^3 c22d^2 c26d* c24d^3 c24s^2 c26g* Mar 26 I thought he was the worst horse in my yard this time last year, but my word he improved; he won a bad hurdle race, and as soon as he hit a fence he loved it, jumping for fun. I may run him back over hurdles first then he'll go for those regional Nationals as well. He's only six, and there's no reason why he can't strengthen up and improve again this year. He'll pay his way, anyway.

Novice Chasers

Time For Spring (Ire) (h125p) 7 b.g Snurge – Burksie (Ire) (Supreme Leader) 2010/11 22d^2 22g* 21s^F 20s 22d* Mar 11 A lovely horse. He'll go chasing—he'll run first in a beginners chase at Exeter over three miles in October. I thought he was quite impressive at Sandown the day he won; I think he got a better ride than Havingotascoobydo that day, but he still beat him fair and square. We tried making the running one day at Plumpton and he didn't jump in front, and we tried him on testing ground at Leicester and that was a waste of time as well. The rest of his runs have all been very good, and I'll be surprised if he can't pick up two or three chases this season.

Time For Spring looks a useful staying chaser in the making

Accordintolawrence (Ire) (h116) 5 b.g Accordion – Giolldante (Ire) (Phardante (Fr)) 2010/11 F16m6 17v* 19d^6 18s* 21g^F Mar 16 He'll go chasing, and I think he'll improve a ton for fences. He won two of his four hurdle races, he's only five, and he's got spring in his jumping. I think he's well handicapped, and we may well go the novice handicap route.

Strongbows Legend (c108p) 6 ch.g Midnight Legend – Miss Crabapple (Sunyboy) 2010/11 16d^2 c18d c21s^2 c24m^3 c26s^F c24d^2 Mar 24 I said at my owners' day that he's the best handicapped horse we've got in the yard off 108. He was bolting up when he fell at Plumpton last season, and he's got bits and pieces of really nice form. He was certainly thrown in at the deep end last year, and I couldn't believe how well he coped with all that. He's always been a great jumper, and he's the sort who could go on and run in all those military races and bolt up. He's not a 108-horse—he's a 125-horse—and he's going to fill into his frame only this season and next. I'd be very disappointed if he can't go and pick up two or three.

Hurdlers

Hildisvini (Ire) (h134p) 5 b.g Milan – Site Mistress (Ire) (Remainder Man) 2010/11 F16s^6 F16s^2 F16s* 16s* 19d* Mar 21 He's thrust into the big time this year because he's won two novice hurdles and he's going to have to run against some top-class horses now. He'll go the Pertemps (Final) route, and if he can't compete he'll go chasing. He's a three-mile, soft-ground chaser, that's what he is, but he's hard as nails and loves his racing.

Tatispout (Fr) (h128) 4 b.f Califet (Fr) – Larmonie (Fr) (Great Palm (USA)) 2010/11 F10d5 15s F10g* 16d 16d^3 16d 16d^3 16m^2 16g^5 16g* :: 2011/12 17g* 16g 16g^2 17g Sep 24 She's grand. If she can't compete in handicap hurdles any longer, then she'll go straight chasing; she'll get an age and sex allowance, and off 10-0 in all those novice chases she could be electric. She's as good a jumper of a fence as we've ever had. I don't think she stayed two miles on soft ground last year, and it was no coincidence that as soon as the better ground came about she improved 20 lb.

Paintball (Ire) (h126+) 4 b.g Le Vie Dei Colori – Camassina (Ire) (Taufan (USA)) 2010/11 16d^2 16s^6 16s* 16g 17g* Apr 13 I made no bones about the fact last season that he wasn't a natural juvenile and would improve with a summer holiday on his back. He's rated 130 at the moment, and he has to run against better horses now, but I've always thought he'd progress this season. We mucked up in the Fred Winter, as I said to ride him handily and he ran away with Dickie Johnson and didn't get up the hill. We put that right there the next time—I thought he won with a little bit in hand in the end—and he'll certainly go to the track with each-way chances in all those decent two-mile handicap hurdles.

Paintball could become a fixture in good two-mile handicap hurdles

Novice Hurdlers

Grandads Horse (h120p) 5 b.g Bollin Eric – Solid Land (Fr) (Solid Illusion (USA)) 2010/11 F16m⁴ F17g³ F17g² F17s* 16g² :: 2011/12 20g* 20m* Sep 7 He's done all right, hasn't he? He's off only 118 at the moment, and I don't know whether we take 7 lb off his back and run somewhere with a double penalty, or go into handicap company. He's a lovely big, strapping horse, and you won't see the best of him until he gets over a fence, but he could be fun before then. When I first got him he didn't give much of a feel in canter, but as soon as he got up to work pace everyone said to me, 'Charlie, this horse can go some!'

Areuwitmenow (Ire) (h109) 6 b.g Beneficial – Clonartic (Ire) (Be My Native (USA)) 2010/11 20s^pu 21d⁵ 25d² 24m² Apr 9 We won't see him until after Christmas. He's a chaser, a three-mile chaser, and he'll be okay; I'm not going to rush him, and he'll be back in February-time.

Rossmore Lad (Ire) (h105p) 6 b.g Beneficial – Celestial Rose (Ire) (Roselier (Fr)) 2010/11 21m² 22g² Apr 19 I think he's well treated off 114, and I'll run him in a handicap with 7 lb off his back. He had wicked sore shins towards the end of last year—we nearly didn't run him at all—so I'd like to think we'll see improvement as he's physically a better horse now. Camden is a good horse, and Rossmore Lad walked through a hurdle that day when second to him at Fontwell.

Getaway Driver (Ire) (h88) 4 br.g Zagreb (USA) – Catch The Mouse (Ire) (Stalker) 2010/11 F17s² F16g⁶ :: 2011/12 16m² 19g May 5 I like him, but I don't think he's anything special. I told Felix (de Giles) to drop him out on his latest start, but I didn't think he'd drop him out five lengths last! He'll need a couple more runs for a mark I'd imagine, and then we'll look to handicap company. He'll jump a fence one day, too.

Bumpers

Magnifique Etoile (F113) 4 b.g Kayf Tara – Star Diva (Ire) (Toulon) 2010/11 F14s³ F16g4 F16d² :: 2011/12 F17g* Sep 24 He was a weak horse last year, and he's never going to be big, but he's improved and improved. I was going to go straight hurdling with him, because he's a brilliant jumper, but I thought that on his form to date he should be winning a bumper and he did just that in great style at Market Rasen recently.

Hayjack (F104) 6 b.g Karinga Bay – Celtic Native (Ire) (Be My Native (USA)) 2010/11 F17g⁵ F17s* F17s² Mar 7 He won a bumper at Hereford last season for Venetia (Williams). We were going to run him, but the ground went against him. He's a lovely big hurdler/chaser in time, and he could be quite nice over two and a half miles on soft.

Hazy Tom (Ire) (F101+) 5 b.g Heron Island (Ire) – The Wounded Cook (Ire) (Muroto) 2010/11 F17m* :: 2011/12 F16m* Sep 23 I was waiting for when that one was going to come out! If you ask my head lad and me which are our horses to follow this season, he'd struggle between Hazy Tom and Be My Present, and I would say Hazy Tom. We don't think we've had as nice a bumper horse as him before, and he made it two from two with a smart performance at Worcester recently. He's won a point-to-point in Ireland already, so longer-term he'll make a jumper. I've got a lot of time for him.

Be My Present (F95+) 4 b.f Presenting – Simply Divine (Ire) (Be My Native (USA)) 2010/11 F16g* Mar 5 She was impressive that day at Kempton when winning against the boys—I haven't had a Presenting with so much speed before, and I loved the way she travelled. She will run in another bumper, and the ultimate aim for her is to get her some black type; we think she's good enough for that, and we'll have a look at the listed bumper at Cheltenham in November.

VISIT TIMEFORM ONLINE

timeform.com The full Timeform service for Britain and Ireland. Timeform Race Cards, with full commentaries and Timeform ratings for £5 each, Race Passes from £2.50 a day and much more. Register free!

timeform.com/free Daily runners and riders plus specially designed short commentaries for an overview of the action at each meeting in Britain, Ireland and North America.

timeform.com/radio Live analysis and commentaries for British racing, plus regular podcasts (also available through iTunes) featuring reviews and interviews.

timeform.com/shop Order Timeform mail order publications and services online

Future Stars

Highlighting the talented trainers and jockeys who've escaped the attentions of the wider public can be as vital as identifying underrated horses. To that end, Timeform's experts have chosen five racing figures—three trainers and two jockeys—who look well worth keeping on side in 2011/12.

Brian Ellison

Name	**BRIAN ELLISON**
Base	Malton, North Yorkshire
First Full Licence	1989
First Jumps Winner	Corbitt's Diamond, Hexham, 10/11/89
Total Winners	540
Best Horse Trained	Latalomne (Timeform Rating 162)

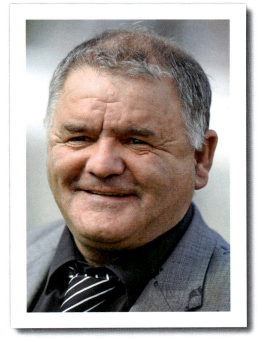

It may seem strange rather perverse to include a trainer as a potential 'Future Star' when he's already saddled more than five hundred winners in a career spanning over twenty years, but there's been such a notable upward shift in Brian Ellison's results in the last season or so—one that almost certainly hasn't been given the credence in the wider racing world it warrants—that the dual-purpose handler fully deserves inclusion in any such list.

Helped by better horses, plus increased investment, since his turn-of-the-century switch from North Yorkshire from his native North East, Ellison has impressed just about as much as any trainer in recent years, to the extent he's now to be considered, pound for pound, as one of the best in his profession.

All horses seem to come alike to Ellison, from juveniles to winners in staying chases, but it is his skill at improving his inmates that has left the deepest impression, especially when it comes to drawing progress out of those he's inherited from other hands. Note for instance Ellison's handling of such as Pravda Street and Mon Brav on the Flat this year, not to mention the likes of Bothy and Bocciani over jumps in 2011/12.

Trainer's Horse To Follow: When **Neptune Equester** is stepped up to three miles and back on softer ground he'll be one to keep on side. He jumped brilliantly when third at Market Rasen in September but just couldn't quicken.

Anthony Honeyball

Name	**ANTHONY HONEYBALL**
Base	Mosterton, Beaminster
First Full Licence	2006
First Jumps Winner	Classic Fair, Taunton, 18/12/06
Total Winners	41
Best Horse Trained	As de Fer (Timeform Rating 136)

There was only ever going to be one destination for Anthony Honeyball when his career as a rider was voluntarily cut short as a twenty-five year old. Honeyball's father, John, sent out The Dikler to win his first race in points, and Honeyball himself hadn't known anything other than horses since leaving school at sixteen to embark upon his life in the saddle; and having learnt the ropes during years spent riding out for such as Paul Nicholls and point-to-point maestro Richard Barber, a future as a trainer was always on the cards.

There's a way to go before Honeyball matches his mentor's exploits, but the early results could hardly have been more positive, save for the 2009/10 season, during which the yard was hit by a virus. That was no more than a blip though, with Honeyball recording huge level-stake profits both seasons either side, while 2011/12 has started even more positively, as a strike-rate in excess of 36% firmly attests.

The quality of the string is improving all the while, and Honeyball's recent exploits in improving markedly the likes of As de Fer, Gan On and Cash Back should ensure the yard continues to thrive.

Trainer's Horse To Follow: I think both early, and late, in the season, **Fountains Flypast** will be interesting. He'll run again in October and be kept going for when the ground is decent during the winter, and in March time he'll go into beginners' chases. He could be useful—if I think he's up to winning handicaps off 120, as I do, then he must be quite tidy.

David O'Meara

Name	**DAVID O'MEARA**
Base	Nawton, York
First Full Licence	2010
First Jumps Winner	Viva Colonia, Wetherby, 30/10/10
Total Winners	6 (plus 69 on Flat)
Best Horse Trained	**Blue Bajan** (Timeform Rating 151)

David O'Meara is hardly the first journeyman jumps jockey to have made a far bigger splash in his second career training horses rather than riding them, and the fledgling handler, who recently entered just his third year in his new venture having taken over the reins from James Hetherton in June 2010, seems to have all the tools required to make another step forward in 2011/12.

Supported by Roger Fell, owner in years gone by of prolific Flat winner Blue Maeve and dual-purpose performer River Logic, O'Meara has made fine strides in his brief time in the training ranks, saddling twenty-five winners on the level in his first year and closing in on the half-century by the end of September of his second: his handling of ex-Andy Turnell inmate Blue Bajan, a potential big-time player back over timber should connections wish to take that path, has made for particularly impressive viewing.

O'Meara has hitherto concentrated less on National Hunt racing, but there's still been more than enough in his work with the likes of Viva Colonia and King In Waiting to suggest he's just as adept at getting the maximum out of a jumper. Indeed, O'Meara's 2011/12 jumps strike-rate at the time of writing stands at a staggering 42%, with a handful of winners to his name and a level-stake profit in excess of £20. Here's hoping, rather expecting, more of the same.

Trainer's Horse To Follow: Our best jumper would be **Viva Colonia**. He improved rapidly this summer—he strengthened up, and Denis (O'Regan) got a great tune out of him. He's off 137 now and he'll contest the likes of the Ladbroke at Ascot, but if he's not up to that he'll go chasing in the New Year— he's already schooled and uses himself very well.

Michael Byrne

Name	**MICHAEL BYRNE**
Attached Stable	Tim Vaughan
First Ride	27/11/09
First Winner	Dipity Doo Dah, Market Rasen, 26/09/10
Total Winners	7
Best Horse Ridden	**Scotsbrook Cloud** (Timeform Rating 132)

It's never a bad thing when a young rider finds himself attached to a yard as prolific as Tim Vaughan's, though that's not to imply that Michael Byrne's promising start as a jockey is linked solely to the prowess of his stable.

Byrne has impressed in little time since his swift switch to the paid ranks last year, opening his account that September with a well-judged come-from-behind ride aboard Dipity Doo Dah in a bumper at Market Rasen.

A move to Vaughan soon arose, and Byrne really served notice of his talents during the summer of this term, steering home six winners in a two-month period, all bar one of which came for his employer.

Byrne still has some room to manoeuvre before his very good value allowance is cut to 5 lb, but even then, with further experience to call upon, he'll be a conditional to keep on side.

Kielan Woods

Name	**KIELAN WOODS**
Attached Stable	Charlie Longsdon
First Ride	27/11/09
First Winner	Heroes Square
Total Winners	15
Best Horse Ridden	**Ostland** (Timeform Rating 134)

Teenage rider Kielan Woods had steered home only three winners in a year-long period in his native Ireland prior to joining Charlie Longsdon's stable. The upturn was almost immediate, though, as the pairing of an evidently very capable young rider with a trainer also going places blended perfectly.

Having had to wait for around a month to receive his licence from the BHA, Woods made up for lost time on finally getting back into the saddle, piloting a winner for his new employer aboard Be My Light on his first day riding in Britain, on just his second ride. It took barely any longer for Woods to show that success aboard a hitherto frustrating mare was no flash in the pan, with Accordintolawrence doubling the jockey's British tally at Fontwell just two days later.

Several more successes have followed for Woods—he's now in double-figures in Britain, fast approaching twenty—and his prevailing 7 lb claim continues to look a steal. It promises to be another productive campaign for both trainer and rider.

JURY

OVER £15,000 PROFIT SINCE LAUNCH*

The expert panel has delivered continuous success over 3 years.

It's the best verdict on the day's racing!

Find out more and view a complete record of all bets advised at timeform.com/jury

*Based on £50 per point at advised prices 10/09/08 – 30/09/11

☎ 01422 330540
timeform.com/shop

TIMEFORM
THE HOME OF WINNERS SINCE 1948

The Team at

There's no better accompaniment to a day's racing than the growing phenomenon that is Timeform Radio. With in-depth coverage of every meeting, including expert opinions, real-time commentaries and big-name interviews, as well as a whole host of podcasts, featuring daily previews and reviews, Timeform Radio is in a league of its own. In this new section, some of Timeform Radio's regular presenters and pundits give us their horse to follow for 2011/12.

Chris Barnett
First Lieutenant (Ire)   h149

6 ch.g Presenting – Fourstargale (Ire) (Fourstars Allstar (USA))

Made a winning debut in the Irish point to point sphere in February 2010 and was soon snapped up by the Gigginstown House Stud as a likely future chaser. Being by Presenting, the new owners had returned to a well-known source of National Hunt winners. Presenting's CV already included top-class chasers such as Denman, Woolcombe Folly, Ballabriggs and War of Attrition, the last-named representing the same owner/trainer combination as First Lieutenant.

First Lieutenant had a cracking first season over hurdles, two of his three wins coming in Grade 1 contests. At Leopardstown in December he edged out Zaidpour in the Future Champions Novices' and then went on to show further improvement when stepped up to twenty-one furlongs in the Baring Bingham at Cheltenham, where he gave another battling display to beat Rock On Ruby by a short head. Trainer Mouse Morris has always seen First Lieutenant as a chaser in the making and there could be even better to come from this big gelding when he goes over fences this season. All being well he will be back at the Cheltenham Festival in March, more than likely in the RSA Chase over three miles than the Arkle over two. **Mouse Morris, Ireland**

Graham Cunningham
Muldoon's Picnic (Ire)   h127
5 b.g King's Theatre (Ire) – Going My Way (Henbit (USA))

Back in the heyday of the music hall in the late-19th century, Muldoon's Picnic was a popular comedy show based at Hyde & Behman's theatre in New York. The phrase has also come to be used for describing any spontaneous gathering of boisterous individuals, and there should certainly be a few glasses raised to the equine Muldoon's Picnic in racecourse bars when he takes centre stage over fences in the coming season. Kim Bailey's gelding showed considerable promise in landing a bumper on his racecourse debut and didn't take long to show useful form over hurdles, winning at Huntingdon first time up before creating an equally-strong impression in defeat in three subsequent starts at Newbury, Doncaster and Aintree. Enthusiastic galloping and accurate jumping were the hallmarks of Muldoon's Picnic's short time over hurdles. He needs only to transfer those assets to fences to be sure of winning races for his resurgent handler. **Kim Bailey**

Rory Delargy
Captain Chris (Ire)   h142+ c156p
7 b.g King's Theatre (Ire) – Function Dream (Ire) (Strong Gale)

There's a temptation in picking one to follow over jumps to find a twice-raced novice hurdler who has the potential to become the next Denman, but taking new blood over established performers is a risky business and I prefer to find one already forged in the furnace of top-class competition. Captain Chris may be an unoriginal choice, then, but I maintain that we haven't come close to seeing the full extent of his talent yet.

Diana Whateley's son of King's Theatre has finished no worse than second since his debut and improved rapidly in the second half of last season to land the Arkle at Cheltenham and the Ryanair Novices' Chase at Punchestown. It's an odd thing to say, but I was equally impressed by his defeats despite those three runners-up spots in novice chases representing lesser form. When beaten by the more precocious Ghizao at Cheltenham and Newbury, and again by Medermit at Sandown, it was notable that while his now-assured jumping was a work in progress, Captain Chris saw his races out thoroughly on each occasion; in fact, he very nearly caught Medermit in the Scilly Isles. Such displays show that he possesses both character and stamina in abundance to go with his proven class, and he's likely to go on to still-loftier heights. Already proven over two and a half miles, Captain Chris is out of the classy mare Function Dream, who was highly adaptable in terms of trip. Whether he'll ever stay the Gold Cup trip is open to debate, but there's little doubt that the three miles of the King George will be within his compass, and there's hardly a Grade 1 chase in the calendar which would be unsuitable for him, meaning that Philip Hobbs can place him when and where he wants. **Philip Hobbs**

Rory sees Captain Chris as one to keep following

Alan Dudman
The Strawberry One   h134
6 ch.m Kadastrof (Fr) – Peppermint Plod (Kinglet)

This dual bumper winner began to thrive over hurdles in the spring and summer, rattling up a hat-trick of wins in novice events at Towcester in May before going on to show useful form when switched to handicaps. The Strawberry One made her handicap bow at Hexham the following month and acquitted herself well against more experienced rivals in finishing second to Maska Pony, and her ability shone through again on her next start in a highly-competitive race at Market Rasen during their valuable summer card. She was held up that day, made ground stylishly and went down fighting to the useful Westlin' Winds, proving her ability to cut it at such an exalted level.

A strong-travelling mare who jumps fluently and is effective at up to twenty-one furlongs, The Strawberry One acts on good to firm and good to soft ground. She's not very big, but she more than makes up for that with her enthusiasm and her battling qualities will continue to stand her in good stead this season.
David Arbuthnot

Will Hayler
Dark Ranger   h104+
5 b.g Where Or When (Ire) – Dark Raider (Ire) (Definite Article)

It has been down to Neil King and Lucy Wadham to fly the flag for jumps racing in Newmarket in recent seasons, and both have done well with strings of limited size and ability. Now the arrival of dual-purpose Group 1-winning trainer Tim Pitt in town will see a few more jumpers using the public schooling facilities on The Links. After making a winning debut over hurdles at Huntingdon last October, things didn't work out for Pitt's Dark Ranger. However, he has an official mark of 107, which looks very tempting not least because he is surely crying out for a stiffer test of stamina over jumps, having shown improved form stepped up markedly in trip on the Flat in 2011. 'I'm pleased someone else thinks he might be well treated, because I'd be disappointed if he's not up to winning off that mark over two and three quarter or three miles,' said Pitt. 'If the ground comes right for him in the spring I'll start looking for the right races.' Having clearly progressed on the Flat this year, there must be a good chance Dark Ranger can build on the promise of his final jumps start last season, a never-nearer fourth to the progressive Ultravox over brush hurdles at Haydock. His stamina now having been proven, expect him to be ridden more prominently now than was the case there and in previous starts. **Tim Pitt**

Paul Jacobs
Rubi Light (Fr)   h132   c162
6 b.g Network (Ger) – Genny Lights (Fr) (Lights Out (Fr))

Sometimes young horses have to be judged as much by their physical make-up as their racing record, and in the long striding, scopey Rubi Light we have a strong example of this. A raw-looking individual who covers an immense amount of ground, the six-year-old started off his 2011/11 campaign by making all to land a Sligo chase, galloping and jumping with real exuberance. Thereafter a handicap success off an official mark of 130 was followed by Rubi Light being pitched into the deep end when second to the very smart Golden Silver before trouncing sound yardstick Roberto Goldback in the Grade 2 Red Mills Chase. But the best was yet to come. Racing on less-testing ground, Rubi Light made light work of the Prestbury Park fences in the Ryanair Chase, stepping over the open ditch down

Rubi Light is Paul's tip for the top

the back as it it was a two-foot obstacle and making eventual winner Albertas Run look decidedly novicey on that line of fences. Rallying to finish third after his sole mistake three out, this raw youngster looks sure to strengthen up into his big frame again this year and will have plenty of opportunities to win some nice prizes. Raced only as far as twenty-one furlongs to date, Rubi Light is well worth a try at three miles. **Robert Hennessy, Ireland**

Alex Steedman
Oscars Well (Ire)   h152
6 b.g Oscar (Ire) – Placid Willow (Ire) (Convinced)

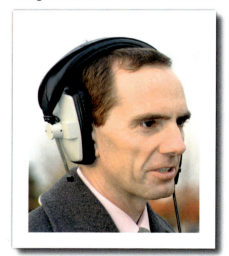

An obvious suggestion Oscars Well may be, but I think there is more to this horse than meets the eye. A sharp hurdler who seemed to get quicker as last season progressed, Oscars Well might well have won the Baring Bingham at Cheltenham but for an overzealous jump at the final hurdle. Two Grade 1 wins prior to that tell their own story; he is a horse of quality but I think he may be pigeon-holed as a middle-distance/staying chase prospect and for me he is better than that. This is a horse with bags of speed and I wouldn't be shocked if he developed into a Champion Hurdle contender. If not, Oscars Well is an obvious contender for two-mile chases building towards the Arkle. I am pretty sure he'll be top class wherever he goes. **Jessica Harrington, Ireland**

Ante-Post Betting

There's a certain romance attached to ante-post betting. Exactly what makes backing a winner several months in advance more exhilarating than doing so the morning of a race remains a mystery but, as with romance itself, to attempt to dissect it would remove all the fun. On the plus side, of course, one can usually secure more attractive odds by wading in at the ante-post stage. On the minus side, should your fancy be forced to miss the race for whatever reason—the excuses in 2010/11 ranged from eleventh-hour injuries to the fear of failing of a post-race drugs test—then you've done your money for good. Alas, anyone wishing a demonstration of the pitfalls of ante-post betting need look no further than this feature in last year's edition, when some dismal luck ensured that we didn't even get a single runner (let alone winner) from any of our nine selections in the stipulated races! Surely lightning can't strike twice…

In truth, it's not all doom and gloom with regards to ante-post betting as the advent of Betfair has arguably reduced the risks for those wishing to play early. Indeed, punters now have the option of laying off bets on the exchanges should their selection's odds shorten significantly during the build-up to the race, which means that one needn't necessarily back a winner in order to make a profit from ante-post punting—our 2011 ante-post Cheltenham Gold Cup selection Diamond Harry, for example, was down to as low as 7/1 (from our advised 25/1) when ruled out by injury late in the day. This development, coupled with the fact that those towards the head of any ante-post market aren't likely to alter dramatically in price unless injury or some other external factor comes into play, means that speculating is certainly the best way to accumulate in the ante-post sphere.

A prime example of this comes in the ante-post market for the 2012 Champion Hurdle, which is headed by title-holder Hurricane Fly at a best price of 7/4, with 10/1 or bigger the rest. There is absolutely no question that Hurricane Fly deserves his place at the head of the market having carried all before him in the latest campaign, emerging unbeaten from five starts at Grade 1 level— he cemented his position as the best two-mile hurdler around with a serene display at Punchestown for the final one of those wins and was awarded Timeform Horse of The Year (ahead of Big Buck's and Long Run) in the latest edition of *Chasers & Hurdlers*. However, 2010/11 was the only trouble-free season that Willie Mullins has enjoyed with Hurricane Fly so far, the somewhat fragile gelding having had to miss the Cheltenham Festival in both 2009 and

2010 due to frustrating setbacks. As a result, 7/4 doesn't look very appealing given such a backdrop and, given his cramped odds, Hurricane Fly isn't one to be interested in until 'non-runner no bet' offers become available. That doesn't mean there isn't value to be gleaned elsewhere in this ante-post market, though. The home-trained pair Spirit Son and Zarkandar, prominent players in the Supreme Novices' and Triumph Hurdle respectively, are closest to Hurricane Fly in the betting, but the half-mile longer Baring Bingham is often the Cheltenham Festival novice to follow when looking for a prospective Champion Hurdle contender. Multiple champions Istabraq and Hardy Eustace both landed this race en route to their historic wins, whilst the likes of Danoli, French Holly and Peddlers Cross all won it before being placed in the Champion twelve months later, the last-named gelding pushing Hurricane Fly close last March. **Oscars Well** might have finished only fourth in the latest renewal of the Baring Bingham, though he'd almost certainly have won but for a luckless mistake at the last and he'd also looked a high-class prospect when winning his three previous starts (including two Grade 1 novices). He appeals as Jessica Harrington's best horse since Moscow Flyer, whose hurdling exploits are often overlooked due to his subsequent legendary chasing career. Harrington was never afraid to take on the mighty Istabraq during this period—the head-to-head between the pair was actually two-one in Moscow Flyer's favour—and clearly isn't scared by Hurricane Fly judging by her decision to keep Oscars Well over hurdles for another season. He'll clearly need to find further improvement to trouble the favourite, but 20/1 appeals as decent each-way value at this stage.

It could be argued that each-way usually isn't the best way to go with ante-post betting, particularly as that option isn't really available to those trading on Betfair, but the safety net of a placed finish is also worth exploring with our King George VI Chase selection **Captain Chris**, who is currently available at a best price of 9/1. Long Run, understandably, is a short-priced favourite in the ante-post market for the Boxing Day showpiece and also the Cheltenham Gold Cup, having shown top-notch form when winning both races in 2010/11. Those results marked a changing of the guard, with the popular veterans Denman and Kauto Star filling the minor placings at Cheltenham, and it could pay to take on Long Run at the ante-post stage given that he's likely to face plenty of fresh rivals in 2011/12. This group seems set to include another Paul Nicholls inmate, the dual Queen Mother Champion Chase winner Master Minded, who is due to be upped in trip following an impressive win over two and a half miles at Aintree on his final start last season. Last season's Arkle winner Captain Chris is also unproven beyond two and a half miles, but he's often given the impression that he'll stay further and could emerge as the greater danger given that he still looks open to improvement. He's currently on the same Timeform rating as Long Run was at the same stage of his career, whilst his very consistent record—he's finished first or second on all ten of his career starts over jumps—suggests he'll be up to bringing home the place money even if unable to dethrone that rival.

The vast majority of Arkle winners, of course, are kept to the minimum trip and can boast an excellent record in the Queen Mother Champion Chase, with Sizing Europe becoming the latest to win both races last March—Remittance Man, Klairon Davis, Flagship Uberalles, Moscow Flyer, Azertyuiop and Voy Por Ustedes are the others to have done the double in the past twenty years. You have to go back to 1986 (Buck House) to find the last Arkle runner-up who's gone one better in the two-mile championship twelve months later, but plenty who've been placed in the Arkle since then have gone on to figure prominently in the Queen Mother (including dual winner Barnbrook Again) and we certainly expect **Finian's Rainbow** to take plenty of beating in Wednesday's showpiece at the 2012 Festival. If anything, Finian's Rainbow shaped like the best horse for much of the way in the latest Arkle, jumping very boldly in front under a forceful ride only to be outstayed by Captain Chris late on. That Arkle second place remains his only defeat from five starts over fences and he looks the safest option at the ante-post stage—Sizing Europe has a history of niggling problems (he was tubed when winning the Queen Mother), whilst 2010 Queen Mother winner Big Zeb will be eleven come next March and is also likely to be without his regular partner Barry Geraghty who'll be claimed to ride Finian's Rainbow.

Nicky Henderson, of course, has saddled more Cheltenham Festival winners than any other trainer currently holding a licence and, hopefully, it won't just be Finian's Rainbow who'll be flying the flag for his stable on the second day of the 2012 Festival. Unbeaten hurdler **Bobs Worth** appeals as a hugely exciting staying novice chasing prospect and, even though it's clearly a risk to back a horse which has yet to jump a fence in public, the 10/1 on offer about him for the RSA Chase still looks reasonable value—particularly as the ante-post market for this race doesn't look anything like so competitive at this stage as the one for the 2012 Arkle. As for the Cheltenham Gold Cup itself, it is difficult to find many concrete alternatives to worthy favourite Long Run, particularly as the likes of Master Minded, Captain Chris, Riverside Theatre and Wishfull Thinking could go for the shorter Ryanair Chase instead. Therefore, it could pay to have a speculative trade on the Paul Nicholls-trained French import **Mon Parrain**, who is currently on offer at 33/1 and significantly bigger odds on Betfair. This imposing five-year-old has created an excellent impression on both starts on British soil to date, running out an effortless wide-margin winner of a three-mile Sandown handicap chase prior to finishing runner-up in the Topham Chase at Aintree. Admittedly a four-length defeat by Always Waining in the latter race hardly reads like Gold Cup form, but Mon Parrain again shaped like a top-class horse in the making that day, jumping superbly in the main and looking all over the winner for most of the way—he's certainly not the first good horse (eg: Crisp and Garrison Savannah) to have been found out by Aintree's long run-in, whilst he possibly paid for racing close up in a fiercely-run race which saw the course record lowered. Connections are reportedly still undecided over this gelding's trip requirements and will make plans after starting him off in the Paddy Power Gold Cup at Cheltenham in November. If he was to win that race impressively, then there should certainly be an opportunity to lay off that Gold Cup bet.

For all that the Cheltenham Festival dominates the National Hunt season, the biggest betting race of the year remains the Grand National and there could be some value at this early stage. A strong mention should go to Prince de Beauchene, who coped splendidly with Aintree's stiff Mildmay fences in April when winning the same race that Don't Push It won twelve months prior to his National win. Prince de Beauchene certainly ticks plenty of boxes as a potential National candidate, though it seems that plans for him are fluid (he's absent in most ante-post lists) after being transferred to Willie Mullins following the ban for his former trainer Howard Johnson this summer. **Western Charmer** (40/1) and **Baby Run** (33/1) are the others who catch our eye as things stand, especially as their prominent style of racing has increasingly proved an asset on the National course in recent years. Western Charmer has a bit of class about him and performed with credit in defeat against some to the leading Irish staying novices of last season prior to finishing a fine second to Organisedconfusion in the Irish Grand National at Fairyhouse on Easter Monday. That race has proved a good trial for Aintree in recent years—Bobbyjo and Numbersixvalverde both won the following season's English version after their Irish wins, whilst 2011 Aintree runner-up Oscar Time had filled the same spot at Fairyhouse twelve months earlier. Another plus for Western Charmer is that his trainer Dessie Hughes clearly knows a thing or two about preparing horses for the National fences, having saddled two winners of the Becher Chase in Black Apalachi and Vic Venturi (the former also finished a fine second in the 2010 National). The 'Aintree factor' shouldn't be ignored when assessing National hopefuls and it's usually desirable to have at least one selection with previous experience of the unique fences. Baby Run certainly falls into that category having claimed a memorable win in the latest renewal of the Fox Hunters' there in April, producing an assured display of jumping under his young jockey Willy Twiston-Davies. Given that Willy has since followed elder brother Sam into the professional ranks, it seems most unlikely that 'family pet' Baby Run will be confined to hunter chases from now on—he finished a fine third in the bet365.com Gold Cup at Sandown when switched to handicap company for his final 2010/11 outing—and this most likeable veteran (he'll be twelve in 2012) should give punters a good run for their money if turning up in the big race itself next April.

After last year's debacle, we're quite keen to just secure an ante-post runner in 2011/12 following last year's whitewash in this section! At least our final selection will guarantee us a runner, that of **Nicky Henderson** at 7/4 to win the National Hunt Trainers' Championship. Paul Nicholls, of course, will again be a very tough nut to crack having won the last six titles, but there were signs in the latest season that his dominance wasn't quite so strong. Indeed, Henderson represents decent value at those odds as he has good claims of being able to outflank his main rival in terms of both quantity and quality (the championship is decided on prize money)—his string swelled to two hundred horses in 2010/11, whilst his big-race team (including the likes of Long Run, Finian's Rainbow and Bobs Worth) is also arguably the strongest in the country at present.

Ante-post Selections		
Selection	Event	Odds
Captain Chris	*King George VI Chase*	(9/1 e-w)
Oscars Well	*Champion Hurdle*	(20/1 e-w)
Bobs Worth	*RSA Chase*	(10/1)
Finian's Rainbow	*Queen Mother Champion Chase*	(10/1)
Mon Parrain	*Cheltenham Gold Cup*	(33/1)
Western Charmer	*Grand National*	(40/1)
Baby Run	*Grand National*	(33/1)
Nicky Henderson	*2011/12 National Hunt trainers' championship*	(7/4)

In Perspective

The daily reports of Timeform's representatives on the course form the basis of *Timeform Perspective*. Their observations, supplemented by those of Timeform's handicappers and comment writers, make *Timeform Perspective* thoroughly informative. Here are some key races from the 2010/11 British jumps season chosen from the Timeform Formbook.

CHELTENHAM Saturday, Nov 13
GOOD to SOFT (Old Course)

2361 Paddy Power Gold Cup Chase (Hcap) (Gr 3)   2½m110y (16)
(1) (164) (4yo+) £85,515

2105*	LITTLE JOSH (IRE) *NA*Twiston-Davies 8-10-5[146] SamTwiston-Davies[3]... 20/1		1
2099[2]	DANCING TORNADO (IRE) *M*Hourigan,Ireland 9-9-13[142] APHeskin[5] 20/1		2¾ 2
4133[3]	LONG RUN (FR) *NJ*Henderson 5-11-1[158] MrsWaley-Cohen[5] 5/2 2/1f		2 3
4537*	MAD MAX (IRE) *NJ*Henderson 8-11-5[157] BarryGeraghty 8 15/2		12 4
1957[2]	Poquelin (FR) *PF*Nicholls 7-11-7[164] IanPopham[5] 16 14/1		6 5
4163*	Great Endeavour (IRE) *DEP*Ipe 6-10-4[142] TimmyMurphy............. 5/1		2¼ 6
4163[2]	Sunnyhillboy (IRE) *Jonjo*O'Neill 7-9-12[139] RichieMcLernon[3] 11 12/1		3¾ 7
1859*	Edgbriar (FR) *PR*Webber 8-10-7[145] (s) DominicElsworth 33/1		4½ 8
1863[3]	Pigeon Island *NA*Twiston-Davies 7-10-0[138] (b) PaddyBrennan 25/1		1½ 9
2096[3]	Catch Me (GER) *EJO'*Grady,Ireland 8-10-5[143] AndrewJMcNamara 8 10/1		1½ 10
1859	Passato (GER) *Miss*JSDavis 6-10-1[139] (t) JamieMoore................ 66/1		14 11
1526[3]	Finger Onthe Pulse (IRE) *TJ*Taaffe,Ireland 9-10-11[149] (t) APMcCoy 20 18/1		5 12
2138[5]	The Sawyer (BEL) *RH*Buckler 10-10-1[146] NathanSweeney[7] 25/1		6 13
2138[f]	Tchico Polos (FR) *PF*Nicholls 6-11-1[153] (t) NoelFehily............... 20/1		f
1859[f]	Gwanako (FR) *PF*Nicholls 7-10-10[148] NickSchofield................. 33/1		f
2084	Can't Buy Time (IRE) *Jonjo*O'Neill 8-10-7[145] DougieCostello....... 50/1		pu
1986[2]	Awesome George *AK*ing 6-9-11[138] CharlieHuxley[3].................. 33/1		pu
2105[3]	Door Boy (IRE) *JH*owardJohnson 7-10-0[138] BrianHughes 40/1		pu

2.35race Mr Tony Bloom 18ran 5m12.79

Invariably one of the best-qualityhandicaps of the season and this renewal lacked nothing in those terms, with the proven class of the likes of Long Run, Poquelin and Mad Max as well as several up-and-comers further down the weights, a pair of whom came to the fore, Little Josh and Dancing Tornado both second-season chasers showing progress; the winner dominated from the off, setting a good pace (eased briefly mid-race), but still seeming to benefit from his position as little got involved, Dancing Tornado worth more credit with that in mind. **Little Josh** is transformed since last season, his jumping now an asset, and that's the key factor to the big progress he's making, defying a stiff-looking mark with a smart performance in this competitive affair, and there is some scope to do even better if he can hold it together; admittedly, his position at the head of affairs seemed an advantage, even though he went fairly hard for the most part, as little made an impact from off the pace, or threatened to for that matter, but his promising rider is worth praise for easing things slightly mid-race before piling it on again from around 4 out, Little Josh showing a most willing response and beginning to tire only in the last 150 yards; he'll reportedly bid for a big-handicap double in the boylesports.com Gold Cup here next month, which will clearly require further improvement even allowing for the fact that race tends to be rather less competitive than this one. **Dancing Tornado** isn't the most fluent of jumpers as a rule (made no notable mistakes here), so he's no banker to repeat this big effort next time, but it was an excellent run on the day, particularly as he came from so far back, still with loads to do approaching 3 out and staying on strongly; if his jumping does hold up, he will remain potentially well treated. **Long Run**'s talent isn't in doubt, capable of better than this in all likelihood, but his jumping has been his Achilles' Heel on both visits here, running a huge race from a high mark this day but likely to have gone close had he not made several mistakes, sloppy at the sixth, seventh and, more crucially, the third last and second last, testament to his ability that he was strong to the finish despite having lost ground and momentum; the King George is his next target and the return to Kempton, where he won the Feltham of course, may be in his favour, but all the same he'll be playing for a place at best if Kauto Star and Imperial Commander are on their game. **Mad Max** will have to improve to defy this mark but shaped for much of this as if he may have it in the locker, within himself until approaching 2 out, looking the main threat to the winner, and the trip perhaps stretched him at a stiff track, the emphasis much more on speed when he was successful in a Grade 2 at Aintree ending last season; he's raced only on good going or softer (acts on heavy). **Poquelin**'s positive comments after the Old Roan stand firm, still a big player in top races around this trip, and this probably just came too soon after Aintree, clearly primed for that day, and he didn't travel so fluently as usual. **Great Endeavour** remains with plenty of mileage from his mark, a 7 lb rise for his impressive win at the Festival when last seen certainly fair, and he'll be all the better for this reappearance, rather fresh, still taking a hold heading to 3 out, after which he tired under a hand ride; there is another valuable handicap to be won with him this season, especially considering he's totally unexposed at 3m+ (improved over hurdles on his only try). **Sunnyhillboy** gradually got to grips with chasing last season, ending on an upward curve (runner-up to Great Endeavour in Festival Plate), and this was an encouraging enough return, poorly placed and not at all knocked about, the run sure to sharpen him up, perhaps for a crack at the valuable boylesports.com Gold Cup at the next meeting here; he stays 21f and is unraced on going firmer than good (acts on soft). **Edgbriar**'s reappearance win came in a less competitive affair, the form already knocked a few times, and on this evidence he'll struggle in these valuable events. **Pigeon Island**'s bad jumping makes him very hard to predict. **Catch Me**'s mark is lenient on his hurdles form but he's not built for chasing and made too many mistakes to get seriously involved in this, already held when badly hampered 2 out; that said, it won't be a surprise if gets closer to his hurdles form on a track which places less emphasis on jumping ability. **Passato** peaked through the summer and no longer seems in anything like the same form. **Finger Onthe Pulse** isn't the most predictable nowadays and this was one of his poor efforts after another 2-month break. **The Sawyer** wasn't himself, game when on song but in trouble soon after halfway here; his yard aren't firing fully. **Tchico Polos** was just beginning to move into contention when taking a heavy fall at the fourth last, doing enough to suggest he remains in form, but it may take time to recover. **Gwanako**'s jumping hasn't been the same since he fell in the Topham (National fences) in April 2009, underlined by his failure to complete on both starts this season, just plugging on when crashing out at the second last here. **Can't Buy Time** is best over longer trips but his jumping was sloppy in any case. **Awesome George** has struggled with his jumping on all 3 chase outings at this track and was detached soon after halfway. **Door Boy** was towards the back when almost brought down by Tchico Polos' fall 4 out, soon eased.

HAYDOCK Saturday, Nov 20
SOFT

2526 Betfair Chase (Lancashire) (Gr 1) (1) (5yo+) 3m (18)
£112,460

4534 uf	IMPERIAL COMMANDER (IRE) *NA Twiston-Davies* 9-11-7 PaddyBrennan	10/11f	1
2090 3	TIDAL BAY (IRE) *JHowardJohnson* 9-11-7 BrianHughes............ 22	16/1	1¼ 2
4762*	PLANET OF SOUND *PJHobbs* 8-11-7 (t) RichardJohnson......... 8	17/2	8 3
2091*	Nacarat (FR) *TRGeorge* 9-11-7 PaulMoloney............................. 15/2	7/1	2¼ 4
4534	What A Friend *PFNicholls* 7-11-7 SamThomas	3/1	2¾ 5
2306 f	Atouchbetweenacara (IRE) *MissVeneta Williams* 9-11-7 AidanColeman	80/1	dist 6
4120*	Chief Dan George (IRE) *JamesMoffatt* 10-11-7 PaddyAspell........	33/1	27 7

3.25race Our Friends in the North 7ran 6m11.03

A high-quality renewal of the Betfair Chase, even without Kauto Star for the first time in 5 years, or any of last season's top novices for that matter, still attracting Gold Cup winner Imperial Commander as well as 3 others who've been successful at Grade 1 level; the winning performance is a bit short of recent standards, Tidal Bay's proximity holding it down, but Imperial Commander had things under control a long way out and was value for plenty extra; the pace was only fair to halfway, set by Atouchbetweenacara, but Paddy Brennan took the intiative on the winner after the ninth, ensuring a good test. **Imperial Commander** didn't have to match his Gold Cup-winning performance to gain a third Grade 1 success but got the job done readily and certainly left the impression he's returned as good as ever, jumping impeccably and always seeming in control after taking over at the tenth, merely pushed out as Tidal Bay came with a late burst; it's impossible to ignore Imperial Commander's patchy record, however, yet to give his running on consecutive starts since operating in top company, a big concern when dealing with his claims for the King George in less than 5 weeks time, especially as he returned with a cut leg after this, whilst he'll have his work cut out if Kauto Star's on-song there, anyway; whatever happens at Kempton, though, there's no doubt Imperial Commander has a big chance of recording back-to-back Gold Cup wins come March. **Tidal Bay** highlighted all that's been said before, that he's very talented but equally as quirky, almost matching his best form in the end but not looking likely to for much of the way, typically awkward when driven after 5 out and consenting to give his all only after the last, flattered by his proximity to Imperial Commander. **Planet of Sound** proved himself high class last term, winning a Grade 1 at Punchestown on his final start, and this was a respectable return from 7 months off, making no mistakes of note and not unduly knocked about once Imperial Commander asserted; he'll reportedly go to Kempton for the King George next. **Nacarat** deserves more credit than the bare result, shaping second best for a long way, still in that position at the last and eventually paying the price for being the only one to give chase to Imperial Commander; he seems as good as ever this season. **What A Friend** was disappointing on his reappearance, especially as he took the eye beforehand, hitting the eleventh and struggling soon after; a dual Grade-1 winner last season, he's a very smart chaser on his day but it's a bit disconcerting that connections felt the need to have his breathing operated on during the summer, especially in the light of how he performed here. **Atouchbetweenacara** was totally out of his depth but his jumping was at least better under a forceful ride and he shouldn't be totally dismissed if returned to handicaps, potentially very well treated of course. **Chief Dan George** ended last season on a high but was in nothing like the same form after 8 months off, admittedly facing a stiff task but beaten a long way out; he stays 4m and is almost certainly being brought along with a spring campaign in mind given his fine record at that time of year.

NEWBURY Saturday, Nov 27
GOOD

2674 Hennessy Gold Cup Chase (Hcap) (Gr 3) (1) 3¼m110y (21)
(182) (4yo+) £99,768

4133pu	DIAMOND HARRY *NickWilliams* 7-10-0[156] DarylJacob	7	6/1	1
4548¹	BURTON PORT (IRE) *NJHenderson* 6-10-1[157] BarryGeraghty...	7	15/2	1¼ 2
4762⁴	DENMAN (IRE) *PFNicholls* 10-11-12[182] SamThomas	9/2	4/1f	14 3
2091²	THE TOTHER ONE (IRE) *PFNicholls* 9-9-9[156] MrMahon⁵.........		28/1	½ 4
2221¹	Niche Market (IRE) *PFNicholls* 9-9-9[156] IanPopham⁵.............		40/1	¾ 5
2084⁶	Carruthers *MBradstock* 7-10-0[156] MattieBatchelor	16	14/1	3¼ 6
3340*	Taranis (FR) *PFNicholls* 9-10-4[160] (i) NickScholfield	12	14/1	4½ 7
2105*	Weird Al (IRE) *IanWilliams* 7-10-0[156] PaddyBrennan	13/2	6/1f	18 8
2525⁵	Hills of Aran *WKGoldsworthy* 8-10-0[156] JamieMoore		100/1	13 9
3678*	Silver By Nature *MissLucindaVRussell* 8-10-0[156] PeterBuchanan		25/1	dist 10
2136²	Madison du Berlais (FR) *DEPipe* 9-10-1[157] (s) TomScudamore......		16/1	f
2275²	Big Fella Thanks *FerdyMurphy* 8-10-0[156] GrahamLee		16 14/1	f
2275³	Hey Big Spender (IRE) *CLTizzard* 7-10-0[156] AidanColeman		25/1	f
	Neptune Collonges (FR) *PFNicholls* 9-10-8[164] APMcCoy		14/1	bd
2091	Barbers Shop *PJHenderson* 8-10-0[156] (b) AndrewTinkler		40/1	pu
4566pu	Dream Alliance (IRE) *PJHobbs* 9-9-9[156] (s) GilesHawkins⁵		66/1	pu
2994*	Pandorama (IRE) *NMeade,Ireland* 7-10-0[156] PaulCarberry...........		8/1	pu
2360	Razor Royale (IRE) *NATwiston-Davies* 8-9-11[156]			
	SamTwiston-Davies³........................		40/1	pu

3.05race Paul Duffy Diamond Partnership 18ran 6m27.85

The Hennessy is not just an early-season highlight but one of the races of the whole campaign and this was an excellent renewal, Denman's presence admittedly meaning that only 6 of them were in the handicap proper, but that didn't stop a pair of progressive second-season chasers pulling clear, both of them with top-class performances as Denman himself gave his running in third; there was a good gallop, as the fast time shows, but it was definitely some advantage to be close up, keeping out of any trouble that occured behind, Madison du Berlais' fall at the fourth in particular having repercussions for those held up. **Diamond Harry** has regularly promised a big performance and delivered even more than expected 8 months after flopping in the RSA Chase, not only showing top-class form but doing so readily, leaving the impression there is better still to come—although he's a way to go to scale the heights of Kauto Star, Imperial Commander and Denman, it must be stressed that Diamond Harry does have the potential to become a Cheltenham Gold Cup contender, if not this season then next, with time on his side too; his jumping gave cause for concern last term but it was a big asset this day, fluent right the way through, enabling him to travel powerfully, not asked for an effort until approaching the last and idling as Burton Port closed on the run-in; he'll reportedly have no more than 1 run between now and Cheltenham in March. **Burton Port** had an excellent novice season over fences, his 5 wins including 3 at Grade 2 level (also runner-up to Weapon's Amnesty in the RSA Chase), but this took him to the next level as he put up a top-class performance to pull so far clear of the rest, and it was despite a less-than-fluent round of jumping, having to regain momentum again after blundering 5 out and strong to the finish, albeit with Diamond Harry idling; he's likely to stay longer trips on this evidence and holds an entry in the Welsh National next month, but there are also plenty of top-level races around this trip for him to contest in the coming months. **Denman** clearly retains all of his ability, this an excellent effort as he tried for a third Hennessy win from an 8 lb higher mark than 12 months earlier, almost matching that form, and it was only a pair of up-and-comers receiving loads of weights that proved too good in the end, Denman showing all his spark as he jumped brilliantly for the most part and was upsides until 3 out (slight error at the next when tiring); he is an outstanding chaser and should in no way be forgotten about with regards to the Gold Cup (won in 2008, runner-up both years since), connections reporting that Denman is likely to head straight there, which is no bad thing given some of his best efforts have come when fresh. **The Tother One** ran well in pure form terms but not for the first time didn't convince with how he went about it, making far too many mistakes to ever be a serious threat; his strong finish does reaffirm that he should be suited by further. **Niche Market** finished third in this race last term and, from an 8 lb higher mark, he achieved a similar level with this typically honest display, jumping safely just 3 weeks after his Wincanton fall (not tongue tied this time), sticking to his task; a return to further is sure to suit and his main target this season is the Grand National. **Carruthers** isn't firing yet but left the impression he will be soon, prominent until after 4 out and not knocked about once held; a very smart and genuine chaser, there are sure to be plenty of opportunities for Carruthers this winter. **Taranis** had things rather fall apart in front of him when winning the Cotswold at Cheltenham on his sole 2009/10 outing and it's possibly misleading in terms of the stamina he showed, effective at much shorter in his prime after all, and he didn't see this out having made smooth progress to 4 out; he's had injury problems and it remains to be seen how much racing he'll stand. **Weird Al**'s potential isn't written off just yet, unbeaten over jumps previously after all, and perhaps coming into this big-field scenario was a bit of a shock to his system having faced no more than 5 rivals previously over fences; he was looked after once his chance had gone too. **Hills of Aran** made mistakes on his return to fences and never threatened to get involved. **Silver By Nature** was on the back foot straight away after a mistake at the first and then hampered by Madison du Berlais' fall; a thorough stayer who acts well on heavy ground, Silver By Nature is worthy of consideration for valuable handicaps over further, starting with the Welsh National (runner-up in 2009). **Madison du Berlais** wasn't fluent at the third and crashed out at the next; he has plenty to prove at present, having ended last season out of sorts. **Big Fella Thanks** is usually a fairly assured jumper but he got no further than the third. **Hey Big Spender**'s jumping is rather indifferent but he was well held when falling at the last here, tired at the time after helping cut out much of the early running.

Neptune Collonges missed last season through injury and had a bad experience on this belated return, brought down at the fourth; he's always been a tough and genuine staying chaser at the highest level. **Barbers Shop** has lost his way, a change of headgear no help (blinkered). **Dream Alliance** went the wrong way after winning the Welsh National last season and gave no sign of a revival. **Pandorama** hit the second hard before being hampered after the fourth and was soon struggling; he'd been unbeaten over fences prior to this, though was withdrawn on vet's advice at the start on his intended reappearance (reportedly bled) earlier this month, so has got a bit to prove at present. **Razor Royale** predictably found life tough from 10 lb out of the weights.

LEOPARDSTOWN Tuesday, Dec 28
SOFT

2817 Lexus Chase (Gr 1) (5yo+) £78,814   3m (17)
2674 pu PANDORAMA (IRE) *NMeade* 7-11-10 PaulCarberry 7/2jf   1
3472 6 MONEY TRIX (IRE) *NickyRichards,GB* 10-11-10 DavyRussell 7/1   6 2
2261 4 JONCOL (IRE) *PaulNolan* 7-11-10 AlainCawley .... 5/1   ¾ 3
2756 4 Glencove Marina (IRE) *EGriffin* 8-11-10 BarryGeraghty 16/1   2½ 4
2108 1 The Listener (IRE) *NickMitchell,GB* 11-11-10 AndrewJMcNamara 10/1   4½ 5
2756 2 J'Y Vole (FR) *WPMullins* 7-11-5 DavyCondon 7/1   9 6
4566 1 Vic Venturi (IRE) *DTHughes* 10-11-10 (s) PaddyFlood 25/1   12 7
2567 4 Siegemaster (IRE) *DTHughes* 9-11-10 (s) RogerLoughran 33/1   7 8
2545 5 Notre Pere (FR) *JTRDreaper* 9-11-10 AELynch .... 14/1   dist 9
2756 pu Mossbank (IRE) *MHourigan* 10-11-10 APHeskin 50/1   4 10
2758 3 Kempes (IRE) *WPMullins* 7-11-10 APMcCoy .... 9/1   ur
2756 5 Cooldine (IRE) *WPMullins* 8-11-10 PaulTownend .... 7/2jf   pu
2.35race Mr R. J. Bagnall 12ran 6m30.00

A competitive renewal of this Grade 1 on paper but it was taken in convincing style by the well-backed Pandorama, the first Irish-trained winner of the race since Beef Or Salmon in 2005 and the only member of this field with the potential to prove a force in the top staying chases in Britain; The Listener set a sound pace. **Pandorama** looks the leading staying chaser in Ireland after this high-class display and should take all the beating in the Hennessy back here in February, losing ground on the leader with a slow jump 3 out but taking over on the bridle approaching the last and asserting in good style for a few smacks after a big jump there; the Cheltenham Gold Cup will reportedly only come under consideration if the ground is softer than good but he was understandably shortened in the betting, this form up there with what Diamond Harry and Burton Port achieved at Newbury. **Money Trix** ran as well as when filling the same position in this last season, not fluent at the tenth and staying on dourly after jumping the last still only in fifth; he was let down by his jumping in the Hennessy here last season but that is the only time he has been out of the first 2 when completing and he'll stay longer distances given the chance. **Joncol** was close to form returned to a more suitable trip, typically jumping slightly right at times waited with on the outside and plugging on under pressure; he followed third place in this with a narrow success in the Hennessy here last term but it's hard to see him doing so again if Pandorama turns up. **Glencove Marina** ran a blinder at a trip which clearly stretched him under the conditions, travelling smoothly most of the way and overhauled by a pair of stouter stayers after jumping the last in a close second. **The Listener** shaped as if retaining most of his ability on his return from 13 months off and is one that could make more of a race of it with the winner in the Hennessy, going with all of his old zest and he made most of the running, jumping boldly apart from when awkward 4 out and headed only off the home turn; he was reportedly sidelined by a tendon injury after a 15-length win in the JNwine.com Champion Chase at Down Royal on his only start last term. **J'Y Vole** ran better than when last in this in 2009/10 but went like a non-stayer, making a mistake in rear at the first, a lesser one at the tenth, and weakening after turning in under pressure just behind the leaders. **Vic Venturi** was never a factor on his first start since falling in the Grand National at Aintree in April, and presumably has that race as his long-term target again; the Becher Chase there and the Grade 2 Bobbyjo at Fairyhouse were among his 3 wins last term. **Siegemaster** wasn't totally disgraced in the face of a stiff task, especially as he blundered at the sixth when in a close second, weakening when slow 3 out. **Notre Pere** ran poorly minus his usual cheekpieces, behind by the eleventh, but is no longer up to this class in any case. **Mossbank** was in touch until 4 out but needs his sights lowering if he is to show some worthwhile form again. **Kempes** had a bit to do in eighth but still seemed to have something left to give when blundering and unseating 2 out. **Cooldine** has questions to answer again after being pulled up in this for the second year in succession, albeit showing up well for a long way this time, blundering 6 out and weakening quickly after jumping 2 out still in fourth, pulled up before the last.

KEMPTON Saturday, Jan 15
GOOD to SOFT

3146 William Hill King George VI Chase (Gr 1) (1)   3m (18)
(5yo+) £102,618

2361 3	LONG RUN (FR) *NickyHenderson* 6-11-10 MrSWaley-Cohen	13/2 9/2	1
2126 *	RIVERSIDE THEATRE *NickyHenderson* 7-11-10 BarryGeraghty	12 10/1	12 2
2226 *	KAUTO STAR (FR) *PaulNicholls* 11-11-10 (t) APMcCoy	4/7	7 3
2526 4	Nacarat (FR) *TomGeorge* 10-11-10 PaddyBrennan	14/1	5 4
2526 3	Planet of Sound *PhilipHobbs* 9-11-10 (t) RichardJohnson	20/1	39 5
2674 1	Madison du Berlais (FR) *DavidPipe* 10-11-10 (s) DannyCook	40/1	10 6
2517 1	Albertas Run (IRE) *JonjoO'Neill* 10-11-10 DougieCostello	33/1	pu
2387 2	Forpadydeplasterer (IRE) *ThomasCooper,Ireland* 9-11-10 RobertThornton	16 14/1	pu
2227 *	The Nightingale (FR) *PaulNicholls* 8-11-10 SamThomas	12 16/1	pu

3.00race Mr Robert Waley-Cohen 9ran 6m02.87

A January staging of the top mid-season chase, the 3-week delay caused by frost and snow after Christmas complicating matters for those who'd been brought to a peak for that original date, and that was perhaps a factor in so few of these runners giving their running here—the market was dominated yet again by Kauto Star, who was sent off at odds on for the fifth season running, though the outcome was very different from the previous 4; there are doubts about the lack of depth (in addition Imperial Commander was a notable absentee, whilst Denman and Diamond Harry weren't considered for the race) but the winner seemed to show form well up to standard for the race, a view supported by the time in what was a well-run contest. **Long Run** had impressed when winning the Feltham over this course and distance on his British debut and returned here to show himself a top-class chaser with a most authoritative display, impressing with the way he travelled and in general jumped, avoiding the mistakes that have littered his efforts round Cheltenham, clearly going better than the favourite from a fair way out and soon in control when sent on 3 out, well on top at the finish; he may yet have more to offer and obviously has the ability to figure prominently in the Cheltenham Gold Cup, but his jumping would need to be a fair bit better than it has been there twice before. **Riverside Theatre** produced an improved effort on his first attempt at 3m and might have done even better still without a bad mistake at the thirteenth, travelling well under a patient ride at the time but set back by it and unable to land a blow when ridden in the straight, staying on to take second; he holds an entry in the Ryanair at Cheltenham and this would suggest he'll be a serious contender for that, whilst something like the Betfair Ascot Chase might be an option before then. **Kauto Star**, who seemed ill at ease beforehand and has looked better in appearance, ran well below expectations for the second time in a year at the very highest level (later reported to have bled slightly), bringing to an end his run of 4 straight wins in this event and raising concerns about his competitiveness in top company; he was clearly not going so well as the winner from a long way out and was flat out after the fourth last, likely to finish no better than second when making a bad mistake 2 out; there must be a chance that age, plus wear and tear, have finally caught up with him and it would be a masterful piece of training to bring him back to anything like his best for this year's renewal of the Cheltenham Gold Cup, though it's worth stressing that he'd have place claims for that race even if judged on this season's form. **Nacarat** ran much as he had in last season's renewal, ensuring a good gallop and seeing off the majority of his rivals but finding the effort telling in the closing stages, no extra once headed (mistake 2 out also didn't help); such tactics have proved more effective in the last 2 renewals of the Racing Post Chase (won in 2009, runner-up in 2010) and it may be he'll take his chance under top weight again there. **Planet of Sound** probably isn't quite up to the highest level but this was still a flat effort on his part, under pressure at the thirteenth and unable to make any impression; he reportedly choked. **Madison du Berlais** turned in a lacklustre effort and just doesn't seem anything like the force of old, ridden along at halfway and soon behind. **Albertas Run** finished runner-up in the 2008 edition of this race but has run well below form in both subsequent renewals, clearly not right on this occasion and perhaps having been set back by his heavy fall last time (he reportedly now faces a spell on the sidelines). **Forpadydeplasterer** wasn't certain to be suited by the step-up to 3m but failed to run a race at all, behind at the tenth and pulled up before the twelfth, clearly not himself; he was later reported to have been clinically abnormal. **The Nightingale** took the eye beforehand but failed to make an impact in much tougher company, making a couple of significant mid-race mistakes and well behind after 5 out, clearly not himself; he was later reported to have a fibrillating heart.

CHELTENHAM Tuesday, Mar 15
GOOD (Old Course)

4192 Stan James Supreme Nov Hdle (Gr 1) (1) 2m110y (8)
(4yo+) £57,010

3585*	AL FEROF (FR) *PaulNicholls* 6-11-7 RWalsh	10/1	1
3602*	SPIRIT SON (FR) *NickyHenderson* 5-11-7 BarryGeraghty	11/2 5/1	2 2
3713*	SPRINTER SACRE (FR) *NickyHenderson* 5-11-7 APMcCoy	11/1	3¼ 3
2701²	Cue Card *ColinTizzard* 5-11-7 JoeTizzard	9/4 7/4f	1¼ 4
3698*	Recession Proof (FR) *JohnQuinn* 5-11-7 RobertThornton	10 12/1	1½ 5
3988*	Rathlin *PJRothwell,Ireland* 6-11-7 JasonMaguire	33/1	7 6
3596²	Zaidpour (FR) *WPMullins,Ireland* 5-11-7 PaulTownend	12 11/1	1½ 7
3291⁵	Spanish Treasure (GER) *AndyTurnell* 5-11-7 NickSchofield	66/1	¾ 8
3596	Far Away So Close (IRE) *PaulNolan,Ireland* 6-11-7 DavyRussell	66/1	4 9
3443*	Gibb River (IRE) *NickyHenderson* 5-11-7 AndrewTinkler	22/1	3¾ 10
3036*	Marsh Warbler *BrianEllison* 4-10-13 FearghalDavis	22/1	7 11
3596⁴	Hidden Universe (IRE) *DKWeld,Ireland* 5-11-7 MrRobbieMcNamara	16/1	10 12
3449*	Magen's Star (IRE) *TStack,Ireland* 6-11-0 DavyCondon	16 14/1	8 13
3880¹	Sheer Genius (IRE) *JohnJosephMurphy,Ireland* 6-11-7 AndrewJMcNamara	150/1	13 14
2521⁴	Dunraven Storm (IRE) *PhilipHobbs* 6-11-7 RichardJohnson	20/1	pu

1.30race Mr J. Hales 15ran 3m52.07

As had been the case last year, much of the build-up to the 2011 Supreme Novices' centred around one horse in long-time favourite Cue Card, but this time around there weren't any notable absentees and a blend of promising National-Hunt breds and good-quality horses from the Flat made for an above-average renewal; the result appeals as being very solid too, with 4 of the market leaders pulling clear off a sound pace after things began to develop fully from 3 out, whilst the presence of recent big-race winner Recession Proof in fifth gives some added substance to the form. **Al Ferof** is now fulfilling all of what his excellent bumper form promised and this very smart performance puts him ahead of most recent Supreme winners—there's no reason to doubt what he's achieved either, suited by this well-run race kept to 2m and staying on strongly from 2 out, having come off the bridle a bit earlier than the other principals; he may have better still to come over hurdles but is built to make a chaser (has a point-winning background) and could well be back as a leading Arkle candidate in 2012 should connections go down that route. **Spirit Son** fully confirmed the promise of his 2 easy wins in lesser company by running a screamer upped further in class and remains open to further improvement given that his relative inexperience seemed to show all round, not helping himself by sweating up and getting rather on edge in the preliminaries (brought late into the paddock), then proving green under pressure having travelled strongly to challenge 2 out, finding enough to lead briefly after the last but hanging markedly right to the near rail as soon as he got there; it's undecided whether he'll stay over hurdles or go chasing next season but, either way, he remains an excellent prospect. **Sprinter Sacre** confirmed himself a smart novice and is a top long-term prospect, arguably the best of this whole bunch, as it's sure to be over fences that he blossoms, the sort to be a big player for next year's Arkle should that be the chosen route; the way Sprinter Sacre travelled was particularly impressive, coming off the bridle last of all and flattening the final flight (jumped fluently otherwise) just as McCoy was getting into full flow, which halted his momentum somewhat; it's worth noting also how well he took this big occasion, in excellent shape and very relaxed beforehand. **Cue Card** had proven himself to be well above-average already, his previous 2 performances of a higher standard than what Al Ferof achieved here, but it's disappointing that he couldn't reproduce that level on this return from 3 months off—admittedly, he'd possibly not had the ideal preparation to have been off for that amount of time, but there was no real excuse as things developed in the race itself, a bit keen in mid-division but not overly so and just underwhelming once the pressure was on after making stylish headway to dispute the lead 2 out, his inclination to hang left up the hill slightly disconcerting; it is still very early days, however, and time may tell that longer trips are his optimum (already proven at 2½m), with fences also an option for 2011/12. **Recession Proof** has had a fantastic season, notching a valuable handicap win, and this was another good effort against the top novices, lacking the speed of the first 4 when things started to fully take shape but seeing things out as well as anything, leaving the impression any further improvement may come back over a longer trip (has won at 19f on heavy ground); he's one to note for the Flat season, incidentally, with his mark potentially very lenient after a quiet 2010 in that sphere. **Rathlin** has quickly made up into a useful novice, acquitting himself really well in face of this stiff task, only 10 days after his maiden win on Irish soil; he's an even better chasing prospect for next season, both bred and built for it (also a winning pointer). **Zaidpour**'s season has been an anti-climax after such a promising start but his previous efforts are still a fairer guide than this, starting to make a move from the rear when blundering 3 out and not unduly knocked about thereafter. **Spanish Treasure** appears to have performed above himself but it's best not to take this at face value for the time being, blundering his way around in rear and merely passing some tiring rivals late on. **Far Away So Close** filled the same spot as in last year's renewal but there's got to be a chance the 2 efforts flatter him to a certain extent, operating some way below this level otherwise. **Gibb River**'s wins have come at a significantly lower level and this seems to expose his limitations somewhat, off the bridle after the fifth and never a threat, his jumping not especially fluent. **Marsh Warbler** faced an ideal scenario when winning the Finale at Chepstow and was simply nothing like so effective in this well-run race on quicker ground, the stronger opposition a side issue given it was his jumping that fell to pieces. **Hidden Universe**'s potential isn't lost, a Grade 1 bumper winner having only his third start over hurdles here, and he clearly wasn't himself for whatever reason, beginning to weaken when baulked 3 out (eased). **Magen's Star** had made a good impression against her own sex in Ireland but just seemed to find this whole occasion too much, worked up beforehand (also raced keenly up with the pace) and let down by her jumping; there's little doubt that she's a useful mare under the right circumnstances. **Sheer Genius** can't be judged on this, totally out of his depth. **Dunraven Storm**'s hurdling career has hit the buffers on his last 2 starts but he's likely to bounce back, stopping quickly after 3 out having raced prominently on this return from 4 months off, reported to have lost a shoe and gone lame behind.

4193 Irish Independent Arkle Challenge Trophy Chase 2m (13)
(Gr 1) (1) (5yo+) £74,113

3846*	CAPTAIN CHRIS (IRE) *PhilipHobbs* 7-11-7 (t) RichardJohnson	15/2 6/1	1
3588*	FINIAN'S RAINBOW (IRE) *NickyHenderson* 8-11-7 BarryGeraghty	9/2 7/2	2¾ 2
3257*	REALT DUBH (IRE) *NoelMeade,Ireland* 7-11-7 PaulCarberry	8 17/2	6 3
3476*	Medermit (FR) *AlanKing* 7-11-7 RobertThornton	3 11/4f	¾ 4
2827*	Ghizao (GER) *PaulNicholls* 7-11-7 TimmyMurphy	7/2 4/1	19 5
3828*	Giorgio Quercus (FR) *NickyHenderson* 6-11-7 PaddyBrennan	33/1	4½ 6
3828²	Dan Breen (IRE) *DavidPipe* 6-11-7 (b) TomScudamore	20/1	½ 7
3476⁴	Rock Noir (FR) *JonjoO'Neill* 6-11-7 (t) APMcCoy	12 14/1	20 8
3588²	Stagecoach Pearl *SueSmith* 7-11-7 ShaneByrne	40/1	hd 9
1389*	West With The Wind *EvanWilliams* 6-11-7 PaulMoloney	33/1	pu

2.05race Mrs Diana L. Whateley 10ran 3m51.78

A smaller field than usual for this championship novice event, but it was run at a typically strong gallop, which tested both jumping and stamina, the winner a stouter stayer than the runner-up after both had jumped well; the form looks up to standard for the race, with the principals likely to make an impact in open company next season. **Captain Chris** finally delivered the sort of performance over fences his hurdling career and physique had promised, running here in preference to the Golden Miller and getting away with the shorter trip due to the strong pace plus the stiff uphill finish, outstaying the runner-up after getting slightly tapped for foot down the hill, his jumping crucially standing up very well despite the test of speed; there will surely be more to come when he returns to further and he's likely to make an impact at a high level next season. **Finian's Rainbow** might have lost his unbeaten record over fences but he emerged with considerable credit, just outstayed late on after helping force a strong gallop, impressing greatly with his jumping and with the way he travelled; he's more likely than the winner to win top 2m chases in open company and, with further improvement on the cards, looks capable of posing a serious threat to the best around next season. **Realt Dubh** ran creditably, coping well with less testing ground than he'd faced in Ireland this season, travelling strongly under a patient ride, looking as if he might do even better until he hit 2 out, his finishing effort (carried head awkwardly under pressure) the one disconcerting thing about his performance; he's sure to make an impact again at this level and will presumably have the Powers Gold Cup or a race at Punchestown on the agenda this spring. **Medermit** had beaten the winner over 2½m at Sandown but wasn't nearly so able to cope with the drop back to 2m, held up further off the pace and lacking the speed to land a blow, urged along from the top of the hill; he's done well over fences this season and may yet gain further success at this level back over further, but he probably lacks the potential of those that finished ahead of him. **Ghizao**, who took the eye beforehand, is best given another chance at this level (particularly as he's got 2 impressive defeats of Captain Chris on his record) as a bad mistake 4 out when still going well behind the leaders surely told against him in the end, still in touch 2 out but weakening after, finishing tired. **Giorgio Quercus** found this much more searching test in a larger field all too much on just his fourth start over fences, held up and never looking likely to make much progress; he'd looked a useful prospect previously and may yet do better when facing less exacting opposition. **Dan Breen**, with blinkers on, just went off too hard with the runner-up and Stagecoach Pearl, doing well to last until 3 out given that his jumping wasn't so fluent as that of the former. **Rock Noir**'s jumping wasn't up to scratch over these even more demanding fences and he never looked likely to take a hand after early mistakes; he may not be the easiest to place, though a return to hurdling must be an option. **Stagecoach Pearl** is probably flattered by some of his front-running efforts in small fields and, with competition for the lead this time, was firmly put his place in this stronger affair. **West With The Wind**'s summer form at Ffos Las perhaps isn't as good as it looks on paper and he was struggling from an early stage on this first start since August, his jumping lacking fluency as well; he may yet prove capable of useful form in calmer waters but isn't likely to be a force at all at this level.

4195 Stan James Champion Hdle Challenge Trophy 2m110y (8)
(Gr 1) (1) (4yo+) £210,937

3259¹	HURRICANE FLY (IRE) *WPMullins,Ireland* 7-11-10 RWalsh 3 11/4f	1
3679*	PEDDLERS CROSS (IRE) *DonaldMcCain* 6-11-10 JasonMaguire . 9/2	1¼ 2
3469*	OSCAR WHISKY (IRE) *NickyHenderson* 6-11-10 BarryGeraghty . 8 7/1	5 3
3259³	Thousand Stars (FR) *WPMullins,Ireland* 7-11-10 PaulTownend.... 33/1	2 4
2701¹	Menorah (IRE) *PhilipHobbs* 6-11-10 RichardJohnson 4 3/1	1¼ 5
2701⁴	Clerk's Choice (IRE) *MichaelBanks* 5-11-10 TomMolloy............. 50/1	2 6
3725⁵	Overturn (IRE) *DonaldMcCain* 7-11-10 GrahamLee 40/1	5 7
3732*	Dunguib (IRE) *PhilipFenton,Ireland* 8-11-10 BrianO'Connell 9 10/1	¾ 8
3145⁴	Khyber Kim *NigelTwiston-Davies* 9-11-10 PaddyBrennan 12/1	½ 9
3679²	Bygones of Brid (IRE) *KarenMcLintock* 8-11-10 TimmyMurphy... 200/1	10 10
3725*	Mille Chief (FR) *AlanKing* 5-11-10 RobertThornton 14 16/1	½ 11

3.20race George Creighton & Mrs Rose Boyd 11ran 3m53.70

This had promised for much of the season to be the strongest Champion Hurdle for several years and, although last year's winner Binocular was an enforced absentee due to concerns he would test positive after being treated for an allergy, it more than lived up to its billing, the first 2 good enough to have won at least 7 of the last 8 runnings; the pace was less strong than might have been expected, with the tempo slower than for the earlier Supreme Novices', picking up only going to 3 out—that said, the qualities traditionally required of a Champion Hurdle winner, a good turn of foot, the ability to travel strongly and slick jumping, were all in evidence from the winner. **Hurricane Fly** is building a superb record, producing one of the best performances in this race since the days of Istabraq, his turn of foot decisive in a race less strongly run than might have been anticipated, though he'd surely have won however the race had been run, impressing with how smoothly he travelled under a patient ride, his jumping fluent and straighter than it had been at Leopardstown, the only slight flaw his drifting right after the last as he was ridden out; there seems little reason why he shouldn't continue to be very hard to beat at the highest level, this effort setting a tough standard for the up-and-coming generation. **Peddlers Cross** ran a tremendous race despite losing his unbeaten record, this performance good enough to have won most recent editions of the Champion Hurdle, his slick jumping and battling qualities very much in evidence, just lacking slightly the turn of foot of the winner at the last after being ridden handily, briefly looking as if he might get back on terms but held as he was carried right in the last 50 yds; he may well switch to fences next season and ought to do really well in that sphere, though a further campaign over hurdles would likely be equally rewarding. **Oscar Whisky** acquitted himself well in a strong renewal of this race, despite slight mistakes at the second and third, pressing on with the runner-up 3 out but unable to quicken into the straight; he has the option of going back over further and presumably the Aintree Hurdle would be a possibility, whilst further good races are likely to come his way next season, particularly given the likely Irish-oriented programme of the winner here. **Thousand Stars** ran as well as he ever has, making the frame behind his stable companion in a Grade 1 for the fourth time, minor placings likely to continue to be the limit of his abilities at such a level; held up this time (raced keenly), he can actually be rated a shade better than the result after being forced wide as he made his effort into the straight. **Menorah** looked extremely well beforehand but was below his best, pushed along to challenge 3 out but unable to quicken with the principals into the straight and held in fourth when making a mistake at the last, fading thereafter; his physique suggests a switch to fences could bring greater reward and he'll surely be a strong contender for the Arkle in a year's time if that route is taken. **Clerk's Choice** has run well on all 3 starts at this track, this his best performance yet, never really threatening the principals but responding well to pressure after being held up and taken wide; this may be his limit as a hurdler, but he has some prospect of making a novice chaser of similar standard. **Overturn**, keen beforehand and in the race itself, wasn't able to match his Christmas Hurdle form, essentially not good enough after dictating a fair pace and already on the retreat when involved in scrimmaging into the straight; he's surely reached his limit as a hurdler and it may be that a switch to fences next season will be the most fruitful option, though a campaign in big Flat handicaps could also be on the cards. **Dunguib**, a bit edgy and tending to sweat beforehand, has been found wanting on both starts in open Grade 1 company and is in danger of having a 'lost' season after an essentially very promising novice campaign, held up and soon outpaced when the tempo increased 3 out; it's hard to see why he should trouble the winner were they to meet at Punchestown and perhaps a step-up in trip at Aintree may be the best means to salvage something, though a full campaign in novice chases next season seems to hold a more likely prospect of success. **Khyber Kim**, runner-up last year, was below his best after a much lighter campaign this time round, the run of the race not suiting him ideally either, soon outpaced when the tempo quickened 3 out; he'll presumably bid for a repeat success in the Aintree Hurdle but has a fair bit to prove regarding his current form. **Bygones of Brid** was out of his depth and on ground that probably wasn't ideal as well. **Mille Chief**'s best form, which had been shown on soft/heavy going, didn't look good enough for him to land a blow in a strong renewal and he struggled as soon as the pace picked up after being held up, eased before the last; he's not an obvious chaser on looks and may not be so easy to place over hurdles either from now on.

```
4197   David Nicholson Mares' Hdle (Gr 2) (1)           2½m (9)
       (4yo+ f+m)  £39,431
 4788*  QUEVEGA (FR) WPMullins,Ireland 7-11-5 RWalsh........... 10/11  5/6f   1
 3233*  SPARKY MAY PatrickRodford 6-11-5 KeiranBurke........... 4/1   10 2
 3849*  OCEAN TRANSIT (IRE) RichardPrice 6-11-0 DavidBass...... 50/1    1 3
 3233³  Alasi PaulWebber 7-11-0 DominicElsworth................ 33/1   ½ 4
 3798²  Stephanie Kate (IRE) CharlieSwan,Ireland 5-11-0 PaulCarberry .. 50/1 3¾ 5
 3233⁶  L'Accordioniste (IRE) NigelTwiston-Davies 6-11-0 PaddyBrennan  9 8/1  2½ 6
 3042¹  Banjaxed Girl NigelTwiston-Davies 7-11-5 SamTwiston-Davies ... 11 8/1  1 7
 2580³  Santera (IRE) JohnFlint 7-11-0 (s) RhysFlint.............. 40/1  1½ 8
 3695⁶  Miss Overdrive AndyTurnell 7-11-0 NickScholfield........ 100/1  2½ 9
 3042⁶  Alegralil DonaldMcCain 6-11-5 JasonMaguire............... 40/1   6 10
        La Vecchia Scuola (IRE) JimGoldie 7-11-0 (s) GrahamLee... 20/1  6 11
 3758³  Princess Rainbow (FR) JennieCandlish 6-11-0 AlanO'Keeffe . 200/1 4½ 12
 3178²  Lonesome Dove (IRE) CharlieSwan,Ireland 6-11-0 DJCasey .. 100/1  ¾ 13
 3042³  Silver Gypsy (IRE) KimBailey 6-11-0 (t) SeanQuinlan .... 25/1  ¾ 14
4.40race Hammer & Trowel Syndicate 14ran 4m48.31
```

A very similar race to the last 2 renewals of this race, with Quevega totally dominating a field that lacked any great depth as she completed a hat-trick of wins without needing to show her very best form; Banjaxed Girl and Silver Gypsy pressed each other into going too hard in front, favouring those held up. **Quevega** is a class apart amongst her own sex, a mare of her standard rarely seen, and she'll dominate this race for a few years to come in all likelihood, still only a 7-y-o after all and completing this hat-trick win just as easily as her previous 2, going powerfully under a patient ride and breezing clear after taking over approaching the last; she followed this with success in the World Series Hurdle at Punchestown last season and will surely take plenty of beating if defending her crown there as well. **Sparky May** failed to improve any more, no match for Quevega, but in doing best of the rest she underlined just how far she's come in this novice season and there are a lot more good mares' events to be won with her; there was an early scare as her rider did well to maintain the partnership after a blunder at the second (bumped by another runner) but otherwise she went smoothly and gave her all despite having no chance with the winner. **Ocean Transit** is clearly thriving but may prove a shade flattered by this bare result, as she benefited from being held up off the strong pace and closed up late without ever threatening. **Alasi** has held her form well this season and caught the eye for much of this, admittedly having things set up for her patient style but still remaining on the bridle for longer than all bar Quevega, tiring only in the last 150 yards; she does have a history of weak finishes, though. **Stephanie Kate** is another who faced a stiff task and did as well as she could, showing the fairly useful form she's capable of under a patient ride which suited. **L'Accordioniste**'s Ascot run was a blip and she's back in better form, still some way off her best in the end here but closer to the pace than ideal and not helped by a couple of scrappy jumps; she has the stature to do at least as well over fences as she has hurdles. **Banjaxed Girl** shaped better than the result suggests, overdoing things in disputing the early lead and worth praise for staying in the mix for as long as she did, headed only on the approach to 2 out; she's a possible for novice chasing next season and has the build of one who'll do well in that sphere. **Santera** was fit from a recent spin on the Flat but isn't up to this level, not at all discredited in the circumstances, particularly as she raced closer to the pace than ideal. **Miss Overdrive** cannot be knocked for this as she ran just about as well as could be expected in the face of a stiff task, but she's definitely not straightforward, sweating beforehand and going about things lazily. **Alegralil** hinted at a return to form after another 2 months off, weakening only after the third last and spared a hard race once held. **La Vecchia Scuola** improved on the Flat last year but was frequently let down by her jumping when last seen in this sphere back in 2008 and made no impact on this belated return after a sloppy round. **Princess Rainbow** had no chance in this company but highlighted her temperament even so, firstly pulling hard and then hanging as she lost touch. **Lonesome Dove** was aimed too high but made far too many mistakes, anyway. **Silver Gypsy** took Banjaxed Girl on for the early lead but there was more behind her capitulation after 3 out than that alone, all perhaps not well.

CHELTENHAM Wednesday, Mar 16
GOOD (Old Course)

4207 Neptune Investment Management Nov Hdle 2m5f (10)
(Baring Bingham) (Gr 1) (1) (4yo+) £57,010

2837*	FIRST LIEUTENANT (IRE) *MFMorris,Ireland* 6-11-7 DavyRussell	13/2 7/1	1
3358²	ROCK ON RUBY (IRE) *PaulNicholls* 6-11-7 (t) DarylJacob	15/2 13/2	sh 2
3539³	SO YOUNG (FR) *WPMullins,Ireland* 5-11-7 RWalsh	2/1f	4½ 3
3596*	Oscars Well (IRE) *MrsJHarrington,Ireland* 6-11-7 RobbiePower	7/2 4/1	2¼ 4
3705³	Megastar *GaryMoore* 6-11-7 JamieMoore	16/1	1½ 5
3814²	Minella Class (IRE) *NickyHenderson* 6-11-7 BarryGeraghty	12 10/1	ns 6
3814*	Aikman (IRE) *JamesEwart* 7-11-7 HarryHaynes	33/1	2½ 7
3358⁶	Ohio Gold (IRE) *ColinTizzard* 5-11-7 JoeTizzard	100/1	1¼ 8
3358³	Habbie Simpson *AlanKing* 6-11-7 RobertThornton	25/1	6 9
3601*	Highland Valley (IRE) *EmmaLavelle* 6-11-7 JackDoyle	50/1	6 10
3341*	Accordintolawrence (IRE) *CharlieLongsdon* 5-11-7 FelixdeGiles	100/1	1
3708²	Tornado Bob (IRE) *DonaldMcCain* 6-11-7 JasonMaguire	10/1	pu

2.05race Gigginstown House Stud 12ran 5m10.34

A smart renewal of the Baring Bingham in terms of the quality on show but it was unsatisfactory in event due to a modest overall pace, things not beginning in earnest until after 3 out (field still bunched at the second last), bringing speed into play more than stamine; what's more, the result would have been different had So Young and Oscars Well not blundered at the last, the latter set to win when making his mistake and the former likely to have beaten First Lieutenant as well without his. **First Lieutenant** confirmed himself a smart and progressive novice with a second Grade 1 win of the season, though both top-level successes have come in rather muddling affairs, better placed than some here (never too far away) and showing a really likeable attitude to get up on the line having been outpaced himself when things first quickened; he wouldn't be at all certain to confirm form with the next 3 if they meet again, but he's a chaser in the making, anyway, and a top novice prospect in that sphere for 2011/12 (likely to stay 3m). **Rock On Ruby**'s second to Bob's Worth in January was on par with an average winner of this race and he duly went close by showing similar form, enhancing an already impressive record in a light career so far, probably more comfortable than some with how things developed—but jumping fluently and looking sure to take advantage of mistakes by the third and fourth as he went 2 lengths clear briefly on the run-in, nailed in the last stride; he's likely to make a chaser, but he may achieve yet more in this sphere given he's had only 3 starts. **So Young** clearly has a huge reputation and, even in defeat, went a long way to justifying the hype with a very promising performance, leaving the form of his 2 wins well behind and sure to have done better still under different circumstances, travelling strongly and just hitting full flow when blundering at the last, having at that stage already quickened past the eventual winner; there isn't a lot to him physically, but he jumps well on the whole and will win top races over hurdles, perhaps starting at Punchestown next month. **Oscars Well** had been progressing markedly and there was nothing about his defeat to question the view he's a top prospect, taking over on the bridle 2 out and still going strongly in front when stumbling on landing after last, costing him all chance and, in all likelihood, a third Grade 1 novice win for all he'd taken a long time to settle; it's yet to be decided whether he'll stay over hurdles or go chasing next season, but either way he's one to look forward to, certainly built and bred for the latter. **Megastar** has still to show what he's about as a hurdler, yet to get the well-run race that's likely to play to his strengths, not always fluent in last place here but sticking to his task and probably not having such a hard race as some; he's on the radar for a valuable handicap win next season, and will be a contender at Aintree before then. **Minella Class**' progress has levelled off for the time being, having every chance under a positive ride here and just not quite up to it; he's had a productive and promising season overall, though, and is very much a chaser in appearance. **Aikman** ran just about as well as could be expected up in grade but had the luxury of an easy lead and was readily left behind once things began in earnest; he does retain some potential for a lower level, though. **Ohio Gold** seemed to improve but it probably shouldn't be taken at face value for the time being given he was always towards the rear in this modestly-run affair. **Habbie Simpson** is better than he showed on the day, rather let down by his jumping; he remains sure to stay 3m. **Highland Valley**'s wins have all come on heavy ground and he again didn't seem at ease under less testing conditions, whilst a couple of mistakes knocked him back as well. **Accordintolawrence** was out of his depth and had already started to struggle when falling 4 out. **Tornado Bob** has made a good impression this season and shouldn't be judged harshly on this, possibly amiss.

4208 RSA Chase (Gr 1) (1) (5yo+) £74,113   3m110y (19)
3594* BOSTONS ANGEL (IRE) *MrsJHarrington,Ireland* 7-11-4   1
       RobbiePower... 16/1
3065² JESSIES DREAM (IRE) *GordonElliott,Ireland* 8-11-4   nk 2
       TimmyMurphy 9 10/1
3485* WAYWARD PRINCE *IanWilliams* 7-11-4 APMcCoy .... 8 15/2   ¾ 3
3594² Magnanimity (IRE) *DTHughes,Ireland* 7-11-4 DavyRussell .... 16/1 ns 4
2697* Time For Rupert (IRE) *PaulWebber* 7-11-4 WillKennedy 9/4 7/4f 5 5
3709* Master of The Hall (IRE) *NickyHenderson* 7-11-4   8 6
       BarryGeraghty 16/1
3065³ Elysian Rock *MFMorris,Ireland* 7-11-4 MartinFerris 150/1 53 7
3594³ Mikael d'Haguenet (FR) *WPMullins,Ireland* 7-11-4 RWalsh........ 8 15/2   f
3594¹ Quel Esprit (FR) *WPMullins,Ireland* 7-11-4 PaulTownend ....   f
3355* The Giant Bolster *DavidBridgwater* 6-11-4 RodiGreene .... 20/1 ur
3700* Aiteen Thirtythree (IRE) *PaulNicholls* 7-11-4 DarylJacob .... 8/1 pu
3458* Wymott (IRE) *DonaldMcCain* 7-11-4 (s) JasonMaguire .... 10 11/1 pu
2.40race Mr E. A. P. Scouller 12ran 6m16.84

Ultimately a disappointing renewal of the top novice event for staying chasers with the standout favourite clearly not himself and none of the other British contenders running as if in top form either; the first 4 finished in a heap in a slow-motion finish to a race run at a fair pace, the winner's performance inferior to that recorded by most recent winners of this event and arguably not even superior to the form shown in the opening NH Chase. **Bostons Angel** gained a third Grade 1 win in a row, none of them by as much as 1 length, testament to his battling qualities and the relatively ordinary nature of the opposition this season, and he makes limited appeal as one who can make his mark at Championship level in open company, particularly with a concern that a series of hard races will leave a mark; this was a particularly gruelling finish as he held on all out, whilst his task was made easier by fallers, the poor showing of the favourite and the runner-up's hanging right. **Jessies Dream** threw away a winning chance by hanging right in the closing stages having travelled best to lead narrowly 2 out, losing the advantage under pressure and unable to get back up as the winner came to the end of his tether; he may well benefit from going back right handed and the Grade 1 at Punchestown would be the obvious next race for him, though the principals here are all much of a muchness and likely to be vulnerable to anything unexposed and promising in that. **Wayward Prince** can improve on this form granted an extreme test of stamina and is likely to do well in his second season so long as a tedency to race lazily doesn't become more pronounced, ridden to stay in contention here and keeping on all the way to the line having again jumped soundly. **Magnanimity** ran very close to his form with the winner from last time and would surely have gone closer still but for mistakes at the twelfth and thirteenth, losing his place at that point but rallying well; he's likely to be well worth a try beyond 3m at some point, though as a smart handicapper in the making rather than a potential Grade 1 chaser. **Time For Rupert** remains by some way the best prospect in this field and has to be given another chance to confirm previous form, his effort here in December a far better performance than that recorded by the winner of this, patently not at his best on the day (later reported to have bled and scoped badly after the race), travelling with no fluency from an early stage and not impressing with his jumping in the way he had previously, though still showing his usual gameness as he stuck on to the finish; he endured a hard race and may not bounce back at Aintree, so it may be best to put him away for next season, when if all is well he has the makings of a serious Gold Cup contender. **Master of The Hall** had won twice over 3m since he flopped here, so the track rather than the distance seems the likely explanation for his weak finishing effort, that and a blunder at the fourteenth, still holding every chance when slightly hampered 3 out but soon weakening; his form doesn't have a lot of depth to it but he clearly has some potential, if kept away from this track. **Elysian Rock** has struggled since stepping up to graded company, though he was still going okay when he made a bad mistake 4 out, another at the next just hastening his retreat. **Mikael d'Haguenet** has had an unfortunate start over fences and fell for the second time in 4 outings, still in touch when he went at the fourteenth with the race yet to develop fully; he'll presumably go to Punchestown if all is well but whether his confidence will enable him to run to his best remains to be seen. **Quel Esprit**'s jumping has caught him out on both starts since his winning chasing debut, strongly pressed in front though still going well enough when falling 3 out on this occasion; his jumping in the main was fluent again and when the odd lapse can be ironed out he clearly has some potential at this level. **The Giant Bolster** had already made one mistake before he blundered and unseated rider at the fifth; he'd made mistakes when winning here last time and clearly has work to do in that regard. **Aiteen Thirtythree** was faced with much his sternest test and disappointed, niggled along from quite early on the final circuit and struggling when hampered 3 out, pulled up before the last; his form is hard to assess with confidence and he has something to prove after this effort. **Wymott** had won 5 of his last 6 races, including all 3 over fences, but much stiffer competition, less testing ground and cheekpieces showed another side of his nature, unwilling from the off and making several mistakes, including a blunder at the ninth; he looks one to treat with caution until he shows this a one-off.

4209 sportingbet.com Queen Mother Champion Chase 2m (13)
(Gr 1) (1) (5yo+) £182,432

3388 ³	SIZING EUROPE (IRE) *Henryde Bromhead,Ireland* 9-11-10 AELynch... 8 10/1	1
3388 ²	BIG ZEB (IRE) *ColmAMurphy,Ireland* 10-11-10 BarryGeraghty 10/3 3/1	5 2
2838 ⁴	CAPTAIN CEE BEE (IRE) *EddieHarty,Ireland* 10-11-10 APMcCoy... 12 14/1	4 3
3751 *	Golden Silver (FR) *WPMullins,Ireland* 9-11-10 PaulTownend..... 10 11/1	1½ 4
3234 ²	Somersby (IRE) *HenriettaKnight* 7-11-10 RobertThornton 8/1	1¾ 5
3697 *	French Opera *NickyHenderson* 8-11-10 AndrewTinkler................ 22/1	3½ 6
3234 ⁶	I'm So Lucky *DavidPipe* 9-11-10 (b+t) TomScudamore 66/1	9 7
3234 *	Master Minded (FR) *PaulNicholls* 8-11-10 RWalsh................. 3 2/1f	6 8
3697	Cornas (NZ) *NickWilliams* 9-11-10 LeightonAspell 150/1	½ 9
3234 ³	Mad Max (IRE) *NickyHenderson* 9-11-10 PaulCarberry 20/1	ns 10
2695 *	Woolcombe Folly (IRE) *PaulNicholls* 8-11-10 DarylJacob 7/1	dh 10

3.20race Ann & Alan Potts Partnership 11ran 3m55.01

With Master Minded, Somersby and Woolcombe Folly all failing to meet expectations by some way this wasn't the Champion Chase it promised to be, though there's no question that Sizing Europe put up a top-class performance in winning decisively; the pace was just fair and those ridden positively (including the winner) were favoured to some extent. **Sizing Europe**'s progress seemed to have come to an end but, in hindsight, there have been excuses for him this season, campaigned over 3m initially and then rather let down by his jumping in the Tied Cottage, and he proved that he is a 2-miler of the highest order with an emphatic success a year after landing the Arkle; admittedly, his task was easier with the big guns not firing as they can, whilst a positive ride was an advantage given they went just a fair pace, but Sizing Europe still deserves credit for how he went about it, travelling and jumping fluently and surging clear after Big Zeb almost got upsides at the last; he's likely to go to Punchestown for the Irish equivalent next month and clearly heads there with a leading chance, for all he's no dominant force. **Big Zeb**'s peak might have come when an impressive winner of this race last year, heading towards the veteran stage now after all, but he's still a top-class performer and lost little in defeat to an improved Sizing Europe, especially as he began his effort from mid-field, jumping sketchily at times like he often can but still travelling smoothly and getting to within less than a length at the last; he's extremely tough and reliable and will continue to win top races. **Captain Cee Bee** is prone to off days, as at Leopardstown in December, but he'd been freshened up since and that paid dividends as he showed himself to be as good as ever, no threat to either of the first 2 but finding plenty after the second last despite having made a couple of minor errors. **Golden Silver** has had an excellent season, most consistent right the way through, and, though not matching the effort that saw him beat Big Zeb in January, he did run much better here than on either of his previous 2 visits to Cheltenham and possibly deserves a bit more credit given he came from further back than any of the principals, going smoothly most of the way and no extra only after challenging for a place at the last; he's likely to be more competitive when attempting to repeat last year's Punchestown win next month. **Somersby** is the youngest of this lot and remains likely to have his day in a Grade 1, though it's likely to be over a longer trip, as has been the impression all along; it wasn't entirely a lack of pace that was the problem this day, however, a blunder at the third last knocking plenty out of him, and it's testament to his attitude that he rallied. **French Opera** is most likeable but will always struggle in Grade 1s, his vulnerability highlighted here, well enough placed but no match. **I'm So Lucky** was out of his depth but at least showed a lot of spark in first-time blinkers until the stiff task told from 2 out. **Master Minded** has shown this season that he genuinely is still a top-class chaser and he'll almost certainly bounce back from this below-par display, a terrible mistake at the second last ending his chance completely, but he was firmly off the bridle at the time anyway; connections reported that he may go to Aintree for the Melling Chase over a longer trip but there has to be some concern of that being so near to hand. **Cornas** isn't a Grade 1 chaser but still could have been expected to fare better, not fluent and always in rear. **Mad Max**'s physical problems have been well documented, his being tubed since last seen in January the latest in a string of operations (also fitted with earplugs here), but it doesn't appear to have made a difference, his weak finish coming even sooner than usual. **Woolcombe Folly**'s handicap win in December is hard to knock but it's a stand-out effort by some way and he struggled to land a blow up against the best around, finding some trouble at the top of the hill and held when making a bad mistake 2 out (quickly pulled up).

```
4212  Weatherbys Champion Bumper              2m110y
       (Standard Open NHF) (Gr 1) (1)
       (4, 5 and 6yo) £31,356
3571*  CHELTENIAN (FR) PhilipHobbs 5-11-5 RichardJohnson ......  14/1    1
3871*  DESTROYER DEPLOYED TimVaughan 5-11-5 AidanColeman .....  5/1    5 2
4013*  AUPCHARLIE (IRE) PECollins,Ireland 5-11-5 MrJPMcKeown ....  33/1   4½ 3
4791²  Go All The Way (IRE) NigelTwiston-Davies 6-11-5           4½ 4
         PaddyBrennan ................................................  20 16/1
2915²  Cinders And Ashes DonaldMcCain 4-10-12 JasonMaguire......  14/1  1¾ 5
3701¹  Ericht (IRE) NickyHenderson 5-11-5 BarryGeraghty.........  6 5/1f  sh 6
4741*  Divine Rhapsody (IRE) PJRothwell,Ireland 5-11-5                   ¾ 7
         PaulCarberry ...............................................  15/2 13/2
2915⁵  Cousin Khee HughieMorrison 4-10-12 SamThomas .......  33/1   ¾ 8
3851*  Oscar Magic (IRE) NigelTwiston-Davies 4-10-12                     1 9
         SamThomas-Davies ..........................................  14 12/1
3858*  The Tracey Shuffle DavidPipe 5-11-5 (s) TomScudamore......  50/1  ½ 10
542*   Double Double (FR) CharlesO'Brien,Ireland 5-11-5                 ½ 11
         MrPaulJMcMahon ............................................  20/1
3466*  Saint Luke (IRE) PeterBowen 6-11-5 TomO'Brien ............  66/1  nk 12
2819*  Star Neuville (FR) JohnJosephHanlon,Ireland 5-11-5 APMcCoy...  14/1  6 13
3810*  Dark Glacier (IRE) ChrisGrant 6-11-5 DenisO'Regan........  50/1  4½ 14
3374*  Tusa Eire (IRE) WPMullins,Ireland 5-11-5 RWalsh..............  20/1  1¾ 15
3104*  Knockalongi OliverSherwood 5-11-5 LeightonAspell ........  100/1  7 16
1895²  Dynamic Approach (IRE) EUHales,Ireland 5-11-5                    7 17
         MrRobbieMcNamara ......................................... 33/1
3701²  Bygones In Brid (IRE) AlanKing 5-11-5 RobertThornton ......  20/1  1¾ 18
3013*  Knight Pass (IRE) WarrenGreatrex 5-11-5 WayneHutchinson......  7/1  6 19
2357*  Master Murphy (IRE) JaneWalton 6-11-5 AlistairFindlay ........ 100/1 12 20
3304*  Felix Yonger (IRE) HowardJohnson 5-11-5 BrianHughes.........  66/1 11 21
1895*  Raise The Beat ColmAMurphy,Ireland 6-11-5 (t) MrMPFogarty ....  7 8/1 21 22
2520*  Twentyfourcarat (IRE) IanWilliams 6-11-5 TimmyMurphy ......  25/1  5 23
3621*  Lord Gale (IRE) WPMullins,Ireland 5-11-5 MrPWMullins........  20/1  pu
5.15race Mr R. S. Brookhouse 24ran 3m51.82
```

The most open renewal of this race in recent years, according to the market at any rate, and plenty had chances in the latter stages, though the winner scored conclusively in the end and the field finished well strung out, the pace having been sound; overall, they were a good-looking bunch and the race will throw up plenty of above-average jumpers over time, even if the winner's performance couldn't quite match that of Dunguib and Cue Card in the last 2 years; for the second successive year British stables dominated in a race formerly regarded as an Irish benefit, the home team taking the first 2 places as well as 5 of the first 6. **Cheltenian**, one of the best types in the paddock, had beaten a subsequent smart winner at Kempton and made similar progress himself, showing himself an excellent prospect for novice hurdling next season and much more beyond if all goes well; he was waited with in touch on the inside, was clearly going as well as anything approaching the straight and was soon in control once he made his move on the inside, kept up to his work as he quickened clear; he was a first French-bred winner of the race, Al Ferof the first such to reach a place when second in 2010. **Destroyer Deployed** had won twice on much more testing ground (over 2f further too) but coped well with these conditions and the marked step up in grade, well placed all the way and finding plenty to take a clear second place, his attitude likely to stand him in good stead when he goes over jumps, when he will stay well. **Aupcharlie** did easily the best of the amateur-ridden runners and the best of the Irish, coming from further off the pace than the first 2 as well, making a very promising move down the hill but that effort perhaps telling as he was unable to quicken when the winner went on; he has plenty of substance and is bound to win races over hurdles. **Go All The Way** is an excellent prospect for novice hurdling, still looking in need of the experience (had left John Kiely for £310,000 at the Doncaster May Sales after debut) but doing really well to make the ground he did in the last 3f as the penny dropped, nearest at the finish; he very much looks the part and will make a chaser later on, while he'll also be well suited by longer trips. **Cinders And Ashes**, who looked really well, emerged with plenty of credit, holding every chance into the straight after being well placed all the way before weakening over 1f out, his stamina perhaps just running out on his first try at this trip. **Ericht** couldn't quite match the form he'd shown at Newbury, ridden more prominently here and just lacking the pace of the principals in the final 2f; he should fill out over the summer and has a clear future as a jumper. **Divine Rhapsody** has done well since last season and was very much the pick of the paddock physically, looking in good shape too, and he's likely to prove one of the best of these over jumps, doing well to finish as close as he did in the end, travelling well held up before getting tapped for foot down the hill, still well back over 2f out before staying on strongly; he'll clearly benefit from more of a test of stamina over jumps. **Cousin Khee** ran creditably, though his forward move over 3f out promised more than it delivered, going well as he made ground but edging left and no extra once more firmly ridden; perhaps he also found the step up to 2m beyond him, and a switch to the Flat rather than a campaign hurdling next season seems the likelier option. **Oscar Magic** was much more patiently ridden than at Kempton and seemed surprisingly green, running wide on the bend passing the stands and going nowhere 4f out before staying on well late in the day; he'd won on soft ground first time up and perhaps such conditions might have suited him better, but he clearly remains a promising sort for hurdling next season. **The Tracey Shuffle**, tried in cheekpieces, found this much more competitive contest beyond him, making most to 3f out but just not good enough to hold his position in the straight under much less testing conditions than encountered previously; his siblings have done well over jumps for this yard and he may well follow suit, though he is rather lacking in substance. **Double Double** would surely have done a lot better with stronger handling, ridden by an amateur unable to claim 7 lb, in a hopeless position 4f out after being held up in a detached last and running on well with minimal assistance after 3f out, nearest at the finish; he's not exactly bred for jumping but clearly has the ability to make some impact. **Saint Luke**, who was sweating, may well need more testing conditions to be seen to best advantage but he belied his odds for a long way, still well there over 2f out before he weakened; he is likely to be of interest in staying novice hurdles next season. **Star Neuville**'s form looked short of the standard required and, even with stronger handling, he shaped as if simply not good enough, ridden to hold every chance 3f out before weakening. **Dark Glacier** looks an out-and-out stayer and surely won't come into his own until getting a thorough test over jumps, losing his prominent position completely over 5f out and dropping to last but one before staying on again late. **Tusa Eire** didn't give himself much chance of getting home, failing to settle waited with and although he was going better than most as he made ground 3f out his effort soon flattened out once ridden more firmly. **Knockalongi**, sold from Rebecca Curtis for £50,000 at the Cheltenham January Sales, failed to settle held up in rear and never looked likely to make an impact, just passing a few beaten horses late on. **Dynamic Approach** was below the form he had shown much earlier in the season, racing prominently but quickly losing his place (being short of room only a minor factor) over 4f out; he's an athletic sort with a decent pedigree for jumping (will stay beyond 2m) and should bounce back once switched to hurdles. **Bygones In Brid** presumably found this coming too soon after Newbury and never figured, held up and always in rear; that previous effort, though, indicates he has the potential to make some impact in novice hurdles next season. **Knight Pass**'s form was perhaps more style than substance and in a truly-run race he fared nowhere near so well, struggling 4f out after taking a good hold in mid-field; he's an athletic sort whose potential can't be written off after one poor effort. **Master Murphy** was out of his depth and soon lost his place when the race began in earnest. **Felix Yonger** may need softer ground to repeat his debut form, stepped up a good deal in class here and struggling 5f out. **Raise The Beat** was presumably amiss on his first start since October, stopping quickly over 4f out. **Twentyfourcarat** would appear to have been grossly flattered at Ascot judged by this effort, well behind by halfway. **Lord Gale**, who unseated rider beforehand, failed to settle and was well held when pulled up over 1f out, racing on much less testing ground than on his debut.

CHELTENHAM Thursday, Mar 17
GOOD (New Course)

4222 Ryanair Chase (Festival) (Gr 1) (1) 2m5f (17)
(5yo+) £154,896

3146 pu	ALBERTAS RUN (IRE) *JonjoO'Neill* 10-11-10 APMcCoy	6/1	1
3234 4	KALAHARI KING (FR) *FerdyMurphy* 10-11-10 GrahamLee	5 7/1	1 2
3730 *	RUBI LIGHT (FR) *RobertHennessy,Ireland* 6-11-10 AELynch	16/1	2 3
2700 *	Poquelin (FR) *PaulNicholls* 8-11-10 RWalsh	5/2 2/1f	4½ 4
4622 5	Voy Por Ustedes (FR) *NickyHenderson* 10-11-10 BarryGeraghty	12 11/1	nk 5
3330 3	J'Y Vole (FR) *WPMullins,Ireland* 8-11-3 PaulTownend	8/1	4 6
3711 5	Tartak (FR) *TomGeorge* 8-11-10 (t) PaddyBrennan	16/1	10 7
3711 2	Gauvain (GER) *NickWilliams* 9-11-10 DarylJacob	10 11/1	6 8
3847 4	Hey Big Spender (IRE) *ColinTizzard* 8-11-10 JoeTizzard	18/1	2¾ 9
3730 2	Roberto Goldback (IRE) *MrsJHarrington,Ireland* 9-11-10 RobbiePower	20 16/1	2½ 10
3710	Breedsbreeze (IRE) *PaulNicholls* 9-11-10 NickScholfield	40/1	pu

2.40race Mr Trevor Hemmings 11ran 5m07.22

Most of these are short of Grade 1 standard, Poquelin standing out on form, and with his below-par showing the race became much more open, with the first 6 having a chance until quite late on, the winner returning to the top-class form he showed when successful in 2010 and perhaps the only one here on this showing who would have enhanced either of the long-established Grade 1 races at the meeting; the pace was sound. **Albertas Run** confirmed beyond much doubt that he's a top-class chaser on his day and enhanced his fine record on good going in the process, looking completely transformed from the horse that had struggled so badly previously this season as he repeated his 2010 win in this with a very gutsy effort from the front, travelling and jumping well before finding plenty when pressed, seeing things out strongly; he followed up in the Melling Chase last season and would hold serious claims again, granted suitable conditions, while connections were considering the Gold Cup as an option and might another year, though he will be 11 in 12 months time and the chances are starting to decline by then. **Kalahari King** justified connections' decision to run in this rather than the Champion Chase, showing form as good as he ever has, very patiently ridden and produced to challenge at the last but finding the winner too resolute a rival to pass; a rematch at Aintree might well be on the cards and another solid effort there seems likely. **Rubi Light** has done really well since switched back to fences this season and was better than ever here, coping fine with less testing ground than previously and sticking to his task after a mistake 3 out saw him flat out (jumped soundly otherwise); he was 2 years younger than any of his rivals here and, whilst he's had quite a lot of racing, he's likely to continue to thrive, including at 3m if tried. **Poquelin** stood out on his form last time but failed to run to that level and was a beaten favourite at this meeting for the third year running, just not travelling with the fluency expected and finding his rally into a place petering out on the run-in, an earlier blunder possibly to blame to an extent; quite a few of his stable-companions performed below expectations over the meeting and he may just not have been quite right. **Voy Por Ustedes**, who had left Alan King, was a late addition to the field and showed he retains a smart level of ability, close enough into the straight but one paced under pressure after, perhaps just short of fitness for all he looked straight enough beforehand; the Melling, a race he's won twice in the past, is perhaps the main aim with him this spring. **J'Y Vole** perhaps just isn't quite as good as she was last season, though she looked a major threat for a long way until a failure to settle took its toll. **Tartak**'s jumping let him down for a second start running, 3 significant errors too many at this level; he's run well at the Grand National meeting for the last 2 years, but he'll need to be a lot more fluent there if he's to make any impact this time round. **Gauvain** was disappointing, his stable not having the meeting it might have hoped for, the primary problem with this one a handful of mistakes, soon losing his position as a result and unable to rally to any extent. **Hey Big Spender** found this step up in class too much, his jumping not helping, trying to move closer when he hit the thirteenth; he'll be better off back in handicaps, given he's only 4 lb higher than when beating a subsequent winner at Warwick. **Roberto Goldback**'s jumping wasn't good enough in a competitive race on less testing ground than he usually encounters, a blunder 4 out when flat out his third error of note; his season so far has been one of under-achievement. **Breedsbreeze** has got worse with each run this season and turned in a listless effort, never travelling in rear and making mistakes.

4223	Ladbrokes World Hdle (Gr 1) (1) (4yo+) £148,226		3m (12)
2833*	BIG BUCK'S (FR) *PaulNicholls* 8-11-10 RWalsh 1/1 10/11f		1
3359*	GRANDS CRUS (FR) *DavidPipe* 6-11-10 (t) TomScudamore 7/2		1¾ 2
3348*	MOURAD (IRE) *WPMullins,Ireland* 6-11-10 PaulTownend 8/1		2¾ 3
3717*	Cross Kennon (IRE) *JennieCandlish* 7-11-10 AlanO'Keeffe 50/1		½ 4
3617²	Rigour Back Bob (IRE) *EJO'Grady,Ireland* 6-11-10 AndrewJMcNamara		½ 5
		80/1	
3617⁶	Berties Dream (IRE) *PaulGilligan,Ireland* 8-11-10 (s) AELynch...... 50/1		2¾ 6
3717⁴	Any Given Day (IRE) *DonaldMcCain* 6-11-10 JasonMaguire 66/1		sh 7
3662*	Fiveforthree (IRE) *WPMullins,Ireland* 9-11-10 DJCasey 12/1		¾ 8
3359³	Restless Harry *RobinDickin* 7-11-10 HenryOliver 40/1		½ 9
3348⁵	Powerstation (IRE) *EamonO'Connell,Ireland* 11-11-10 DavyRussell		6 10
		50/1	
4532²	Souffleur *PeterBowen* 8-11-10 TomO'Brien 100/1		15 11
2698⁴	Zaynar (FR) *NickyHenderson* 6-11-10 (s) BarryGeraghty 16 12/1		¾ 12
2914*	Ashkazar (FR) *DavidPipe* 7-11-10 TimmyMurphy 22/1		30 13

3.20race The Stewart Family 13ran 5m50.86

The emergence of Grands Crus gave the 2011 World Hurdle a new dimension, providing a genuine form challenger to Big Buck's, and that pair duly fought out a thrilling finish; a steady pace greatly dilutes the bare form, however, the time more than 10 seconds slower than the Pertemps Final, and the leading pair were significantly more superior to the rest than they were able to show on the day. **Big Buck's** continued his domination of this division as he completed a hat-trick of World Hurdle wins and it's hard to see him being defeated anytime soon, passing through a new challenge as he faced Grands Crus for the first time here and completing it in much the same style as previously; unfortunately, the steady gallop stopped him from producing the sort of performance of which he's surely well capable, but he had plenty more in the locker, typically responding generously to forge to the front turning in (despite Walsh having dropped his whip) and idling quite markedly on the run-in (hung left); he's an exceptional racehorse and it's a credit to connections to have constantly delivered him spot on for these big occasions. **Grands Crus** will have his day in the limelight, only a 6-y-o after all, and this second at the very top level underlines just how far he's come this season, losing absolutely nothing in defeat to an outstanding rival in Big Buck's, worth credit in fact for serving it up to him like he did given he'd conceded a head start in a race that wasn't truly run, travelling strongly as usual and almost getting upsides on the run-in; connections talked afterwards about the possibility of Grands Crus going chasing next season, and he'll be as exciting a novice chase prospect as there's been for years. **Mourad** had little chance with 2 rivals from right out of the top-drawer, flattered by his proximity to them in a steadily-run race but still giving his own running, sticking to his task without mounting a serious challenge; there's no doubt he'll continue to win good races, particularly back in Ireland. **Cross Kennon** confirmed the improvement he'd shown at Haydock, possibly even bettering that slightly, though dictating the steady pace clearly benefited him to some extent in getting so close to the first 3, albeit probably value for his beating of the remainder. **Rigour Back Bob** ran as well as could be expected at this level and would probably have finished fourth but for meeting trouble shortly after 3 out, ending up in the rear before a strong finish; he's no better than this, however. **Berties Dream** has got back on track returned to hurdles the last twice, seeming to show here that he retains all of what he showed to win the Albert Bartlett last term, but it's hardly the most solid guide given the messy nature of the race. **Any Given Day** seemed to run creditably but never got involved properly and was almost certainly flattered on the day; this can't be used as evidence that he's fully effective at 3m, either. **Fiveforthree**'s reappearance win isn't firm proof that he retains all of his ability after missing last season, and a weakish finish here after he'd briefly challenged for a place was disconcerting. **Restless Harry** will always be vulnerable at this level but at least continues in form, sure to have finished closer but for being short of room as things started to develop. **Powerstation** is on the slide aged 11, his second to Mourad in December his only creditable effort this season. **Souffleur** hadn't been seen for almost a year since second to Big Buck's at Aintree and was very rusty; he'll presumably head there again next time, but he'll have a bit to prove. **Zaynar**'s ability isn't in question but his temperament has been in doubt for a while and he's one to treat with caution after this moody display with cheekpieces refitted. **Ashkazar** seemed to go wrong after being hampered 4 out.

CHELTENHAM Friday, Mar 18

GOOD (New Course)

4250 JCB Triumph Hdle (Gr 1) (1) (4yo) £57,010 2m1f (8)

3845[*]	ZARKANDAR (IRE) *PaulNicholls* 4-11-0 DarylJacob		13/2		1
3593[*]	UNACCOMPANIED (IRE) *DKWeld,Ireland* 4-10-7 PaulTownend	6	11/2	2¼	2
3232[*]	GRANDOUET (FR) *NickyHenderson* 4-11-0 BarryGeraghty	7	13/2	2¾	3
3036[4]	Sam Winner (FR) *PaulNicholls* 4-11-0 RWalsh	6	4/1f	nk	4
3762[3]	Sir Pitt *AlisonThorpe* 4-11-0 DonalFahy		200/1	2½	5
3593[2]	Sailors Warn (IRE) *EJO'Grady,Ireland* 4-11-0 AndrewJMcNamara		33/1	1½	6
3715[2]	Third Intention (IRE) *ColinTizzard* 4-11-0 JoeTizzard		11/1	½	7
3715[4]	Local Hero (GER) *SteveGollings* 4-11-0 RhysFlint		20/1	½	8
3552[*]	Brampour (IRE) *PaulNicholls* 4-11-0 HarrySkelton		20/1	½	9
3728[*]	Smad Place (FR) *AlanKing* 4-11-0 RobertThornton	9	11/1	nk	10
3845[6]	Aikideau (FR) *RichardRowe* 4-11-0 LeightonAspell		100/1	1½	11
3488[2]	Kuilsriver (IRE) *AlisonThorpe* 4-11-0 (t) JasonMaguire		125/1	3¼	12
3733	Walter de La Mare (IRE) *JohnJosephMurphy,Ireland* 4-11-0 RobbiePower		200/1	3¾	13
3845[2]	Molotof (FR) *NickyHenderson* 4-11-0 AndrewTinkler		16/1	3¼	14
2972[*]	First Fandango *TimVaughan* 4-11-0 (v+t) SamThomas		50/1	2¾	15
3715[*]	Houblon des Obeaux (FR) *VenetiaWilliams* 4-11-0 AidanColeman		22/1	1¾	16
3522[*]	High Ransom *MickyHammond* 4-10-7 (s) BarryKeniry		125/1	9	17
3593	Tillahow (IRE) *MFMorris,Ireland* 4-11-0 DavyRussell		80/1	10	18
2358	Architrave *TimVaughan* 4-11-0 RichardJohnson		40/1	1	19
3552[f]	Trop Fort (FR) *DavidPipe* 4-11-0 TomScudamore		50/1	3¼	20
3057[4]	Mister Carter (IRE) *TStack,Ireland* 4-11-0 WJLee		50/1		ur
3919	New Den *JimBoyle* 4-11-0 (s+t) CampbellGillies		250/1		pu
3547[*]	A Media Luz (FR) *NickyHenderson* 4-10-7 APMcCoy	10	12/1		pu

1.30race Potensis Limited & Mr Chris Giles 23ran 3m53.99

A most competitive renewal of the juvenile championship, with virtually all of the season's leading juveniles in the field, and the form should be viewed positively, for all that the field wasn't that well strung out at the finish despite a true gallop—the ground, which was close to good to firm, almost certainly played its part in that; the winner's performance is well up to standard for the race and he, along with quite a few of the others, has the potential to make an impact in open company next season. **Zarkandar** was keen beforehand, though not so edgy as he'd been at Kempton, and showed himself the best juvenile seen this season with another taking performance, one which suggests he has strong claims of making up into a Champion Hurdle contender next season, likely to be effective at 2m in good company given the way he travelled and the turn of foot he showed to go the front before the last, ridden out towards the finish; he has good claims of a follow-up success at Aintree, with that track unlikely to pose any problems for him. **Unaccompanied** acquitted herself really well on her third start over hurdles, having more to offer and presumably a leading candidate for Grade 1 success at Punchestown, coming from a similar position to the winner, travelling equally well but just lacking his turn of foot at the last, nevertheless keeping on well; as well as having the potential to progress as a hurdler, she presumably has more to offer on the Flat, her stamina by no means fully tested in that sphere. **Grandouet** has done well over hurdles this season and has a bright future, whether kept hurdling or switched to fences in 2011/12, impressing with the way he travelled here, racing closer to the pace than the pair that beat him, still on the bridle before the last but unable to quicken when ridden; he comes from a very stout family on the dam's side of his pedigree and is likely to be at least as effective over further. **Sam Winner** had the best previous form but couldn't quite match that level, running an extraordinary race, not always fluent and losing his place in mid-division completely 3 out, having only one behind at the next (rider briefly accepted matters) before flying home under strong pressure to pass most of the field from the home turn, closing down the principals at the line; he's likely to stay further on this evidence, though it's also possible that lazy tendencies played a part in this display. **Sir Pitt** looked as well as anything beforehand and belied his SP with a much improved effort, the different test presumably bringing out latent ability, travelling smoothly held up and making good headway to challenge 2 out, just unable to quicken in the straight; he's clearly well up to winning races on this evidence and he is sure to stay beyond 2m. **Sailors Warn** ran well on less testing ground than previously, taking a good hold in a share of the lead and weakening only going to the last; he lacks size and may not have much more to offer, however, for all that his form is progressive to this point. **Third Intention** ran creditably on form though is probably capable of a bit better again, his jumping lacking fluency after a mistake at the first, still able to travel smoothly until after 3 out but a bit out of his ground as a result when the race was taking shape. **Local Hero** ran creditably and it says much for his willingness that he did so after an indifferent round of jumping, going nowhere after 3 out but sticking to his task well without being able to land a blow; he's done well over hurdles but perhaps needs a rest after this (was carrying little condition beforehand). **Brampour** might have been expected to improve for this sort of test but he made only limited progress, having every chance when making a mistake 2 out and weakening as if not good enough at the last; he lacks size and this may be as good as he is. **Smad Place** ran creditably and may yet show himself better than his form to date indicates, his 2 runs in Grade 1 company not showing him to advantage for differing reasons, getting run off his feet after 3 out here before staying on again late; he's likely to be well suited by a step-up in trip. **Aikideau** had been well supported in the Adonis and belatedly showed that that market confidence wasn't totally misguided, appearing to show useful form this time, albeit possibly flattered in staying on late (edged left) having been well back before 2 out; he has the ability to win an ordinary race at least. **Kuilsriver** appeared to excel himself in face of a stiff task, well suited by the different type of test, different tactics employed too instead of front running, well off the pace 3 out but staying on through beaten horses late on. **Walter de La Mare**, very much on his toes, had presumably found the ground against him on his hurdling debut and acquitted himself well in face of his quixotic task, never a factor but staying on late in the day, seeming to show a fairly useful level of form. **Molotof**'s Kempton second has been well advertised at this meeting and he has the potential to do very well next season, whether as a novice hurdler or switched to fences, not looking to have thrived since that race and simply not in the same form here, albeit shaping a fair bit better than the distances beaten suggest, not seeing the race out after travelling smoothly close up to 2 out, eased after a mistake at the last. **First Fandango**, tried visored, essentially wasn't good enough upped in class, well enough placed after 3 out but ridden and soon losing ground; he may yet have more to offer faced with a stiffer test of stamina and/or a return to softer ground. **Houblon des Obeaux** almost certainly needs softer ground to be seen to best advantage on this evidence, making the running but flat to the boards soon after 3 out and weakening before the next, running well below form. **High Ransom** has often worn headgear on the Flat but the addition of cheekpieces for the first time over hurdles seemingly did little for her, admittedly in the face of a stiff task, making mistakes and always among the stragglers. **Tillahow**, who had raced on softer ground previously over hurdles, was below form and never really recovered from a mistake at the third, under pressure in rear and going nowhere after 3 out. **Architrave** was well below his best on his first start in 4 months, weakening after 3 out having raced close up. **Trop Fort**, who lacks size and substance, was always towards the rear after making a mistake at the first and essentially shaped as if lacking the experience for this sort of test. **Mister Carter** may well be capable of better under these sort of conditions judged on his Flat form and he was still to be asked fully for his effort when unseating 2 out here, though plenty were still in contention at that stage. **New Den**, tried tongue tied, was wasting his time at this level. **A Media Luz**'s headstrong nature proved her undoing as, having been on her toes beforehand, she failed to settle in the race itself, well placed down the hill but weakening quickly after a mistake 2 out; she's got something to prove after this, for all that her best form ought to make her competitive at this level.

4252 Albert Bartlett Nov Hdle (Spa) (Gr 1) (1)   3m (12)
(4yo+) £57,010

3358 [5]	BOBS WORTH (IRE) *Nicky Henderson* 6-11-7 Barry Geraghty	5/2 15/8f	1
3153 [5]	MOSSLEY (IRE) *Nicky Henderson* 5-11-7 APMcCoy	12/1 2¼	2
3716 [2]	COURT IN MOTION (IRE) *Emma Lavelle* 6-11-7 Jack Doyle	9/1	6 3
3358	Champion Court (IRE) *Martin Keighley* 6-11-7 Warren Marston	12 16/1	5 4
3477 [1]	Kilcrea Kim (IRE) *Philip Hobbs* 6-11-7 Richard Johnson	8 6/1	1¼ 5
3787 [2]	Ackertac (IRE) *Nigel Twiston-Davies* 6-11-7 Paddy Brennan	40/1	6 6
3699 [7]	Our Island (IRE) *Tim Vaughan* 6-11-7 Tom Scudamore	33/1	3¼ 7
3669 [2]	Teaforthree (IRE) *Rebecca Curtis* 7-11-7 Aidan Coleman	28/1	hd 8
3428 [1]	Allee Garde (FR) *WPMullins,Ireland* 6-11-7 DJCasey	66/1	1 9
3142 [2]	Sybarite (FR) *Nigel Twiston-Davies* 5-11-7 Sam Twiston-Davies	25/1 4½	10
3237 [2]	No Secrets (IRE) *Warren Greatrex* 7-11-7 Wayne Hutchinson	50/1 3¼	11
3723 [1]	Jetnova (IRE) *AlanKing* 6-11-7 Robert Thornton	40/1	f
4131	Flulin Evan*Williams* 6-11-7 Paul Moloney	66/1	pu
3390 [1]	Gagewell Flyer (IRE) *WPMullins,Ireland* 7-11-7 Paul Townend	8 15/2	pu
3461 [1]	Join Together (IRE) *PaulNicholls* 6-11-7 RWalsh	15/2 8/1	pu
3482 [1]	Moonlight Drive (IRE) *John Quinn* 5-11-7 Graham Lee	20/1	pu
3591 [1]	Radetsky March (IRE) *Mark Bradstock* 8-11-7 Jason Maguire	66/1	pu
3450 [R]	Start Me Up (IRE) *Charlie Swan,Ireland* 7-11-7 Davy Russell	80/1	pu

2.40race The Not Afraid Partnership 18ran 5m42.05

This race has quickly established itself as a genuine Grade 1 contest and, whilst it might be argued that the winner and third would have made the Baring Bingham an even stronger contest than it was already, the form here was every bit as strong as that of the longer-established contest; it was run at a sound pace and, although plenty had a chance 2 out, there were soon only 3 in it as the winner and third kicked on. **Bobs Worth** gained a fourth win from 4 starts over hurdles, switched late to this race from an expected run in the Baring Bingham and showing plenty of stamina after he'd cruised through the race, responding well after jumping left at the last, then drifting right under pressure; he could make up into a high-class staying hurdler next season if connections choose that route but, like so many here, he has the make and shape of a chaser, so could return to this meeting as a leading contender for the RSA Chase—either way, he's very much one to follow. **Mossley** showed his running last time to be all wrong back under these less testing conditions, this a gritty effort as he responded to pressure to chase home his stable companion, just not good enough to close him down after the last; he may well have more to offer over hurdles but, like so many of this field, his future almost certainly lies over fences. **Court In Motion** was running in the wrong race, performing creditably but simply lacking the required stamina after cruising to a share of the lead into the straight, going as well as the winner at that stage but just not seeing things out nearly so well; he's another who looks a smashing prospect for chasing next season. **Champion Court**, with his stable in better form now, was quickly back on track and coped well with the longer trip, shaping a bit better than the bare result in all probability too, held up taking a good hold and still going strongly after 3 out, but untidy at the next and rather letting the first 3 steal a march on him; he'd be well worth trying in the Sefton at Aintree, particularly if ridden a bit more positively, and has a really bright future over fences beyond that. **Kilcrea Kim** ran respectably, unable to quicken after 2 out having been close up on the inside all the way, the less testing ground possibly just telling against him; he's shown himself a useful performer over hurdles and has the physique to suggest there'll be even better to come as a chaser. **Ackertac** matched the improvement shown in handicap company last time, though he never really threatened and just kept on steadily, looking a thorough stayer; the greater tests of stamina available over fences are likely to show him to advantage if he takes to chasing. **Our Island** ended up running creditably though it was hard work after he'd dropped to the rear before halfway, just keeping on steadily in the closing stages, again looking very much a stayer; he's another who may well come into his own when able to tackle marathon distances over fences. **Teaforthree** ran creditably on less testing ground than previously, chasing the pace for much of the way and every chance when blundering 2 out, just not good enough thereafter; he has the size for chasing and has already won a point, that surely the route with him next season. **Allee Garde** was highly tried on just his second start over hurdles and didn't really know enough to show what he could do, though he shaped better than the distances beaten indicate, blundering at the second and held up, then hampered 2 out and spared a hard race; he should stay 3m. **Sybarite** was on his toes beforehand and was nowhere near his best, on the back foot almost from the off after a mistake at the first, his rider never really seeming happy with him; his stable had a poor week and he's best judged on previous efforts, fences surely the option next season, though he may remain a novice over hurdles should connections take a more patient approach; he should stay 3m, lack of stamina clearly not the problem here. **No Secrets**, on his toes beforehand, ran a lot better than the bare result suggests, again travelling strongly in front for a long way (jumped well) and headed only after 2 out, tying up badly as his exertions told, lack of stamina clearly also a possible factor on this first start at 3m. **Jetnova** was unlikely to have troubled the first 3 but still performing with plenty of credit when falling 2 out, just in behind the leaders at the time and not fully asked for his effort; he is likely to be effective at 3m and looks just the sort to make a better chaser next season. **Fiulin** was out of his depth again and stopped quickly before 3 out, though stamina admittedly might have been an issue over this markedly longer trip. **Gagewell Flyer** was taking a big step-up in trip and it looked beyond him, seeming to be going well enough under a patient ride after 3 out but not picking up when ridden and then hampered at the next. **Join Together** hadn't been far behind the runner-up here on his penultimate start but was in nothing like the same form this time, losing his place completely soon after halfway; his stable had a successful week but there were some very disappointing efforts in amongst those wins. **Moonlight Drive** lacked experience for this level and perhaps found the ground against him too, so he's worth another chance back at a more realistic level to confirm the promise of his win last time; he's likely to make a chaser next season as well. **Radetsky March** had it to do at this level and just wasn't good enough to hold his prominent position after 3 out. **Start Me Up**'s form looked short of the standard required but he was shaping a good deal better than that indicated upped to 3m for the first time when badly hampered 2 out (when still to be asked for his effort), unable to recover; he's clearly worth another chance at this trip.

4253 totesport Cheltenham Gold Cup Chase 3¼m110y (22)
(Gr 1) (1) (5yo+) £285,050

3146*	LONG RUN (FR) *NickyHenderson* 6-11-10 MrSWaley-Cohen	4 7/2f	1
2674³	DENMAN (IRE) *PaulNicholls* 11-11-10 SamThomas	11 8/1	7 2
3146³	KAUTO STAR (FR) *PaulNicholls* 11-11-10 (t) RWalsh	13/2 5/1	4 3
3696²	What A Friend *PaulNicholls* 8-11-10 (b) DarylJacob	25/1	ns 4
2693*	Midnight Chase *NeilMulholland* 9-11-10 TomScudamore	11 9/1	8 5
3357²	Tidal Bay (IRE) *HowardJohnson* 10-11-10 BrianHughes	16/1	3¾ 6
2817*	Pandorama (IRE) *NoelMeade,Ireland* 8-11-10 PaulCarberry	14/1	sh 7
3357*	Neptune Collonges (FR) *PaulNicholls* 10-11-10 RobertThornton	33/1	3½ 8
3718⁴	Carruthers *MarkBradstock* 8-11-10 MattieBatchelor	66/1	34 9
3597⁴	China Rock (IRE) *MFMorris,Ireland* 8-11-10 BarryGeraghty	25/1	pu
2526*	Imperial Commander (IRE) *NigelTwiston-Davies* 10-11-10 PaddyBrennan	9/2 4/1	pu
3597*	Kempes (IRE) *WPMullins,Ireland* 8-11-10 (t) APMcCoy	7 9/1	pu
2674	Weird Al (IRE) *IanWilliams* 8-11-10 JasonMaguire	20/1	pu

3.20race Mr Robert Waley-Cohen 13ran 6m29.96

A most memorable renewal of National Hunt's blue riband event, bringing together —amongst others—a truly top-notch up-and-comer in Long Run and a pair of outstanding veterans in Denman and Kauto Star, neither of whom were at their imperious best but both ran hugely creditable races to be placed and provide plenty of substance to the form itself; the winner's bare rating is slightly lower than the previous 3 Gold Cups yet still some way ahead of the overall standard in recent years, testament to an outstanding era of staying chasers, and there's no reason whatsoever to doubt this result—a sound gallop was ensured by Midnight Chase (underlined by a course record time) and the principals asserted quickly once the screw was really turned after 4 out; Imperial Commander was the only high-profile disappointment of the race, whilst Diamond Harry and Weapon's Amnesty were the obvious absentees from an otherwise fully-loaded line-up. **Long Run**'s emergence as an exceptional performer has been swift, only 5 months ago beaten in a handicap here from a BHA mark of 158, but that's an irrelevance now as with his 2 wins since he's joined the likes of Desert Orchid, Best Mate and Kauto Star in an elite group who have taken both the King George and Gold Cup in the same season, with his achievement all the more noteworthy given he's the first 6-y-o since Mill House in 1963 to land this most prestigious prize; admittedly, it wasn't all plain-sailing for him as things went, not for the first time showing a tendency to make mistakes (notably at the tenth and twelfth)—a niggling concern looking ahead—but that it failed to get him off the bridle highlights just how much ability Long Run has and he powered clear after taking over approaching the final fence, not having any problem with the extra 2½f, albeit on quickish ground; his next target is undecided, with Aintree, Punchestown and a return to France all reported as possible options, but whereever he goes he'll clearly be the one to beat and, given his age, Long Run has unquestionable potential to develop into one of the true greats of steeplechasing; incidentally, this provided trainer Nicky Henderson with a first Gold Cup, whilst Sam Waley-Cohen became the first amateur to win the race for some 30 years. **Denman**'s record in this race befits a truly top-class chaser, runner-up in each of the 3 years since winning in 2008, and although not quite the force he was, this was still a performance that would have landed plenty of average Gold Cups in years gone by, unfortunate in a way to bump into such an excellent youngster in Long Run; patiently ridden, he jumped impeccably (as he always has at this track) and responded well for pressure from 5 out, duelling with Kauto Star from 3 out to 2 out and typically gallant as he stuck to his task as best he could once the winner pounced soon after; he's had such a light campaign that perhaps he'll have at least one more big performance to give, but this gruelling race will have taken a lot out of him and surely another break is in order. **Kauto Star** is no longer capable of the outstanding performances that saw him achieve the highest Timeform rating of the modern era but he gave a much better showing than when filling the same position behind Long Run in the King George 2 months earlier, still showing top-class form on this occasion, and he went about it with great enthusiasm too, jumping soundly on the whole under a positive ride and just unable to see things out like he used to from 2 out; as with Denman, this big effort is likely to have taken a lot out of him and he's probably best freshened up. **What A Friend** ran a career-best effort, unsurprisingly taking well to first-time blinkers given he's a quirky sort, travelling smoothly to 4 out and looking more straightforward than has sometimes been the case (another new jockey here) as he found plenty despite having hit 2 out; he took the totesport Bowl at Aintree last season, but a tilt at the Grand National itself could be on the cards for him there this time around and he'll clearly hold an excellent chance on form for that, though it's worth noting that the headgear isn't guaranteed to work so well again a second time. **Midnight Chase** is one of the most improved horses of the last 12 months and, although not up this very stiff task, he acquitted himself as well as could be expected, setting a sound pace until Kauto Star took over with a circuit to go and then giving his all under strong pressure from after the sixteenth; he's tough, likeable and high-class, so will be very competitive in lesser graded races. **Tidal Bay** is such a difficult ride and did his usual thing here, making a couple of mistakes and dropping right out before belatedly consenting to run on when it was too late; this was a creditable effort in form terms but he's no betting proposition. **Pandorama**'s Lexus win showed what he's capable of and it's best not to judge him on this, facing quicker ground than is probably ideal (goes extremely well in the mud) and also badly hampered as he went for a gap up Long Run's inside just after the tenth. **Neptune Collonges** thrived in a small field here last time but is perhaps reliant on such circumstances to show his form nowadays, showing little interest from an early stage after rather missing the break and not jumping anything like so well as usual either. **Carruthers** hasn't matched his performances of last season this time around but being unable to get to the front seemed the main problem here, not well positioned as the starter let them go and never travelling after slow jumps at the first 2 fences; he's still one to bear in mind for handicaps given comments at Haydock. **China Rock** shaped a lot better than his being pulled up suggests, jumping soundly up with the pace and looking held but still in touch when losing his action around 3 out, quickly eased and dismounted; he has improved this season and should win more good races in 2011/12. **Imperial Commander** may never get back to the peak that saw him win this race decisively in 2010, a 10-y-o now who has had his share of injury problems (including this winter), whilst clouting the fourth last here reportedly led to him returning lame and also with a broken blood vessel; he had travelled and jumped exhuberantly up to that point, however, which suggests he retains plenty of that ability. **Kempes** faced his stiffest task yet and was let down by his jumping, unable to make an impression before being pulled up after 5 out; he was tongue tied, incidentally. **Weird Al** lost his place well before halfway and was reported afterwards to have bled; he'd undergone a breathing operation since the Hennessy in late-November and clearly has a bit to prove at present.

AINTREE Thursday, Apr 7
GOOD to SOFT

4562 BGC Partners Liverpool Hdle (Gr 1) (1) 3m110y (13)
(4yo+) £57,010

4223¹	BIG BUCK'S (FR) *PaulNicholls* 8-11-7 RWalsh	4/6f	1
4223²	GRANDS CRUS (FR) *DavidPipe* 6-11-7 (t) TomScudamore	7/2 3/1	5 2
4308²	WON IN THE DARK (IRE) *SabrinaJHarty,Ireland* 7-11-7 AELynch	66/1	7 3
4210¹	Carlito Brigante (IRE) *GordonElliott,Ireland* 5-11-7 (t) DavyRussell	10/1	12 4
4221⁴	Knockara Beau (IRE) *GeorgeCharlton* 8-11-7 JanFaltejsek	33/1	12 5
4195	Khyber Kim *NigelTwiston-Davies* 9-11-7 PaddyBrennan	18 16/1	5 6
2084	Possol (FR) *HenryDaly* 8-11-7 RichardJohnson	80/1	28 7
2664	Markington *PeterBowen* 8-11-7 (b) TomO'Brien	200/1	19 8
2698	Sentry Duty (FR) *NickyHenderson* 9-11-7 BarryGeraghty	25/1	35 9
4221	Gwanako (FR) *PaulNicholls* 8-11-7 DarylJacob	100/1	16 10
3868⁴	Karabak (FR) *AlanKing* 8-11-7 (b) APMcCoy	20/1	pu

2.00race The Stewart Family 11ran 6m10.25

A good gallop was set by Knockara Beau in the latest renewal of this Grade 1 and it ensured a solid-looking result, with Big Buck's able to show his class with a performance right from the top drawer, himself and Grands Crus dominating in the straight as could have been expected. **Big Buck's** is a brilliant racehorse and, unlike at Cheltenham, had the opportunity to really show as much, producing just about his best performance yet as he quite literally brushed aside a top-class rival in Grands Crus, the good gallop setting things up perfectly for him to do so, hitting no flat spot this time, cruising as the runner-up tried to throw it down to him in the straight and sealing things with 3 slick jumps before shaken up to assert on the run-in, value for at least twice the winning margin; it's likely to be a long time before another staying hurdler of the calibre of Big Buck's comes along and he's sure to continue to dominate this sphere, though it would be great to see him try chasing again at some stage next season given he's still only an 8-y-o. **Grands Crus**, in a way, is unlucky to be around at the same time as one so outstanding as Big Buck's and, though he perhaps wasn't fully on song, he is again worth praise for his comprehensive beating of the rest here, able to be more decisive in that regard than at Cheltenham in this well-run race, driven upsides 3 out and pulling clear of the rest despite being unable to get Big

Buck's off the bridle; it's worth reaffirming what an exciting prospect Grands Crus is for novice chases in 2010/11. **Won In The Dark** has had a subdued season overall but returned to his very best from out of the blue, seeming to benefit from the step-up to 3m, travelling well to the home turn and keeping on, albeit without threatening the first 2; he isn't the most reliable, however, so whether he repeats this is another matter. **Carlito Brigante** is capable of making a bigger impact at this level another day, shaping third best here until his stamina ran dry, travelling strongly until approaching 3 out and clearly stretched by the longer trip. **Knockara Beau** perhaps wasn't over his Cheltenham exertions, failing to rally so well as usual once headed and slightly below form, but he's sure to bounce back. **Khyber Kim** isn't a 3-miler but that's only partly to blame for this latest below-par display, simply not the same force this season as in 2009/10. **Possol** has presumably had his problems to have been off since late-October (when shaping as if amiss) and was firmly put in his place once things began in earnest; he was probably flattered by his third in this race last year. **Markington** had no chance in this company but to be detached as early as the fourth is testament to his bad attitude. **Sentry Duty** has regularly failed to fire on the big stage and, returning from 4 months off, didn't travel like he can after a couple of sloppy jumps. **Gwanako** had a very stiff task and stopped quickly after 4 out. **Karabak** is possibly losing interest, essentially disappointing since winning the Relkeel in December, and first-time blinkers were tried to no avail here, struggling after the ninth; he's got plenty to prove at present.

4564 totesport Bowl Chase (Gr 1) (1) (5yo+) £84,780 3m1f (19)
3847³ NACARAT (FR) *TomGeorge* 10-11-7 (t) PaddyBrennan........... 9/2 7/2 1
4194² CAROLE'S LEGACY *NickyHenderson* 7-11-0 APMcCoy 5 4/1 6 2
3883¹ FOLLOW THE PLAN (IRE) *OliverMcKiernan,Ireland* 8-11-7
                      TomDoyle 40/1 3¾ 3
3711³ Deep Purple *EvanWilliams* 10-11-7 PaulMoloney 12/1 7 4
4253² Denman (IRE) *PaulNicholls* 11-11-7 RWalsh 6/5 5/4f 8 5
3569* Punchestowns (FR) *NickyHenderson* 8-11-7 BarryGeraghty...... 11/2 6/1 14 6
3.05race Mr Simon W. Clarke 6ran 6m31.36s

Denman's poor effort dominates the fallout of this Grade 1 chase and unquestionably weakens the overall form, leaving a pretty uncompetitive race by top-level standards, and it was modestly-run too, with the winner disputing an uneven gallop with Deep Purple and picking things up fully only from the thirteenth. **Nacarat** is a top-class chaser in his own right when things click and deserves credit for how comfortably he did this from the front, whether or not Denman's flop created an excellent opening by Grade 1 standards, admittedly allowed to dispute a modest pace (with Paddy Brennan excelling) and gaining the upper hand when quickening a few lengths clear at the thirteenth but still jumping superbly and always in control, his hanging left between the last 2 fences an indication that he was dossing in the late stages; he will remain vulnerable to the very best around but is a likeable/uncomplicated sort and should win more good races. **Carole's Legacy** never fails to give her running and was typically game in defeat, rather caught out when the pace quickened but sticking to her task to keep Nacarat honest in the straight; this Grade 1 placing in open company will add considerably to her value as a broodmare. **Follow The Plan** will find it tough going in any Grade 1 in all likelihood but acquitted himself as well as could be expected in face of a stiff task, especially as he barely stays this far, going freely in rear and unable to pick up after still looking a potential threat between 3 out and 2 out. **Deep Purple**'s best is probably behind him and he was no match once the tempo increased here, despite having disputed the stop-start gallop with Nacarat. **Denman**'s big effort in the Gold Cup had obviously left a mark, unsurprisingly so to be honest, and it's essentially best to write off this unusually laboured display; there's still a chance he'll have another big performance to come once freshened up for next season. **Punchestowns** simply doesn't jump well enough for him to compete at this level over fences but, in truth, there's probably more behind his current slump in form than that and he isn't one to be interested in at present, even if reverted to hurdles.

AINTREE Friday, Apr 8
GOOD

```
4586   John Smith's Melling Chase (Gr 1) (1)            2½m (16)
       (5yo+) £98,910
4209   MASTER MINDED (FR) PaulNicholls 8-11-10 RWalsh ......... 5 11/2    1
4222*  ALBERTAS RUN (IRE) JonjoO'Neill 10-11-10 APMcCoy ...... 3 11/4f   9 2
4209⁵  SOMERSBY (IRE) HenriettaKnight 7-11-10 RobertThornton .... 5/1    1½ 3
4222   Tartak (FR) TomGeorge 8-11-10 (t) PaddyBrennan ........ 16 14/1  2¾ 4
4209⁶  French Opera NickyHenderson 8-11-10 BarryGeraghty ...... 11/1   3¾ 5
4209   Mad Max (IRE) NickyHenderson 9-11-10 PaulCarberry ..... 14 11/1  ¾ 6
2756*  Tranquil Sea (IRE) EJO'Grady,Ireland 9-11-10
         AndrewJMcNamara ................................... 15/2 8/1  31 7
4428⁶  Made In Taipan (IRE) ThomasMullins,Ireland 9-11-10
         RobbiePower ....................................... 40/1     10 8
4222²  Kalahari King (FR) FerdyMurphy 10-11-10 GrahamLee ....... 9/2    pu
4566 ʳᵗʳ Chaninbar (FR) MiltonHarris 8-11-10 (b+t) SeanQuinlan.. 100/1  rtr
3.05race Mr Clive D. Smith 10ran 4m54.20s
```

The most competitive Melling for a while, even allowing for the underperformances of both Kalahari King and Tranquil Sea, with Master Minded back close to his top-class best as he proved far too good for last year's winner, his performance good enough to have won last month's Champion Chase; a strong early pace set by Mad Max steadied briefly before the sixth, though it picked up again more than far enough out to ensure a true test. **Master Minded** firmly put to bed any lingering talk of his demise, putting up an imperious display in claiming this third Grade 1 win of the season, easing alongside 2 out and treating a top-class pair facing their optimum conditions with disdain as he stretched clear with comfort, the return to 2½m surely of less significance than a race that saw him to better advantage than either the Victor Chandler (when all out to hold Somersby) or the Champion Chase; the lure of trying to replace the ageing Kauto Star in next year's King George will doubtless be a hard one for connections to resist, though regaining his Champion Chase crown after 2 defeats in that race would be no less meritorious. **Albertas Run** has peaked at both major spring Festivals for the last 2 years, not going with quite the same zest as at Cheltenham but losing little in defeat all the same in his bid to repeat last season's Ryanair/Melling double, finding only an outstanding rival too strong and probably value for a bigger margin over the staying-on third after making successive mistakes at the tenth and eleventh as things were really taking shape; his 2011/12 campaign seems likely to follow a similar pattern to this one, though he'll be 11 by the time Cheltenham and Aintree come round. **Somersby** took his run of placed efforts to 6 from his last 7 starts, meeting a better Master Minded here than the one he pushed so close at Ascot but again not helping his own chance with a mistake, in front going strongly when a slow leap 3 out saw him shuffled back; his late rally did highlight he'll prove at least as good at 2½m+ as shorter, however, and it remains a mere matter of time before he opens his Grade 1 account. **Tartak** did much to show he's still a high-class chaser as he made the frame in this race for the second year in a row, though the mistakes 5 out and 4 out that knocked him back are a recurring theme with him, doing well to finish where he did with those in mind as he rallied well; he's essentially a contender for a place only at Grade 1 level, though. **French Opera** is a very smart chaser and no better on balance, though he'd have gone closer to matching his Newbury form here had he jumped with his usual fluency, uncharacteristic mistakes at the second and seventh seeing him out of rhythm. **Mad Max** raised his game at this meeting for the second successive year, and his weak finish could be overlooked for a change given he'd forced the pace, still holding a narrow lead 2 out before he gave way; placing him to advantage gets no easier, however. **Tranquil Sea** hasn't fired on his last 2 runs in Britain, though his absence since winning at Fairyhouse before Christmas suggests things simply haven't gone smoothly with him, doing nothing to alleviate such fears by stopping to nothing from 4 out here. **Made In Taipan** has lost something in consistency this season, out of his depth here or not. **Kalahari King** presumably hadn't recovered from his Ryanair second to run such a lacklustre race, though predicting him has generally become a more difficult task this season. **Chaninbar** completed a quick-fire hat-trick of refusals and is one to leave severely alone.

	AINTREE Saturday, Apr 9	
	GOOD	

4599	John Smith's Maghull Nov Chase (Gr 1) (1) (5yo+) £56,632	2m (11)
	What should have been the fourth last fence was omitted due to a stricken jockey	
4193²	FINIAN'S RAINBOW (IRE) *Nicky Henderson* 8-11-4 BarryGeraghty 4/5 10/11f	1
4193⁵	GHIZAO (GER) *Paul Nicholls* 7-11-4 RWalsh 3/1	2 2
4519*	DAN BREEN (IRE) *David Pipe* 6-11-4 JasonMaguire........... 10 8/1	22 3
4133³	Starluck (IRE) *Alan Fleming* 6-11-4 APMcCoy.................. 11/2 9/2	18 4
2737³	Gilbarry (IRE) *Malcolm Jefferson* 6-11-4 GrahamLee........... 22/1	3¾ 5
3373	Romanesco (FR) *Alison Thorpe* 6-11-4 SamTwiston-Davies.......... 50/1	70 6
4475⁶	Classic Fly (FR) *Arthur Whiting* 8-11-4 (t) PeterToole................... 100/1	f
2.15race Mr Michael Buckley 7ran 3m54.53		

No real depth to this year's Maghull, with the pair that dominated the betting having it between them more or less throughout, and the result could well have been different had Ghizao not blundered 2 out when beginning to throw it down to the front-running Finian's Rainbow; what should have been 4 out was omitted due to a stricken rider. **Finian's Rainbow** followed up his excellent effort in the Arkle with a Grade 1 win of his own, though in truth it doesn't show anything new, not having to match his Cheltenham form in this less competitive affair and unlikely to have won had Ghizao not blundered 2 out; he did jump well again, however, a slight error at the sixth his only blip, and the way that he responded to pressure is also a positive—he remains a high-class prospect for next season. **Ghizao** possibly hasn't shown his best yet, potentially a bigger player in open company next term than defeats at both Cheltenham and here might imply, as on both occasions a single mistake has cost him (generally a sound jumper), travelling best here and about to take over when getting in too tight to the second last, the way he rallied afterwards testament to a good attitude; he could make amends at Punchestown if all is well. **Dan Breen** isn't in the same league as the first 2 and could never get on terms with more patient tactics adopted for the first time, under pressure by 4 out; he won't be easy to place next season, with a BHA mark of 148 very much on the stiff side. **Starluck** suddenly doesn't seem cut out for chasing, struggling with his jumping in better company the last twice; reverting to hurdles looks a more sensible option than tackling handicap chases. **Gilbarry** isn't up to this standard but his jumping is a concern even for more realistic tasks, not fluent at the second and struggling after hitting the fourth. **Romanesco** was out of his depth on this first start for new connections (sold out of Henry de Bromhead's stable £11,000 Ascot February Sales) and was always detached after a blunder at the first, continuing to make mistakes thereafter. **Classic Fly** fell heavily at the first.

4600 John Smith's Aintree Hdle (Gr 1) (1) 2½m (11)
(4yo+) £90,432

4195³	OSCAR WHISKY (IRE) *NickyHenderson* 6-11-7 BarryGeraghty	6/1	1
4195⁴	THOUSAND STARS (FR) *WPMullins,Ireland* 7-11-7 MsKWalsh	14 16/1	nk 2
4251⁵	SALDEN LICHT *AlanKing* 7-11-7 RobertThornton	25/1	10 3
3475*	Binocular (FR) *NickyHenderson* 7-11-7 APMcCoy	15/8 7/4	2½ 4
3617³	Oscar Dan Dan (IRE) *ThomasMullins,Ireland* 9-11-7 PaulCarberry	40/1	hd 5
4131¹	Ronaldo des Mottes (FR) *DavidPipe* 6-11-7 TimmyMurphy	50/1	2¾ 6
4195²	Peddlers Cross (IRE) *DonaldMcCain* 6-11-7 JasonMaguire	13/8 11/8f	7 7
3868*	Celestial Halo (IRE) *PaulNicholls* 7-11-7 (b+t) RWalsh	9 8/1	3 8

2.50race Walters Plant Hire Ltd 8ran 4m45.24

Disappointing runs from Peddlers Cross and Binocular meant this wasn't quite the race it promised to be but there was still high-class form on show from the pair that pulled clear; Celestial Halo ensured a sound pace. **Oscar Whisky** is not only a high-class performer but tough, versatile and uncomplicated with it, attributes that will surely continue to stand him in good stead in top races, reverted to this longer trip to gain his first Grade 1 win here and doing it in gutsy fashion, taking over from Celestial Halo at the seventh (always close up) and piling on the pressure soon after, at least 3 lengths clear for much of the straight and finding just enough to hold off one that was waited with, albeit with his task made easier with Binocular and Peddlers Cross not on song. **Thousand Stars** is very similar to the winner, tough and versatile himself, and he proved as much with another big effort on the back of finishing fourth in the Champion, ridden patiently at this longer trip and coming with a strong run after the second last; he endured a very hard race (rider subsequently received a whip ban) and may be best freshened up rather than going to Punchestown. **Salden Licht** is vulnerable at this level but gave a good account of himself, sticking to his task up the straight without ever threatening the winner, seeing out the longer trip as expected. **Binocular**'s Christmas Hurdle performance proves that he's been about as good as ever this season but it has been turbulent otherwise, missing the chance to retain his Champion Hurdle crown but unlikely to have been competitive at Cheltenham anyway on the evidence of this flat display, the longer trip not solely to blame for all he's a doubtful stayer at 2½m; that said, he'll no doubt still be a player in the top 2m races again next term. **Oscar Dan Dan** isn't quite up to competing with the best but is very reliable and ran a typically solid race despite seeming to find it an insufficient test of stamina. **Ronaldo des Mottes** showed that he retains all of his ability, facing a stiff task but running creditably, and he promised a bit more with how he travelled for a long way, weakening only after 2 out trying this trip for the first time; he still has mileage for valuable handicap hurdles around 2m. **Peddlers Cross** boasts a brilliant overall record and his second in the Champion must have just taken a bit too much out of him to be able to show his form less than 4 weeks on, clearly not himself as he failed to respond to pressure in the straight. **Celestial Halo** isn't quite the force he was but off-days like this are still rare for him over hurdles (possibly amiss).

Timeform's 'Top Hundred'

	Hurdlers
176+	Big Buck's
172	Hurricane Fly
171	Grands Crus
166	Peddlers Cross
164	Solwhit
163	Binocular
162	Oscar Whisky
162	Silviniaco Conti
162	Thousand Stars
161	Overturn
160	Menorah
159	Quevega
158	Al Ferof
158	Dunguib
158	Mourad
157p	Spirit Son
157	Australia Day
157	Celestial Halo
157	Cross Kennon
157	Organisateur
157	Rigour Back Bob
156	Carlito Brigante
156	Karabak
156	Luska Lad
155§	Ashkazar
155	Bahrain Storm
155	Cue Card
155	Salden Licht
155	Starluck
155	Won In The Dark
154?	Berties Dream
154§	Zaynar
154	Any Given Day
154	Clerk's Choice
153p	Bobs Worth
153	Fiveforthree
153	Get Me Out of Here
152	Nearby
152	Oscars Well
152	Restless Harry
152	Voler La Vedette
152	Walkon
151+	Shot From The Hip
151	James de Vassy
151	Jumbo Rio
151	Lough Derg
151	Mille Chief
151	Powerstation
150p	Sprinter Sacre
150	Fair Along
150	Final Approach
150	Mossley

150	Oscar Dan Dan
150	Stonemaster
149	Court In Motion
149	First Lieutenant
149	Jack Cool
149	Knockara Beau
149	Rock On Ruby
148§	Mobaasher
148	Alaivan
148	Cristal Bonus
148	Shinrock Paddy
147§	Trenchant
147	Dancing Tornado
147	Donnas Palm
147	Mossey Joe
147	Sanctuaire
147	Soldatino
146p	Sir des Champs
146+	Hidden Cyclone
146§	Battle Group
146	Aitmatov
146	Buena Vista
146	Khyber Kim
146	Micheal Flips
146	Quartz de Thaix
146	Recession Proof
146	Sir Harry Ormesher
146	Solix
146	Working Title
145p	Tocca Ferro
145+	Pittoni
145	Backspin
145	Bella Haze
145	Footy Facts
145	Ronaldo des Mottes
145	Son of Flicka
145	So Young
145	Summit Meeting
144	Askanna
144	Banjaxed Girl
144	Black Jack Blues
144	Blackstairmountain
144	Bygones of Brid
144	Duc de Regniere
144	Oneeightofamile
144	Ski Sunday
144	Tornado Bob
144	Zaidpour
	Chasers
184	Long Run
175	Denman
175	Master Minded
172	Big Zeb

171	Sizing Europe
170+	Imperial Commander
168§	Twist Magic
168	Somersby
167	Golden Silver
167	Riverside Theatre
167	Woolcombe Folly
166	Kauto Star
166	What A Friend
165p	Diamond Harry
165	Albertas Run
165	Monet's Garden
165	Wishfull Thinking
164	Kalahari King
164	Nacarat
164	Pandorama
164	Poquelin
163	Burton Port
162	Captain Cee Bee
162	Rubi Light
161	Neptune Collonges
160§	Tidal Bay
160	Midnight Chase
159	Ballabriggs
159	Don't Push It
159	Kempes
159	The Nightingale
158	China Rock
158	Garde Champetre
158	Hey Big Spender
158	Joncol
158	Money Trix
158	Tranquil Sea
157	Petit Robin
157	Silver By Nature
156p	Captain Chris
156p	Time For Rupert
156+	Voy Por Ustedes
156	Follow The Plan
156	French Opera
156	Synchronised
156	Tartak
156	Tchico Polos
155	Deep Purple
155	Gauvain
155	Glencove Marina
155	Roberto Goldback
155	Scotsirish
154p	Finian's Rainbow
154p	Mon Parrain
154	Oiseau de Nuit
153	Cooldine
153	Great Endeavour

153	Little Josh		136	Marsh Warbler		121p	Samain
153	Majestic Concorde		136	Smad Place		121	Destroyer Deployed
153	Quinz		134p	Tonic Mellysse		119	Rock On Ruby
153	Rare Bob		133	Aikideau		117	Cinders And Ashes
153	Siegemaster		132	Plan A		117	Close House
152+	Quito de LA Roque		130+	Palawi		117	Keys
152+	Tataniano		130	Current Event		117	Mount Benbulben
152d	Breedsbreeze		130	Ultravox		117	The Real Article
152	Barker		**Novice Hurdlers**			116	Ericht
152	Carole's Legacy		158	Al Ferof		116	Mono Man
152	Oscar Time		157p	Spirit Son		116	Swincombe Flame
152	Psycho		155	Cue Card		115	Celtic Folklore
151+	Planet of Sound		153p	Bobs Worth		115	Colonel Mortimer
151§	Chaninbar		152	Oscars Well		115	Jenari
151	Bensalem		151+	Shot From The Hip		114	Aupcharlie
151	Blazing Bailey		150p	Sprinter Sacre		114	Endless Intrigue
151	Cornas		150	Mossley		**Hunter Chasers**	
151	J'Y Vole		149	Court In Motion		139	Baby Run
151	Mad Max		149	First Lieutenant		138	Herons Well *
151	Noble Prince		149	Jack Cool		137	Zemsky
151d	Notre Pere		149	Rock On Ruby		135x	Otage de Brion *
151	Or Noir de Somoza		147	Mossey Joe		134p	On The Fringe
151	Punchestowns		146+	Hidden Cyclone		133x	Lord Henry *
151	The Listener		146§	Battle Group		133	Salsify
150p	Ghizao		146	Recession Proof		130	I Have Dreamed *
150x	Mahogany Blaze		145	Backspin		129+	Roulez Cool
150	Big Fella Thanks		145	So Young		129x	Turko
150	Dooneys Gate		144	Askanna		129	Templer *
150	Let Yourself Go		144	Oneeightofamile		128	Boxer Georg
150	Massini's Maguire		144	Tornado Bob		127+	Viking Splash
150	Realt Dubh		144	Zaidpour		127§	King Johns Castle *
150	Watch My Back		**Novice Chasers**			127	Dead Or Alive *
149+	Forpadydeplasterer		165	Wishfull Thinking		126x	Take The Stand
149+	The Midnight Club		156p	Captain Chris		126	Marblehead *
149+	Weird Al		156p	Time For Rupert		126	Turthen *
149x	Zaarito		154p	Finian's Rainbow		125§	Silver Adonis *
149	Beshabar		153	Quinz		125	Takeroc
149	Chicago Grey		152+	Quito de La Roque		125	Whizzaar
149	I'msingingtheblues		151	Noble Prince			
149	In Compliance		150p	Ghizao			
149	Junior		150	Realt Dubh			
149	Made In Taipan		149	Beshabar			
149	The Fonze		149	Chicago Grey			
149	Trafford Lad		148	Jessies Dream			
Juvenile Hurdlers			147	Bostons Angel			
155p	Zarkandar		146p	Flat Out			
154	Grandouet		146	Hell's Bay			
146	Sam Winner		146	Magnanimity			
143	Kumbeshwar		146	Medermit			
142+	Unaccompanied		146	Mikael d'Haguenet			
140	Molotof		146	Wayward Prince			
140	Sir Pitt		145+	Quel Esprit			
138	Houblon des Obeaux		**National Hunt Flat Horses**				
138	Sailors Warn		128	Cheltenian			
137+	Third Intention		127	Lovethehigherlaw			
137	Local Hero		126	Steps To Freedom			
136	Brampour		122	Montbazon			
136	Indian Daudaie		122	Waaheb			

* = Highest rating achieved in a non-hunter

NB: Silviniaco Conti (162), Organisateur (157) and Clerk's Choice (154) all won novice hurdles in 2010/11 but haven't been included in the above list due their novice status expiring at the end of October.

Racecourse Characteristics

The following A-Z guide covers all racecourses in England, Scotland and Wales that stage racing over the Jumps. A thumbnail sketch is provided of each racecourse's characteristics.

AINTREE

The Grand National course is triangular with its apex (at the Canal Turn) the furthest point from the stands. It covers two and a quarter miles and is perfectly flat throughout. Inside is the easier Mildmay course, providing a circuit of one and a half miles, which has birch fences. A major feature of the Mildmay course is its sharpness; the fences there are appreciably stiffer than used to be the case. The Grand National is run over two complete circuits taking in sixteen spruce fences first time round and fourteen the second, and, in spite of modifications to the fences in recent years, the race still provides one of the toughest tests ever devised for horse and rider. The run from the final fence to the winning post is 494 yards long and includes an elbow.

ASCOT

The triangular, right-handed circuit is approximately a mile and three quarters round; the turns are easy and the course is galloping in nature. The sides of the triangle away from the stands have four fences each, and the circuit is completed by two plain fences in the straight of two furlongs. After being closed for two seasons due to major redevelopment work, NH racing returned to Ascot in 2006/7. The fences are still stiff, though improved drainage means conditions don't get so testing as they once did.

AYR

The Ayr course is a left-handed circuit of one and a half miles comprising nine fences, with well-graduated turns. There is a steady downhill run to the home turn and a gentle rise to the finish. There is a run-in of 210 yards. When the going is firm the course is sharp, but conditions regularly get extremely gruelling, making for a thorough test.

BANGOR-ON-DEE

Bangor has a left-handed circuit of approximately one and a half miles. It's a fair test of jumping, with nine fences in a circuit, and the run-in is about a furlong. The track is fairly sharp because of its many bends, the paddock bend being especially tight.

CARLISLE

The course is right-handed, pear-shaped and undulating, a mile and five furlongs in extent. The track is a particularly stiff one and the uphill home stretch is very severe. There are nine fences to a circuit with a run-in of 300 yards. Perhaps due to the nature of the track, the fences are among the easiest in the country. A long-striding galloper suited by a real test of stamina is an ideal type for Carlisle.

CARTMEL

This tight, undulating, left-handed circuit is a little over a mile round. There are six fences to a circuit and the winning post is a little over a furlong from the turn into the finishing straight, which divides the course and which the horses enter after two circuits for races over seventeen furlongs or three circuits for three and a quarter miles. The fences are tricky, with four coming in quick succession in the back straight; the run of half a mile from the last fence is the longest in the country.

CATTERICK BRIDGE

The Catterick course is a left-handed, oval-shaped circuit of around a mile and a quarter, with eight fences and a run-in of about 280 yards. Races over two miles and three miles one and a half furlongs start on an extension to the straight and over two miles the first fence is jumped before joining the round course. Catterick's undulations and sharp turns make it unsuitable for the long-striding galloper and ideal for the nippy, front-running type.

CHELTENHAM

There are two left-handed courses at Cheltenham, the Old Course and the New Course. The Old Course is oval in shape and about one and a half miles in extent. There are nine fences to a circuit, with recent modifications for 2010/11 meaning there will now be two fences jumped in the home straight.

The New Course leaves the old track at the furthest point from the stands and runs parallel to it before rejoining at the entrance to the finishing straight. This circuit is a little longer than the Old Course and has ten fences, two of which are jumped in the final straight.

The most telling feature of the Old and the New Courses is their testing nature. The fences are stiff and the last half mile is uphill, with a run-in of just over a furlong. The hurdle races over the two tracks are quite different in complexion, with only two flights jumped in the final 6f on the New Course. The four-mile and two-and-a-half-mile starts are on an extension, with five fences, which bisects both courses almost at right angles. The two-mile start is also on this extension, and two fences are jumped before reaching the main circuit.

There is also a cross-country course at Cheltenham, laid out in the centre of the conventional tracks.

CHEPSTOW

Chepstow is a left-handed, undulating, oval course, nearly two miles round with eleven fences to a circuit, a five-furlong home straight, and a run-in of 250 yards. Conditions can be very testing. With five fences in the straight, the first part of which is downhill, front runners do well here.

DONCASTER

The Doncaster course is a left-handed pear-shaped circuit of approximately two miles, and has eleven fences—including four in the home straight—with a run-in of 240 yards. Only one fence is jumped twice in races over two miles. The course is flat apart from one slight hill about one and a quarter miles from the finish. The track is well drained and often produces conditions which naturally favour horses with more speed than stamina.

EXETER

This is a hilly course, galloping in nature. Conditions can get extremely testing in midwinter and the exact opposite in drier periods, the course being without an artificial watering system. Its right-handed two-mile circuit is laid out in a long oval, with eleven fences and a run-in of around 170 yards. The chase course is on the outside of the hurdles one, but the inside track is often used on the home turn regardless of whether the races are over fences or not. The half-mile home straight is on the rise all the way to the finish.

FAKENHAM

Fakenham is an undulating, very sharp track, ideal for the handy, front-running type and unsuitable for the long-striding animal. The left-handed, square-shaped track has a circuit of a mile and a run-in of 250 yards. There are six fences to a circuit and, probably on account of most races being well run, the course takes more jumping than most which cater for horses of lesser ability.

FFOS LAS

A wide, galloping, left-handed circuit of 1½ miles, with a straight of just over 4f. It has no undulations but a very slight rise over the course of the back straight and the opposite in the home straight. There are short run-ins for both hurdles and chases. Early indications are that it is a very fair track, though there has been a tendency at the first few meetings for the races to be steadily run, meaning the fields haven't got stretched and large numbers of runners have still been in contention turning for home.

FOLKESTONE

The course is right-handed and approximately eleven furlongs round. The turns are easy, but the undulations can put a long-striding horse off balance. There are seven fences to a circuit, which are relatively easy, and the run-in is about a furlong.

FONTWELL PARK

There are two types of track at Fontwell, the hurdle course being left-handed, an oval about a mile in circumference with four flights, and the chase course a figure of eight with six fences which are all in the two straight intersections linked with the hurdle course. Fontwell is not a course for the big, long-striding horse, and it can cause problems for inexperienced chasers.

HAYDOCK PARK

The 2007/8 season was the first since redevelopment work at Haydock resulted in a resiting of the chase course. All jump races are now run on the old hurdle course, using portable fences instead of the traditional ones, some of which had a slight drop on landing. There are four fences (instead of five) in the back straight, with the open ditch now the second there instead of the last, whilst there are still four fences and a water jump in the home straight. The 440-yard run-in is no more, however, its length significantly reduced as only the water jump is omitted on the final circuit. The new chase course has a tighter configuration than the old one and doesn't test jumping to the same extent.

HEREFORD

Hereford's right-handed circuit of about a mile and a half is almost square and has nine fences, of which the first after the winning post has to be taken on a turn. The home turn, which is on falling ground, is pretty sharp but the other bends are easy.

HEXHAM

Hexham has an undulating left-handed circuit of a mile and a half with ten fences. Although the fences are easy the course is very testing; the long back straight runs steeply downhill for most of the way but there is a steep climb from the end of the back straight to the home straight, which levels out in front of the stands. The finish is on a spur, which has one fence and a run-in of a furlong.

HUNTINGDON

The course is right-handed, oval with easy bends, and is a flat, fast track about one and a half miles in length. There are nine fences to a circuit, some of them rather tricky. Huntingdon favours horses with speed over stamina, sluggards seen to best advantage only under extremely testing conditions.

KELSO

The left-handed Kelso course has two tracks, the oval hurdle course of approximately a mile and a quarter and the chase course of approximately eleven furlongs. There are nine fences to be jumped in a complete circuit of the chase course; the last two aren't jumped on the final circuit and the first open ditch isn't taken at the start of the chases over four miles. The run-in, which is on an elbow, is a tiring one of 440 yards.

The hurdle track is tight, with a particularly sharp bend after the stands.

KEMPTON PARK

Kempton is a very fair test for a jumper; it is a flat, triangular circuit of one mile five furlongs and is right handed. There are nine fences to a circuit, three of them in the home straight, and although they are quite stiff they present few problems to a sound jumper. After the laying of an all-weather course, which necessitated the removal of the water jump, NH racing returned in 2006/7.

LEICESTER

The right-handed course is rectangular in shape, a mile and three quarters in extent and has ten fences. Leicester is a stiff test and the last three furlongs are uphill. The run-in of 250 yards has a slight elbow on the chase course 150 yards from the winning post. Races over hurdles are run on the Flat course and the going tends to be a good deal more testing than over fences.

LINGFIELD PARK

Lingfield is about a mile and a half in length, triangular and taken left-handed, sharp, has several gradients and a tight downhill turn into the straight. Nine relatively easy fences are jumped on a complete circuit. Bumper races are now usually run on the all-weather track.

LUDLOW

Ludlow is a sharp, right-handed, oval track, with a nine-fence chase circuit about a mile and a half and a run-in of 250 yards. The fences are easy. The hurdle course, which runs on the outside of the chase course, has easier turns. Whereas the chase course is flat, the hurdle course has slight undulations but they rarely provide difficulties for a long-striding horse.

MARKET RASEN

There is a right-handed, oval circuit of a mile and a quarter, seven relatively easy fences and a run-in of 250 yards at Market Rasen. The track is sharp, covered with minor undulations, and favours the handy, nippy type of horse.

MUSSELBURGH

A right-handed oval track a little over a mile and a quarter in extent, almost flat with sharp bends, favouring the handy type of animal and also front runners. There are eight fences (four in each straight) or six flights of hurdles (three in each straight nowadays) to a circuit. The two-mile start is on a spur on the last bend.

NEWBURY

The oval Newbury course, with eleven fences to the circuit, is about a mile and three quarters in circumference and is set inside the Flat track, following a left-handed line. It is one of the fairest courses in the country, favouring no particular type of horse. The home straight is five furlongs with three plain fences, an open ditch (the water jump being omitted on the final circuit) and a run-in of 255 yards. There are seven hurdles to a circuit, four in the back straight and three in the home straight with a long run to the third last. The course is galloping in nature, with easy bends, plenty of room and few significant undulations.

NEWCASTLE

The jumps track is laid out inside the Flat course, its left-handed circuit of one and three quarter miles containing ten fences. There is a steady rise from the fifth last to the winning post and the course puts a premium on stamina, with the fences being on the stiff side. The ground is often testing here, too.

NEWTON ABBOT

Newton Abbot has a flat, oval, tight, left-handed circuit of about nine furlongs that favours the handy sort of horse. There are seven relatively easy fences to a circuit, and a very short run-in. The nineteen-furlong start over hurdles is on a spur after the winning post and the first hurdle is jumped only once.

PERTH

Perth is a right-handed circuit of one and a quarter miles, with eight fences to the circuit. The course has sweeping turns and quite a flat running surface. The water jump is in front of the stands and is left out on the run-in, leaving a long run from the last fence to the winning post.

PLUMPTON

The oblong-shaped course is only nine furlongs in circumference and has tight, left-handed bends, steep undulations, and an uphill home straight. The climb becomes pretty steep near the finish but the course is not a particularly stiff one; it favours the handy and quick-jumping types. There are six fences to a circuit and the run-in is 200 yards.

SANDOWN PARK

Sandown is a right-handed, oval-shaped course of thirteen furlongs, with a straight run-in of four furlongs. There is a separate straight course which runs across the main circuit over which all five-furlong races are decided. From the mile-and-a-quarter starting gate, the Eclipse Stakes course, the track is level to the turn into the straight, from there it is uphill until less than a furlong from the winning post, the last hundred yards being more or less level. The five-furlong track is perfectly straight and rises steadily throughout. Apart from the minor gradients between the main winning post and the mile-and-a-quarter starting gate, there are no undulations to throw a long-striding horse off balance, and all races over the round course are very much against the collar from the turn into the straight. The course is, in fact, a fairly testing one, and over all distances the ability to see the trip out well is important.

SEDGEFIELD

The circuit is approximately a mile and a quarter, oval, and taken left-handed. It is essentially sharp in character and the eight fences are fairly easy, though some uphill sections of the undulating ground, notably the final 150 yards, are punishing. The run-in is 200 yards.

SOUTHWELL

The Southwell track is laid out in a fairly tight, level oval of less than a mile and a quarter. In 2002/3 the circuit was divided into a summer and a winter track, with the slightly larger summer track on the outside of the winter one. The runners go left-handed. There are seven portable fences to a circuit which are stiff ones for a minor track. The brush-type hurdles can also catch out less fluent jumpers.

STRATFORD-ON-AVON

This sharp track is flat, triangular in shape and has a left-handed circuit of a mile and a quarter, taking in eight fences. One of the fences in the home straight was removed in the summer of 2007, but a water jump was introduced at the start of the following season just before the winning line and is obviously bypassed on the final circuit.

TAUNTON

The right-handed course is a long oval, about a mile and a quarter round, and has seven fences, four in the back straight and three in the home straight. The fences are easy enough but, due the the sharp nature of the track, catch out plenty more runners than might be expected. The bend after the winning post is tight and the chase run-in short.

TOWCESTER

Towcester is a right-handed course, a mile and three quarters round, and is the stiffest track in the country. The last mile or so is very punishing, with a steep climb to the home turn and a continuing rise past the winning post. Stamina is at a premium and conditions can get very testing. There are ten fences on the circuit, two (small obstacles) in the finishing straight, but they seldom present problems, with the exception of the two downhill ones running away from the stands. The run-in is 200 yards.

UTTOXETER

The course is an oval of approximately a mile and a quarter with a long, sweeping, left-handed bend into the straight and a sharper one after the winning post. The hurdle course in particular suits the handier type of horse. There are minor undulations and the back straight has slight bends. The ground can get extremely testing, so that few horses act on it. There are eight fences, with a run-in of around 170 yards. Races of two miles, three and a quarter miles and four and a half miles are started on a spur on the last bend.

WARWICK

Warwick's left-handed course is a mile and three quarters round with ten fences to a circuit. Five of them come close together in the back straight and sound jumping is at a premium. The bends are rather tight and the track is a sharp one, favouring the handy horse. There is a run-in of 250 yards.

WETHERBY

The course is left-handed, with easy turns and follows a long oval circuit of a mile and a half, during which nine fences are jumped, the four in the home straight now on the inside of the hurdles track. It provides a very fair test for any horse, but is ideal for the free-running, long-striding individual with plenty of jumping ability.

WINCANTON

Wincanton is a level course with an oval, right-handed circuit of around a mile and a half containing nine fences. It is essentially sharp in nature and, as such, provides a stiffish test with regards to jumping. The run from the last fence is only about 200 yards.

WORCESTER

The course is laid out in the shape of a long oval of thirteen furlongs, flat throughout with easy, left-handed turns. There are nine well-sited fences, five in the back straight, four in the home straight, and a run-in of 220 yards. Brush-type hurdles are used at Worcester and can cause jumping problems. Severe flooding in summer 2007 caused considerable damage to both the racing surface and stands.

Index

A

Accordintolawrence	75, 83, 109
Ackertac	31, 119
Aikideau	117
Aikman	4, 5, 6, 109, 126
Aiteen Thirtythree	110
Alasi	107
Albertas Run	90, 102, 114, 124
Alegralil	108
Al Ferof	103
Allee Garde	119
Amaury de Lusignan	4, 6, 35
A Media Luz	118
Any Given Day	116
Architrave	118
Areuwitmenow	77
Arthurian Legend	68
Ashkazar	12, 116
Atouchbetweenacara	98
Aupcharlie	112
Awesome George	97

B

Baby Run	94, 95
Back In Focus	49, 50
Bally Legend	4, 7, 8
Balthazar King	67
Banjaxed Girl	107, 108
Barbatos	4, 8
Barbers Shop	100
Baseball Ted	73
Bear's Affair	8, 9
Beautiful Sound	50
Be My Present	78
Berties Dream	116
Big Buck's	91, 115, 116, 122
Big Fella Thanks	100
Big Zeb	93, 111
Binocular	105, 126
Bobs Worth	12, 29, 93, 95, 118
Bold Optimist	51
Bostons Angel	109
Brampour	117
Breedsbreeze	115
Bubbly Breeze	4, 9, 10
Burton Port	99, 101
Bygones In Brid	113
Bygones of Brid	107

C

Caheronaun	51, 52
Can't Buy Time	97
Cappagh	67
Captain Cee Bee	111
Captain Chris	32, 33, 63, 65, 66, 70, 86, 87, 92, 93, 95, 104, 105
Carlito Brigante	16, 50, 123
Carole's Legacy	24, 44, 123
Carruthers	100, 122
Catch Me	97
Cedre Bleu	4, 10
Celestial Halo	126
Champion Court	4, 9, 11, 12, 37, 119
Chaninbar	125
Chartreux	4, 12, 13
Cheltenian	23, 24, 112
Chief Dan George	98
China Rock	122
Cinders And Ashes	112
Classic Fly	125
Clerk's Choice	106
Cooldine	101
Cornas	112
Court In Motion	27, 49, 119
Cousin Khee	113
Cross Kennon	38, 116
Cue Card	103

D

Dan Breen	105, 125
Dancing Tornado	96
Dare Me	70
Dark Glacier	4, 13, 113
Dark Ranger	88
Deep Purple	123
Denman	20, 65, 85, 86, 92, 99, 102, 120, 121, 123, 124
Destroyer Deployed	112
Diamond Harry	91, 99, 101, 102, 120
Diocles	4, 14
Divine Rhapsody	113
Door Boy	97
Double Double	113
Dream Alliance	100
Dream Function	70
Duke of Lucca	68
Dunguib	106, 112
Dunraven Storm	69, 104
Dynamic Approach	113

E

Edgbriar	97
Elysian Rock	110
Ericht	113

F

Fair Along	66
Far Away So Close	104
Felix Yonger	51, 114
Filbert	70
Fingal Bay	70
Finger Onthe Pulse	97
Finian's Rainbow	32, 33, 93, 95, 105, 125
First Fandango	118
First Lieutenant	53, 85, 108
Fishoutofwater	4, 14, 15
Fiulin	120
Fiveforthree	116
Flying Award	4, 15
Follow The Plan	123
For Bill	52
For Non Stop	4, 16, 17
Forpadydeplasterer	102
Fountains Flypast	81
Freddie Brown	4, 17
French Opera	111, 124

G

Gagewell Flyer	120
Gauvain	115
Getaway Driver	77
Ghizao	87, 105, 125
Gibb River	36, 104
Gilbarry	125
Giorgio Quercus	105
Glencove Marina	101
Global Power	4, 18
Go All The Way	112
Golden Silver	89, 111
Grandads Horse	77
Grandouet	117
Grands Crus	16, 115, 116, 122, 123
Great Endeavour	97
Gwanako	97, 123

H

Habbie Simpson	109
Havingotascoobydo	4, 18, 19, 74
Hayjack	77
Hazy Tom	78
Hey Big Spender	100, 115
Hidden Cyclone	53, 54
Hidden Keel	71, 72
Hidden Universe	104
Highland Valley	109
High Ransom	118
Hildisvini	71, 75
Hills of Aran	100
Houblon des Obeaux	118
Hurricane Fly	91, 92, 106

I

Imperial Commander	97, 98, 99, 102, 122
I'm So Lucky	111

J

Jessies Dream	50, 109
Jetnova	4, 19, 119
Jetson	18, 54
Join Together	120
Joncol	101
J'Y Vole	101, 115

K

Kalahari King	114, 124, 125
Karabak	123
Kauto Star	47, 92, 97, 98, 99, 101, 102, 120, 121, 124
Kempes	101, 122
Khyber Kim	107, 123
Kilcrea Kim	4, 20, 21, 68, 119
King Vuvuzela	55
Knight Pass	114
Knockalongi	113
Knockara Beau	122, 123
Kuilsriver	118

L

L'Accordioniste	107
La Vecchia Scuola	108
Little Josh	96
Local Hero	117
Lonesome Dove	108
Long Run	91, 92, 93, 95, 96, 102, 120, 121
Lord Gale	114
Lovethehigherlaw	54, 55, 56, 60
Lovey Dovey	4, 21

M

Made In Taipan	125
Madison du Berlais	99, 100, 102
Mad Max	96, 97, 112, 124, 125

Magen's Star	104
Magnanimity	110
Magnifique Etoile	77
Markington	123
Marsh Warbler	104
Master Minded	92, 93, 111, 124
Master Murphy	114
Master of The Hall	110
Medermit	19, 87, 105
Megastar	15, 109
Menorah	67, 68, 106
Midnight Chase	120, 121
Mikael d'Haguenet	110
Mille Chief	19, 107
Milo Milan	4, 22
Minella Boys	73
Minella Class	6, 109
Miss Overdrive	108
Mister Carter	118
Molly Round	4, 22, 23
Molotof	118
Money Trix	101
Mon Parrain	94, 95
Montbazon	4, 23, 24
Moonlight Drive	42, 120
Moscow Chancer	4, 24, 25
Mossbank	101
Mossley	119
Mourad	116
Muldoon's Picnic	86
My Shamwari	69

N

Nacarat	24, 98, 102, 123, 124
Nearby	68
Nearest The Pin	56, 57
Neptune Collonges	100, 121
Neptune Equester	80
New Den	118
Next To Nowhere	4, 25
Niche Market	99
No Secrets	119
Notre Pere	101

O

Ocean Transit	107
Ohio Gold	109
Oscar Dan Dan	126
Oscar Magic	113
Oscars Well	57, 58, 90, 92, 95, 108
Oscar Whisky	32, 106, 126
Ostland	73
Our Island	119
Overturn	106

P

Paintball	4, 26, 27, 75, 76
Pandorama	100, 101, 121
Passato	97
Peddlers Cross	33, 92, 106, 126
Penny Max	4, 27
Persian Snow	70
Pigeon Island	97
Pittoni	58, 59
Planet of Sound	65, 70, 98, 102
Poquelin	96, 97, 114
Possol	123
Powerstation	116
Prince de Beauchene	49, 59, 60, 94
Princess Rainbow	108
Punchestowns	124

Q

Qhilimar	73
Quel Elite	4, 27, 28
Quel Esprit	110
Quevega	107
Quinz	66

R

Radetsky March	27, 120
Raise The Beat	114
Rathlin	104
Razor Royale	100
Realt Dubh	105
Recession Proof	14, 103
Restless Harry	116
Rey Nacarado	73
Rigour Back Bob	116
Riverside Theatre	93, 102
Roberto Goldback	89, 115
Rock Noir	105
Rock of Deauville	4, 28, 29
Rock On Ruby	85, 108
Romanesco	125
Ronaldo des Mottes	126
Rose of The Moon	4, 29
Rossmore Lad	77
Royal Guardsman	4, 29, 30
Rubi Light	89, 90, 114

S

Sailors Warn	117
Saint Luke	113
Salden Licht	126
Salubrious	4, 30, 31
Samain	60
Sam Winner	117
Santera	107
Sentry Duty	123
Seren Rouge	4, 31, 47
Sheer Genius	104
Siegemaster	101
Silver By Nature	100
Silver Gypsy	107, 108
Simonsig	4, 32
Sir des Champs	61
Sir Pitt	117
Sizing Europe	93, 111
Smad Place	117
Somersby	111, 124
Songe	72, 73
Souffleur	116
So Young	108
Spanish Treasure	104
Sparky May	107
Spirit Son	8, 10, 34, 92, 103
Sprinter Sacre	4, 32, 33, 103
Stagecoach Pearl	105
Starluck	125
Star Neuville	113
Start Me Up	120
Stephanie Kate	107
Storm Brig	4, 34
Strongbows Legend	4, 34, 35, 75
Sunley Peace	4, 35, 36
Sunnyhillboy	97
Swincombe Flame	4, 36, 37
Sybarite	4, 12, 37, 38, 119

T

Taranis	100
Tarn Hows	4, 38
Tartak	115, 124
Tatispout	75
Tchico Polos	97
Teaforthree	119
Tenor Nivernais	4, 39, 40
The Giant Bolster	110
The Listener	101
The Nightingale	102
The Sawyer	97
The Strawberry One	88
The Tother One	99
The Tracey Shuffle	113
Third Intention	117
Thousand Stars	106, 126
Tidal Bay	98, 121
Tillahow	118
Time For Rupert	110
Time For Spring	74
Tornado Bob	4, 40, 41, 109
Tranquil Sea	124, 125
Trop Fort	118
Trustan Times	4, 41, 42, 47
Tusa Eire	113
Twentyfourcarat	114

U

Unaccompanied	117

V

Veiled	4, 43, 44
Victor Lynch	4, 44
Victors Serenade	45
Vic Venturi	101
Viva Colonia	81, 82
Voy Por Ustedes	10, 93, 115

W

Walter de La Mare	118
Water Garden	4, 45, 46
Wayward Prince	110
Weird Al	100, 122
Western Charmer	94, 95
West With The Wind	105
What A Friend	98, 121
Whoops A Daisy	4, 46
Wishfull Thinking	63, 64, 65, 93
Won In The Dark	123
Woolcombe Folly	85, 111, 112
Wymott	110

Y

Yurok	4, 31, 42, 47

Z

Zaidpour	53, 57, 58, 85, 104
Zarkandar	92, 116
Zaynar	116